DEWITCHED

E.L. SARNOFF

THE UNTOLD STORY OF THE EVIL QUEEN

This is a work of fiction. Names, characters, places, and incidents are products of the author's imagination or are used fictitiously and are not to be construed as real. Any resemblance to actual events, locales, organizations or persons, living or dead, is entirely coincidental.

NICHOLS CANYON PRESS
Los Angeles, CA USA

DEWITCHED: The Untold Story of the Evil Queen
By E.L. Sarnoff

ISBN-13: 978-0615673165
ISBN-10: 0615673163

Cover and Interior: Streetlight Graphics

For Lilly and Isabella,
The lights inside my heart

DEWITCHED

E-vil [Middle English, from Old English yfel]

adj.
1. Morally bad or wrong; wicked
2. Causing ruin, injury, or pain; harmful
3. Characterized by or indicating future misfortune; ominous
4. Bad or blameworthy by report; infamous
5. Characterized by anger or spite; malicious

n.
1. The quality of being morally bad or wrong; wickedness
2. That which causes harm, misfortune, or destruction
3. An evil force, power, or personification
4. Something that is a cause or source of suffering, injury, or destruction

BOOK ONE

*Look in the mirror and one thing's sure;
what we see is not who we are.*

—Richard Bach

CHAPTER 1

A mirror can be your best friend. Or your worst enemy. The only thing you can count on is brutal honesty.

I talk to my mirror. Lots of women do. Except mine talks back. It's magic.

Time for our daily chat. I head down the long corridor toward the chamber where I keep my magic mirror, but I'm distracted by the sound of singing. I detour over to a window and peek between the thick, tightly drawn drapes.

Below in my castle courtyard, she's standing idly by the wishing well. My stepdaughter. Snow White. Why the hell is she wasting her time wishing when she should be washing? Well, I suppose I'll give her a little break today. After all, it's her birthday. Her sixteenth.

Birds and butterflies dance around her. I don't get it. Her whole life, I've piled her with a crapload of chores and dressed her in rags, yet she still looks ravishing.

I try hard not to scowl; the last thing I need is a deep, ugly crease between my brows. I know. I'm going to double her workload. What a perfect birthday present!

Enough. I yank the drapes closed and quicken my pace down the corridor. At the end, I crank open a heavy mahogany door.

The windowless room is dark and bare, lit only by candlelight. My mirror faces me. I stride up to it and meet my shadowy reflection.

"Mirror, mirror on the wall,

Who's the fairest one of all?"

Awaiting an answer, I admire my candle-lit face, flickering in the smoky glass. My creamy, unblemished skin. My cat-green eyes. My full red lips. And those high cheekbones.

I grow impatient. What's taking so long? There's only answer. ME!

Finally, the mirror responds:

> "You are fair indeed, My Queen,
> But there is someone fairer who is Sweet Sixteen."

I let out a gasp so loud it echoes. The mirror continues:

> "Even in darkness she is a bright light,
> A princess who goes by the name Snow White."

Her? Blood rushes to my head. I pace the chamber, zigzagging from corner to corner, in a frenzy. My mirror is a traitor! I rip off my crown and aim it at the glass. About to smash it into smithereens, I get an even better idea. Something I should have done ages ago…

Eliminate the competition. And I have just the perfect person to do it.

My faithful Huntsman.

Snow White can wish as much as she wants. This birthday will be her last.

———

The Huntsman cowers before me as I sit high on my gem-studded throne. Despite his imposing height and girth, the bearded man appears small to me today. Almost frail.

"Take Snow White deep into the forest and bring me back her heart," I command.

"But—"

"There are no buts. Do as I say, and I will reward you." I jingle a bag of gold coins.

"But—"

My icy stare silences him.

He bows his head. "Yes, My Queen."

The hesitancy in his voice irks me. "If you fail me, you will pay the consequences." With a wry smile curled on my lips, I slide a finger across my neck.

The Huntsman says nothing. He pivots around and plods toward the throne room's massive double doors.

"Wait!" I shout out.

The Huntsman spins around. His forest-green eyes glimmer with the hope I've changed my mind.

"Use this to bring me back her heart." I toss him a small jeweled box. He catches it. His eyes downcast, he stuffs it inside his leather satchel, then disappears.

I grimace with regret. Such an elegant coffin. A potato sack would have sufficed.

———

All afternoon, I've been pacing the chamber that houses my magic mirror, struggling not to glance at it. We're not speaking.

What's taking that big-footed fool so long? I mean, how hard is it to plunge a dagger into a twig of a girl, rip out her heart, and bring it back? It doesn't have to be gift-wrapped. In fact, I hate bows. They remind me of her.

The minutes crawl like hours. I'm getting antsy. Where the hell is he?

The door to my chamber swings open. Finally, The Huntsman, holding the jeweled box.

"Give it to me," I order though I'm not sure what I'm going to do with my little souvenir. Dinner for the help perhaps?

The Huntsman's lowers his head and silently hands me the box. He's out the door before I can offer him the gold coins. Fine. I'll save some money.

I give the box a little shake. It's in there okay. I swear I can hear it still beating. Mission accomplished.

I stride up to my mirror and break into a wicked smile. Time for a little tête-à-tête.

> "Mirror, mirror on the wall,
> Now, who's the fairest one of all?"

Studying my reflection, I await the answer with the eagerness of a child about to get a sweet.

Silence. What's the problem? It's not like I'm asking it to solve an impossible what-came-first riddle. I shoot my mirror a dirty look. Finally, it responds:

> "My Queen, you are the fairest that I see…"

Yes! I *am* the fairest! My magic mirror can hold it right there. But the bigmouth rattles on:

> "But near the hills where the Seven Dwarfs dwell,
> Snow White is still alive and well,
> And there is none so fair as she."

What? That two-timing wimp didn't kill her? She's still alive? A stabbing pain pierces my heart. I don't know whom I hate more—The Huntsman or my mirror.

Clutching the box, I storm out the door and race down the corridor. "You're history!" I scream out, but it's no use. The betrayer is gone, nowhere in sight.

I stomp back to my chamber and hurl the box at my mirror. I miss. It hits a wall. My mouth twitches, in horror, as its bloody contents splatter across it.

I have no choice. I've got to take care of Snow White myself.

Easier said than done. Over the past two weeks, I've ventured twice to the cottage where Snow White has taken refuge with a bunch of lowlife dwarfs. Seven of them—just like my smart-ass looking glass said.

The first time, I disguised myself as an old corset peddler and asphyxiated the wench with laces I was selling. So I thought until my magic mirror told me she was still alive and well. The second, in a different but equally repugnant peasant disguise, I talked her into trying out a comb I poisoned. After having the pleasure of watching her crumple to the floor once again, I had the misfortune of hearing my magic mirror report that I had failed yet another time. Damn my mirror. And damn those dwarfs. After each attempt, they somehow must have rescued the tart before she took her final breath.

This time, I'm done wasting my time. Those runts can say adieu to their precious princess because I've come up with a foolproof plan. I'm wearing my newest and, I must say, best disguise. A butt-ugly hag get-up I picked up for nothing at a thrift store. To make sure Snow White doesn't recognize me, I've dyed my long hair gray, blackened out my front tooth, and added a honker of a nose made out of putty.

I stare at my reflection in my magic mirror. I don't even recognize myself. The wart on my nose is such a nice touch. My disguise is brilliant! Best of all, this is the last time I'll ever have to sacrifice my beauty to have Snow White out of my life.

Dressed to kill, I wind my way down the rickety stairs that lead to my favorite playroom. My dungeon. Time to check on my evil potion. It's been brewing for hours.

Perfect! The mixture in the cauldron has come to a boil. The cackling bubbles are like music to my ears. I give it a stir with a long femur bone—probably the remains of one of my late husband's prisoners.

"It's as easy as pie," said the instructions. I wouldn't know since I've never made one. All I can say is that this is the most fun I've ever had.

Following the recipe to a tee, I throw in the final lethal ingredient—a dash of dragonstone extract. The potion sizzles, and snakes of smoke curl around me. I smile proudly. The mistress of disguise can chalk up another talent.

Now, for the tricky part. Carefully, I dip half of a big red apple that I handpicked from my orchard into the gurgling mixture. I count to three and strategically place it on top of a basket filled with other ripe apples.

"Satisfaction guaranteed or I'll refund your money one hundred percent," promised the sorcerer who sold me the potion. "One bite and Snow White will be asleep forever." Frightening simplicity! And there's nothing those damn dwarfs can do.

I can practically make the trek to the Seven Dwarfs' cottage blindfolded. That's not to say I enjoy it. In fact, I hate it. First, I have to row a boat across my moat to get to land and endure an hour of sunshine on my flawless, vanilla skin. Then I have to trudge through a dark forest with its monstrous trees and wild beasts and risk my life. Or worse, scratch my face. Let's put it this way: I'm not exactly what you'd call the outdoorsy type. And I despise the sun.

Thank goodness, this trip will be my last. Near the edge of the forest, their so-cute-I-could-puke cottage comes into view. Holding the basket of apples in one hand, I crouch down behind a tree and impatiently wait for the dwarfs to leave. After twenty or so time-wasting minutes, the bearded mini-men file out, carrying their work tools. Snow White plants a kiss on each of them. It'll be their last.

The tiniest one of the bunch is the last to exit. I count them again to play it safe. Seven for sure. In a perfect line, they march toward the mountains that lie behind their house. In no time, they disappear. *Hi ho. Hi ho.* It's showtime!

I spring to my feet, my target in sight, when a loud hissing sound stops me in my tracks. My eyes shift left and right, then up. My heart jumps. Dangling from a branch right above me is a monstrous green and yellow snake. With its jaws wide open, it coils toward me. I'm paralyzed with fear. I don't know what I dread more—its venom or the fang marks it will leave behind. I hold my breath as its black forked tongue flicks my cheek. That does it. I grab an apple and hurl it at the serpent. Without looking back, I run.

My relief is short-lived. A terrifying thought flashes into my head. Oh no! What if it was the poison apple I threw? I glance down at my basket and relax. It's still there. Better yet, I'm still here. Nothing is going to screw up my perfect plan. *Nothing!*

As I near the cottage, I spy an open window. Switching into hag mode, I hobble up to it and pop my head inside. Snow White's in the kitchen, singing (ugh!) as she scrubs a long wooden table. Always the perfect little homemaker. Not for long. Miss Tidy Whitey's cleaning days will soon be over.

"Hello, dearie," I call out in my finest hag voice. "I've got some delicious apples for sale."

Startled, Snow White whirls around. Her face, drop-dead gorgeous as ever, nauseates me.

"I'm not allowed to talk to strangers anymore," she says in her sickening sweet voice.

"But I'm just a poor old woman trying to make ends meet. And these apples will make a delicious apple pie." I hold up my special apple. "You must try one."

"What if it's poisonous?"

She's smartened up. No worries. I'll show her how good it tastes. With a loud crunch, I bite into the apple. "See. I'm good as new. Now, you try it."

Hesitantly, Snow White strolls up to the window and takes the apple. She beholds the shiny fruit in her hand. Why is she stalling? *Just take a bite. Come on. Do it already.* My heart pounds in anticipation.

At last, she raises the apple toward her face. It's like a slow motion dream. Her lips part. Her mouth opens. Finally, her teeth sink into the other side of my juicy red apple. *Crunch*. What a lovely sound! Her big brown eyes roll back into her head, and she collapses to the stone floor in a crumpled heap. I smile wickedly.

Eternal sleep! At last!

Victory surges inside me. I'm tingling with excitement. I can't wait to get back to my castle to ask my magic mirror one simple little question…

And with Snow White out of the picture, this time for good, there can only be one simple little answer…

The sound of heavy footsteps interrupts my reverie. The front door bursts open. My heart skips a beat. It's those damn dwarfs! What are they doing back so early?

I'd better get out of here. Fast!

Too late. One of the runts has spotted me. "Stop her!" he yells, pointing his grubby little finger.

Having no choice, I dive through the window and make a mad dash for the mountains. The pint-sized twerps chase after me. I toss the basket of apples, hoping to trip them. I steal a look behind me. No luck. They're picking up speed and getting closer. How the hell can they run so fast on those stumpy legs?

A sudden gust of wind fills my cape like a sail, making it impossible for me to move any faster. My hair whips across my face as I glance back one more time. The dwarfs are gaining on me. Calling upon every muscle in my body, I force myself forward.

An explosive clap of thunder startles me. I almost trip. As I regain my footing, the sky opens, and torrential rain starts pouring down. Dragonballs! The one day it had to rain in Lalaland.

The earth quickly becomes a mud bath. Drenched, I slip and slide across the treacherous ground with the pack of dwarfs still on my back. And then…a dead end. I'm smack against the mountains.

"Get her!" shouts one of the dwarfs.

I gaze up at the jagged wall of rocks. I have no choice but to start climbing.

Gripping the wet, slippery rocks, I clamber up the steep terrain. The pouring rain is blinding me, and I have to keep dodging all manner of falling debris. The dwarfs are still right behind me and show no sign of slowing down. They must be part mountain goat. I, on the other hand, am panting like a dog. And my thighs are screaming they're on fire. Once I get back to my castle, I swear I'm going to get out more and start an exercise regime. The Fairest is also going to become The Fittest.

The slope grows steeper and steeper. I'm practically on all fours. Ahead of me is a giant boulder. I scramble behind it. I can run no more. Not because I'm out of steam. I've reached the edge of the mountain. A cliff. There is no place to go but down. Far, far down.

I'm trapped! I peek around the boulder. The dwarfs are so close I can feel their breath on my face. Brainstorm! I'm going to flatten the runts. All seven of them at once! With all the strength I can muster, I push the massive rock. It won't budge. I try again, this time using my entire body. Nothing. Not even an inch!

Claps of thunder synchronize with my thudding heart. I'm about to give up when the sky sends a bolt of lightning directly at the dwarfs. What good luck! They're going to fry. What bad luck! They leap back just in time to avoid their fiery demise. My face grows wide-eyed with horror as nature etches a deep jagged line across the surface of the rocky precipice. *Crack!* It's breaking off. I'm going down!

Blood flees to the bottoms of my feet as I squeeze my eyes shut. Life is so unfair. I'm finally again *Fairest of All,* and I'm going to be a goner! An icy sting shoots up my legs, then zaps my body. Is this how death feels? Daring to open my eyes, I find myself under water. I've landed in a river! I hold my breath, but as I sink deeper, my lungs may burst. Death still awaits me. I finally hit rock bottom. Instantly, I catapult upward.

My head powers through the surface of the water. I'm alive! Desperate for air, I open my mouth wide, catching raindrops on my tongue. Victory is mine. It's time to wave bye-bye to that pack of vertically challenged losers. I look up, but I might as well kiss my life goodbye. The boulder is toppling toward me at dizzying speed!

A bolt of raw energy surges through my veins. Kicking and stroking furiously, I battle the fierce current and swim away a split second before the boulder crashes into the water. I hold on to dear life as the waves of its aftermath thrash me around like an angry dragon's tail.

The next thing I know I'm lying facedown on a hard, muddy surface. Land! The river must have washed me ashore. As I stagger to my feet, my eyes light up. Straight ahead of me is my majestic castle sitting high and mighty on its perch. I can practically hear my magic mirror welcoming me home.

Except there's no way my mirror will recognize me. Soaked to the bone, I must look like a drowned witch.

Not wasting a second, I rip off my stinking-wet hag rag and the nose. I toss everything into the river and let the current carry it away. It's a good thing I threw on a backpack last minute with my don't-leave-home-without-them necessities. It's sopping wet, but otherwise intact. I tear it open, slip on my black velvet cloak, and apply my favorite red lipstick, charcoal brow liner, and creamy foundation with sun protection.

The final touch: my gold crown. I cradle it in my hands and admire it. It's worthy of only one legendary beauty— yours truly.

Mirror, mirror. Ready or not, here I come. Suddenly, two bone-crushing hands grip my arms. I crank my head around and practically choke when I come face to face with my assailant. The Huntsman!

"You're under arrest for murder!"

CHAPTER 2

Ha! They'll never prove me guilty, I tell myself as spectators clamor into the courtroom where I'm being tried for Snow White's murder. I bet every fairy-tale freak in the world is here. Giants. Gnomes. Ogres. Trolls. You name it. It's a circus. And I'm the star.

Chained to a wooden chair that's bolted to the floor, I laugh silently as the freaks make a beeline for the best seats. Sitting here, at least, beats being holed up in that cold, mirrorless dungeon for a month. Reporters from the *Fairytale Tattler* are lined up, falling over each other to get a good look at me. I plaster a charming smile on my face. Trust me, I'm going to give them a great story. With a happy ending.

The judge, a big fat woman, with spiky hair the color of a blood orange and a small gold crown, strolls up to her bench like a queen to her throne. "Order in the Court!" she roars in a deep, husky voice. She pounds her gavel. The room shakes. Obviously, she's got a big fat temper too.

She calls the first witness. The Huntsman. As he lumbers up to the stand, rage and regret consume me. I should have never trusted the spineless twit. I should have done him in when he brought me back some beast's heart, pretending it was Snow White's. I should have ripped out *his* heart. Yes, that's what I should have done.

I cringe as he confesses everything…how I bribed him to take Snow White into the forest and kill her…threatened his life. So, it was boar's heart he brought back. The wuss!

His forest green eyes stay riveted on me as a tear trickles

down his thick dark beard. "I just couldn't bring myself to harm that sweet, beautiful girl."

Beautiful? My blood curdles. I want to sink my teeth into him like a mad dog.

The Huntsman faces the judge. "Your honor, Jane needs help." His voice wavers. "Before she does more evil."

How dare he call me by my first name! And how the hell does he know it?

The judge turns her jowly face toward me. I count her chins. Three!

"So what do you have to say for yourself?" she asks.

I quickly compose myself. Time for a little self-defense. Rising, I tell the court, in my calmest voice, that what The Huntsman said is all a bunch of lies. To get back at me for firing him. And with Snow White dead, he can't prove a thing. "There's not an evil bone in my body," I add, almost with a laugh.

Okay. I lied. I'm going to destroy this insolent traitor and those damn dwarfs as soon as soon as I'm free.

The judge looks back at The Huntsman and presses her heart-shaped lips into a hard, grim line. My heart hammers.

"Dismissed!" she thunders with a bang of her gavel.

Inwardly, I breathe a sigh of relief.

The Huntsman plods out of the courtroom, not once taking his eyes off me.

I sit back down. Score one for me.

"Next witness," hollers the judge.

The Seven Dwarfs march into the court with a vengeance. They're in their grungy work clothes. Good. That's not going to help with their credibility.

"Do you recognize this woman?" asks the judge.

Fourteen eyes lay rest on me.

My body doesn't move a muscle. But inside my heart is racing. *Stay calm. Just stay calm.*

The dwarfs study my face, then shake their heads in unison.

"We've never seen her before," says the one wearing spectacles.

Ha! I'm out of here. Not so fast. The dwarf at the end of the lineup bashfully comes forward. I hold my breath.

"The woman who poisoned our beloved Snow White was a witch, not a beauty."

How sweet of him to say! I purse my lips and blow the runt a kiss. He blushes.

The tiniest one with the big ears opens his mouth, but the judge bangs her gavel before he can utter a word.

"Dismissed!" she shouts, rolling her eyes with impatience.

The little suckers file out of the courtroom, and I breathe another deep sigh of relief. Smart thing I tossed my disguise into that river. There's no evidence to prove I killed Snow White. In no time, I'll be free to go back to my castle and lay it on the line with my magic mirror. "Let's get one thing straight, smart one. *I'm* the fairest one of all."

The judge's thunderous voice catapults me back to reality. "Will the last witness please step forward?"

My eyes flicker around the courtroom. Who the hell is she talking about? There *are* no other witnesses. Well, except for that snake which I'm sure won't be slithering in here anytime soon.

There's a loud, collective gasp as the witness enters the courtroom. My mouth drops to the floor. It can't be! But it is! *Snow White!*

Wearing the same puff-sleeve rag she's always worn and that same revolting red velvet bow, she waltzes toward the stand.

My eyes fix on her face. Her lips are as red as blood, her hair as black as ebony, and her skin as white as snow. In fact, her skin is fairer than ever. Damn it! There's nothing like a deep sleep to make your complexion glow. My body shakes with envy.

Facing the stunned courtroom, she tells the judge how the dwarfs kept her preserved in a glass coffin. The "sweeties" just couldn't bear to part with her.

I don't get it. She was dwarf-proof dead.

"So, how exactly did you get here?" snaps the judge, her interest piqued.

"This morning, a handsome prince rode by and woke me with a kiss," she says dreamily.

With nothing but a kiss? Rage is shooting through me like a thousand crossbows. I paid a fortune for that evil potion. I deserve a refund.

"We're getting married," she beams.

What! She's going to live happily ever after? I'm close to imploding as the courtroom erupts into raucous cheers and applause.

"Order in the court!" roars the judge, jiggling her layers of jowls.

As the courtroom quiets, Snow White's eyes meet mine. Tears stream down her cheeks. "I feel for you," she says.

I feel for her too. An unbearable hatred that makes me want to jump out of my skin. I want to kill her! I want her dead!

The judge reaches down under her bench and holds up something as if it were a dead rat.

My hag rag! It must have washed up on shore. My heart leaps to my throat. I'm doomed!

"Miss White, do you recognize this?" asks the judge, puckering her lips in disgust.

Terror washes over Snow White's porcelain face.

"Yes, the woman who gave me the apple was wearing that," she says, her voice trembling.

The judge shoots me a contemptuous look and then bangs her gavel. "Off with her head!" she roars.

I'm numb. My life is over!

"Your Honor, please be lenient on her," pleads Snow White. "Everyone deserves a second chance."

"Yes, I do deserve a second chance—this time to get it right and destroy you once and for all, Snow White!"

My stepdaughter blanches, her snow-white skin turning whiter than ever. The judge fires me another dirty look and slams her gavel once more.

"I hereby sentence The Evil Queen to one hundred years in prison!"

One hundred years! The words reverberate in my head. One hundred years! What will I look like when I come out? That is, *if* I come out. The headline in tomorrow's *Fairytale Tattler* flashes through my head: *"Evil Queen's Fairest Days are Over!"*

CHAPTER 3

I'm back in that mirrorless dungeon. It's the kind in the middle of nowhere you can never escape even if you think you can. I'm devoid of all worldly contact, except for a lowly guard. A dim-witted green ogre who brings me meals. Lousy meals I barely touch. Trust me, I'd rather eat green curds and whey.

Every day, I beg him to go to my castle to fetch my magic mirror. I want to know what I look like. Where I stand. I've even promised him a royal position if does me this one itsy bitsy favor. He can be my new Huntsman. No deal.

Seven years. That's how long I've been here. The only way I know is by the monthly magazines the guard brings me. His wife works at some beauty center and gets all these style and beauty magazines free. *Palace Digest, Princess, Royal Style* to name a few. Rather than throwing them out when she's done with them, her husband, the ogre, passes them on to me.

The magazines have helped me pass the time away. Even better, they've kept me up on the latest beauty trends. If I ever get out of this hellhole, I know what I have to do. Go to a spa! That's what all the fairy-tale princesses are doing these days. I grit my teeth every time I think about Snow White living the spa-life—happily ever after—while I'm rotting away in this cell.

Yes, spa treatments! With a few deep-cleansing facials, body scrubs, and massages—okay, and a little makeup—I'll knock Snow White right off her pedestal. And I'll show my

stupid-ass looking glass—in fact, any crappy looking glass—
who's *Fairest of All.*

While I'm reading about the anti-aging benefits of bulbadox juice (I could kick myself for wasting it on that evil
potion) in my latest *Princess* magazine, a jingling sound
distracts me. I look up. It's the ogre, and he's dangling a large
metal key.

"You're getting out of here."

Did I hear that right?

"Read this." He holds up a brochure with an illustration of
a castle on the cover.

Tossing my magazine, I wrench it away from him through
the rusty iron bars. I start reading.

WELCOME TO FARAWAY

*FARAWAY is a unique treatment center that will give
you the tools to find your inner princess. It's a magical
place where recovery and self-discovery happen every
day. Guests reside in a magnificent castle where they
can chill out and relax. Our tranquil center also
features an enchanted forest, lush gardens, and a
lovely hillside view.*

*We offer a personalized therapy program, developed
by our renowned staff to meet your individual needs.
Our unique program offers a variety of proven clinical
methods, including one-on-one therapy and supportive
group sessions. As part of our multi-faceted program,
we offer hiking, Arts and Crafts, nutrition, yoga, and
fine dining. You will eat like royalty.*

*Once we feel you are ready, you will re-enter the
enchanted world of fairy tales and participate in
our apprenticeship program. Each assignment is
customized to meet your special needs and skills.*

When it is completed to our satisfaction, you will be able to resume your fairy-tale life.

We, at Faraway, provide a comprehensive mind-body experience that treats the needs of the whole person. No wonder our graduates report that their lives are better and more fulfilling in every possible way. You'll look and feel more beautiful, inside and out. Get ready to live happily ever after!

You'll look and feel more beautiful. I read the words over and over as the guard unlocks my cell door. I can't believe it! I'm being sent to a spa! I'm being given a second chance to reclaim what is rightfully mine—my crown and my title, *Fairest of All.*

———◆———

From a distance, Faraway promises to be everything the leaflet said it would be. Perched high on a hill, the castle looks quite luxurious. It's even surrounded by a high stonewall and a moat. There's nothing like privacy.

The coach crosses the drawbridge. As it follows the yellow brick road toward the guardhouse, my heartbeat accelerates. I can hardly wait for my first spa treatment. And, at last, to look at myself in a mirror.

The guard, a friendly giant named Gulliver, unlocks the massive iron gate and lets us in. The driver pulls up to the castle where a plump fairy godmother-type in a green uniform with wings is waving. Of course, she must be a spa attendant. Clever! A fairy spa-mother.

"Welcome to Faraway!" she says in one of those bubbly voices I so hate. "We've been expecting you, dearie."

Dearie? Is she kidding? Doesn't she mean "My Queen"? Or "Your Majesty" or "Your Highness"? I'd even settle for "Queenie."

Before I can set her straight, she whisks me inside the castle.

Inside, Faraway doesn't quite measure up to what I expected. The "grand entrance" is not so grand. The walls are painted dingy yellow, and in some places, there are signs of chipping. The shabby furnishings, for sure, are from some junk store. Nowhere is there evidence of the lush lounging areas I've read about in those beauty magazines. Perhaps, the place is about to undergo major renovations. It seriously does need an extreme makeover.

"Here, fill this out." The fairy spa-mother hands me a sheet of parchment and a quill.

"Please answer all the questions below," it states on top. Of course, the admissions form.

1. *What are your goals here at Faraway?*
   To get beautiful, then split.

2. *Do you have any hobbies and talents?*
   Disguises. Also, making evil potions.

3. *List some of the evil things you've done.*
   Not enough space to write answer.

4. *Have you ever had a best friend?*
   My magic mirror, but we're not speaking.

5. *Have you ever been in love with someone?*
   Does "myself" count?

6. *I care about other people. TRUE OR FALSE?*
   Trick question! Not answering!

7. *What could improve your life?*
   A facial, massage, and definitely a new mirror.

8. *How do you feel about your mother?*
   NO ANSWER! It's none of your damn business.

9. *What are you most afraid of?*
   Sunburn.

10. *On a scale of 1-10, with 1=My life is a horror story and 10=My life is a fairy tale, how would you rate your life?*
    10! I'm here, right?

Strange questions, but easy enough. Except for Question #8. Some things are personal. *Very* personal. Besides, what does my mother have to do with getting a facial or massage? She's the last person I want to think about. *Ever!*

The fairy spa-mother snatches the application and reads it over. "Come with me for your first treatment." She bounces into the air and then flies down the hall.

Yes! At last! She's taking me for a facial. Anyone with two eyes can see I desperately need one. Following her, I wonder why I don't see any princesses with blue facial masks and fluffy white robes. And how come there aren't any mirrors on the walls?

Along the way, I pass a young woman, who's so skinny it's scary, mopping the floors. A good sign of a quality spa, I tell myself, having once read to beware of unsanitary conditions. She shoots me a smirk.

The loser's just jealous. I almost feel sorry for her. I pick up my pace to catch up with the fairy spa-mother.

She finally touches down in front of a door at the end of the corridor. The words "Private Do Not Enter" are scrawled across it. A treatment room. I can't wait to step inside.

To my surprise, the room is small and sparse. There's a simple wooden chair, a small set of drawers, and a bucket of water. And it, too, is painted insipid yellow. Whoever did the interior decorating around this place should be fired.

The fairy spa-mother shoves me onto the chair and drapes a shabby yellow smock over my head.

"Hey, where's my fluffy white robe?" I ask, shocked to be treated with such indignity. When I'm done with my facial, the first thing I'm going to do is complain and get her fired.

Two thumb-sized pixies, dressed in stretchy white uniforms, come buzzing into the room. One has green hair; the other purple. They circle my head in opposite directions.

"Say hello to the Hair Fairies." The fairy spa-mother grins. "They'll be taking over from here." She flies out the door, slamming it behind her.

The two pixies immediately examine my hair, strand by strand.

"I haven't had a good shampoo in ages," I tell them as they run a spiky comb through my mane. Aah. It feels so good against my itchy scalp. At last, I'm beginning to feel like I'm at a spa.

Not for long. Without the courtesy of a warning, they dump the bucket of water over my head.

Aagh! It's ice cold. I jump up from the chair.

Snip. Snip. The sound comes at me faster. *Snip. Snip. Snip. Snip. Snip.*

What the hell? They're chopping off my hair!

"I order you to stop!" I cry out, my voice more panic than power-driven.

The fairies accelerate their pace, each clutching a handle of a bone-shearing scissors.

I swat at them frantically, but they're too damn fast. Panic turns to dread. What if the maniacs butcher my face with the razor-sharp blades? I shield it with both hands.

"You have lice," tisks the purple-haired fairy.

I scratch my head and gasp. "I want my hair back!"

"Don't worry, it'll grow back," says her green-haired partner as another clump tumbles to the floor.

Grow back? It took me my entire life to grow my raven-black hair past my butt. That's it. I'm going to snatch the scissors and clip their wings. Then stomp on them.

Too late. They fling the scissors across the room. I gaze down at a foot-high mountain of hair. My hair! Sick to my stomach, I run my fingers through what remains of it. All two inches.

"Give me a mirror!" I scream.

"There are no mirrors at Faraway," says the green-haired fairy as she nosedives into the layers of hair and starts tossing them into the bucket.

No mirrors? She must be joking. No mirrors?? What kind of spa is this?

"You're ready to meet Elzmerelda, your roommate," says the other, scooping up more of my precious locks.

Roommate? Even in that disgusting dungeon, I had my own private room. Maybe it was just a stinky cell, but at least it was all mine.

"You're going to adore her," she continues. "She's one of our favorite inmates. She's done so well here."

"We always try to pair up a new patient with a recovering one," the green-haired fairy adds. "We have found that a recovering addict can serve as an excellent role model for someone who has not yet set out on their road to renewal."

Inmates? Patients? Addicts? I read in those beauty magazines—even in that brochure—that people at spas are called "guests."

"What about my massage? My facial? My seaweed wrap? My aromatherapy bath?"

The two pixies stare at me as if they haven't understood a word I've said.

My voice takes on desperation. "Or how about a swim in the mineral pool?" I read many spas have them. "I happen to be an excellent swimmer."

The purple-haired pixie raises her brows as if I'm some kind of nutcase. "Honey, the only 'pool' we have here is a moat. And trust me, you don't want to be swimming in that disease-infested swamp."

"I demand to see a list of spa services," I say in my most authoritative voice.

"This is not a spa," say the pixies in unison.

Of course. I've been sent to the wrong place. It's a mistake. A terrible, stupid mistake!

"Faraway is a recovery center for people who are addicted to evil," says the green-haired fairy in a matter-of-fact voice.

A recovery center for addicts? I should have known it sounded too good to be true. It was all a bunch of lies. A horrible bunch of lies! I should start a lawsuit! That's what I should do!

Suddenly, it all sinks in. I've been tricked. Faraway isn't a spa. It's an insane asylum!

Sloshing through my pile of hair, I bolt to the door.

I jiggle the knob, but it's jammed. I slam my body against the hard slab of wood, hoping I can ram it down. Not even a dent. My hip roars with pain.

"I order you to let me out of here!" I scream.

The duo fires me a look that says I *am* crazy.

Beads of sweat are erupting all over me. Nausea rises to my chest, and the room closes in on me. And then blackness.

CHAPTER 4

B irds are attacking me! They're circling my head. Ow! One of them is pecking my nose. Wakening from my nightmare, I snap open my eyes. Wait! This is *not* a bad dream. Birds *are* all over me! They're trying to pull down my bed covers.

"Get lost!" I scream, swatting at them. I swear if one makes a dent on my face, they're all dead.

Where am I? A ray of light filters through the darkness. I'm in a small square room. There's a set of drawers, a couple of doors, and an empty bed next to mine.

A singsong voice pierces the air. "Rise and shine!"

A gangly woman in a drab flannel nightgown lopes toward me. She's got to be at least six feet tall, and even in the dim light, I can tell she's no beauty queen. Her nose is long and pointy; her eyes too close together, and her lips pale and thin. She adjusts a yellow bow over her mousy brown hair.

"Who are you?" I ask, still swatting at the birds.

"I'm your new roomie, Elzmerelda," she says in a tone so cheerful it makes me want to swat her. "How was your first night at Faraway?"

Faraway? Then it hits me. Hard like a hammer to my head. My new reality. A living nightmare. I'm trapped in a loony bin with a lunatic. I've got to get out of here!

"Lalalalalalalalalalalalalalalalalalalalalalala…." Singing on top of her lungs, the lunatic pirouettes over to the window and pulls the curtains apart. Sunshine instantly floods the room through a grille of metal bars.

The jolt of bright light makes me squint. Shit! Squinting will give me lines! And lines will make me look old! I struggle desperately to pull a blanket over my head, but the damn birds won't let me.

"It's another beautiful sunny day," the loony trills, peeking outside.

She *is* nuts. Doesn't she know how bad the sun is for your skin? Freckles! Wrinkles! Age spots! Crow's feet! You can even die! "Close the damn curtains!" I order as more birds whoosh through the bars and swarm me.

Ignoring me, the homely beanpole slips into a puff-sleeve dress that matches her bow. It's so Snow White, I want to puke.

"You still haven't told me about your first night," she says.

After that dreadful haircut, I can't remember a thing. I bet those wicked hair fairies poisoned me. With that comb they used. The nerve of them stealing my idea! I'm going to add that to my list of grievances when I get out of this joint and sue.

More birds! I dodge them while the lunatic brushes her limp waist-length hair.

Jealousy gnaws at me. How come she got to keep her worthless tresses? I stroke my head, hoping for magic. Forget it! My hair's still the length of your average front lawn.

The loony shoots me a wide toothy grin that makes me want to knock out her large, crooked teeth. "You need to get dressed," she says, prancing over to a closet. She returns with a bright yellow gown folded over her spindly arms. She lays it flat on my bed.

"What's that?" I ask, eyeing the hideous garment as if it's carrying the plague. Doesn't she know I don't do colors? I only wear black.

"The Good Fairies made it for you. It'll make you cheery."

I also don't do cheery.

She makes her bed. "Hurry! You don't want to be late for breakfast."

Screw breakfast! I just need a cup of black coffee. Trust me, I'm even more evil without one.

"Lalala! Lalala!" She won't stop.

What am I waiting for? While her back is turned, I bolt out of bed, charge through the swarm of birds, and sprint to the nearest door. I jerk the door open and slam it behind me on the beak freaks.

Dragonballs! Wrong door! The foul odor lets me know immediately where I am. The bathroom. Yet another reminder I'm not at spa. There's a bucket for a tub, chamber pot, chipped pitcher, and a few ragged towels. Something's missing. *A mirror!*

It's not possible. Every halfway decent bathroom has a mirror, right? I check inside every drawer, under the tub, between the towels…even in the wretched chamber pot. Zilch!

I storm back into the bedroom "Where did you hide the mirror?" I shout at Elzmerelda.

"Don't you remember?" She grins. "Mirrors aren't allowed at Faraway."

My body shakes, and sweat runs down the back of my knees.

I'm having major mirror withdrawal.

CHAPTER 5

Why the hell are we outside? More bloody sunshine! I've got a splitting headache and feel jittery all over. I need a cup of coffee. Desperately.

"This is our Enchanted Garden," beams Elzmerelda. "We grow our own vegetables, fruits, and grains."

It's all one big green blur to me. I'm getting edgier and edgier. A rabbit scampers by me. I want to crush it. Turn it into rabbit stew. Seriously, if don't get my daily dose of caffeine soon, I *am* going to cause some major damage.

"Get me my coffee!" I order.

A single, simple cup of black coffee. What's so difficult about that? Even in that decrepit dungeon, I always got my morning coffee.

"Oh, we don't drink coffee at Faraway," she says in that sickening singsong voice. "We only drink herbal tea. It's part of the healing process."

My life is over. I'm never going to make it out of here without my coffee.

"Here's a basket." The loony hands me the extra one she's holding. She's so relentlessly cheery a fire-breathing dragon couldn't melt her smiley façade.

I've had it. Coffee or no coffee. I've got to get out of here. My eyes search in every direction for an exit until Miss Cheerful and Deranged yanks me toward a patch of berries.

"What kind of tea do you like?" she asks. "My favorite's chamomile."

Mine is anything that will shut her up. Permanently.

"Lalalala!" sings a stout, silver-haired woman in a red frock and bonnet, waving a wand. When she turns her back, I catch sight of a pair of wings and a butt as big as a warthog's.

"People, let me hear you sing it louder!" shouts another big butt woman in an identical green getup. I recognize her immediately. She's that rude fairy spa-mother I met yesterday.

"Bring it on!" cheers a third wand-waving, winged woman in blue who could easily be the shorter, roly-poly sister of the first two.

How can they be so energetic so early in the morning? I bet *they* get coffee!

Singing their "lalalalas" in perfect harmony, the trio is supervising a pathetic group of losers who are picking berries and attempting to sing along. There's a troll with glazed eyes and a pronounced limp, a woman about my age but triple my size, and the scary-skinny chick I saw mopping floors yesterday. She bears a strong resemblance to my new "roomie," except she's anything but cheerful. Who are all these freaks?

"This is the way we start our day," Elzmerelda tells me. "The Good Fairies believe singing brings out the best in people."

Is she kidding? It's bringing out the worst in me. This "lala" stuff is driving me crazy. I know. It's a conspiracy to prove I really *do* belong in this nuthouse.

"And they believe a rustic diet will restore our souls." *Doesn't she ever shut up? I want to rip her tongue out.* "We only eat things made from fresh fruits, veggies, grains, and eggs we gather ourselves."

Peasant diet is more like it. What happened to the "you will eat like royalty" promise? Another lie. I *am* going to sue!

Elzmerelda frolics over to the others, leaving me alone. Brainstorm! While no one's watching, I'll run away and escape. The front gate can't be too far off. Ha! By the time they notice I'm missing, I'll be long gone.

So long, losers. I've hardly taken five steps when the three Badass Fairies touchdown in front of me and grab me forcefully by my arms. I try to wrestle myself free but am no match for their astounding strength. They're like a pack of winged behemoths.

"Hello, I'm Fanta," says the one in green.

"I'm Flossie," says the one in red.

"And I'm Fairweather," says the one in blue. "And you must be our new resident, Jane Yvel."

My real name. I haven't used it in years. At that dungeon, everyone called me The Evil Queen. Everyone!

"Welcome to Faraway!" they say together.

"Come join us for breakfast," says Flossie as they haul me back to the berry patch. "We've baked some fresh muffins."

All I want to do is tear off a pair of their wings and blow out of here.

"Don't you love the Good Fairies?" asks Elzmerelda, biting into her muffin.

Seriously, I want to poison them but have to admit the muffin's delicious. Warm, buttery, melt-in-your-mouth delicious. I haven't eaten anything this good in years. It's even gotten me over my coffee fixation.

Elzmerelda babbles on. "They used to be Sleeping Beauty's fairy godmothers. When they retired, they came here. Now, they're certified life coaches."

Life coaches? What kind of nonsense job is that?

"They also teach cooking, sewing, and Arts and Crafts. Their classes are so much fun!"

Hardly my idea of fun. Maybe, there's an advanced class on making evil potions.

"And on Sunday's, they hold a talent show."

"Don't trust them; they're spies," says another voice. It's the scary skinny girl that resembles Elzmerelda. Picking crumbs off the top of her muffin, she saunters over to the bench where we're sitting.

"Jane, this is my sister, Sasperilla," says Elzmerelda.

Sasperilla gives me the once-over with her dark, beady eyes.

"Why are you two here?" I ask.

"Mother made us come," says Sasperilla, her tone bitter.

"She thinks if we get more in touch with our inner princess, we'll marry royalty," chimes in Elzmerelda.

"It's all our stepsister's fault." Sasperilla rolls a crumb between her bony fingers. "If that cunning little bitch hadn't snuck out of her room with the other glass slipper, Prince Charming would have been mine!"

"Cinderella's not a b...bad person," says Elzmerelda.

Sasperilla snorts. "Puh-lease. It takes one to know one. Right, Jane?"

So, she thinks *I'm* a bitch. Just wait. I'll show her.

Another woman strolls over to us. The obese one. She has delicate features and long, lustrous red hair that I would kill for. I'd almost call her pretty if she weren't so damn fat and freckled.

"Sasperilla, can I have your muffin?" she asks.

"Be my guest." The skinny bitch tosses her the barely touched muffin. "One woman's dread is another woman's bread."

Elzmerelda shakes her head in frustration. "Sassy, you're never going to get of here if you don't start eating like a normal person."

Sasperilla scoffs at her sister. "Everyone knows princes only marry skinny girls. If I wanted to marry a poor cobbler, I'd look like Winifred."

The heavy woman forces a smile. "At least, my husband's a good man and loves me."

"Yeah, right," snickers Sasperilla. "He loves you so much he had you committed here."

Winifred's hazel eyes flare. "Here, you can keep your

muffin." She flings it back at the skinny bitch.

"Fattie!" screams Sasperilla, flicking crumbs off her frilly gown as if they're deadly insects.

Winifred's freckles explode like fireworks, turning her whole face red. Clenching her fists, she looks ready to charge.

Great. The party's about to get bigger. The ugly troll is limping our way. His stony eyes fixate on me. What's your problem, mister? On second thought, I *don't* want to know. I've had it with these whackos.

"How's everyone doing?" It's Fanta. Her two big-butt sisters join her just in time to prevent a brawl between Sasperilla and Winifred.

"People, finish up," says Flossie.

"It's time for your morning meditation," says Fairweather.
Meditation? Now, what poison are they springing on me? Elzmerelda tells me that meditation teaches us to stay focused on the present while turbulent thoughts and emotions swirl through our heads. "Getting in touch with your inner spirituality is another part of the healing process."

Inner spirituality? What the hell is she talking about? It gets worse. She rambles on, spewing more mumbo jumbo like "life affirmation," "self-realization," and "emotional awareness."

"It's a stupid waste of time!" snorts Sasperilla.

Reluctantly, the skinny bitch sits down on the grass with her sister, the fatty, and the catatonic troll in a cross-legged pose. Fanta leads them in some ridiculous "hang-out-in-the-light" incantation. I refuse to join in.

Flossie takes me aside. "Don't worry, dear. Grass stains don't hurt so please find a place with the others." She gently takes me by the hand and then shoves me to the ground. The nerve of her! I'm going to file a complaint for excessive force. *Fairy brutality!* When they find out I'm a queen, they'll shut this place down. And I'll be free to go!

Right now, I have no choice but to chant along while Flossie keeps her stink eye on me. She'll probably batter me with her wand if I don't cooperate. And break my nose and knock out my teeth! I'll never ever be *Fairest of All* again! Talking about turbulent thoughts! Chanting isn't going to help me.

"Close your eyes and repeat after me," says Fanta. Waving her wand, she chants:

> "I am here to be helped.
> To share. To be one with me.
> On whatever level, I can find myself
> To become the me I need to be."

I have no idea what these words mean. But when I say them, a peacefulness saturates my body and mind. I'm no longer on this planet. I'm in a higher place. A place where everything is possible. Even going back to my castle and forgiving my mirror.

"Isn't Fanta amazing?" singsongs Elzmerelda when our meditation ends. "She and her sisters were once able to put an entire kingdom to sleep."

I hate to admit it, but I've never felt so good. I feel a glimmer of hope. Maybe, this place is some kind of spa after all. Okay, it's a little run down and caters to a bunch of crazies, but nonetheless, it's got spa potential.

Fairweather waddles up to me. She hands me a map showing the layout of the castle and grounds. "My dear, it's time for you to meet your personal therapist."

A therapist? Faraway *is* a real spa! At last, I'm getting a massage. A facial and quick body wrap can't be far behind. In no time, they'll let me out of this joint. Renewed! Refreshed! Revitalized! Ready to reclaim my place as *Fairest of All*.

———⟡———

Following the directions of the map, I find myself humping the never-ending spiral staircase of a towering turret. With every step, I get more and more winded. The massage room is located at the very top. What a stupid place to put it! Then again, maybe they deliberately want you to feel wasted to appreciate your massage. That's *if* you make it. I may not.

At last, I reach my destination. Breathing heavily, I stagger into a small circular room. It's sparsely decorated with only a simple round wall clock and a single piece of furniture—a burgundy velvet chaise lounge. Although worn and faded, the chaise looks comfortable and inviting. This must be where I lie down and get my massage. Wasting no time, I sink into it. I'm so ready to surrender my body.

Just as I relax, a tiny winged creature zips in like a streak of lightning, drenching me in a shower of sparkling dust. I cough. *What the—*

"Hello, Jane. I'm Shrinkerbell, but you can all me Shrink. I'll be your personal therapist here at Faraway."

What kind of massage therapist is this? She's the size of a sparrow, with hands no bigger than a bird's claws and thick round spectacles that make her look bug-eyed. Buzzing around the room, she's as calming as a mosquito.

"So that you know, Tinkerbell is my fraternal twin. She got the looks; I got the brains." She runs one of her tiny hands through a messy pouf of blond hair. "Who do you think came up with the Peter Pan complex? Me, that's who! It kills me that my in-your-face sister always gets the credit."

Why is she telling me all this stuff? She's taking precious time away from my massage. I'm going to demand an extra fifteen minutes if she doesn't get going.

She swoops down from the ceiling. "Sorry for getting carried away with my issues. We're here to talk about yours. First, do you have any questions?"

"Yes. Can you go deep?" I read in one of those beauty magazines that a deep tissue massage can magically restore your beauty.

"Yes, I like to go as deep as possible with all my clients. My goal is to find the underlying causes of their problems."

Great, because I feel like crap. I'm not sure if it's the lack of coffee, the climb, or mirror withdrawal. I still have a pounding headache, and my body is aching all over. Plus, that damn dust is stinging my eyes.

"Just one other little question. Can I borrow a mirror before we begin?" Someone around this joint has got to have one.

"Ah, yes," she replies.

Finally! A mirror!

"I've read your case history. Quite complex, indeed. Has anyone ever told you what you look like?"

"Actually, I had a magic mirror that did a pretty good job until this little shrew named Snow White got it distracted."

She zooms in closer and circles my head. Talking about someone being in your face.

"Your nose is too long; your lips are too big; your cheekbones are too high, and your eyes, although a lovely shade of green, are too far apart."

Her words hit me like a cannonball. "Liar!"

"Jane, having to face the truth is the start of recovery."

"Give me a mirror!" I demand.

She pulls out a tiny glass object from a pocket.

"Give me that!" I grab for it.

She zips off before I can snatch it. "No, Jane, this is *my* magic mirror."

Clasping the small object in her tiny hands, she examines every inch of my face. I try again to snag the mirror, but her trail of fairy dust is blinding me.

"Ah! I've discovered a freckle."

A freckle!? I bolt to a sitting position, clutching my stomach like someone's punched it. I knew all the sunshine around this place would do me in. I'll never be the fairest again! I'm ruined!

A mixture of rage and despair boils inside me. Grasping at air, I finally snatch the looking glass and hold it up to my face. I don't see a damn thing. That's because it's a magnifying glass, not a mirror. I refuse to believe her. She's deliberately messing with my head. She deserves to die!

I hold out my hands and get ready to smoosh her between my palms. *Clap!* She flits off just in the nick of time.

I rub my prickling hands together as she flutters overhead out of reach.

"You have numerous imperfections, but they come together in an interesting, attractive way. Remember, Jane, the whole is greater than the sum of its parts."

"Are we done here?" I say, gritting my teeth.

"No, Jane, we've just begun."

A chime from the clock sounds.

"Time's up for today. I'll see you here tomorrow at the same time."

Like a shooting star, she's gone, leaving a streak of sparkling fairy dust in her wake.

I choke. Obviously, I'm not getting a massage.

Every muscle in my body is twitching from that bogus therapist. She thinks I'm going to see her tomorrow? Not a chance in hell. I'm going to figure a way out of here. The good news is I've got a map. Following it, I head back to my room. I'll take a quick nap to unknot my body and brain, then study it. Seriously, how hard can it be?

The moment I step foot inside the castle, Fairweather thrusts a bucket and mop at me.

"Ha-ha! It's your day to do the floors," snickers Sasperilla.

Flossie tosses her a feather duster. "You'll be keeping her company."

Scary-Skinny scrunches up her face in disgust.

Rage is rising inside me. I demand to know what's going on.

"Everyday, after morning meditation, we have castle clean-up," explains Elzmerelda as she polishes a bureau. "The

Good Fairies believe that hard work builds strong bodies and minds."

Is she joking? Haven't those cheapskates heard of the word "servant"?

"Jane, what are you waiting for? Get going!" snaps Fanta, jabbing her wand into my back.

These Badass Fairies aren't life coaches; they're slave drivers.

"During clean-up, we all take turns meeting with Shrink," Elzmerelda tells me after they fly off. "Winnie's meeting with her now. Then it's Sassy's turn, What's-His-Name's, and finally mine."

I'm hardly listening to a word she's saying. I'm too busy squeezing water out of the mop.

Sasperilla tickles my nose with her duster. "Having fun yet?"

It's bad enough I'm doing slave labor, but there's no way I'm putting up with Skinny Bitch's sarcasm. I toss the bucket of dirty water at her. She shrieks.

"Now, I am." I smile. She looks like a drowned rat.

Before Sasperilla can retaliate, Fanta flies in, touching down between us.

"Look what she did to me!" screeches Sasperilla, wringing out her soggy curls.

"You can talk all about it with Shrink." Grabbing her by the elbow, Fanta steers her toward the front door.

Sasperilla turns her head and sticks her tongue out at me. I give her my always-effective icy stare.

"Get back to work," Fanta barks at me.

The Badass Fairy's words echo in my head, and I'm suddenly a little girl again, scrubbing the gritty stone floor of the cramped, one-story flat I share with my mother. A chorus of voices coming from outside distracts me, and I peek out the window. Children are playing on the street. They're laughing, singing, having fun. How I long to join them! "Jane, what are you doing?" yells my mother. Yanking me by my hair, she shoves my head into the bucket of dirty water. I hold my breath, counting the seconds, not daring to open my eyes to the sting of the septic suds. Thirty-one…thirty-two…thirty-three… Finally, she jerks me out. She throws a mop at me and hisses, "Get back to work!"

I mop the castle floor frantically to erase the memory. *I hate you, Fanta.*

CHAPTER 6

All this dreadful mopping has worked up my appetite. I'm starving. Finally, Flossie reappears and announces lunch.

This time our meal is indoors in a large banquet hall, if you can call it that. There's nothing more than a few rectangular wooden tables with chairs and a buffet. The walls, like everything else in this dump, are painted yellow, and the floor-to-ceiling windows allow the sun to shine through brightly. There's just no escaping the sun around this joint.

Fairweather toddles up to me. "Jane, you're on table setting duty. The silverware is in the buffet. And tonight after dinner, you have clean-up. Now, get going!"

The nerve of her bossing me around! Hasn't someone told these Badass Fairies that I'm a queen? Hello! *I* am the one who gives orders. Even in that dreary dungeon, they treated me with the respect I deserve. They didn't make me do these awful fit-for-a-servant chores. And maybe the food wasn't so great, but at least I got room service. If I don't escape this joint, I'm going to demand a transfer back there.

"Lunch is one of our best meals!" says Elzmerelda. Holding a plate full of assorted cheeses, salads, and breads, she takes a seat at the last table I'm setting.

I fling the rest of the silverware on the table and head over to the lunch line. Ravenous, I pile up my plate. Miss Scary-

Skinny is in front of me. She hesitantly puts a few greens on her plate. Miss Fat-and-Freckled, who's behind me, eats for two, loading way more on her plate than me. She slyly sneaks an extra piece of bread into her pocket. Fanta catches her in the act and immediately confiscates it.

"Remember, Winifred, you are what you eat," she chides.

Scary-Skinny directs a couple of pig-like snorts at the overweight woman.

"And the same goes for you, Sasperilla," snaps the plump fairy. "You're not leaving this room until you eat this piece of bread. And I'll be watching every bite."

"See, I told you they were spies!" sneers Sasperilla.

I'm beginning to believe her.

———❦———

I take a seat at Elzmerelda's table, between Sasperilla and Winifred. The troll, the last in line, teeter-totters over to another table and eats alone.

"So, what are you here for?" I ask Winifred after a bite of a surprisingly tasty cheese.

The fat woman gulps down a mouthful of buttered bread. "I had what they call a psychotic breakdown." She gazes down at her plate, shamefully. "I tried to kill my own children."

Cripes! And they thought I was evil. I merely tried to kill my stepdaughter. We weren't even related by blood.

"Ha! I bet she tried to eat them!" snickers Sasperilla as she expertly sneaks her bread under the table.

Winifred chokes. Elzmerelda pats her on her back and shakes her head in dismay at her sister.

"And what about Gimpy over there?" I ask, pointing to the troll, who reminds me of those loathsome dwarfs. He keeps staring at me and is getting on my nerves.

"Oh, it's very sad," says Elzmerelda, squinting in his direction. "The Good Fairies told us he's a notorious criminal. An extortionist!"

That's not sad. It's just a *little* evil.

"But then some queen outsmarted him. He was so mad he stomped his foot into the ground. Waist deep! Then he tried to tear off his other leg."

That explains his limp. "How did he end up here?"

"The queen made her husband pull him out, then had him committed."

She's the evil one!

"He couldn't remember a thing. Not even his name."

"He has a classic case of dissociative amnesia according to Dr. Grimm," interjects Winifred.

"Who's Dr. Grimm?" I ask.

"An ogre with big ears who's out to get us," butts in Sasperilla.

"Don't listen to her. He leads our group therapy sessions. You'll meet him right after lunch," says Winifred.

Maybe, they call it group therapy because we give each other massages? Fat chance.

"We have to call that little guy 'What's-His-Name' until he can remember his real name," says Elzmerelda. "Dr. Grimm says that'll be his first step toward recovery."

"Puh-lease!" Sasperilla rolls her eyes. "He's a vertically challenged moron. I can't believe I have to associate with people like him."

Personally, I can't believe I have to associate with any of these freaks. I don't need a magic mirror to tell me where I stand among this sorry bunch of losers.

"So, why are *you* here, Miss Needs-to-Know-Every-body's-Business?" asks Sasperilla.

"I thought I was here for a makeover." There's no way I'm sharing my life with these nut-jobs.

"You *are* here for a makeover. Only not the kind you were expecting," says Winifred.

"What do you mean?"

"Trust me, you'll see."

Group is held in a small room on the main floor of the castle. Yet more of that dismal minimalist look—there are just six wooden chairs arranged in a circle. We each take a seat, leaving one for Dr. Grimm.

The chair is hard as nails. It's digging into my back, not to mention killing my butt. Comfort is clearly not a priority around this sham-of-a-spa.

"Stop staring at me, you mindless midget," snaps Sasperilla at What's-His-Name.

"He's not staring at you," comes her sister to his defense. "He's staring at Jane."

She's right, and I wish he'd stop it already.

Sasperilla crinkles her nose. "Why don't you wear your spectacles? Mother paid a fortune for them. Or is it that you're afraid they'll make you uglier than you already are?"

Elzmerelda shrivels. "Sassy, please don't tell her I lost them."

Sasperilla shoots her sister a smirk but wipes it off her face when a tall, stringy man slumps into the room. He takes the vacant seat next to her. This must be Dr. Grimm.

"Good afternoon, group," he says solemnly.

Grimm looks like his name. Gloomy and depressing. Dressed in a droopy black waistcoat, he seriously should be leading a funeral procession, not a group therapy session. His beaky nose and straggly gray hair don't help nor does his unkempt beard—easily a nest for one of those rude birds. And Sasperilla's right again. His ears are big. At least five inches long.

"I'd like everyone to say hello to Jane," he says. "Our new group member."

Sasperilla feigns a yawn. "We've already met the bitch."

"Sasperilla," says Grimm sternly, "you know we don't use that kind of language in group. Please apologize to Jane."

"Sooory." She twists one of her long corkscrew curls

around a bony finger, clearly not.

"So, Jane, is there something you'd like to share with us today?" asks Grimm.

"Yes, my back is killing me."

Stroking his beard, Grimm gazes at me with bewilderment.

Sasperilla snorts with laughter. "He meant about your life."

Is she kidding? There's *nothing* I want to share with her or any of these psychos.

Grimm leans forward. "Jane, there has to be at least one thing you'd like to share."

Fine. "I'm a Queen." The way they treat me around this place they must have no clue.

"Wow!" says Elzmerelda in awe. "I knew you had to be royalty!"

"Big deal!" says Sasperilla. "Royals are a dime a dozen."

"That's not true," says Winifred. "I read that only five percent of Lalaland's population is a king or queen."

What's-His-Name's eyes twinkle, finally showing some life.

"Does the word 'queen' jog your memory?" Grimm asks him.

Rocking his body, What's-His-Name chants "n-nice queen" over and over. He *is* a major head case.

"Good." Grimm nods. "Try to remember more things about this nice queen."

"Hold on. I want to know more about *this* 'Queen'," cuts in Sasperilla. "So, *Jane,* were you born into royalty *or* did you marry into it?"

"I married a King." Wait! Why am I telling this skinny bitch *anything* about my life?

"Did your mother bring you up to marry royalty? Teach you all the tricks?"

My mother. My stomach turns over.

"Leave my mother out of this!" I yell.

"Jane, do you want to tell us something about your

mother?" asks Grimm.

"Go to hell! All of you!"

"Jane, I will remind you that we have a no tolerance policy for foul language. Just because you're royalty doesn't mean you get special treatment. We've had several kings and queens here before. I even recall an Emperor. The bottom line is everyone is treated as equals."

That's obvious. I don't need a lecture from some shlump of a head doctor to make that clear to me. What's just as obvious: I don't belong here.

"Group is over," announces Grimm as I spring to my feet.

Finally! There's nothing I want to do more than say farewell to these losers. With the exception of poisoning them, Grimm included.

I've made up my mind. Whatever it takes, I've got to escape this madhouse.

———— ❧ ————

"People, it's time to indulge your creativity," announces Fairweather upon meeting us in the corridor.

"What's going on?" I ask Elzmerelda.

She explains that every day after group we attend one of three workshops: "Enchanted Arts & Crafts" with Fairweather, "Sew-La-Ti-Do" with Flossie, or "The Magic of Cooking" with Fanta.

"The Good Fairies believe creativity nourishes the soul and builds self-esteem," she says.

What dragon dung! There's only one thing I want to create. An escape plan.

———— ❧ ————

I end up in the cooking workshop with Winifred. It takes place in the castle's kitchen, which is surprisingly well equipped and elaborate compared to the rest of this rundown dump.

Fanta tells us that today's project is to make a "delicious crusty bread."

"I'm going to leave you two girls on your own. I'll come back in a little while." She stops short at the door. "Jane, please make sure that Winifred doesn't eat the dough before you bake it." And then she's gone.

Great! A chance to escape.

"I love making bread," says Winifred, already gathering pans, bowls, and utensils. "It's so therapeutic. It lets you take out all your hurt and anger on the dough, but still the bread turns out delicious."

She's obviously made bread before. Good. I'll let her do all the work. When she's not looking, I'll split. With a little luck, I'll be able to sneak a piece for my journey home.

Luck is not in my cards. Winifred immediately puts me to work.

"Jane, we need water, yeast, butter, and flour," she says with authority.

How am I supposed to know where they are? I've never been in this kitchen. In fact, I haven't been in a kitchen for years. When I was Queen, I had cooks.

"Hurry, Jane. We don't have all day!"

Maybe it's time to remind her that I'm still a queen and don't take orders from anyone.

With her hands planted on her wide hips, she taps her foot as though she's counting down to an attack. The thought of her two hundred-pound body tackling mine motivates me. I'm not ready to die. I have a future ahead of me. A title to recapture.

I manage to find all the ingredients. Winifred mixes them together in a large earthenware bowl.

"Now we have our dough," she says.

She sprinkles our butcher-block worktable with some of the flour and places the mixture on the surface. "Now, comes the fun part. We get to knead it."

We? I want nothing to do with this big glob of goo.

"Watch." She plunges her hands into the dough and starts

to push, pull, and fold it. "Kneading is great for releasing stress. Try it."

Cautiously, I put my hands into the dough and copy her motions. It's soft and warm. And you know what? It *does* feel good!

"I used to think that making bread was like making love," says Winifred, her voice wistful.

A spark of interest kindles inside me.

"When I first got married, I would caress the dough and stretch it gently. Over time, I started to whack and squeeze it hard."

Something in her relationship changed. Despite my curiosity, I let it go.

"Think about someone you hate and pretend he or she is the dough," she tells me.

Shrink! Grimm! This fat chick and the rest of those pathetic loonies! I hate them all! To my surprise, I find myself tugging at the dough and bashing it. I break into a sweat as I work the dough harder and harder.

"Good job, Jane." Winifred takes the dough from me and forms it into a round shape. Still flat as a board, it hardly resembles a loaf of bread.

"Do we bake it now?" I ask.

"No." She places a towel over the dough. "We have to wait a half-hour for it to rise."

What! Now, I have to hang out with her?

"Would you care for some chamomile tea?" she asks.

A cup of coffee would be more like it. Strong and black.

"Sure," I tell her.

She boils some water in the cauldron and then returns with a tray holding two cups of tea and a plate full of biscuits. "Have one," she says. "They must be left over from yesterday's class."

I bite into a tasty biscuit and notice she's not eating one. She stares at me, salivating with envy.

"You're so lucky you're so thin. I bet you can eat anything

you want and never gain a pound."

I feel a tinge of pity. It must be awful to be that fat.

"My husband won't make love to me anymore," she says forlornly.

I wonder why she would *ever* want to make love to the creep who sent her here.

"So, what's your husband like?" she asks.

This is getting way too personal. I wish the damn dough would rise.

"He's dead," I say.

"I'm sorry."

"Don't be. He was a lot older than me."

"Do you miss him?"

"Of course!" What a big fat liar I am! Why would I miss him? Our brief marriage was a joke. Old King Cold spent all his time doting on his daughter Snow White. Little Miss Perfect. I was almost happy when he died. Except I got stuck with taking care of the imp.

Winifred returns her attention to the dough. She removes the towel. I'm shocked. The dough has risen. It's double its size!

She gently runs her fingers across the top. "Touch it. It's like the skin of a baby."

Hesitantly, I stroke the dough. It *is* like the skin of a baby. Smooth and silky. So new to the world. The memory of the infant I never got a chance to know fills my head. Trembling, I pull my hand away.

"Are you okay?" Winifred asks.

"I'm fine," I stammer. The painful memory fades.

"Good. One last thing before we put it into the hearth," says Winifred. "I'm going to let you do the honors."

"Now, what do I have to do?" I ask, not really wanting to know.

"Imagine your worst enemy and punch it as hard as you can."

Is she serious? Okay. Here goes. I look down at the perfect white mound, and to my astonishment, it comes alive. Oh my God! It's Snow White! Hatred shoots through my veins.

With my right hand curled into a tight fist, I punch the dough with a force I never knew I had. But as I strike the mound, it's no longer Snow White. The dough has morphed. It's turned into the one person I've dreaded ever seeing again. Nelle Yvel. *My mother!* I shriek. The dough deflates. I shriek again.

"Perfect!" Winifred places the dough in the hearth. "Now, we have to wait until it bakes."

More waiting? The image of my mother has knocked me for a loop. I'm drained and shaken.

In no time, a delicious aroma wafts through the air. It gets my mind off my mother. My heartbeat returns to normal.

"What's the point of all this hard work?" I ask. "I mean, the bread's just going to get eaten or turn moldy."

"Look on the bright side. You've created something that will nourish others," replies Winifred. "When I bake delicious bread for my family, it's my way of telling them I love them."

Her eyes grow watery.

"So, in other words, you're baking love?" I say with uncertainty.

"I never thought about it that way." She takes a sip of tea.

"Once my children got lost in the woods and scattered pieces of my bread to help them find their way back home." A tear spills into her tea. "I miss them."

Our conversation comes to a dead end, and we drink our tea in silence. The tantalizing smell of the baking bread grows stronger. It's making me hungry. Finally, Winifred removes the dough from the hearth. To my amazement, it's a big crusty loaf of bread. Winifred must be some kind of magician.

"Have some," she says.

I tear off a piece of the warm bread and stuff it in my mouth. My eyes light up. It's so good! Winifred bites into a chunk and moans with pleasure. Within minutes, we devour the entire loaf.

Winifred's face falls. Why is she suddenly so glum?

"When Fanta finds out that I've eaten so much bread, she'll ban me from dinner."

"Don't worry. I'll tell her I ate the entire loaf."

"Thanks, Jane. I owe you." A cheek-to-cheek smile spreads across her chubby face.

I've made a decision. I'm taking Winifred off my hate list.

"Jane, how did it go today?" asks Elzmerelda.

We're back in our room, freshening up for dinner. I say nothing.

"It was awful for me at first too. Don't worry. It gets better. Honestly."

Honestly? There's no way I'm hanging around this dump to find out.

"Well, got to go. I have Dinner Prep tonight. See you later." She skitters out the door.

Good. She's gone. I can use this free time alone to plot my escape. Except I'm too exhausted to think. I plunk down on my bed and close my eyes.

When I re-open them, it's pitch-black. For a second, I have no idea where I am. Elzmerelda's singsong voice regrettably reminds me.

"I brought you back some dinner." After lighting a candle, she lays a tray on my bed.

"What time is it?" I ask groggily, raising myself to a sitting position.

"It's after nine. You fell asleep. When I came back to get you, I didn't have the heart to wake you."

I gulp down my soup and wipe the bowl clean with the bread. Shit! I missed clean-up. One of those Badass Fairies will probably give me one hundred lashes.

As if reading my mind, Elzmerelda says, "Don't worry. I covered clean-up for you."

Why is she so nice to me? I don't get it. If it's because she wants me to be nice to her, she can forget it. I don't do nice.

Elzmerelda clears the tray, then slips into her nightgown. She crawls into bed and blows out the candle.

"Sweet dreams, Jane."

No one has ever said that to me before. I shut my eyes again, but sleep betrays me. I can't get the image of my mother out of my head.

CHAPTER 7

My next day at Faraway begins no better than the first. The chirpy birds wake me up too early; the sun attacks me; my caffeine deprivation gives me a headache, and Elzmerelda's cheerfulness drives me nuts.

At breakfast, we gather fresh eggs in addition to berries. In a nearby shed, Winifred shows me how easy it is take an egg from one of the nesting hens. Trust me, it's not. The nasty chickens are in constant attack mode. I narrowly escape being their breakfast.

I'm happy to go back to berry picking. I've actually gotten better at it. As I'm counting my haul, someone screams in the distance.

It's Sasperilla, and she's running toward us faster than any Gingerbread Man can. "Help! A wild beast is after me!"

Out of the clearing leaps a beautiful spotted fawn.

Elzmerelda makes a squinty face. "He's lost!"

"The poor baby," says Winifred. "I bet he's trying to find his mother."

The animal prances up to us. I admire his lithe body and long, graceful legs.

"Get him away from me!" shrieks Sasperilla, flailing her stick-thin arms.

Elzmerelda tries to calm down her sister. "Sassy, he's not going to bite you."

For some reason, the animal is attracted to me. It nuzzles its head up against my body and helps itself to the berries in my basket.

"The poor thing must be starving," says Winifred. She orders Sasperilla to find some nuts and acorns. More than happy to oblige, Miss Scared and Skinny scurries off.

Watching this gentle creature, I'm transported to my childhood again. I'm dancing barefoot in the street. Passersby notice I have no shoes and throw an extra coin into my tin. I don't dare tell them that my mother forbid me to wear shoes so they would feel sorry for me and be generous with their alms.

A kind-looking man dressed in regal clothes watches me dance. He must be from a faraway land because he uses words I don't know. "*Bambina*, you are destined for greatness." He tosses a gold coin into my tin. I smile. My mother will be pleased.

Not long after the man strolls away, I feel a warm, wet tickling sensation on my toes. I glance down. At my feet is an adorable brown and white spotted puppy that won't stop licking me. When he gazes up at me with his big take-me-home eyes, I know he's mine. I name him Bambi.

Wagging his tail, he follows me home. He's so cute and smart. When I call out to him, he knows his name and runs up to me. I'm sure my mother will let me keep him because of the gold coin. I'm wrong.

"Jane, how dare you bring home this flea-ridden beast?" she shrieks. "The last thing we need is another mouth to feed!"

To my horror, she kicks the little dog. It whimpers. My poor little Bambi! As I fall to my knees to shield him with my body, a fiery pain rips across my back. I look up only to receive another lashing from my mother, gripping a frayed leather belt laced with my blood. "He'd better be gone when I come back," she hisses. Emptying the tin with the gold coin, she stomps toward the front door, slamming it behind her as she leaves.

I scoop Bambi up in my arms. He licks my hot, salty tears. I can't part with him. I cry myself to sleep, with the little pup hidden under my thin woolen blanket, curled up in the crook of my knees.

When I open my eyes in the morning, Bambi's gone. "He ran away," says my smirking mother.

Fresh tears sprinkle down my face. Grabbing my tin, I race to the village square where I dance, hoping he'll be there. I dance all day until my feet bleed. The pup never shows up. Night falls. Hobbling from street to street, I shout out his name until I'm hoarse and cannot take another step. "Bambi! Bambi! Bambi!"

"Do you know someone named Bambi?" asks Elzmerelda, snapping me back to reality.

"Where is he?" I ask.

Winifred eyes me strangely. "Do you mean the deer? Sasperilla came back and scared him off. Remember?"

She must think I'm delusional. Maybe I *am* losing it.

———❦———

We begin our morning meditation standing, with our arms raised to the sky.

"Draw in the sunshine," instructs Fanta.

So, now they're going to fry our insides. When I die from all this sunshine, they'll probably find sunspots on my bones.

Surprisingly, the posture brightens my spirits. It makes me stronger. Energized.

Flossie leads us through a series of movements she calls "sun salutations." They're a bunch of weird poses that require a lot of flexibility. I can't believe how flexible the Badass Fairy is. Fluidly moving from one pose to the next, she's like a dancer.

Following along, I glance at the others. Elzmerelda is as graceful as a gazelle. Even maimed What's-His-Name and super-plus size Winifred move with ease. Distracted, Sasperilla shoots me a what-are-you-staring-at look. Right back at you, bitch. She loses her balance and falls. She grimaces; I smile. Wickedly.

I focus my attention back on Fanta. She chants, *"Om ravaye namah."*

Gulp! She's casting a spell on us! She's going to turn us all into frogs!

"Let it all go," she says. "And say OMmmmm."

Reluctantly, I close my eyes, take a deep breath, and prepare for the worse. When I open them, I'm surprised. I'm not some ugly ribitting frog princess. Oddly, I'm at peace with myself.

So relaxed, I'm not looking forward to my second session with Shrink, especially after all the insults she threw in my face yesterday. The nerve of her! She'll be sorry if she pulls that stuff on me today. I'll have her on her knees, begging for forgiveness. Then I'll stomp on her and turn her into pixie juice.

"Hello, Jane," says Shrink in her no-nonsense voice as she flies into her office.

Lying on the velvet chaise, I tilt my head up slightly and gaze at her with disdain.

"Jane is an interesting name," she begins. "It rhymes with both 'plain' and 'vain.' Which one are you—a plain Jane or a vain Jane?"

Plain Jane. The two words send a chill down my spine. It's been so long since I've heard them, yet I can still hear my mother's deprecating voice as if it were only yesterday. "You waste of human space. You're nothing but a plain Jane."

"Well, Jane, which one are you?" Shrink's words hurl me back to the moment.

"I'm not answering that question."

"Well, then I'll answer it for you. You're a vain Jane. That's why your best friend was a mirror."

How does she know that my best friend was a mirror? Of course, she read my "admissions form." Some enrollment application! It was just a bunch of trick questions to reveal my secrets. Sasperilla was right; they're *all* spies around this place.

"What did you use to ask your mirror?"

"None of your business."

"Jane, that's *not* what you used to say to your mirror. Now, tell me, what you really asked it."

"Mirror, mirror on the wall, who's the fairest one of all?" I blurt out, unable to control myself.

"And why did you ask your mirror this question?"

"Because it told me I was the fairest."

"And why did you need to hear this?"

"B-because…" I squirm.

"Because you needed instant gratification," steps in Shrink. "Instant gratification is a fundamental part of an addict's personality."

"I am *not* an addict!" I shout, straightening up.

"And what happened when your mirror told you someone else was the fairest one of all?"

"I tried to kill her!" Wait! Why am I telling her all these things? What's wrong with me?

"Yes, your addiction to beauty drove you to evil."

"Stop it!" I grip the arms of the chaise. "You think you know everything about me, but you don't!"

"Jane, you are here because you have a problem. And I am here to help you overcome your problem."

"The *only* problem I have is that I'm stuck in this nuthouse. I didn't ask to come here!"

"You agreed to come here."

"It was all a bunch of lies! I was tricked! I thought I was being sent to a spa! I want to go back that dungeon!"

"It's too late. You *can't* go back."

What! I'm stuck here? Rage crescendos inside me.

"Here's the deal," she says to my face. "Everyday at this time for the next three weeks, you are going to talk to me about your life. I will listen with a third ear and find the underlying cause of your addiction. Then I will share this discovery with you, and we will work together toward a complete recovery."

I'm about to explode. There's no way I'm going to spend three weeks opening up to this flying bug of a woman who has some invisible third ear.

"You can't keep me here!" I shout. "I'll run away. Escape! In fact, I'm going to say good-bye to this dump right now."

I bolt off the chaise and head straight for the door.

"Good luck," says Shrink. "But may I remind you of the high stone wall, the locked gate, and the armed guardsman. And I almost forgot, there's a moat."

I stop dead in my tracks. Why did she have to remind me? Rage becomes despair. I'm stuck in this madhouse!

The chime sounds.

"Time's up for today, Jane. I'll see you here tomorrow."

Leaving a blinding trail of fairy dust, she zips out the door.

I've got to get out of here. I've got to! Before that insidious bug of a woman who calls herself a therapist makes me completely insane. That also rhymes with Jane. I tremble as I put them together. *Insane Jane.*

CHAPTER 8

G roup, I'd like you to meet our newest Faraway resident," Dr. Grimm says as we file in for our afternoon session.

The last thing I want to do is meet another nutter.

Standing—or should I say posing—next to him is a tall, buff man in an open blousy shirt, shiny black boots, and tight white britches. In one hand, he holds a feathered felt hat; the other is hidden behind his back.

He's definitely an improvement in the man-department over What's-His-Name. His deep-set eyes are gray-blue like the sea, and a shadow of a beard lines his tan, weathered skin. Plus, he has the most fabulous hair I've ever seen—at least, on a man. Thick, black, glossy hair that grazes his shoulders and makes me miss mine. He catches me staring at him and winks. I pretend not to see it.

"This is James Hook," says Grimm.

"*Captain* James Hook," the man corrects with an air of arrogance. "King of the Pirates."

"Are you sure you're a king? You don't look like one to me," says Sasperilla, eying him from head to toe. Elzmerelda, flushed, also stares at him.

"Yo, Ho, Ho!" cackles the pirate. "I'm a legend. Ask anyone."

Yeah, a legend in his own mind. He's so full of himself.

"Group, today we are going to join hands to connect with one and other," says Grimm.

Another waste-of-time activity.

"Who would like to hold Hook's hand?"

Our eyes dart from one to another. Elzmerelda takes a step forward, then hesitates.

"Fine. I'll do it," says Sasperilla as if she's doing us all a big favor.

"The pleasure is mine." Holding out his hat, Hook bows graciously and offers the skinny bitch his hand. The one he's kept hidden behind his back.

"Aagh!" Sasperilla jumps back. "I'm not holding *that!*"

My mouth drops. Hook's hand is *not* a hand. It's an iron claw!

"You poor thing! What happened to your hand?" asks Winifred.

Hook ignores her. His eyes linger on places of my body he has no right staring at. I want to take that hook and hang him by his eyeballs.

Grimm repeats, "Who would like to hold Hook's hand?"

Again, there's silence. No one volunteers. Hook keeps leering at me. Forget it! I'm not going near him. Finally, What's-His-Name teeters over to him. Except he takes the swine's good hand.

"I'll hold his other hand," says Elzmerelda bravely. She blushes as she wraps her long, spidery fingers around the pirate's grotesque hook.

"Thank you, Elzmerelda," says Grimm, stepping away. "Now, I'd like the rest of you to join in please and form a circle."

I move next to Elzmerelda, and Winifred next to me. That leaves Sasperilla who's forced to stand between Winifred and What's-His-Name.

"Why do I always get stuck next to *him*?" Skinny Bitch grumbles.

What's-His-Name squeezes her bony hand so hard she winces. He's growing on me. I can't say the same about Hook.

Standing diagonally across from me, he shoots me a smirk. I give him my signature scornful stare, the one I perfected in my magic mirror—cold, distant, and belittling. Instead of getting my message, he purses his lips and blows me a kiss.

The boar! He reminds me of the creeps my mother would bring home. The thought sends a shiver to the base of my spine. He had better stay away from me. Far away!

"Who would like to share today?" asks Grimm, standing in the middle of our circle.

Elzmerelda, breaking loose of my grip, raises her hand halfway. "I've always wanted to meet a real pirate." She gazes dreamily at Hook.

"Why is that?" asks Grimm.

"To go on an adventure and sail the high seas." She takes hold of my hand again.

"That's really brave," interjects Winifred.

"Winifred, you seem to admire bravery," says Grimm. "Often, the qualities we admire in others are the very traits we lack and covet in ourselves."

Bravery is sure not my problem. If that pirate doesn't stop ogling me, I swear I'm going to yank off his hook and whack him with it. And I know exactly where.

Dr. Grimm presses on. "So, Elzmerelda, why do you want to go on a high seas adventure?"

"I've always wanted to get away." Her palm is suddenly cold and clammy.

"From whom?" asks Grimm.

Silence. Elzmerelda's bravery has melted into fear.

Sasperilla folds her arms across her concave chest. "You're wasting everyone's time. Tell him already."

"Mother!" her sister blurts out at last.

Sasperilla's eyes narrow into knife-like slits.

"Why your mother?" asks Grimm.

I shudder. He'd better never ask me why *I* dreamt of escaping my mother!

"B-b-because I want to live my own life!" splutters Elzmerelda. "I'm tired of her telling me what to do, what to wear, and whom to marry!"

Sasperilla gasps. "You indignant ingrate! I'm telling

Mother on you when I see her!"

"Tell on me; I don't care." Elzmerelda's voice shakes. "And besides, you've always told on me. You've always wanted to get me into trouble with Mother."

"My children are always telling on each other," comments Winifred. "They just want attention."

"That's an excellent observation, Winifred," says Grimm. "Sasperilla, does your mother give you enough attention?"

"Never! She always dotes on Elzmerelda because she thinks she's the pretty one."

"That is so not true!" protests Elzmerelda.

An "is so/ is not" battle erupts and lasts until What's-His-Name lets out a startling roar that stops both sisters in their tracks.

With the slightest trace of a smile, Grimm thanks the troll. His eyes shift from one sister to the other. "Fighting is not an acceptable way to resolve conflicts. I want the two of you to work on alternative means."

Despite Grimm's ultimatum, Sasperilla won't give up. She manages to get in the last word.

"Guess what! I hope you sail away and get eaten by a whale, you little twit!"

Her hurtful words bring tears to Elzmerelda's eyes. An unexpected wave of sadness sweeps over me. I know how it feels to be abandoned. To feel unloved. Elzmerelda's quiet sobs tug at my heart. If Hook's back to leering at me, I'm oblivious.

After group, Elzmerelda begs me to go to Arts and Crafts with her.

"I'm sure if we're in class together Sasperilla won't come," she says. "I don't think she likes you."

That's an understatement. The skinny bitch hates me. Though I was looking forward to cooking again with Winifred,

I cave in to Elzmerelda's plea. Unfortunately, Sasperilla's already in the classroom when we get there. What's-His-Name is there too.

Fairweather announces that today's theme is jewelry. The only piece of jewelry I want to make is a lucky charm—the key to Faraway's front gate to free myself from this prison. Instead, I opt to make a paper chain necklace. When it comes to art, I have little talent.

At a long metal table, Elzmerelda works as far away as possible from her sister. "What are you making?" I ask.

"Jewelry for feet—shoes!" she says proudly.

I examine her project. She's constructed a pair of high-heeled shoes out of papier-mâché, painted them gold, and encrusted them with multi-color sequins. You know what, she's actually talented.

At the back of the room, What's-His-Name sits at a spinning wheel. He's making something out of straw.

He limps over to me, holding his creation. "F-for you," he stutters.

It's a delicate golden bracelet with my name woven into it. "QUEEN." Nice! Finally, someone respects me around this joint.

"Wonderful!" says Fairweather. "This is the first time he's connected with someone at Faraway."

I take the bracelet from him and slip it over my hand. It falls apart. What's-His-Name looks crestfallen.

"It's the thought that counts," Fairweather tells him. "Next time, think of incorporating *your* name."

Sasperilla saunters over to her sister. "Watch'ya making?" she asks nosily.

Elzmerelda ignores her.

Sasperilla snatches the shoes and tosses them onto the floor. "Let me be the first to try them on."

"No!" cries Elzmerelda. But it's too late. Sasperilla squeezes her long, bony feet into the sparkly shoes and completely destroys them. They're nothing but a bunch of cardboard scraps.

Elzmerelda bursts into tears. "I worked so hard on them!"

"Such a pity!" tisks Sasperilla. "Because they went so nicely with what I'm wearing."

I want to strangle the skinny bitch with the chain I've made. Too bad it's only made of paper.

***

Elzmerelda will not get out of bed for dinner. She's bundled under her covers, still sobbing.

"Come on, Elz, you've got to eat something." It's the first time I've called her Elz for short.

"I'm not hungry," she sniffles.

There's a loud knock at the door. It swings open. Winifred.

"I brought you something," she says, plopping down on Elz's bed. She digs into a pocket and plucks out a huge bar of chocolate.

Elz sits up as Winifred brushes away her tears. "Winnie, they'll punish you if they catch you with that."

"Let them." The chubster shrugs. "They can take everything else away from me, but they can't take away my chocolate. I have a secret stash in my room, so eat your heart out."

Elz breaks off a chunk and savors it. "I feel so much better. You're the best, Winnie!"

Winnie devours a large piece as well and sighs. There's still a small piece left.

"You know, you're going to get pimples from eating so much chocolate," I tell them.

"That is such an old wives' tale," laughs Winnie.

I have to admit she does have gorgeous skin if you don't count the freckles. Maybe she's right.

"Have a piece," she offers.

Hesitantly, I take the last piece of chocolate. As it melts in my mouth…euphoria! I want more.

Winnie must be a mind reader. She whips out three more

bars and lays them on the bed. Like vultures, we dive in and devour them. With every bite, we moan with ecstasy. The chocolate must have magical powers.

"Come on, girlfriends," grins Elz after licking the last bit of chocolate off her fingers. "Let's not be late for dinner."

The three of us band together at one table while Sasperilla sits by herself picking at her food at another. She makes a face at us. We ignore her.

"Isn't Hook adorable?" asks Elz giddily.

"Not my type," says Winnie, cutting into a hunk of cheese. "And besides, I'm married."

He's a total jerk, I say to myself, not wanting to offend Elz.

As if on cue, Mr. Total Jerk strides up to us. He straddles the empty chair next to mine.

"You don't mind if I join you lovely ladies?" he asks, jabbing his hook into a slice of bread.

Elz flushes. "Is it okay with you girls?"

"Sure," shrugs Winnie.

"No problem," I say coolly. *Liar!* I don't want him anywhere near me.

"Why are you here at Faraway?" Winnie asks him.

"I'm searching for my inner princess."

The mockery in his voice makes me want to barf.

"That's so beautiful," coos Elz.

"I wish my husband would find his," says Winnie.

I think she truly means it.

"What's it like to be a pirate?" asks Elz with wide-eyed infatuation.

Hook recites the sordid details of his exploits as though he's rehearsed them for days. Winnie and I roll our eyes. Elz, unlike us, hangs on to every word.

"Have you ever made someone walk the plank?" she asks

in awe.

"Countless times," boasts Hook.

"Wow!" exclaims Elz. The more dangerous he seems, the more attracted to him she becomes. Why can't she see that this guy's a creep?

A certified creep! To my utter disgust, the swashbuckler rubs his good hand up and down my thigh under the table. I jerk away. Who the hell does he think he is?

Winnie shoots me a perplexed look. Elz, immersed in Hook's storytelling, doesn't notice a thing.

"So, how did you lose your hand?" she asks.

A dark, sinister cloud falls over the swine. "Some faggot named Peter Pan cut if off and fed it to a crocodile." His eyes become two steel blades. "Trust me, he'll pay one day."

The name Peter Pan sounds familiar to me. Where have I heard it before? I know. Shrink mentioned it during our first session. Something about a Peter Pan complex and her sister Tinkerbell.

I can't help myself. "Do you know a Tinkerbell?"

Hook reddens with rage. "She's the real reason I'm here! That two-timing imp! I should have never trusted her to lead me to Peter Pan."

I would almost give *my* hand to sit in on a session between Shrink and Hook. It could get personal. Maybe, he'll smoosh her.

Hook seethes. "Man, could I use a bottle of rum!"

"Let me pour you some tea," says Elz sweetly.

"Real men don't drink tea." He storms off but doesn't get far.

"Where do you think you're going, mister?" asks Fanta, yanking him back by a handful of his gorgeous hair.

"You're on clean-up duty tonight," smiles Flossie. "Remember?"

"Move it," snaps Fairweather.

Ha! You deserve clean-up duty, you pig.

Just my luck. I'm on clean-up duty with Hook. So is Sasperilla.

Hook scrapes the dishes with his handy iron claw, then passes them to me to scrub. I'm careful not to let him get too close. Sasperilla, meanwhile, sits idly on a counter, twirling her corkscrew curls. I bet, before Faraway, she never lifted a wannabe royal finger in her life.

"So, Hook, if you're *really* King of the Pirates, you've probably found lots of buried treasure," she says sheepishly.

"Yo, Ho, Ho!" laughs Hook. "Babe, I'm worth millions!"

Babe? He'd better not try that one on me. And I'm so not falling for his filthy rich act. I know his type. How many times did my mother fall for the same bullshit? The same asshole!

Sasperilla's face lights up. She hops off the counter and heads our way. "Why don't you let *me* give those dirty dishes to Jane after you've scraped them?"

She worms her emaciated body between us. As much as I despise the skinny bitch, I'm glad swineface is no longer breathing in my face.

"So, Hook, what exactly are you going to do with all that money?" she purrs, brushing up against him.

"I'm going to sail away with some babe to some romantic island and build myself a castle."

Sasperilla's eyes flutter.

"So, babe, do you want to go out on the town for a drink with me one night?"

Sasperilla is positively drooling. As her lips part to say "yes," Hook leans over her and leers at me.

"So, babe, we're on?"

Sasperilla cringes.

So do I. I want to throw a plate at the swine. There is no town. And there is no babe. Take that back. I want to throw the entire sink full of plates at him. Instead, I croon seductively.

And convincingly.

"Sure. As long as you can get past the crocodile in the moat."

Crash! When I say "crocodile," Hook drops the stack of dishes he's holding.

"OW!" screeches Sasperilla. "That was my foot!"

Clean-up has suddenly become fun.

———❦———

Exhausted, I retreat to my room. It's pitch-black. I tread lightly so I don't wake up Elz.

As I slip on my nightgown, Elz's voice filters through the darkness. "Jane, can I tell you a secret?"

"Sure." To be honest, it's the last thing I want to hear. I've heard way too much crap for one day.

"I think I'm in love with Hook."

I don't know what to say. After all she's been through today, I can't bring myself to tell her what I think of him.

"Great." I crawl into bed. "Good night."

"Sweet dreams, Jane."

"Sweet dreams to you too, Elz." I only hope Hook's not in them.

CHAPTER 9

When I awaken in the morning, Elz is bawling. I don't get it. Last night, she was deliriously in love; now; she's deliriously in tears. I make a mental note: Reminder! My roomie is a loony. Proceed with caution.

"What's the matter?" I ask.

"I'm so ugly," she whimpers.

"No, you're not." Who am I kidding? She's as ugly as sin.

"Yes, I am!" she insists. "In Lalaland, everyone called me Cinderella's ugly stepsister. Hook will never fall for me."

She's right. What she needs is an extreme makeover.

I may be a master of disguise, but I'm not a makeover magician. Still, I've got to give it a shot. The poor girl is desperate.

Using every trick I know, I style her limp hair, make her bite down on her thin lips to give them a little color, and pluck a few of her unsightly chin hairs. One final touch—I tell her to lose the hair bow.

"How do I look?" she asks.

For once, I'm glad there are no mirrors at Faraway. She definitely looks more attractive. But you can only go so far with what you have. Okay. Let me put it this way: I haven't exactly transformed her into a Rehab Goddess.

"I don't feel beautiful," she mopes.

"Elz, that's exactly your problem," says Winnie, who has stopped by on her way to breakfast. "Beauty is an attitude."

"What do you mean?" I ask.

"Men are attracted to women who *think* they're beautiful."

What does this two hundred-pound bruiser of a woman know about beauty that I don't?

"And besides, there are other attributes far more important than mere physical beauty for attracting a man," she continues.

Now, she's really got me curious. Elz is also all ears.

"It's simple. Be confident. Be playful. Be interested. Men are fascinated by women who find them fascinating."

What is she—some kind of seduction genie?

"Winnie, how do you know all this sh…stuff?" I ask with a tone of distrust.

"I landed a husband," she says before forlornness edges out the pride on her face. "You know, I was thin once."

At breakfast, Elz flutters around The Enchanted Garden, singing her "lalalas" louder than ever.

"Careful," I overhear Winnie whisper to her. "Let him know you exist, but don't be too obvious."

To my amazement, Winnie's words of wisdom work like a charm. Hook strides up to Elz and checks out her pillar-like body. Even in flats, she's several inches taller than him.

"Elzmerelda, you're looking particularly lovely today," he says, flashing his pearly white teeth.

"Really?" She sounds more disbelieving than flattered.

He sneaks a wink at me. Asswipe! Fortunately, Elz is too enraptured to notice. I just don't get what she sees in this pompous asshole.

"Push-lease!" comes a sarcastic voice nearby. It's Sasperilla. She moseys over to us.

"Captain, why are you wasting your time with her?" Smiling coyly, she bats her eyelashes. "Everyone says *I'm* the pretty one."

Elz frowns but says nothing.

Sasperilla twirls around to show herself off. Her frilly pink frock does little for her other than to expose the beveled edges of her rib cage.

Hook gives her the once-over. "Babe, you should put some meat on those bones."

Sasperilla turns as pink as her dress and stomps off. I'm grateful for Hook's brutal honesty despite how much I despise him.

"So, Jane—" he says, moving closer to me.

I cut him off. "Later. It's time for morning meditation."

"I'll be meditating about you, babe."

And I'll be in some other world where he doesn't exist.

I head over to Shrink's office for my session after morning meditation.

Reclining in the chaise, I shift restlessly waiting for her to show up. Why do I always have to see bugface right after morning meditation and mess up the rest of my day? I mean, after meditation, I'm always so relaxed and empowered. After Shrink, I'm always so stressed and damaged. It's not fair. I'm going to ask for a schedule change. I've been here long enough. Four forever days. I deserve it.

"Today, Jane, we're going to play a little game," says Shrink as she finally flits into her office.

Big whoop.

"Did you ever play any games as a child?"

Only one game comes to mind. When my mother was out with her latest male conquest, I would sneak into her room and dress up in one of her pretty gowns. Then, I would stand in front of her treasured mirror and pretend I was a beautiful princess, waiting for my handsome prince to come and take me away. Far away to a magnificent palace in a magical land. Far, far away from my mother.

"I used to play make-believe," I say, omitting the details of my childhood fantasy.

"Perfect! Because that's exactly what we're going to play today. A game of make-believe."

Ha! This should be fun.

"Jane, if you were an object, what would you be?"

What kind of stupid question is that? I have no clue.

"Jane, I'm waiting for an answer," Shrink buzzes around the room impatiently.

I survey my surroundings. "This chaise lounge," I finally blurt out.

"Why did you pick this chaise?"

"It happens to be here, right?"

"No, Jane. There must be a better reason. You could have picked the door, the clock, or your shoes. They're here too."

She has a point. Where is she going with this mind game?

Hovering above me, she looks straight into my eyes. "So, Jane, why did you *really* pick the chaise?"

"Because it reminds me of myself." Why am I'm saying this? I don't look like a piece of furniture.

"How so, Jane?" Shrink's interest is stirred.

I sit up straight and examine the worn out chaise. My eyes take in its elegant lines and graceful curves. It's actually a shame it's so tattered.

"Because it's long and lean like me," I say.

"Yes, Jane, it is." She seems pleased with my answer.

"At some time, it must have been beautiful."

"What makes you say that?"

"It has good bones. I suppose, if it were re-upholstered, it would be beautiful again."

"Jane, do you think you need to be re-upholstered?"

"That's a ridiculous question!" I laugh. Though when I think about it, I could use a new head of hair.

"Fine, Jane. Then, answer this. What's the difference between you and the chaise?"

Okay, now she wants to prove I'm stupid. Anyone with a

brain knows the difference.

"Um…. I'm a person and the chaise is a piece of furniture?" I say with obvious sarcasm.

"That's right, Jane. The chaise is an object. What's the difference between a person and an object?"

Another stupid question! Who does she think I am—some dopey dwarf? Well, two can play at this game.

"Duh! A person can see and feel; an object can't."

"Jane, enough with the attitude," says Shrink harshly. "Now, close your eyes and imagine the life of this chaise."

Reluctantly, I close my eyes and fantasize where this chaise once lived. For sure, it must have inhabited a beautiful palace, full of riches and regal people. Generation after generation lounged on it until it was worn out and ultimately given away.

"It must have belonged to a royal family," I tell her after opening my eyes.

"Yes. It did. A queen once nursed her twin infant sons on it. They grew up to be a kind, handsome princes."

In my head, I picture a woman cradling a baby boy in her arms. Her head is lowered, her lips pressed against his warm, silky skull. When she lifts her head, I see her face and jolt. The mother with the child is *me*!

"Jane, I'm going to ask you again; what's the difference between you and this chaise?"

My lips quiver. "This chaise has known love."

"Jane, did your mother love you?"

A painful knot forms in my stomach. I don't want to talk about my mother. I can't! Just in time, the chime sounds.

"Jane, time's up for today. I'll see you here tomorrow."

Slowly, I peel myself off the chaise. I don't want to leave it. Not today.

———

At lunch, I have no appetite. And I'm in no mood for conversation. I half-listen as Elz picks Winnie's brain about her next move with Hook.

"Don't forget to play hard-to-get. Remember, men are basically thrill seekers engaged by hunting instincts," instructs Winnie.

The conversation turns to me. "Jane, how come you're so quiet?" asks Elz.

"Was therapy rough?" asks Winnie.

How does she know? She's a relationship guru *and* a mind reader?

"I thought therapy's supposed to make you feel better."

"Actually, most of the time it doesn't." Winnie passes me a bowl. "Have some of my vegetable soup. *This* will make you feel better."

I sip a tablespoon of the warm, hearty soup. And guess what, it does make me feel better. I scoff down the entire bowl.

By the time group rolls around, I'm back to myself. And contemplating an escape plan.

In group, Elz heeds Winnie's play-hard-to-get advice and sits as far away from Hook as she can. I end up sitting next to him. Regrettably.

"So, babe, how 'bout it tonight?" he whispers in my ear.

Pressing his thigh against mine, he gives me his smarmy you-don't-know-what-you're-missing-out-on smile.

I edge away from him before I punch him where it hurts and focus my attention on Grimm.

"Today, we're going on a group hike in The Enchanted Forest."

Fine with me. At least, I won't be stuck sitting next to swineface for an hour.

"We're going to engage in a non-visual intimate encounter with trees," Grimm continues.

Great. This morning I had to pretend I was a piece of

furniture, and now I have to hump a tree. Rehab is just all fun and games.

"I have randomly paired you up. Winifred will be with What's-His-Name; Elzmerelda will be with…"

Elz looks longingly at Hook, hoping he'll be her partner.

"…her sister, Sasperilla."

"No way!" shrieks Sasperilla. "I'm not partnering with *her*!"

Poor Elz cannot hide her disappointment.

"…and finally, Jane will be with…"

I hear his name before Grimm says it. My luck! I'm stuck with Hook!

The rogue won't leave me alone. As Grimm explains our tree game, his hook toys with the buttons on my dress. I inch away from him, only to have him move closer. Maybe some rabid squirrel will bite his nuts.

"The way this exercise works is that one person is blind-folded while his or her partner directs them to a tree that fits their personality. Blah, blah, blah, blah." I'm so distracted by Hook that I hardly hear a word Grimm's saying. The next thing I know, we're flipping a coin to determine which partner will be blindfolded first. It's going to be What's-His-Name, Sasperilla, and me.

"What this exercise does is build responsibility and trust in a fun way," says Grimm.

Sasperilla plants her hands on her jutting hipbones and fumes. "Elzmerelda's out to get me! I can't trust her!"

"You can trust *me*, babe." Hook slaps my ass.

Cripes! How am I going trust him when he's out to get me?

Grimm is such a liar. This is *not* going to be fun.

Grimm has assigned us different paths so that we don't bump into one and other. Just as I thought, being alone—and blind-folded—with Hook in the middle of the forest is no walk in the park. I can hardly wait for this stupid tree-hugging game to end.

"So, Jane, what kind of trees are you into?" asks Hook. "I bet you like them big and hard."

I'm not answering that question.

"Have you ever felt the flow of life energy in a tree?"

"No," I reply dryly.

"You've been missing out on a life-changing experience."

"Just tell me where to go." I can sense he's no longer standing next to me. His voice sounds distant.

"Take ten giant steps ahead of you and then ten to the right. I think you'll find your perfect tree."

I'm anxious. "Hook, weren't you supposed to hold my hand and lead me to the tree?"

"Babe, that's a different game," he chuckles.

I admit I really wasn't paying attention while Grimm was explaining the rules. The good news is that I don't have to hold the asshole's hand—his hooked one or good one. Cautiously, I take one step after another. As I veer to the right, I hear a howl and then…

I'm thirteen again, somewhere in the middle of a dark forest, hunting for magical leaves that my mother uses to beautify her complexion. She's been seeing a King and doesn't want him to think she's a day over twenty-nine. As I reach for a leafy clump, a voice startles me. "This is no place for a beautiful young girl to be by herself." I whirl around. Facing me is a burly bearded man whose eyes are the color of evergreens. In his hand is the biggest knife I've ever seen—it's at least two-feet long. He stomps toward me. My heart races. He's coming after me! I bolt. As I run for my life, gnarled branches tear my dress and claw my skin. Vines wrap around my limbs, and thorns bite into me. The trees have become monsters, trying to gobble me up alive. And the heavy crunching steps of the knife-wielding man are close behind me. Fear propels my legs to run faster and to fight the burning sensation filling my lungs. At last freedom. And then home. Breathless, I swing open the front door, never so happy to see my mother. Her eyes narrow into slithers of glass. "Where are my leaves?" she hisses. I open my mouth to tell her about the man, but—*whack!* —a groan leaks out instead. She's smacked me with my tin. My cheek stinging, I grab it and flee...

"You're almost there."

Hook's voice whisks me back to reality. It sounds like he's moved closer to me, but in my disoriented state, I can't tell exactly where he is.

"Only two more giant steps."

Eager for this game to end, I take them.

"Now, wrap your arms around the trunk and press your lips against the bark."

I hug the tree. Its rough bark scrapes my face, leaving it raw and prickly; its sap burns my lips. I've had enough. But the tree wants more. It wraps its limbs around me, pressing my body against its hard trunk. So tight, I can't break loose. The more I resist, the more it sucks the life out of me. Oh my God! This tree *is* a monster.

A shocked voice screams out. Elz.

"Jane! How could you do this to me! I thought you were my friend!"

With all my muscle-power, I wrench myself from the monster. Right in front of me is an erect Hook, wearing a proud smirk on his slimy lips. The pig! I should have known!

"Elz, it's not what you think!" Oh, God! What have I done?

"I may need glasses, but I have eyes," she cries.

"Yo, Ho, Ho." Hook laughs snidely.

Game over! I slap him hard across the face. "I'd rather hug a one-eyed ogre than you!"

Stunned, he rubs the bright red welt I've left on his cheek.

Elz runs off into the woods, leaving her twig-of-a-sister behind.

"Don't leave me, you traitor!" shrieks Sasperilla. Still wearing her blindfold, she slams into a tree.

"I think I broke my nose!" she wails. "Somebody help me!"

As I flee from Hook, I'm shaking like a leaf.

CHAPTER 10

I usually dread my sessions with Shrink, but today I can hardly wait. It's been an awful twenty-four hours. Elz has totally avoided me. She sat by herself at breakfast and refused to lead a chant with me during morning meditation. She didn't even wish me sweet dreams last night. It's as if I don't exist.

Lying in the chaise, I grow impatient. Shrink is usually late, but not this late. After fifteen minutes or so, I decide to split. I'm furious with Shrink for not showing up. Of all days!

Rising, I notice Shrink's bug-eyed spectacles peeking out from under the chaise. That's strange. I bend over and pick them up. The rims are dented. Maybe, she crashed into something. Seriously, with all that fairy dust, it's easy to be blindsided.

Perhaps, she's somewhere under the chaise. Stooping down to my knees, I run my hand beneath it. Uh oh! Something warm and fleshy. My heart skips a beat. A dead body? To my relief, it's only a mouse. It scuttles away.

Taking a deep breath, I stand up. And there she is. Behind the chaise, sprawled out on her back. Her eyes are shut, and her little wings are outstretched. Her blond hair has fallen loose and cradles her shoulders. She looks like a fallen butterfly.

"Shrink, wake up," I say, crouching over her.

She doesn't move.

"Shrink, wake up!" I shout. "Wake up!" I fold her wings up and down like an accordion, but she still doesn't budge.

Oh no! Maybe she's dead. A fat tear rolls down my cheek onto her teeny weeny body.

"Is it raining in here? How many times do I have to tell them to fix that damn leak in the roof?"

Shrink! She's alive! Feistier than ever.

"So, Jane, where were we?" she asks as she spirals into the air.

With a sigh of relief, I sink back into the chaise and talk about what happened yesterday with Hook. The words flow out of my mouth like a raging rapid.

"Why are you upset that Elzmerelda is not talking to you?"

"It's not fair. I didn't do anything."

"That's not really why you're upset."

"Okay, I feel rejected."

"Yes, you feel rejected. But if Hook rejected you, you wouldn't feel bad, would you?

"Hardly." *I'd do a happy dance.*

"Do you understand why you feel bad about Elzmerelda's behavior?"

I shake my head "no."

"Jane, you feel bad because Elzmerelda is your friend."

Silence.

"Have you ever had a friend before?"

Another flashback. This one to a little girl who's seen me at the window. She's motioning with her hand for me to come outside and play with her. My mother isn't home. An opportunity. I toss my dust rag, dash out the front door, and slam into her on the landing. My mother, her lips clamped as tightly as her fists. "Where the hell do you think you're going, Jane?" Before I can utter a word, she shoves me back into the house, with such force I tumble, scraping my knees on the cold stone floor. A warm river of blood seeps through my torn muslin skirt.

Tears burn my eyes as I shake my head. I never saw that little girl again.

Shrink adjusts her lopsided, dented glasses.

"Jane, let me tell you something about friends. Friends

care about each other. You care about Elzmerelda. That's why you're upset she's mad at you."

I take in what she's just said. I miss Elz terribly. "Will she ever talk to me again?" I ask tentatively.

"Yes, because she cares about you. Tell her the truth and give her a little time."

The chime sounds.

"Time's up for today, Jane. I'll see you here tomorrow."

As I step out of her office, feeling much better, she calls out to me.

"By the way, Jane, thank you for finding my spectacles. No more triple air flips for me."

For the rest of the day, Elz continues to give me the cold shoulder. She won't sit next to me at lunch and avoids me in group. When I join her in Arts and Crafts, she switches to sewing. Finally, we're forced together for dinner prep.

In the kitchen, we hang out at different ends. I prepare the salad while she handles the main course. She's still not talking to me. I sing a few refrains of "lalala," hoping that'll break the ice, but it's as if she's deaf. She completely ignores me.

Fine! Let her be an ice queen; two can play at this game, and I can play it better. I'll just pretend she's not here.

Singing louder (okay, so I'm deliberately being annoying; she deserves it), I tear up greens and slice tomatoes. A sudden sharp pain makes me yelp. Shit! I've sliced my finger. The cut is deep; blood is gushing out all over my hand. A rush of nausea passes through me. I can't stand the sight of blood. It sickens me. That's why I never had the courage to plunge a knife into Snow White's heart myself and had to send that worthless Huntsman to do it for me.

My finger won't stop bleeding. To tell the truth, I haven't seen this much blood in my entire life. Except for the time I lost my child. A bed full of blood, my body soaked red. The painful memory stays with me as I gaze down at the scarlet puddle that's spreading by my feet. I'm getting woozy.

Elz rushes over to me. "Oh my God! You're bleeding to death!"

She's right. I'm seeing stars. My life is almost over!

Elz grabs a dishtowel and presses it firmly against my wound.

"Jane, hold this tightly against your finger!"

Wincing, I do exactly what she tells me. The cut's so deep that blood seeps through the thick cloth. I turn my head away.

My finger throbs. I'm getting woozier and woozier. I don't think I can hang on much longer. "Am I really going to die?" I ask Elz, knowing full well it's only a matter of time.

Elz is too busy to answer me. She's feverishly tearing her white petticoat into long, ragged strips. Removing the blood-soaked towel, she begins to wrap them around my finger until it's mummified. I take a deep breath as she ties the ends of the last strip together into a neat little bow at the base.

"I think we've got it under control," she says, grinning proudly at her handiwork.

"Elz, you saved my life!"

"You weren't *really* going to die," she singsongs.

What! She tricked me into thinking I was going to die! What a mean way to get back at me! And for something I didn't even do.

I glance down at my big-bandaged finger with its silly little bow. My rage melts into relief.

"Elz, thanks for being there for me."

"It's okay. You'd do the same."

Would I? I wonder as she finishes making the salad for me.

I need to know. "Elz, why are you so nice to me?"

"Because you have a big heart." She smiles.

No one has ever told me that. In fact, during my trial, the tabloids called me cruel and heartless. I'm on the verge of tears.

"About yesterday—"

She doesn't let me finish. "Forget it."

Does she know what really happened? Right now, it doesn't matter.

"Friends?" I say.

"Best friends!" she beams as tears trickle down her cheeks.

"Why are you crying?"

"The same reason you are."

I do something I've never done before. Not to anyone. I hug her.

CHAPTER 11

R ise and shine, Jane!"
It's great to hear Elz's wake-up call again. Yet, it's still a struggle for me to get up and face the sunshine despite being here almost a week. And truth be told, I'm still not one hundred percent over my caffeine addiction.

"Hurry! I need your help!"

I blink my eyes open. Elz is more cheerful than ever.

"What's going on?" I ask.

"It's Visitor's Day. Mother will be here for dinner. I can't wait for you to meet her."

I'm confused. I thought she wanted to get away from her mother.

"Jane, will you help me pick out something to wear? I want to look my best."

Okay. I'll help. She's thrilled with the dress I choose. Another version of the hideous Snow White costume she always wears.

"I wish I could see myself in a mirror!"

"Pretend I'm your mirror." In a deep, put-on voice, I tell her she looks beautiful.

"You're the best friend I could ever have!"

I think about my magic mirror and silently curse it. Why couldn't it be there for me?

A hug from Elz brings me back into the moment. I'm happy how things turned out between us. Shrink will be proud of me.

"Who's coming to visit you?" asks Elz cheerfully.

"No one." I shrug. "I'm not allowed yet. I haven't been here for a full week." Though it feels like a lifetime.

"Look on the bright side as Winnie would say. Next week, you can have a visitor."

Yes, maybe next week, that dumb-ass dungeon guard will show up. Or that whack-job judge. Of course, how could I forget? *Snow White and the Seven Dwarfs!* Come on! Who am I kidding? I have no one to visit me. No one!

Hold on. With any luck, I won't be here next week. The thought of escaping brightens my spirits. Slightly.

<hr>

The first person I encounter at breakfast is Hook. I'm still furious with him for pulling that stunt in The Enchanted Forest. Behaving as if nothing happened, he notices my bandaged finger.

"Yo, babe. Can I kiss your boo-boo and make it better?"

It happens to be my right middle finger. I shove it into to his face. He smirks, but I think he's gotten the message. He turns his attention to Elz. Good.

"Elzmerelda, I must say you're looking mighty fine this morning." His eyes travel down her beanpole body with a few unnecessary stops. "What's the occasion?"

"Mother's coming! I'd love for you to meet her."

"Wait till Mother hears what you did to me the other day!"

It's Sasperilla. A thick bandage covers her swollen nose, and under her bloodshot eyes, she's all black and blue. I bite my lip hard not to laugh.

Winnie, carrying a basketful of berries, lumbers over to us.

"My husband's coming," she sighs before popping berry after berry into her mouth.

Our resident expert on relationships is clearly dreading his visit. "Are your children coming as well?" I ask.

She lowers her eyes. "No, I don't want them to see me

here." She polishes off the berries.

"Dr. Grimm thinks it's a good idea for my husband to join us in group," she says at last. "I'm not so sure."

I'm actually looking forward to meeting him. If he's not nice to her, I'm going to take him out.

———

I've been eager to meet with Shrink all morning. I couldn't even focus during meditation.

Proudly, I tell her that Elz and I made up. We're best friends again. Everything's better than ever.

"Good," she says flatly.

Is that all she can say? I thought for sure she'd do a single flip. And doesn't she at least want to know what happened to my finger?

Clenching a rolled up sheet of parchment that's twice her size, Shrink hovers over me and scowls. I don't get it. Have I done something wrong?

"Jane, you lied to me yesterday," she says angrily. "You told me that you never had a friend. But on this assessment, you wrote that you not only had a friend, but a best friend."

What is she talking about? I can hardly remember anything I wrote on that stupid questionnaire. It seems like a hundred years ago.

"It says right here that your 'magic mirror' was your best friend."

"Give me that!" I wrench the assessment away from her and read it. Damn it! She's right. We even briefly talked about my mirror in one of our first sessions. How could I forget?

"Jane, why was this mirror your best friend?"

"It talked to me. It said nice things about me. What's wrong with that?"

"Were you alone when you talked with it?"

"Yes."

"So, you talked to it when you were lonely."

"No! When I was alone." I hate it when she puts words in my mouth.

"Fine. What happened to your mirror?"

"That kiss-ass looking glass betrayed me." Hatred courses through my veins. "The traitor!"

"Friends don't betray each other. Especially best friends."

She's playing with my head. And I don't like it. Not one bit.

She flutters closer. "Jane, the mirror wasn't your friend. It was a thing. A thing that couldn't really see, feel, hear...or talk."

What is she saying? That my mirror *wasn't* really magic? But I heard it talk. I swear I did.

"Jane, the voice you heard was your subconscious talking."

I squirm. More Shrink-speak. What the hell is *she* talking about?

"This inner voice told you things you craved to hear."

"Like how beautiful I was?"

"Yes, Jane. And things you feared to hear."

"You mean…"

"That some young girl was fairer than you."

My blood is bubbling like the evil potion that sent me here.

Shrink looks hard into my eyes.

"Jane, you may have played a game of pretend with your so-called magic mirror. But it played a game of reality with you."

Anger mingles with confusion. I hate Shrink! And I don't believe a word she's just said. My mirror *was* magic!

She takes a spin around the room before I can swat her.

She returns, hovering above me but not within reach. "By the way, Jane, how do you feel about Visitor's Day?"

Her words slash through me. How can she be so cruel? I wish this session would end.

To my relief, the chime sounds.

"Time's up for today, Jane. I'll see you here tomorrow."

I'm in no mood for group. I don't even care any more about meeting Winnie's husband. I'm sick of this place. I'm sick of singing "lalala" and picking berries; I'm sick of washing dishes and mopping floors; I'm sick of people telling me what to do; I'm sick of not saying whatever-the-hell I want to. Most of all, I'm sick of being humiliated, shot down to nothing by some know-it-all bug of a woman who tells me bodacious lies about my magic mirror. From now on, I'm staying focused on my one and only goal—getting out of this hellhole. There's no way I can stick it out here for two more weeks. More than ever, I need to get back to my castle. And that damn mirror.

Waiting for group to start, I contemplate an escape plan. But it's futile; Faraway's a fortress; there's no way out. Out of the blue, I have an epiphany. I'll bribe that giant of a guard, Gulliver. They probably pay him bubkus, so he'll jump at the chance to make a little extra dough. But wait, where am I going to get the money? Dragonballs! This isn't going to work.

I unfortunately have to put a new escape plan on hold when Winnie walks in with her husband John. With his strong chin and nose and head full of wavy auburn hair, he could be what I call good-looking, if years of hard work hadn't prematurely aged him. He nervously takes a seat between Winnie and Grimm, who welcomes him to the group. Sasperilla glares at him as if he's carrying some infectious disease.

"Does anyone have a question for John?" begins Grimm.

Elz raises her hand. "Why can't women find shoes that fit?"

"Good one!" snorts Sasperilla.

"Elzmerelda, that's not the kind of question I had in mind," says Grimm, somewhat exasperated.

All eyes turn to What's-His-Name. He's rolling on the

floor, in a fit of hysterical laughter.

Grimm thumbs his bristly beard and nods approvingly. "Good. You've remembered your sense of humor. Now, I want you to get up and concentrate on remembering your name."

"C'mon, say it, matey," shouts Hook.

What's-His-Name makes an unintelligible grunting sound. "Ruhruhruh." Frustrated, he limps back to his seat next to mine. I give his stubby hand a gentle squeeze. At least, he tried.

No one has any further questions for John; Grimm takes over.

"John, how do you feel?"

"Tired."

That's obvious by the dark circles and creases around his eyes.

Grimm continues. "Why do you feel tired?"

"I have to work and take care of the kids by myself. It's exhausting."

"Did your wife have to take care of them by herself?"

John fidgets with his fingers. "I suppose."

"No, John, the answer is 'yes.' Say it, 'yes, my wife had to take care of the kids by herself.'"

He reluctantly repeats Grimm's words. Anger is rising in Winnie like bread in an oven. I'm worried. Where's Grimm going with these questions?

"John, do you think your wife ever got tired of taking care of your children?"

"I don't know," he mumbles. Grimm's wearing him down.

"Why don't you know?"

"Because I never asked her."

Winnie leaps up, her freckles flickering with fury. "You've never asked me anything about my life!"

"Winifred, can you elaborate?" asks Grimm.

"All he's ever done is come home with his filthy hands, demand dinner, and go to sleep!" she shouts with rage I've never witnessed before.

"Is that true, John?" asks Grimm.

John stares down at his large, leathery hands. "Yes," he says finally.

"How do you think your wife feels about your behavior?"

"I guess she's not happy. That's why she's here."

"Yes, John, that's one of the reasons she's here. Why else is she here?"

"Because she's as fat as a cow!" blurts out Sasperilla. "Anyone with eyes can see that."

Winnie is verging on tears. I want to kill Sasperilla.

John gazes at his wife with a mixture of pity and disgust. "She overeats."

"Why do you think she overeats?" asks Grimm.

He shakes his head. "I don't know."

"I eat because you never pay attention to me!" shouts Winnie.

"John, your wife is an emotional overeater. Food comforts her. It's a substitution for love."

John says nothing. Grimm perseveres.

"Why do you think she tried to eat your children?"

What! She actually tried to eat her own children?

Winnie's face contorts with pain. John's turns ashen. Thunderstruck, we all gape with shock. Except for Sasperilla, who's got I-told-you-so written all over her.

"Leave Hansel and Gretel out of this!" Collapsing back onto her chair, Winnie bursts into a tempest of tears.

I feel painfully helpless.

"Ha!" snickers Sasperilla. "It's no wonder she's not fatter. I bet eating plump kids can really pack on the pounds."

Elz is horrified. "Sassy, that's a terrible thing to say."

Sasperilla huffs. "Can't anyone take a joke around this place?"

"Too bad you don't have enough fat on your bones to whet Winnie's appetite," chortles Hook.

I have to give it to Hook. His sick joke shuts the skinny bitch up. For Winnie, it's no laughing matter. Bawling her eyes out, she faces her husband.

"I wasn't really going to eat them! I just wanted you to notice me! For once!"

"I didn't recognize you! You turned into a fat ugly witch!"

"You turned me into that!"

Grimm, showing no emotion, turns to her. "No, Winifred, you did it to yourself. You have to take some ownership of your problem."

The ogre! My friend's having a total breakdown! And he doesn't give a dragon's ass!

"John, when was the last time you made love to your wife?" asks Grimm, still showing no sympathy.

"I don't remember." His tone is flat, his eyes distant.

"When was the last time you told your wife she is beautiful?"

Shaking his head, he slumps deeper into his chair. "I don't remember."

I can't contain myself any longer. "Every woman needs to be told she's beautiful!"

"Who ever told you you're beautiful?" snaps Sasperilla.

"Sasperilla, put a lid on it," orders Grimm.

The skinny bitch makes a face but doesn't utter another word.

Thank goodness, I don't have to tell her—or any of them—about my mirror.

Hook shoots me one of his smarmy smiles. "Jane's right. Flattery is the way to a woman's heart."

Just not mine, you pompous asshole. I'm back to hating him.

Grimm takes control again. "John, did you ever think your wife was beautiful?"

He stares at his sobbing wife. "Yes." His eyes grow watery. "When I first met her, I thought she was the most beautiful woman on earth."

"I was a lot thinner then," sniffles Winnie.

"And I was a lot younger," says John softly.

Their eyes meet.

"John, what do you want?" Grimm leans in to him.

Without taking his eyes off Winnie, John parts his quivering lips. "I want her back." No longer able to hold back tears, he slides closer to her. "Sweetheart, please come home. I miss you. The kids miss you. We can't live without you."

My skin prickles as he takes her into his arms.

Winnie melts. "I miss you so much. And the children too."

John strokes her long red hair. "I'm sorry, sweetheart. I promise things will be different; I can't lose you again."

"I'm sorry too," says Winnie.

John squeezes her wide, inviting body. "I love you, Winifred."

"I love you too," whispers Winnie.

Their lips meet, the two of them oblivious to our voyeuristic stares. Envy comes over me unlike any I've ever felt.

So, this must be love.

—⁂—

By dinnertime, I'm totally drained. All I want to do is crawl into bed, pull the covers over my head, and close my eyes. The last thing I want to do is have dinner with Elz, Sasperilla, and their mother. And to be honest, I should be working on an escape plan.

When I arrive at the banquet hall, Winnie and her husband, holding hands, are intimately engaged in conversation at the table in the corner. At another table, What's-His-Name is busily chatting with Hook. My spirits rise a little—at least, he's not sitting alone for once.

Elz is at our usual table with Sasperilla and their mother, whose back is to me. As I head over to them, I overhear their conversation.

"Sasperilla, what in heavens happened to your nose?" asks their mother, sounding more disgusted than concerned.

"It's all Elzmerelda's fault!"

"It was an accident," protests Elz. "I didn't mean for it to happen."

"Did so!"

"Did not!"

"Well, let's hope it doesn't leave a scar because no prince is going to marry a marred woman," says their mother, cutting their argument short.

Elz is relieved to see me. She introduces me to her mother, Lady Germaine, who bears a striking resemblance to Sasperilla. She's tall and bony with a pointy, aristocratic nose and sharp, jutting chin that could probably cut through glass. Dressed in an austere high-neck gray dress that matches the color of her upswept hair, she nods with a coldness that sends a chill up my spine. Her eyes fixate on my bandaged finger before shifting back to her daughters.

"I'm beginning to think I've sent you two to an emergency room, not a rehabilitation center," she says, her voice brimming with contempt.

Sasperilla pushes a few peas around her plate with her fork.

"Why aren't you eating, Sasperilla?" Lady Germaine asks.

"Mother, I'm having an issue with the food here. I'm eating less and less but getting bigger and bigger." She gives me a hard kick under the table. "Jane, don't you agree I look fat?"

"Yes!" I say, unable to resist. Truthfully, she's scary-skinnier than ever.

"I knew it!" Sasperilla shoves her plate away. "I'm going to have to stop eating altogether!"

Seriously, how much skinnier can she get? My imagination doesn't get far. Hook, as dapper as ever, swaggers up to our table. Sasperilla fixes her curls, then grimaces when she catches him winking at me. Luckily, Elz doesn't notice. Her face radiates with excitement as she introduces Hook to her mother.

Lady Germaine runs her frosty eyes over him. They stay glued on his hook.

"So, *Captain*, exactly what royal army do you command?" she asks, her tone haughty and suspicious.

"Lady, *I* am a pirate," he replies, full of macho pride.

Lady Germaine puckers her face in disgust while Elz gazes at Hook adoringly.

"Mother, when I get out of here, I want to sail away with him."

Lady Germaine arches her brows. "What are you talking about, Elzmerelda? Have you gone *completely* mad?"

"Yes, Mother," jumps in Sasperilla. "She's totally lost her mind. She should be permanently confined to a mental institution."

"Elzmerelda, you know perfectly well that I have spent considerable time and money grooming both you and your sister to marry a prince."

"Mother, *I'm* perfect marriage material." Sasperilla smiles smugly.

"Actually, I do know of one available prince. His name is Gallant. His wife died several years ago, and now he's ready to remarry. We'd better hurry because I've heard there may be a princess-in-waiting ahead of you."

"Then what are we waiting for?" Sasperilla leaps up like a frog. "Sign me out of here!"

"Actually, I thought he would be perfect for Elzmerelda."

Sasperilla's beady eyes narrow. "You always favor her!"

"No, she doesn't," protests Elz.

"Don't lie, Elzmerelda. You were always Mother's favorite."

"Was not!"

"Was so!"

"I don't even want to marry a prince!" Elz's words shoot out like a burst of flames.

Lady Germaine gasps. Her pale skin flushes.

Fueled by her newfound determination and courage, Elz

pushes her chair away from the table, stands up, and squarely faces her mother.

Go for it, Elz, I root silently.

"Mother, I'm tired of you shoving your agenda down my throat. You can't control my life!"

Lady Germaine tries to say something but can't get her lips to move. Her face grows redder.

"Mother, did you ever think that's why Sasperilla doesn't eat? Food is the one thing you can't shove down her throat. The one thing you can't control."

Sasperilla's eyes bug out. Ha! Elz has hit on a nerve. *Don't stop, roomie.*

"Mother, your agenda is *not* mine. I don't want to live out your dream! I want to marry someone who loves me for who I am!"

Lady Germaine clutches her chest. She hyperventilates, chokes, and finally keels over. Her head hangs limply in her bowl of salad, and her spindly arms dangle by her side. Cripes! She's barely breathing.

"Mother, Mother! Wake up!" shouts Elz. She shakes her mother like a rattle, but there's no response.

"Can't someone do something?" scoffs Sasperilla.

Hook yanks up Lady Germaine's head and presses his lips against hers, rhythmically blowing air into her mouth. "I saved a near-be-drowned matey this way," he manages to say between breaths.

The three of us don't blink an eye as he breathes life into Lady Germaine.

"What's the matter?" asks Sasperilla impatiently.

Hook comes up for air. "The matter is she's dead."

"Elzmerelda, you killed her!" hisses Sasperilla.

"Oh God!" wails Elz. "What have I done?"

I'm speechless.

Still in her dress-up clothes, Elz is curled up in a ball on her bed. I've tried to convince her that she's not responsible for her mother's death. It hasn't helped. She cannot stop crying.

Without asking, I crawl into her bed, lay my head down on her tear-soaked pillow, and cradle her shaking body in mine. Her sobbing grows softer. Neither of us says a word.

"Jane," she says at last, "I've never asked you about your mother."

"I don't remember her," I lie. The truth is I don't want to remember her.

"Is she dead?"

"Yes." Another lie. Okay, it's a half-lie. In my heart, my mother is dead. I don't know what became of her. What's more, I don't care.

"I'm sorry, Jane."

Don't be. I tell Elz she needs to get some sleep. In fact, we both do.

"Sweet dreams, Jane."

"Sweet dreams, Elz." How odd to say that after what's happened tonight.

I'm lulled to sleep by Elz's soft sobs and the rhythmic heaving of her body. In the middle of the night, I wake up screaming and drenched with sweat. I've just killed my mother in my dream.

CHAPTER 12

Lady Germaine is buried the next morning in a simple ceremony just outside The Enchanted Forest. Everyone at Faraway attends, staff and inmates alike. Winnie's husband is also there. All activities, including therapy sessions, have been suspended.

Winnie and I flank Elz, holding her up by the arms for support. Her face is spotted, and her eyes are swollen-red from crying. She looks awful. Sasperilla stands by herself, twirling her curls. She looks bored.

In his eulogy, Dr. Grimm calls Lady Germaine "a beautiful, kind woman who loved her daughters more than anything." Maybe, he never met her.

"Would anyone like to say something?" he asks at the conclusion of his tribute.

Elz bursts into tears once again. "Poor Cinderella lost her mother, and I was so mean to her. Do you think she can ever forgive me?"

Sasperilla furrows her brows. "Puh-lease. She should be apologizing to *us* for screwing up *our* lives!"

Grimm smiles. Seriously, how can he be smiling at a time like this?

"Elzmerelda, by acknowledging your dysfunctional behavior and asking for forgiveness, it shows you're on your way to a full recovery. You'll be ready to leave Faraway soon."

"I just want my mother back!" Elz wails.

"Get over it!" snaps Sasperilla. "Mother was a bitch, and you know it!"

"How could you say that?" Elz croaks. "Everything she did, she did for us."

Sasperilla breaks into jeering laughter. "You're so pathetically naïve, Elzmerelda. Everything she did, she did for *herself!*"

Elz presses her hands against her ears and sings "lalala" as loud as she can, attempting to drown out Sasperilla's voice.

"I know you can hear me," taunts Sasperilla. "Honestly, do you really think Mother wanted us to marry royalty so that *we* could live happily ever after?"

Elz sings louder.

"Duh! She only wanted to keep herself out of the poorhouse."

Poor Elz is close to collapsing. I can't hold back any longer. Someone's got to protect Elz from her despicable sister.

"You don't really know what a self-centered, wicked mother is!" I lash out.

"And you do, Miss Know-It-All?" sneers the skinny bitch. "Why don't you tell us more about Mommy?"

I'm trapped by my own words. I don't want to talk about my mother. Not now! Not ever!

But Grimm gloms on to the idea. "Yes, let's talk about our mothers. Who would like to share?" His eyes jump from face to face before landing on mine.

A giant knot forms in my stomach. I'm *not* sharing.

To my relief, Hook steps forward. "I loved my mother." His trembling voice surprises me. "She deserved a better life."

"Why is that?" asks Grimm.

Hook's eyes wander into space and grow watery. Can Mr. Macho actually be on the brink of tears?

Shrink swoops in and looks straight at him. "You grew up in a noble house that seemed normal. But inside, it wasn't, James; was it?"

Hook lowers his head. "My father drank."

"A lot?"

Hook nods.

"And what did your father do when he drank?" she asks.

Silence.

"Answer me, James."

"He hit my mother," he says at last, his lips quivering.

"So, your father abused your mother. Like you do to others."

His voice rises with anger. "I don't abuse anyone!"

Yes, you do, you swine! I want to shout out. *Admit it!* The loving, compassionate look on Elz's face makes me bite my tongue. Shrink jumps into the silence.

"James, let me remind you. You've made countless people walk the plank. You kidnapped an innocent young Indian maiden named Tiger Lily and threatened her. You even tortured a helpless little fairy."

She must be referring to her twin Tinkerbell. Do I detect some feelings?

Hook fiddles nervously with his hook.

"And let's not forget the fact that you crashed your ship because you were drinking and almost killed your crew!" she adds.

"Who told you that?" Hook barks.

"Your shipmate, Mr. Smee. You should thank him. He's the one who you needed help and had you committed to Faraway."

Hook's face reddens with rage. "So that's who landed me here. That traitor!"

"Hook, you're in denial," says Grimm, taking over. "Your deviant behavior is a natural progression. You learned it from your father."

Like father like son. A horrible thought occurs to me. Like mother like daughter? Am I just an extension of my wicked mother? Nausea slithers through me as Grimm perseveres.

"What happened to your mother?"

Hook descends into darkness. "She died when I was ten."

"How did she die?"

A tear escapes his eye and rolls down his swarthy face. "She jumped into a river." He swallows hard. "A crocodile attacked her."

That explains Hook's morbid fear of crocodiles. It goes way beyond his missing hand. More tears spring from his eyes. I almost feel sorry for him.

Grimm pushes on. "How did you feel?"

Hook's eyes turn to steel. "I wanted to kill my father!"

Sasperilla suddenly interrupts. "This is all so fascinating, but can't we wrap things up? It's cutting into my grieving time."

"Shut up, Sasperilla!" shouts Winnie, ready to pounce on her.

Sasperilla crinkles her bandaged nose and winces.

John proudly puts an arm around his outspoken wife. The Badass Fairies give her a collective thumbs-up. Thanking her, Grimm plows ahead with Hook.

"Who do you see when you make people walk the plank?"

Hook's face contorts. "Who do you think, you idiot? My father! He destroyed my mother. The bastard deserved to die!"

I'm eager to find out if Hook's father is still alive, but Grimm takes his questions in a different direction.

"So, why did you want to destroy Peter Pan?"

"Because he cut off my hand." Hook bitterly flings his iron claw at Grimm. "What does Peter Pan have to do with my mother?"

"Dig deeper, Hook. Why did you *really* want to kill Peter Pan?"

Silence. Hook's anger dissolves into despair.

"I wished I could be a boy like him. And have Wendy," he says at last, his voice hoarse and tearful.

"Yes, Hook. By eliminating Peter Pan, you could have Wendy for yourself. To take care of you like a little boy. Admit it, Hook, you wanted Wendy to be your mother."

"It's true," he says, choking on his words. "I wanted her to be my mother."

"And when she rejected you, you tried to kill her."

"Stop it!" Hook breaks down in tears, his shoulders heaving. I feel his pain. We're cut from the same cloth.

Elz dashes over to the broken pirate and hugs him. "Thank you for sharing. You wanted your mother back. Like me."

Hook bawls in Elz's arms. Like a little boy.

Sasperilla's veins pop with jealousy. "I've had it with all this nonsense!" She stomps off.

"Mama, mama!"

What's a baby doing here? Wait a minute! I recognize that voice. It's What's-His-Name. He's crawling on the ground like a one-year old!

"Me R-rumpelstiltskin," he says in a baby-talk voice.

Can it be? What's-His-Name has remembered his name! Grimm and Shrink exchange a smile. We're free to go.

Hook spends the rest of the day with Elz. Winnie spends it with her husband John, who must go back to their children in the evening. Rumpelstiltskin spends it telling every living and non-living thing alike his name. And I spend it hopelessly plotting my escape.

Thank goodness, I didn't have to talk about *my* mother. It's only a matter of time before I'll be forced to expose everything. Every painful thing! I've got to get out of here. I've got to!

CHAPTER 13

S unday. A day of rest. There are no scheduled activities or therapy sessions. Thank goodness. After the past two days of breakouts, breakthroughs, and breakdowns, I've had enough. Finally, I can focus on my escape plan.

At breakfast, Fairweather reminds us that today is talent show day. "The show must go on!" she declares.

Dragonballs!

"We all feel it'll be therapeutic. What everyone needs right now is a little fun!" says Fanta. Flossie adds that the three of them will be available to assist anyone who needs help with their act.

The only act that interests me is making myself disappear. I've been here almost a week and still haven't come up with a single idea that works.

As I pop a boysenberry into my mouth, I have an unexpected breakthrough of my own. *Boysen. Poison.* Duh! I'll find some poisonous berries and feed them to Shrink, Grimm, and those three blubbery fairies. Kind of like my old Snow White trick! Why didn't I think of this before? With all the berries around this place, there's got to be a few lethal ones; I mean, I only need five of them. Oh, yeah, and one for that armed guard Gulliver.

My eyes dart from bush to bush. How will I figure out which berries are poison? It's not like I can go on a tasting spree. With the way my luck's been going, the first one I sample will be poisonous, and I'll be the one to go. I know. I can try them out on Sasperilla. The skinny bitch deserves to

die. There's just one big problem. Sasperilla won't eat a thing!
Just another lamebrain idea. I'll never get out of here.

Over lunch, Elz is eager to discuss our plans for the talent show. She's surprisingly chipper given all she's been through. Hook, who's seated between us, probably has something to do with it. I'm still not sure I trust him even after his emotional breakthrough yesterday. In fact, I'm surprised he's not wrought with anger after what Shrink and Grimm put him through. Maybe Elz is the quick fix he needs.

Elz tells us she's going to sing; Winnie's going to juggle, and Rump, who hasn't stopped saying, "R-rumpelstiltskin is my name," is obviously doing some kind of jig. He's already practicing in the corner. The clickity-click of his clogs grates on my nerves.

"What are you going to do?" Elz asks me.

"I have no clue."

Hook eyes me lustfully. "Maybe you and I can do a little number together."

I've changed my mind. I *definitely* don't trust him.

Elz, who's missed Hook's come-on, offers to sing along. A trio.

"I can't sing," I say. Honestly, I have one of the worst singing voices in the world. My "lalas" scare off forest critters.

"I bet you have some other secret talent," Elz insists.

"Her only talent is trying to look like me!" says Sasperilla, pushing her way into our conversation. "Have you noticed how little she eats?"

I eat more than I've ever eaten around this place, but it's not worth arguing with the skinny bitch. But she's reminded me that I *do* have a talent! I can look like other people. I'm a master of disguise! I fooled my very own stepdaughter in those hag get-ups. Every one of them was brilliant.

"I'm going to do an impersonation."

"Of whom?" asks Elz, dying of curiosity.

"It's going to be a surprise."

I smile wickedly. I've just hatched the perfect escape plan.

The talent show is right after dinner. I have less than six hours to get it together. To transform myself into Fanta and walk straight out the gates of Faraway.

Wasting no time, I obtain some green fabric from Flossie and ask her to help me design a frock that's like the one she and her sisters wear. She helps me make the pattern, then hands me a needle and thread.

"Good luck, dear," she says. "I must help Fairweather and Fanta set up the banquet hall for the show." She flies off.

How dare she leave me! I don't know the first thing about sewing. Now, I'm sorry I blew off her workshop.

Fumbling with the needle, I start sewing the pieces together. My stitches zigzag all over the fabric, and beads of blood are everywhere from pricking my fingers so many times. But somehow, I manage to finish. I hold up my costume. After all is said and done, it's surprisingly quite good. Time to try it on.

Something's wrong. *Very wrong.* I can't get the dress over my head. Crap! I've sewn the edges of the neckline together. I rip them apart and slip on the dress. No problem—except for the sleeve I've accidentally torn off. The dress is ruined! And there's no more green fabric.

I'm totally screwed. How am I going to disguise myself as Fanta if I don't have a costume? Don't panic! Think! *Think!* I can't blow my perfect plan.

And then, the obvious comes to me. I still have a map of Faraway, the one Fairweather gave me when I first got here. I'll check out where the three fairies sleep, sneak into their room, and "borrow" one of Fanta's outfits. Frightening simplicity! Why didn't I think of this before? Let's just hope they don't keep their room locked.

The fairies' chamber is located on the second floor of the castle. Luck, for once, is on my side. The door's unlocked. I slip inside. The room is small but fastidious with their three beds lined up in a row. There are two doors—one must be the closet. *Eenie, meenie, miney, moe.*

Bingo! The first one I open is filled with identical fairy outfits in red, blue, and green. Fanta won't notice she's missing a thing. I help myself to one of her cheesy green frocks and a matching bonnet. Then I spot a pair of wings. Why not go all the way! Who knows, maybe they'll enable me to fly. I hide everything under my long skirt and split.

It's time to get really creative. I find Fairweather in the Arts and Crafts room and ask her for some flesh-colored putty and gold paint along with a brush and black crayon. The busybody's curious to find out what I'm up to. I tell her she's in for a surprise. Wait till she sees me disguised as her sister!

Armed with all my materials, I head outside. All is need is a thick stick. I find one instantly and paint it gold. Ta-dah. My magic wand is complete. Maybe it's not as magical as Fanta's, but it'll get me out the front gate.

Now, it's time for me to work *my* magic. I hurry back to my room, relieved that Elz is not there. I undress and slip Fanta's gown over my head. The dress hangs loosely on my thin frame as I expected. No worries. I crumple up a couple of hand towels and stuff them into my brassiere. Ha! I've got boobs! Big, sagging ones that hang down to my waist just like Fanta's. Moving right along, I take my pillow and stuff it into my bloomers. I now have a butt as big as the Badass Fairy's. It actually might be a little bigger, but come on, who's going to measure?

Okay. Now for the challenging part that can make or break my disguise. Carefully, I apply the putty to my cheeks and my chin and blend it in with my skin. If only I had a mirror! I run my fingers over the surface of my face and crack a smile. My new plump cheeks and extra chin are works of art! I add a little putty to the tip of my nose and mold it to look exactly like Fanta's upturned snout. Finally, I take the crayon and soften my arched eyebrows. As much as I wish I had one, I don't need a mirror to tell me I've done it again!

I put on the bonnet, making sure it covers my snippets of hair, slip on the wings, and grab my magic wand. It's showtime! And what do you know! The wings *are* magic! I'm actually flying out the door.

I stealthily fly into the banquet hall. No one notices me in the back of the room, hovering near the ceiling. All the better to make my grand entrance.

Dinner is over, and Hook starts off the show. "Yo Ho, Yo Ho, a pirate's wife for me," he sings with bravura. I have to admit his rich baritone voice is fantastic. Everyone, except Sasperilla, applauds wildly. Beaming, Elzmerelda gives him a standing ovation.

Next up is Rumpelstiltskin. Hopping from leg to leg, he recites:

> "Y-yesterday I was b-blank, but t-today I knew
> That once u-upon a t-time I used to spin
> S-straw into g-gold for a s-selected few,
> And the name I am c-called is R-rumpelstiltskin."

Okay. He's not going to win any awards for being funny, but he's got everyone laughing, including me. Grimm was right. Once Rumpelstiltskin remembered his name, his memory would start coming back to him. And the other good news, he's stuttering less.

Winnie, the third to go, performs an amazing juggling act, using muffins she ends up tossing into the audience. More claps and cheers. Elzmerelda follows her with a love song in her sweet soprano voice. From my vantage point, it's obvious she's directing it at Hook. The swine blows her a kiss. I hope he's not leading her on.

"Sasperilla, your next," says Fairweather, who's been emceeing the show.

"There's no way I'm participating in this freak show!" The skinny bitch makes a face. Ha! Her one and only talent. Ignoring a loud boo from Hook, she goes right back to playing with her food.

Finally, it's my turn.

"Has anyone seen Jane?" asks Fairweather.

On cue, I swoop down onto the buffet. The landing's a little rough, but I make it. Fairweather's eyes pop. "Fanta, is that you?"

"I'm over here!" shouts a voice in the audience. It's the real Fanta.

Fairweather does a double take and is speechless. In fact, everyone's gaping with shock. I'm not sure if it's because I can fly or because they're seeing double.

I get right into it. In my best Fanta voice, I announce, "For our evening meditation…" I'm stopped by laughter in the audience. "… I'd like everyone to close their eyes and chant to the moon with me." Waving my wand, I chant:

> "We have all that we need,
> Full blessed children of space;
> Light shines full on our face,
> Giving Love, Illumination, Peace."

I suspend my wand in mid-air and take a bow to signal my act is over. There's no applause whatsoever. Only dead silence. Everyone in the room is in a trance. My little chant has worked like magic. To be honest, it was more fun putting people to sleep this way than with a poison apple. It's time to knock Snow White off her pedestal. *Mirror, mirror, I'm coming home!*

I take one last look at the dozing group of inmates and staffers. An unexpected melancholy descends on me. I'm going to miss this motley crew of losers and monsters. Especially Elz and Winnie. Maybe one day, we'll see each other again.

Enough. There's no more time to reflect. I've got to stick to the plan and leave while they're all still asleep. Tossing my "magic" wand, I leap into the air and take flight.

———

Flying is not as easy as it looks. Or as fun. Because the moon is a mere sliver, it's hard to see anything in the dark of the night. I'm also not used to avoiding things like treetops, stars, and flying objects. I almost crash into an oncoming bat and narrowly miss catching my wings on the tip of a tree branch.

Finally, I get the flying thing down. And because I studied my map, I have some sense of where I'm going. Good. I can see the fortress wall in the distance. It's just beyond The Enchanted Forest. All I have to do is get past that stupid armed giant at the gate, and I'll be free!

Suddenly, out of nowhere, a blast of heat scorches my backside. A shooting star? A thunderous roar tells me this is not a cosmic phenomenon. I twist my neck and look behind me. My eyes make contact with a pair of angry, yellow, glow-in-the-dark ones. Two outstretched wings that must span fifty feet flap as madly as my heart. A monstrous, fire-breathing dragon is after me!

Unable to fly any faster, I zigzag across the night sky, hoping to lose the beast. Or at least tire it. No luck. The dragon chases me in hot pursuit. Panic sets in as the monster gains ground on me. It lets out another fierce roar. Something's burning. Oh no! My wings have caught fire! I'm doomed.

My high-speed flying is reduced to a crawl. Then to a dead halt. Fanta's magical wings have completely lost their powers. The dragon flies away, satisfied with its victory, as I tailspin toward the earth.

This was so not part of the plan. My life is over. I squeeze my eyes closed, not wanting to see the ugly end. A loud, ripping sound jolts them open. My crash-and-burn fall has been intercepted by a tree limb. Hanging by the sleeve of my dress, I'm dangling like an ornament on a Christmas tree. Fanta's wings, now smoldering, are mere gossamers of what they once were.

How am I going to get down? A thought. Maybe if I shout out to that giant guard Gulliver, he'll hear me. I bet he'll be able to reach up and bring me down to safety. A strange splintering sound steals my attention. *Crack! Crack! Snap!* The tree branch is breaking off. Just when I thought I could smell freedom, I'm freefalling to Earth, clinging to a branch. For the second time tonight, I can kiss my life good-bye...

Or not. I land hard on a soft pile of compost. What good luck! And thank goodness for all my padding. I'm sore all over, but otherwise okay. I pick myself up, wipe off the yucky mulch, and yank off my tattered wings. They're of no further use. I have no choice but to travel by foot.

When I take my first step, a sharp pain shoots up my right ankle. I wince. I must have sprained it. If this is nature's way of stopping me, forget it. I break off a limb of the branch. Using it as crutch, I take off.

Despite my injury, I hobble through the dark forest with its monstrous trees and unknown sounds at astonishing speed. My childhood fears have come back to haunt me, so the quicker I can get out of here the better. My eyes dart left and right, watchful for thorny branches that will whip themselves around me, evil spirits who will jump out from nowhere and attack me, and that fire-breathing dragon. Who knows where it's lurking. Fighting the pain in my foot, I pick up my pace.

At last, I reach the guardhouse. Gulliver waves to me. I hold my breath.

"Why good evening, Fanta. What brings you here?" he asks.

Either he's dumber than he sounds or I'm a genius. Whatever it is, I've fooled him. He thinks I'm Fanta!

"Oh, I thought I'd take a little stroll." I falter for an excuse. "You know, it gets so claustrophobic being inside that castle."

The giant gawks at me. My heart hammers. Maybe he doesn't understand the word "claustrophobic." Worse, maybe he's questioning my Fanta voice. It ultimately doesn't matter. He unlocks the gate with a large key and lets me out. "Have a nice walk," he says and then relocks the gate.

Yes! I'm out. Free at last! I want to jump for joy. But wait! The drawbridge is up! I can't cross over to Lalaland! My body pulsates with anger and frustration. What am I going to do? *Don't panic. Think, Jane! Think!*

My pulse rate slows down, and my emotions settle. I survey the dark, swampy moat. It's about a half-mile wide. I have no choice. I know what I have to do. Jump into it and swim across to the other side. I'm a strong swimmer. I can do it! I've *got* to!

Wasting no time, I toss my makeshift crutch and dive into the black, stagnant water. It feels thick and warm like a blanket, but the stench is nauseating. A few minutes into my swim, a massive, rancid blob of flesh and fur assaults me. A monster! I frantically wrestle the muddy beast until I realize it's only a dead boar. As dead as the boar whose heart The Huntsman stole. It floats away, and I swim on.

With each sludge-squeezing stroke, I grow more fatigued. Every muscle is cramping from the strain. Finally, I reach land. Heaving, I drag myself out of the muck and struggle to my feet. Dripping wet with scum, I stink. I'm exhausted. And I'm in agony. But I'm free. Really free! At last! Next stop: a real spa for a little beautification and then home to my castle. And my magic mirror.

"What are *you* doing here?"

The voice, a familiar one, startles me. I spin around and face a strapping, bearded man with unforgettable green eyes. The Huntsman! What's *he* doing here?

There's no way I'm letting him get in the way of my freedom this time with all I've been through. I make a run for it, hobbling as fast as I can. The Huntsman races after me. Every step is more painful than the one before, but pure willpower keeps me moving. The crunching sound of his heavy footsteps grows fainter. He must be losing steam. I run faster. Suddenly, I find myself tumbling to the ground; something—a rock?—has tripped me. As I scramble to get up, The Huntsman tackles me from behind. Kicking and screaming, I try desperately to free myself from his grip. I'm no match for his brutal strength.

Holding me down with the weight of his body, he pulls something out from his satchel.

My eyes widen. It's his two-foot knife, and he's pointing it my way!

"How would you like me to cut out *your* heart?" he breathes down my throat.

"Ha! You don't have the courage." I spit at him.

I'm wrong. Dead wrong. Without blinking an eye, I watch him lower the blade to my chest. Fear grips my insides. My life is over. This time for sure. I squeeze my eyes shut. An image of myself as a child reaching out to my mother flashes into my mind. They say you never know what you'll see when you're about to die.

One, two, three...I'm counting the seconds to my last breath. On the count of four, I'm yanked to a standing position.

The Huntsman throws me over his broad shoulders. "You belong at Faraway."

CHAPTER 14

F everishly, I twist and turn. Nightmare after nightmare assaults me, each one more frightening than the one before it. Dragons torch me. Monstrous trees strangle me. Sea serpents drown me. And giant knives cut me apart.

Periodically, I wake up, drenched with sweat. Sometimes it's pitch-black. I'm terrified and scream. Other times it's bright. Oh, how the light hurts my eyes. Objects and people float by me, but they're all a blur. Not knowing where I am, I drift back into unconsciousness to escape the pain.

The horrific dreams won't stop. One, in particular, keeps recurring. I'm a child again. An ugly witch holds me prisoner in a rat-infested cell. What am I doing here? I've been good. *"Let me go! Please!"* Howling with laughter, she sears me with her branding iron. Oh, the pain! But I don't let her see me scream. I can't! Biting my trembling lips, I reach deep into her pocket and wrap my fingers around the large metal key she keeps there. *Do it!* In one swift move, I stab the cold metal into the thick green vein that snakes up her neck. "You, bitch!" she shrieks as a fountain of blood spurts out of the puncture. Soaked with her blood, I quickly unlock the cell door. I run faster than I ever have, only to have the raving mad witch chase after me. My lungs burn as much as my seared skin. Finally, I can run no more. I've come to the end of the earth. And so has she. I have no choice but to jump off the edge into the gray sea miles below. *Splash!* I stroke furiously. I'm free! But, free to do what? The sea never ends. My tears mingle with the salt of the cruel sea as I wonder: Will I be swimming forever?

"I'm so tired!" I cry out, desperately hoping the sea will take pity on me and carry me back to land.

"Of course, my dear, you're tired," says a sweet voice.

The sea has heard my plea and now seems so nice!

I slowly pry open my eyes, one at a time. Yes, I'm on land! I can smell flowers. People are clamoring around me. My vision is cloudy. I can't make them out.

"You've been delirious with a raging fever for over a week," says the voice I heard in my dream.

"Thank goodness, it's finally broken," says a second one.

"You almost died, dear," says a third.

I blink my eyes several times. Slowly, everything comes into focus. I'm back at Faraway, lying in my bed. A vase of wild flowers sits on a stand next to me, and the Badass Fairies are hovering over me.

"You must have picked up something from that disease-ridden moat," says Fairweather as she gently wipes my forehead with a damp cloth.

"I had to throw out my dress and bonnet!" tisks Fanta. "Flossie was able to repair the tears, but no matter how much I tried, I couldn't get out the stains or that awful smell."

The events that have brought me here come back to me with the mad rush of a rockslide.

"You're lucky that nasty crocodile we keep in the moat didn't eat you alive," adds Fanta.

There's really a crocodile in the moat? I thought I was making that up when I gave Hook the brush off. Truth be told, I'd be better off dead than back here. I wish the crocodile had gotten me. Or The Huntsman had killed me.

I'm near tears when Winnie tiptoes into the room. She's holding a tray with a tea caddy and cup. Her presence brightens my spirits a little.

"Hi," I say feebly.

She smiles at me. She looks different. Maybe my vision is still impaired. As she gets closer, I realize my eyesight's just fine. She's lost weight. She's a lot thinner.

"We'll leave you two alone," says Flossie. She and her sisters fly out the door.

Winnie carefully sits down on my bed, placing the tray on the nightstand. She plumps another pillow under my head, then pours me a cup of tea. She holds it up for me. I feel like a helpless child.

"I always give tea to my children when they're sick. It makes them feel better." Her soft voice spreads itself like a blanket on my chilled body.

I take a sip of the hot beverage. Chamomile. Elz's favorite.

"Where's Elz?" I ask, sounding a little stronger. Her bed doesn't look like it's been slept in for a while.

"She's gone."

I bolt up, knocking the teacup out of Winnie's hand. "She's dead?"

"No, no, Jane! She's *not* dead! She's gone back to Lalaland. The staff felt she was ready to start a post-rehab apprenticeship."

My heart sinks. Elz is gone? I didn't get a chance to say good-bye to her.

"You missed her going away party. It would have been more fun if you'd been there." Winnie reaches into her pocket and hands me a folded up sheet of parchment. "Elz made this for you."

I unfold it. Before me, is a childlike drawing of two smiley girls hugging each other, one very tall and thin with long brown hair and a bow; the other, not as tall or thin, with short dark hair and a crown. Below the picture, the words "BEST FRIENDS FOREVER" are printed in big block letters.

I burst into tears. "I wish I was dead!"

"Jane, you must never say that! *Never!*" Winnie holds me close to her. "Let's get some fresh air. It'll do you good."

She helps me out of bed, letting me grip her body for support. Though I'm no longer in any pain, it takes all my effort to stand up. Clutching Winnie's arm, I take my first step.

My legs wobble. My body trembles. I'm much weaker than I thought.

As I limp down the corridor with the only friend I have left at Faraway, I feel something I haven't felt since I was a little girl. Vulnerable. The Evil Queen, who once upon a time was not afraid to kill, is now afraid to die.

———⋙———

At lunch, a huge banner above the buffet welcomes me back. Everyone has signed it, except for Sasperilla. Rumpelstiltskin's signature, written in large, ornate letters, sticks out like a sore thumb. He must really be proud of his name. I'm touched; it takes everything I have to hold back tears.

The best part of being back from the dead is that everyone's so nice to me. They bring me my meal and volunteer to do my yucky chores. Even Hook's on good behavior though I'm not sure how long that'll last.

I'm surprised, to say the least, when Sasperilla sits down next to me and wraps one of her scrawny arms around my shoulders. Could she have she possibly become a new person while I was sick?

"I have a welcome back present for you," she says.

With a wide smile, she dumps her plate of food on mine and then saunters off. Shame on me for thinking she could be nice. She's just jealous I've lost weight from my illness.

After lunch, I retreat to my room. I'm still not well enough to go to group or meet with Shrink. Which is fine by me because I dread going to either.

Slumped on the edge of my bed, I stare at the empty bed next to mine. God, I miss Elz. Her homely face. Her fashion-challenged bows. Even her annoying singsong voice and her "lalalas." Who's going to get me up in the morning? Those stupid birds probably won't even show up now that she's gone.

I suppose I should enjoy having the room to myself. It's

only a matter of time until I get a new roomie. A new loony who won't replace my Elz. As I pull my covers over me, I take another look at the card she made. *"Best Friends Forever."* Holding it next to my heart, I close my eyes.

CHAPTER 15

L alala! To my surprise, the birds fly in the next morning and pull down my covers. Hello, my little feathered friends! I'm feeling much stronger. And I'm starving—guess I must have slept right through dinner last night.

After breakfast, I feel well enough to join the others for morning meditation. Our sun salutations make me even stronger. I'm ready to face Shrink.

The climb up to Shrink's office isn't easy for me. I have to stop several times to catch my breath. When I finally get there, she's waiting for me. That's a first.

"Jane, it's good to see you," she smiles. "You've been through an ordeal. Would you like to talk about it?"

"Not really," I say, collapsing onto the chaise. "I want to know when I'm getting out of here."

"That's up to you, Jane." Shrink does a figure eight across the room, then hovers over me.

"What do you mean?"

"What I mean is that you have to want to get better."

"I do." Surprisingly, I really mean it.

"Good. Then you must trust me. You must start opening up about your past so that I can understand the roots of your addiction and help you recover."

My past. The words run cold through my veins.

"For tomorrow, I'd like you to write down as much as possible of what you remember about your childhood. Where you were born. Your earliest memories. Your relationship with your father as well as—"

"My father?" I cut her off. "I don't know who he is."

"Good. Include that detail. It's important. And, of course, don't forget about your relationship with your mother."

My mother! My stomach knots up into a painful ball. Why can't I just pretend she's dead?

"You wrote on your assessment that your relationship with your mother was no one's business. Well, it's mine. I need to know about it."

I take a deep breath. I'm not sure if I can go through with this.

"We're running out of time for today, Jane. Do you have any questions?"

"Why didn't The Huntsman kill me?" My eyes tear up. "I deserved to die."

"No, Jane, you didn't deserve to die. You deserved to *live*. That's why he spared your life." She pauses. "Did you know that he's the one who committed you to Faraway?"

The Huntsman committed me?

The all-too-familiar chime sounds.

"Time's up for today, Jane. I'll see you here tomorrow." She shoots out of the room, covering me in a cloud of fairy dust.

I linger on the chaise, unable to stop thinking about The Huntsman. Shrink practically made it sound like I should fall to my knees and thank him. Give me a break! The hatred I feel toward him cannot be put into words. There's no one who's more deliberately and underhandedly messed up my life. Not even Snow White. She couldn't help being born beautiful.

After lunch at group, Grimm introduces two new members to me.

The first is a teenage boy in tan overalls named Pinocchio. I would actually call him beautiful if it wasn't for his nose. It's as long as a parsnip.

"Why are you here?" I ask.

The boy stares at me. His expressive brown eyes remind me of my puppy Bambi. "There's nothing wrong with me," he says.

He's got to be kidding. Seriously, with a nose like that, he's at least got to have girl problems. Suddenly, something happens that makes me almost fall off my chair. His nose grows three inches!

Grimm frowns. "Pinocchio, tell her the truth."

"Okay, I'm a pathological liar. My father won't stand for it anymore. So he sent me here."

To my astonishment, the boy's nose shrinks considerably.

"Good, Pinocchio," says Grimm. "You told Jane the truth."

Whoof! This place has gotten even more whacked.

The other new member is a frail, silver-haired man in a formal frock coat and bow tie, who must be in his seventies.

"I'm the Wizard. The Great and Powerful Wizard of Oz!" he proclaims.

"Yo, Oz. Show Jane some of your magic tricks!" mocks Hook.

The elderly man's face and body twitch. He flushes with embarrassment.

Sasperilla bursts out laughing. "Maybe we should call him 'The Wizard of Spaz.'"

God! Can she get any meaner?

"And, Sasperilla, we should call you 'The Wicked Bitch of the West!'" says Hook.

"W-wicked Bitch! W-wicked Bitch!" chants Rump.

Go, Rump! His words shut the scrawn up. My hero.

To my surprise, Grimm moves the focus of the group on to me.

"Jane, would you like to share anything with us today?"

Is he out of his mind too? What makes him think I now have a reason to share my life with these whackos? "Thanks, but no thanks."

"Fine. Does anyone have any questions for Jane?"

Hook raises his missing hand. "So, babe, do you want to 'hook up' later?"

That's it. I've had it. It's time to set him straight. "First, my name's not 'babe'; it's Jane. And second, I'd rather make it with a one-legged stinky cheese man."

Stunned, Hook rocks back on his chair and topples over. He mutters a curse. Ha! Serves him right.

"Group's over for today," announces Grimm.

Hallelujah! I can't take a minute more of these pathetic losers. I'm going to work hard with Shrink to get out of Loserville once and for all.

After dinner, I return to my room and work on Shrink's writing assignment. I have writer's block. I can't get started. Or maybe it's more because I don't want to. Okay, I admit it. I'm afraid of writing down my past.

It's a good thing there was a roll of parchment waiting for me. Each time, I begin with "I was born," I can't write another word and tear up the sheet. There's a mountain of shreds next to my bed.

I need a new approach to my life story. Wait! That's it! I'll try writing my life like a story. I start over again and the words flow.

> Once upon a time, there was a little girl named Jane who lived alone with her poor but beautiful mother, Nelle. Little Jane was always curious about her father, but whenever she would ask her mother where he was, she would reply, "Who knows!"

> On her fifth birthday, Jane's mother handed her a rusty, old tin cup. Every day from that day on, she had to walk miles to the village square where she would dance until her feet bled. Passersby dropped coins into her tin. When it was all filled up, she would

limp back home. Her mother would take all the money and spend it on new clothes and makeup. She never bought Jane anything, not even a tiny toy.

The little girl's mother had a large mirror that she kept in her bedroom. It was her favorite possession. She loved to look at herself in the shiny glass. Every night, she would dress up and admire her reflection. Then she would go out, leaving Jane all alone.

One night, Jane snuck into her mother's room. She put on one of her mother's pretty dresses and looked at herself in the mirror. "Mirror, mirror, on the wall. Who's the fairest one of all?" she asked. To her delight, the mirror replied, "Your mother is fair, but her beauty is bland; You, My Queen, are the fairest in the land."

Jane loved this game of make-believe. She secretly played it again and again. Then one evening, her mother came home early and surprised her. "How dare you dress up in my beautiful clothes and look into my mirror!" she screamed. She beat Jane so hard that the little girl could not dance for weeks.

When Jane grew up, she married a King and became a Queen. She never had to worry about her mother or money. Ever again.

THE END

I quickly reread my story. It's perfect. I even got in the no-father detail. Shrink will be pleased. Exhausted, I crawl into bed, surprisingly looking forward to my session with Shrink in the morning. I'm one step closer to going home to my castle. And my magic mirror.

CHAPTER 16

After morning meditation, I'm stress-free and determined. All the better to see Shrink. I'm not going to let her get to me today, I promise myself as I head over to her office with my story in hand. Actually, I bet she'll treat me with the respect I deserve now that I'm opening up about my past.

Clutching the story to my chest, I lie restlessly on the chaise, waiting for her arrival. Things are back to normal. She's late.

Finally, she flies in like a storm, showering me in fairy dust. Without a word, she wrenches what I've written away from me. My eyes stay glued on her as she shoves her glasses onto her head and immerses herself in my words. She's actually quite pretty without those ridiculous bug-eyed spectacles. Maybe, if she's nice to me today, I'll do her a favor and tell her to stop wearing them.

She rolls up the parchment and flips her glasses back over her face. "Jane, you're quite a wordsmith. You should consider a career as a writer."

Is that *all* she can say after I've spent hours pouring my heart out? I honestly thought she'd do a somersault and, at least, schedule my release.

"What's interesting about your story is that it's written in third person and is completely devoid of emotion."

"It just came out that way," I say defensively. "Every time I started with the word 'I,' I got writer's block."

"That tells me you don't like being the little girl in the story. You want to be detached from her."

I tremble. It's true. "I hated my childhood!" I blurt out.

"Good, Jane. You're showing some emotion. Now, tell me why you hated it."

The tears that have been welling up in my eyes roll down my face. "My mother."

"Why your mother?"

Memories flee my head like prisoners that have been holed up for life. Tears of grief mingle with tears of relief as I start spewing the horrific things she did to me. The beatings… the burns… the dunkings…the lies…the nights alone…

"She abused you, didn't she?"

I wipe my tears and nod.

Shrink looks at me kindly. "Jane, it's understandable why you're crying. You are in pain. You're revisiting painful memories that you've suppressed for many years."

She lets me weep for a few minutes before continuing.

"Jane, let's dig deeper. Can you remember the meanest thing your mother ever did?"

How can I ever forget? "I found a little puppy. She killed it!"

I sob as I relive the memory. I'm doing the chore I dread the most—washing a load of my mother's soiled clothes—in the river near our flat. Oh, how I hate the rancid odor left behind by her conquests; it nauseates me. Scrubbing the last of her many gowns, I glimpse a furry little body drifting by. Bambi! The river's strong current is pulling him down stream. I have to save him! I jump into the river, and though I've never swum before, swimming comes naturally to me. All my mother's dunkings have taught me how to hold my breath under water, and my arms are strong from years of hard labor. Battling the current, I catch up to my puppy and manage to pull him to shore. He stares at me with those big brown eyes, the same eyes that melted my heart when I first found him. Except now he's a lifeless, little bundle of wet, matted fur. Tied tightly around his neck is a green scarf. My mother's! My hands trembling, I unknot it and fling it back into the river as if it were a deadly snake. As it slithers out of sight, I cradle Bambi in my arms and watch my river of tears flow onto his cold, still body. I bury my sweet puppy, and for days, I remove the mud embedded deep beneath my fingernails to forget.

"Are you okay, Jane?"

Shrink's voice brings me back to the moment. To my horror, I've bitten my fingernails down to the quick. They're red-raw and sting from my tears.

"I don't know why I'm crying so much," I splutter. "I had my puppy for less than a day."

"It's okay to cry." Shrink gently flicks away my tears. "People get very attached to their pets no matter how long they've had them. You loved Bambi, and he loved you back."

My tears let up a little. I did love him.

Shrink presses on. "Jane, did you love your mother?"

My blood churns. I hated her for all she did to me. And for what she did to Bambi. "I wanted to love her," I say at last.

"Did she love you?"

"No!" I bolt upright. "She only loved herself!"

Shrink flutters closer to me. "How do you know that?"

I close my eyes and see my mother all dressed up, leaning into her mirror. In a scarlet (her favorite color) dress, cinched tightly to accentuate her tiny waist and plump up her breasts; her thick, dark hair draping her shoulders like a cape; her thin, painted red lips pursed. "The only thing she ever kissed was her own reflection."

"Ah, you're referring to the mirror in your story."

I bite my quivering lip and nod.

"Did your mother spend a lot of time in front of this mirror?"

I nod again.

"Jane, your mother was addicted to beauty. She was a narcissist."

I'm in no mood for her fancy Shrink-speak words.

"Your mother's narcissism explains your addiction to beauty. You, like your mother, are a narcissist."

"Stop it!" I cup my ears, remembering how she and Grimm tried to trick Hook into admitting he was an alcoholic like his father.

"Jane, parents are role models. We model our behavior after them. Even if we hate the things they do. You need to admit that you're a narcissist to recover from your addiction."

"I'm not my mother!"

"No, Jane, you're not your mother."

"I'm better than my mother!"

"Is that what you wanted your mother's mirror to say when you played make-believe with it?"

"I wanted it to tell me I was beautiful! And it did!"

Shrinks hovers over me and looks directly into my eyes.

"Remember, Jane, your mirror *wasn't* magic. It didn't talk. That's what you *wanted* to hear. You *imagined* it saying you were beautiful because no one ever made you feel that way. Because no one ever loved you."

Her words come at me like a shower of spears. Sobs shake my body. I hate Shrink! I want this session to end.

As if I willed it, the chime sounds.

"Jane, your story might say 'The End,' but we've got a long way to go. I'll see you here tomorrow."

I retreat to my room, collapse on my bed, and stare blankly at the crumbling ceiling. It's as if all my blood has been drained from inside me. I'm sorry now that I opened up to Shrink about my past. She's using it to torture me, not help me. She still wants to prove that I was delusional about my magic mirror. And it's wearing me down.

I have no appetite for lunch and decide to skip group as well. I'm in no mood to be shot down by Grimm and a troupe of loonies. Hunger finally gets the better of me, and I show up for dinner. Hook brushes up against me as I listlessly work my way down the buffet table.

"Yo, Jane, where were you during group? We missed you."

"None of your business."

"Well, you missed a good session. My matey Rump finally remembered something about the queen he extorted. They're going to let him out of this joint any day."

Rump's getting out too? A new wave of depression washes over me.

I push past the swine and take a seat at a table by myself. I'm not up for any conversation, especially with any of these nutcases.

Half-way through my meal, the boy with the parsnip nose sits down next to me. Pinocchio. What does he want?

He stares at me with his sad puppy eyes. "I want to tell you that you're beautiful."

To my astonishment, his nose shrinks. He must be telling the truth!

"Jane, come with me outside for a walk. Please?"

I cannot say no to those eyes.

Quietly, we slip away.

The warm summer air is calming as we walk in silence through The Enchanted Forest. Moonlight beams between the trees. With Pinocchio by my side, I'm not afraid.

"Pinocchio, is there something you want to tell me?" I say at last.

"Jane, a blue fairy made me a boy," he says.

"With her magic wand?" I can't help laughing.

"Yes. Now, I need a real woman to make me a man."

He gazes at me with his puppy-brown eyes. They make me think again of my little stray Bambi. Of how much he needed me.

Slowly, the beautiful boy-man undresses me. I do not flinch. Only my breasts quiver against the summer breeze.

He stares at me. The scars left behind by my mother's beatings shimmer in the moonlight. No one has ever seen them, not even my precious mirror.

Pinocchio's eyes do not move; it's as if he's looking right through me. "You've suffered, Jane. That's why I knew I could trust you."

He peels off his clothes and stands naked before me. His body, though slight, is as beautifully sculpted as his face. The full moon illuminates his nascent muscles and smooth porcelain skin. It's the body of a boy ready to be born into manhood.

He clasps my hands and pulls me closer. His mouth moves toward mine. I can taste his warm breath.

Suddenly, his nose grows. At least six inches, maybe more! He jumps back and glances down at the flesh between his legs, ashamed.

"Jane, I can't."

Silently, I watch his nose shrink to half its size.

He begins to weep.

I wrap my arms around him and caress his silky chestnut hair. The connection between us is powerful, almost magical. Seeing ourselves for who we really are, we've become each other's mirror.

"We should go back," he says.

"No, stay here with me," I say softly. I cannot go back to the loneliness of my empty room. At least, not tonight. I want to be with him.

Together, we lie down side by side on the warm earth. I stare at the starry sky and silently curse the full moon for not being there to help me with my escape.

"Jane, I never had a mother," Pinocchio whispers.

Lucky you.

"But if I had, I wish she could have been you."

A tear travels down my cheek. Our souls belong together.

"You know, Jane, the Blue Fairy once told me that when you wish upon a star, your dreams come true. Let's each pick a star and make a wish for one another."

I take his hand in mine. Neither of us says another word. Under the watchful gaze of the stars and moon, two lost souls, who have saved each other, fall fast asleep.

CHAPTER 17

At breakfast, I gather berries with Pinocchio. We speak only through our eyes. Something inside each of us has changed. We're happier, freer, wiser. I'm not even filled with dread when I report to my session with Shrink.

"So, Jane, let's pick up where we left off yesterday," Shrink says as she whizzes into her office.

Her entry takes me by surprise. Reclining on the chaise, I've been lost in thought about my night with Pinocchio. That's something she's never going to know about, though a part of me wants to tell her everything.

She zooms in close to me. "I reread your story. It ends rather abruptly. And there's quite a big gap in time. The little girl stops dancing, then she's all grown up and marries a king. What happened in between?"

My chest tightens. Reliving my past is no easier today. "My mother went out with a lot of men."

"What kind of men?"

"Creeps. All of them. Even the rich ones."

"What made them creeps?"

"They drank. Cursed. And stunk." I scrunch my nose, still smelling the stench they left behind. A combination of stale beer, sweat, and semen.

"Did they ever—"

I cut her off. I know where she's going. "No! My mother didn't want me around. She kept me locked in a closet."

"Was she jealous of you? Like how you were jealous of Snow White."

I shudder. I never thought about my mother being jealous of me. Maybe it's true. Like mother like daughter?

Hovering close to me at eye level, Shrink looks at me with intimidating intensity.

"Jane, I'm going to ask you a question, and I don't want you to interrupt. Did any of your mother's suitors ever touch you?"

The blood inside me rushes to my head. I feel like I'm going to implode. I can no longer keep it in.

"Snow White's father came into my bed!"

If Shrink is shocked, she does not show it.

Tears flood my eyes as I relive the event that changed my life forever. "My mother had finally seduced a King. A widower with a young daughter. She was set to marry him."

Shrink jumps in. "How did you feel about that?"

"I was excited about living in a big castle. And having a little sister. And now that my mother had gotten what she wanted, I was sure she would stop beating me—"

"And love you?"

Silence. How does she know?

"What happened?"

"We spent the night before the wedding at my castle. I mean, his."

"You lured the King?"

Her hurtful question jolts me upright.

"No! Never! He was drunk and forced himself on me."

My tears cannot blur the memory of his lustful assault. Hard. Harder. Heartless.

"Go on," says Shrink, her voice still showing no emotion.

I find myself talking in present tense, the words crawling out like shell-shocked warriors.

"Suddenly, the chamber door slams open and a voice screams out, 'How dare you wreck my life, you rotten little witch!' My mother! Her bulging eyes fixate on me like a cobra ready to strike. The King rolls off me and—"

Crack! The sound explodes in my head. A razor-sharp

pain rips across my chest. And then another loud crack, this one more agonizing. I clench the worn arms of the chaise, my body writhing.

"Jane, tell me, what's going on?" Shrink's voice cuts through the memory and pain.

"My mother…she's whipping me with The King's thick leather belt, the one he tore off his robe and flung to the floor. With every strike she hisses, 'Witch! Witch! Witch!'"

Shrink lets me take a long pause, then asks, "What did The King do when your mother attacked you?"

The scene unfolds in my head as I recount the nightmarish events that follow. "The King, regaining his senses, struggles to wrestle the belt away from my mother. Then a tiny porcelain figure, lit up by moonlight, runs into the room and cries out, "Papa! Papa!" Snow White. The King's precious three-year old daughter. To my horror, my mother swings the belt at her. *Crack!* The helpless child cries out in pain. The King, horrified, lunges at my mother to try and stop her, only to be whipped by her himself. Snow White wails louder, and I run to her side. To protect her. My mother charges toward me, wielding the belt. Prepared for the worst, I huddle over Snow White. But just at that moment, a large man bursts into the room and takes the blow for me. Saving me. His eyes meet mine, and I recognize him immediately. He's the bearded man with the knife I encountered in the forest not long ago."

"Who was this man?" asks Shrink.

"The King's Huntsman." I do not tell her about our previous encounter.

"The same Huntsman you sent to kill Snow White?"

I nod weakly.

"Jane, are you okay?"

The madness of that night swells in my head. I press my fingers against my pounding temples and muster the strength to continue. The scene plays on despite how much I wish I could pull the curtains on it.

"The Huntsman, undeterred by my mother's wrath,

pounces on her, knocking her to the floor. 'Take her away,' commands The King, holding the still sobbing Snow White in his arms. The Huntsman yanks my mother to her feet, gripping her by both arms. The enraged King confronts her: 'If I ever see you again, I shall destroy you!'"

Shrink gets in a question. "How did your mother react?"

I close my eyes and knead the back of my neck. The memory of my mother fighting The Huntsman as he hauls her out of the castle fills my head. Kicking. Clawing. Howling. Foaming. She's become a monster.

"She says one day we'll all be sorry," I say, reopening my eyes.

I'll never forget the venomous look in her eyes as she hissed those words. *Never.*

"Did you ever see her again?" asks Shrink.

I shake my head. I was happy she was out of my life.

Shrink heaves a sigh. "I must admit it's quite a page-turner of a story. What happened next?"

My sobbing subsides a little, and I switch over to past tense. "I married The King."

"Why?" asks Shrink, a hint of surprise in her voice.

"I had no choice. I was carrying his child."

"His second child," notes Shrink. "What happened to the child?"

Sadness sweeps over me as I remember the pain, the blood...so much blood. "It was a very difficult birth. I survived, but the baby, he died."

I sob heavily again, burying my soaked face in my hands. My poor little baby! I held him for only a minute. But I'll never forget the touch of his dewy skin or his silky curls. Or the heartbreaking expression on his beautiful face that cried out for life, not death, as the midwife pulled him away.

I don't know long I've been crying when Shrink's voice sounds in my head. "So, Jane, you lost The King's son. His only heir. How did he feel?"

I raise my head slowly, remembering how much I wanted

The King to hold and comfort me. Instead, he ranted, blaming me for the infant's death. And then he punished me.

"He banned me from his bed." My voice is hoarse from crying.

"That's a lot for a young woman to handle. The loss of a child and spousal abandonment. Plus the trauma of your mother. How old were you?"

"Thirteen." So long ago yet now it feels like only yesterday.

"You were practically a child yourself," Shrink says with a gentle flutter of her wings. "How did you feel?"

"I felt nothing." Sadness had numbed my heart

"What happened to The King's other child, Snow White?"

"She grew more and more beautiful every day. The King doted on her."

"But he didn't dote on you, his wife." She's getting tough with me again. "How did you feel about that?"

"I was jealous. I thought The King loved her more because she was more beautiful than me."

"What did you do?"

"I was alone most of the time. I spent hours standing in front of my mirror—"

Shrink interrupts me. "What mirror?"

"My mother's. She had ordered The King's men to move it from our flat to the castle."

"Ah, the mirror from your childhood. Remember, Jane, there was *nothing* magic about it."

My stomach muscles clench at her words. I still don't believe her. I go on, taking precaution to make her think I do. I so badly want out of this place.

"Every day, I stood before it, making myself as beautiful as possible, until I *believed* I was the fairest of all. The King still paid no attention to me. The more he ignored me, the more time I spent with my mirror."

Shrink nods. "Of course. The more he ignored you, the more you felt unloved. Continue."

While I'm sure I've fooled her, her words make my blood run cold. I take a deep breath before going on. "The King went off to war and left me in charge of Snow White."

"How did you feel about that?"

"At first, I resented it. Then I saw an opportunity to bring her down. So I dressed her in rags and treated her like a servant."

"Understandable. You modeled your parenting after your mother's."

Like mother like daughter. An image of Snow White on her hands and knees scrubbing floors flashes into my head. Singing no less! No matter how poorly I treated her, her beauty remained intact. In fact, with every passing day, her beauty was more evident. I was nervous that my little plan was backfiring.

"And tell me, what was going on between you and your mirror?" asks Shrink, interrupting my thoughts.

"My mirror continued to assure me that I was still the fairest of all." I pause. "Then it gave me a scare."

"How so?" asks Shrink sharply.

"On the day Snow White turned seven, it told me she would one day be fairer than me."

"Correction." Scowling, Shrink adjusts her spectacles. "Your mirror *didn't* say a word. You were merely facing reality."

"Right." I nod like one of those bobblehead toys. Why can't I believe that my mirror wasn't magic?

Shrink gives me a fleeting smile. "How did you feel when you realized that Snow White could possibly be more attractive than you?"

"I panicked. I worked her harder. Fed her practically nothing."

"You wanted her out of your life."

I say nothing.

"Just like how your mother wanted you out of her life."

"No! It's not like that!" I shout back.

"I don't understand, Jane. Explain to me what you mean."

"I thought that if I could starve or work her to death, The King would finally love me."

"In other words, Jane, you were still searching for love. Desperate for it, in fact."

I'm so confused. How did this suddenly get back to love?

"What happened to The King?" asks Shrink.

"He died in battle."

"How did you feel?"

"On one hand, I was glad he was dead because he didn't love me. On the other, I regretted I never had the chance to make him love me."

"How did Snow White react?"

"She cried a lot. She missed her father terribly."

"How did that make you feel, Jane?"

"It made me hate her more." *More than anyone or anything.*

"Why, Jane? The King was dead. It no longer mattered."

"She wrecked my life!"

"Like how you *thought* you wrecked your mother's?"

Shrink's question brings on another round of tears. I'm unbearably sad and perplexed. What if I'd never slept with The King? What if he had married my mother instead of me? What if I had never talked to my mirror? The what-ifs pile up like dirt, burying me alive. Would things have turned out a lot differently?

Shrink's voice cuts through the madness. "Jane, listen, to me. You didn't wreck your mother's life. She wrecked it herself."

"I just wanted her to love me!" I cry out, from somewhere deep inside my soul.

"Your mother was sick. She was incapable of loving you."

Shrink's words swirl around in my head. They do little to console me. No matter what I did, I could never own a place in my mother's heart. My chest heaves in pain as I cry uncontrollably.

Shrink gently brushes away my tears. "Jane, you have to move beyond your past and come face to face with the person you've become. But *not* in a mirror."

The chime sounds. My sobs drown it out.

"Time's up, Jane. I'll see you here tomorrow." Like a flash of light, Shrink disappears.

Unable to move, I realize my vanity had blinded me. It wasn't Snow White's beauty I envied. It was her knowledge. She knew what love was.

I'm practically a zombie as I do lunch set-up with Winnie. She, in contrast, is like a wind-up toy.

"Jane, I won't be in group today," she says cheerfully.

"How come?" I should feel a pang of jealousy, but I'm too worn out from my session with Shrink to feel anything.

"I'll tell you later. I have a meeting with Shrink."

She's skipping a meal to see Shrink? I don't get it. On second thought, maybe that's how she's been losing weight.

"Who would like to share today?" begins Grimm.

"I would," says Pinocchio.

My heart skips a beat. Oh no! He's going to tell everyone about last night!

He stands up. "I'm gay," he announces.

Hook leaps up. "I'm not sitting next to some fag!"

Rage races through my bloodstream. "He's a person! If you had half the heart he had, I'd find you appealing."

Hook snarls. "So, that's it, Jane. You like your men to be pretty boys."

"Sit down, Hook!" orders Grimm.

Hook reluctantly lowers himself to his chair, sitting as far away as possible from Pinocchio.

I gaze at the beautiful boy-man. His nose has returned to normal size. It's exquisite. As if someone sculpted it to perfection.

"Thank you for sharing, Pinocchio," says Grimm, looking pleased. "Now that you've come out with the truth of who you are, you no longer have to live a life of lies."

Pinocchio's eyes connect with mine. We exchange a smile, knowing we'll always have our unspoken moment of truth.

Grimm's eyes rotate around the group, stopping on each of us. "We all hide behind protective screens. Each of you must come forward—like Pinocchio bravely just did—and face the reality of who you really are."

Oz begins to sob. His face twitches; his body shakes.

"I'm not a great and powerful wizard. I'm a fake. My name is really Oscar Zoroaster Phadrig Isaac Norman Henkel Emmannuel Ambroise Diggs. I'm just a washed-up old magician."

"Ha! You're a joke!" snickers Sasperilla.

Grimm ignores her. "Oscar, getting old is difficult. Sometimes, we need to reinvent ourselves. Rewriting our lives is good as long as it doesn't hurt anyone."

The wannabe wizard hangs his head low. "I've let down so many people." His spasms lessen.

"Oscar, you've acknowledged your problem. That's healthy," says Grimm.

He addresses the group as a whole. "Sometimes we put a pompous title in front of our name like Wizard, Queen, or Captain to make us feel self-important. It's a tell-tale sign of an addict. They tend to have a tremendous sense of self-importance and an extremely low sense of self-esteem."

Hook and I exchange a nervous glance. It doesn't take a genius to know Grimm's referring to us.

"Are you implying *I'm* not important?" snaps Sasperilla.

"Sasperilla, have you ever thought you've sought to marry royalty to gain a title and self-importance?"

Sasperilla is taken aback. I have to admit Grimm is good.

He's really getting to her.

"You are important, Sasperilla." The skinny bitch smiles smugly. "Except not as important as you think." Her smile falls off her face like a scab.

"You suffer from an enormous amount of insecurity. You starve yourself to give yourself a sense of empowerment."

Sasperilla fumes. "I'm not taking this bullshit from some dweeb who puts the self-important title 'Doctor' in front of his name. You're as phony as the rest of us!"

Although I wouldn't mind seeing Grimm come apart for once, he's unfazed by her words.

"Sasperilla, I worked hard for my title; you, on the other hand, think you're entitled. The truth is, you're entitled to nothing. Not even to tomorrow."

Grimm's words shut Miss Bitchy-and-Entitled up.

"Would anyone else like to share?" asks Grimm.

"I would." A giant lump forms in my throat. I've just uttered the two words I've most dreaded saying in group.

"What a joke!" snorts Sasperilla. "The selfish, self-centered bitch is actually going to share?"

Pinocchio springs to his feet. "You're wrong! Jane is a beautiful, sensitive woman."

"Like you're an expert on women!" snickers the skinny bitch.

Poor Pinocchio looks like a hurt puppy. I want to rescue him.

"Sh-shut up, Sasperilla!" roars Rump as in her face as he can get without touching her.

She cowers in her chair. *Thanks, Rump.*

Slowly, I stand up. I clear my throat to free the words. "I have a problem. I'm addicted to beauty."

I've finally said it.

"Puh-lease. That's a problem? Every woman is," sneers Sasperilla.

Pinocchio gazes at me with his soulful eyes. He gives me the courage to continue.

"My addiction to beauty drove me to do terrible things."

"Can you elaborate?" asks Grimm.

"I tried to kill my stepdaughter Snow White. I was jealous of her," I say tearfully.

The entire group is in a frozen state of shock. Except for Sasperilla who leaps out of her seat.

"I'm getting out of here before she does something terrible to me!" she shrieks.

Grimm shoves her back onto her chair. "Don't move, Sasperilla!"

She shrivels like a child who's about to get spanked.

Grimm refocuses his attention back on me.

"Jane, are you sorry you tried to kill Snow White?"

If he'd asked me that question when I first got to Faraway, the answer would have been a loud and clear "NO!" Now, I'm unsure.

"Well, Jane, yes or no?"

"YES!" I finally blurt out, sobbing uncontrollably. "I wouldn't be here! Would I? I wouldn't be so fu…" Sobs trump my words, and my voice trails off.

"Jane, you've made a tremendous breakthrough!" Grimm steps behind me and gently squeezes my heaving shoulders. "Group's over for today."

One by one, my fellow inmates follow him out, staring at me as I weep. All except Pinocchio who sits down beside me and holds my hand. My misery gives way to an unexpected lightness of being. Peace.

———

At dinner, I tell Winnie about my breakthrough. She's all ears, and I'm surprised how much calmer I am. I feel closer to her than I ever have. After a proud hug, she eagerly tells me her news.

"Jane, I'm going home tomorrow! Shrink and Grimm think I'm ready to start my post-rehab apprenticeship."

My heart sinks like a cannonball. I should feel happy for her. But I don't. And, it's not jealousy. It's sadness. An awful eat-your-heart-up-alive sadness. First Elz. Now, Winnie. I'm losing another friend.

"That's wonderful!" Finding my voice, I give her a perfunctory hug. "What will you be doing?"

"Shrink won't tell me until the very last minute."

My eyes grow watery. "I'm going to miss you, Winnie."

"The same," says Winnie, wiping away my tears. "You'll be released soon too."

The tears keep coming. I haven't cried so much in one day since the loss of my child.

"Will you come to my birthday party after dinner?"

Birthday party? That's odd. She's never mentioned an upcoming birthday.

"It's not really a birthday party," she continues. "It's more of a going away party, but there's a birthday cake because you're starting your life anew."

"Of course, I'll be there." I force a smile. "I wouldn't miss it for the world."

After dinner, we all gather around a mammoth, candle-lit chocolate cake the Badass Fairies have baked in honor of Winnie and sing "Happy Birthday." A big smile spreads across every face in the banquet hall, except Sasperilla's

"I should be getting out here, not her!" she snivels.

The day she gets out of Faraway is the day I'm checking myself back in. That is, assuming I make it out of here.

"Make a wish, Winnie, and blow out the candles," says Fanta.

With a smile, Winnie closes her eyes for a few seconds. When she re-opens them, she inhales deeply and then extinguishes the candles with one big breath.

Cheers and applause. She's radiant. I bet she wished for

something good for her kids.

Fairweather cuts the cake and then hands out a slice to everyone.

"No thank you," says Winnie with all the will power she can muster.

I notice how baggy her dress is. She's lost a ton of weight since her husband's visit.

"Winnie, you've got to try it!" I insist. "Have a bite of mine."

She caves in. "Okay, just one teeny weeny bite."

I feed her a forkful of my cake. Then I take a bite. The two of us moan in ecstasy. I'm reminded of the night she, Elz, and I devoured her secret stash of chocolate. The memory makes me smile wistfully.

Sasperilla loiters over to us. "Winifred, I have a going away present for you." Smirking, she thrusts her plate of cake at Winnie.

"And I have one for you," says Winnie.

Before I can blink an eye, she smooshes the cake plate into the hollows of skinny bitch's smirking face.

Sasperilla shrieks, unable to get her chocolate-covered jaw to close.

"I've always wanted to do that!" grins Winnie.

God, I'm going to miss her.

CHAPTER 18

By breakfast, Winnie's already gone. I've been spared a tear-fest.

"You look like you've lost your best friend," says Pinocchio.

"I have." *Two of them,* I add silently.

He takes my hands in his.

"Thanks for being there for me in group yesterday," I say.

"The same to you. That was a pretty heavy session. I'm glad I came out. Grimm told me I'll be getting out of here pretty soon."

Now, my new best friend is on his way out? With a heavy heart, I wander through The Enchanted Garden, aimlessly gathering fruit.

"Yo, Ho, Ho!"

I whirl around and find Hook standing behind me. He stabs a cherry I've picked with the sharp tip of his hook, then licks it with his tongue. Disgust rises in my chest.

"I came clean about my drinking." He swallows the cherry whole. "I'm going back to Lalaland at the end of the week."

What! He should be going straight to hell.

"So, *Jane*, what about it?" he says, moving closer to me.

"What about what?" I move away.

"You and me. It's your last chance."

"You and I belong in Neverland."

Hooks smirks. What part of "never" doesn't he understand?

Before I can pivot away, he hooks me by my neck and yanks me toward him.

"You're hurting me! Get that claw of yours off me!" I scream.

Hook releases me and edges away. "I get it. It's my hand, isn't it?"

I actually feel a tinge of pity for him.

"No, Hook, it's not your hand," I say, more gently. "It's just that I'm not that into you."

"You don't need to explain." He storms off.

Some men obviously can't take rejection.

———————

After morning meditation, I trudge up to Shrink's office, feeling blue every step of the way. Shrink flies in, full of energy, and circles around me.

"I heard you had a major breakthrough in group yesterday," she says brightly.

"I suppose. I admitted I was addicted to beauty."

"How do you feel?"

Should I tell her depressed, lonely, or confused? Or all of the above?

"Winnie's gone," I find myself saying instead.

"How do you feel about that?"

"I don't know."

"Do you feel jealous?"

"No, I'm happy for her. She deserves to go home to her family. She's a good person."

"That's a healthy reaction. I must say, however, that your look belies your happiness."

"What do you mean?"

"Jane, you seem sad."

"I am sad!" My voice rises. "I miss her. Is that okay?"

"It's more than okay. It's excellent. You've connected to another person."

She's right. I've also connected to Elz, Pinocchio, Rump, and, in some way, Hook too.

"What's special about Winifred?" asks Shrink.

"She cared about me. We had fun together."

"Did you care about her?"

"Yes, of course, I cared about her." I'm getting irritable. Where is she going with these stupid questions?

"Remember, that's what friendship's all about. Caring. Being there for each other in good times as well as bad."

My mind flashes back to Winnie caring for me when I was sick. Other memories drift through my head…Elz fixing my bloody mess of a finger…Pinocchio standing up for me in group… Rump telling Sasperilla off.

Shrink hovers over me. "Jane, if I asked you today to write down the answer to this question—Do you have a best friend?—what would it be?"

I've answered that question before. On that bogus admissions form.

"Can there be two answers?"

Shrink's face tenses up. "Only if you have to."

"Then, Winifred and Elzmerelda."

Shrink's face relaxes. "That's wonderful, Jane. I thought for a minute you were going to say Winifred and your 'magic' mirror."

It takes a moment for her words to sink in. My mirror, magic or not, is no longer my best friend. I hardly miss it.

"Will I ever get to see them again?" I ask.

"Yes, Jane."

In my next life, I suppose.

"Start packing your bag. You'll be going back to Lalaland tomorrow morning. Both Dr. Grimm and I believe you've made significant progress here and are ready to continue your recovery there."

I'm leaving Faraway? Bolting up, I gaze at Shrink with a mixture of shock, disbelief, and pure joy.

"But I still have evil thoughts." Wait! Why am I telling her that when I've just gotten this great news?

"Give me an example."

"Sometimes, I want to strangle Sasperilla." I don't dare tell her about my pixie juice fantasy.

"Many patients have said they've wanted to kill me." So, I'm not alone. "But there's a big difference between thinking evil and doing evil."

I listen intently.

"Everyone has evil thoughts. Even I do."

"Like what?" I ask, intrigued.

"I'd love to put my show-off sister Tink to shame once and for all and…Enough about me! We're here to talk about you."

She pauses reflectively. "Jane, do you think you've changed?"

I'd better be careful how I answer her questions. The last thing I want to do is blow my chance of getting out of here. I nod. "Yes, I feel like I've turned a corner."

"No, Jane, you haven't turned a corner."

Oh no! I've blown it.

"You've become a whole new person. Someone who has shown compassion and kindness; someone who has demonstrated the meaning of friendship; someone who has felt both joy and sadness; someone who has even saved a life."

Yes, hers! My skin tingles. I *have* done all these things!

Shrink smiles at me warmly. "Jane, you *are* ready."

The chime sounds.

"Time's up for today, Jane. I'll see you here tomorrow. It'll be our last session together."

Shrink zooms out of her office, covering me, as usual, in a pouf of fairy dust. But today, it feels magical. I can't believe it! I'm going home! To my castle! At last!

———————

On my way to group after lunch, Hook grabs me in the corridor and pins me against the wall. After I've rejected him a gazillion times—even a few hours ago—why won't he give up? At least, I won't have to put up with him much longer. I'm going home in less than twenty-four hours.

"Come on, Jane. You know you want me," he says, pressing his chest hard against mine.

"Hook, the only thing I want is to go to group. Don't make me late for my last session."

He flicks his tongue at me.

I've had it. With all I've got, I kick him in the shin.

Wincing, he backs away.

"Why did you do that?" he asks, massaging the dent I've left on his shiny black boot.

"I hate you."

"You love me." He winces again.

Suffer, swineface! I march down the hall to group with Hook hobbling behind me. I'm going to share again today. It's time to tell everyone what a pompous asshole he is. They deserve to know.

When I get to group, the door's closed. Damn! They've started without me.

Tentatively, I open the door.

"HAPPY BIRTHDAY!" Everyone's there singing on top of their lungs. My fellow inmates, Grimm, Shrink, and the Badass Fairies. Even Gulliver and the two hair fairies. I never thought I'd ever be happy to see them again.

I feel bad I was so mean to Hook. He was just trying to bide time so I wouldn't blow my surprise party.

"Hook, you're okay," I say with a humble smile.

He shoots a smile back at me. It's not one of his smarmy smirks. This one's genuine. Almost sentimental. Yes, we've been through a lot. I'll miss him in some strange way.

I gape at my cake, perched on a chair in the middle of our circle. It's a towering confection frosted in a bright yellow. For the first time, that color is beautiful to me. A dozen or so flickering candles—all colors of the rainbow—sit on the top layer.

"Dear, blow out your candles and make a wish," says

Flossie.

I behold the cake. No one has ever baked one in my honor. My heart swells with emotion. I want it to last forever. Finally, with one big breath, I extinguish the candles. A head-to-toe tingly sensation spreads through my body. I've been reborn.

Grimm slices the cake. "Who would like to share?" Ha! He's trying to be funny.

For the remainder of the session, we feast on the scrumptious cake. We exchange hugs and "I'll miss you's." How close we've all become in such a short time, old inmates and new ones alike. Everyone wishes me good luck, except Sasperilla.

"Can someone please tell me why she's getting out and I'm not?" she sulks. No one's listening.

Rump teeters over to me. "I-I made this for you."

It's another woven name bracelet. This time it says "JANE." He carefully puts it on my wrist.

Tears trickle down my face. "It's beautiful, Rump. I'll never take it off." I bend down to hug my little hero. He blushes.

I'm going to miss my Faraway family. I really am. I'll let you in on a secret. I wished for everyone here to live happily ever after. Except maybe Sasperilla.

When I return to my room in the evening, giddy with happiness, I discover I have a new roommate. She's lanky like me, with sinewy arms, intense violet eyes, and raven black hair that's cropped as short as mine. Slumped on the edge of Elz's bed, she looks glum.

"Hi," I say cheerfully. I'm not going to let anyone get me down, now that I'm going home. "I'm Jane. Who are you?"

"Gothel." Her voice is deep and husky, almost like a man's. She runs a hand through her hair and grimaces.

"Lice?" I ask.

"Hell no," she snarls. "Two frickin' fairies butchered my

hair like Rapunzel's. They wanted to give me a dose of my own medicine."

I'm not up for hearing her life story. "Don't worry. It'll grow back."

She lets out a scathing snort.

"How's your first day going otherwise?"

"It sucked."

"Don't worry. It gets better." *Honestly.*

"Dragon dung!"

I wonder if she knows I'm getting out of here tomorrow. I'll break the news to her in the morning.

"Sweet dreams," I say, climbing into bed.

"Fuck you."

Whoof! She's got a long road to recovery.

CHAPTER 19

"Good morning, birdies," I chirp as they pull down my covers. "I'm going home today!"

I don't need caffeine to get me out of bed. I'm pumped up enough.

"Lalalala," I sing on top of my lungs. It's my last day at Faraway.

"Shut up!" grumbles my new roommate Gothel. Her head is buried under her pillow. I don't blame her. My singing is painful.

"Why are you so friggin' cheerful?" she asks, finally getting out of bed.

It's time to tell her. "It's my last day here. I'm going back to Lalaland this morning."

"Go to hell." She swats at the birds. "And take these freaks with beaks with you."

I know just how she feels. Trapped and hopeless. "Don't worry," I say. "You'll get out of here one day too."

Breakfast. After today, no more berry picking. And no more sunshine. Tomorrow, when I wake up, I'm going to have real meal. A big cup of steaming black coffee served to me in bed. My bed in my castle. And then, my magic mirror and I are going to have a little chat about the future.

Hook swaggers up to me. Now, what does he want?

"Jane, I want to apologize for my behavior and wish you

good luck back in Lalaland."

Wow. He actually has a conscience. Maybe the swine really is on the road to recovery.

He brushes up against me. "So, do you think you can introduce me to your new roommate? She's a real babe!"

Some things just never change.

My last morning meditation with Fanta, Flossie, and Fairweather. With my eyes closed, I chant my final OM. When I open them, I decide I'm going to make meditation a part of my new life. It releases stress and empowers me. I'm going to send peace and healing into the world and make those three Badass Fairies proud of me.

I bound up the spiral stairs to Shrink's office, taking two steps at a time and counting each one. I think back to the first time I made the climb and was panting every step of the way. Now, it's effortless. I reach Shrink's office in no time—333 steps in all.

I lie down in the chaise in the same position I've assumed every day at this time for the last three weeks (except for the time I was ill). Instead of relaxing, my heartbeat accelerates from excitement and anticipation.

As usual, Shrink's late. How rude of her! The least she could have done is get here on time knowing how eager I am to go home.

At last, she makes her grand entrance, flying into the room at lightning speed. Fairy dust surrounds me.

"Jane, since it's our last session together, I've brought you a little going away present."

A present for me?

She hands me a small blue box that's wrapped with a

messy white bow.

"Sorry about the wrapping. I'm not good at those kinds of things."

"It's okay." I'm touched by the gesture. Besides, I'm not a bow person anyway.

I carefully unwrap the package. Inside is a shiny gold locket on a chain. It's beautiful.

"I'd like you to stand up and open the locket," Shrink says.

I rise and almost collapse back onto the chaise. Inside the gold case is a mirror, about the size of the magnifying glass Shrink used in our first session.

"Jane, take a look at yourself."

I'm trembling all over. The locket shakes in my hand. It's been over seven years since I've seen myself in a mirror.

Slowly, I raise the mirror to my face. My heart hammers with apprehension.

I gasp as I meet my own eyes. My face looks fuller with my short hair, and I've got not just one freckle, but many. I even have a few fine lines.

As I study my reflection, the shock dies down. Actually, I don't look that bad with my hair this length. It brings out my high cheekbones and wide-set eyes. I could get used to it. And I could probably cover up the freckles and lines with some makeup. I risk a smile. And my reflection smiles back.

"Jane, who do you see?" asks Shrink.

What is this? Some kind of trick question? "Me!" I snap.

"Yes, Jane, when you stand up close to a mirror, you are the whole universe."

Where is she going with this?

"Now, we're going to play a game."

Not another one of her stupid games! Doesn't she know how eager I am to go home?

"I want you to move the mirror away from you about a foot."

Fine. I'll do anything to get out of here. I extend my arm.

Magically, the freckles and fine lines disappear.

"Now, who else do you see?" asks Shrink, hovering behind me.

"I can see you."

"Yes, Jane. You are no longer the only one in the universe. Now, move the mirror further away from you, and tell me what else you see."

"I see the wall clock," I say after moving the mirror another foot away from me. For the first time, I notice the hands don't move. The clock can chime, but it can't tell time. No wonder Shrink's always late.

"Yes, Jane, the further away you are, the more you discover."

I'm shocked by the results of her little experiment. I don't know what to say.

Flying halfway around my head to face me, she continues her lecture.

"Interestingly, a mirror can be a gateway to the world around you. A tool for learning and growing. But if used incorrectly, it can be an instrument for evil."

I process what she's saying. It's a lot of information.

"Jane, by connecting with other people at Faraway, you've traveled beyond yourself, beyond the close-up in your mirror."

All at once, memories of all the people I've connected with at Faraway swirl around in my head. My best friends Elz and Winnie who were always there for me. Kind Rump. Sweet Pinocchio. Even full-of-himself Hook and nasty Sasperilla. Good times and bad times. We've been through so much together. Swamped with emotion, I sob.

Still holding the mirror at a distance, I watch the tears roll down my face. I've never seen myself cry. I *am* a different person. I snap the locket shut.

Shrink helps me brush away my tears. "You must continue your journey when you return to the land of fairy tales."

"I'm not fully recovered?" I sniffle.

"Jane, the road is long, and there's still a distance to go. You must find the true meaning of beauty."

"How do I do that?" I ask, my throat burning.

"All I will tell you is that beauty is not in your face. It is a light inside your heart."

I fidget with the locket. Her words make no sense to me.

"Our time's almost up. Is there anything you'd like to ask me?"

"Has my castle been cleaned up for my return?"

"Ah, yes, I almost forgot to tell you. You'll be boarding at a prince's castle. You'll be the personal assistant to his PIW."

My heart tumbles like it's fallen down a wishing well. How could she do this to me? I was so looking forward to going home.

"What's a PIW?" The words fly out of my mouth like angry bees. I'm back to despising her.

"A Princess-in-Waiting. This job, if you wish to call it that, will test all the interpersonal skills you've learned here and help you discover the true meaning of beauty. If you succeed and hence fully recover from your addiction, you'll be free to return to your castle. And resume your life."

I am disappointed, resentful, and anxious. Almost sick. "And what if I fail?"

"I'm afraid you won't be able to remain in Lalaland nor will you have another chance."

The hair on the back of my neck bristles. I have to stay hopeful and focused. I must!

"Jane, we have time for one last question. Make it a good one."

I swallow hard, pushing the anger and pain down my throat. There *is* something I've been thinking about since I've been here. "Are people born evil or do they become evil?"

Shrink flutters up and down like a yo-yo. "That is a good

question, Jane. One I've wrestled with myself. We could talk about it for hours. All I will say now is that people are like apples."

Apples? My stomach churns. Why couldn't she say watermelons, or bananas, or some other fruit when there are so many to choose from? I bet she's trying to prove that she still knows how to get to me. How cruel! Especially on my last day here.

I resist the urge to swat her as she continues. "All of us start off as blossoms, then mature into beautiful fruit. A few of us remain perfect while most others get blemishes. Those that stray too far from the tree often get stepped on or infested by a worm. They can grow rotten to the core."

Like Sasperilla. As much as it unnerves me, I have to admit her apple theory makes sense.

"I almost forgot," she adds as if an afterthought, "people, like apples, can be poisoned by the human hand."

Her words sting me like a hornet. I want to hurt this insipid insect of a woman just like she's hurt me.

"And *I* almost forgot," I blurt out, "you should lose the glasses and wear your hair down. You'd look a lot prettier."

For a split-second, she's speechless. That's a first. Then she thanks me for the beauty advice. "And by the way, I never thanked you for saving my life."

Shrink smiles at me warmly. My anger melts away. I smile back. I'm actually going to miss her. I slip the mirrored locket over my head. It lies on my chest, close to my heart. Another round of tears is on its way.

I'm saved by the chime. It's the last time I'll ever hear it.

"Jane, it's time for you to re-enter the world of fairy tales and find that light."

A coach to take me back must be waiting for me. I rise from the chaise.

Before I can take a step, Shrink spins around my body

like a tornado. Her tiny figure becomes a blur as her sparkling fairy dust envelops me.

My feet are no longer on the ground. It's as if my body is leaving me. I'm being transported to another world!

Shrink's fairy dust was magical after all.

BOOK TWO

Beauty is as Beauty does.

—Anonymous

CHAPTER 20

One minute, I'm in Shrink's office; the next, I'm standing at the entrance of an imposing castle. Unfortunately, it's not mine.

I'm surprised when a little a girl wearing a red velvet bow opens the oak door. She is, in a word, exquisite. Her skin is as white as lilies, her lips as red as rosebuds, and her hair as golden as a harvest moon. She can't be more than seven. The age Snow White was when my mirror first betrayed me. Sheesh! I've hardly stepped foot in Lalaland, and I've already got Snow White on my brain.

Her chocolate brown eyes twinkle with a hint of mischief. "You must be Marcella's latest assistant."

I'm not sure what she means by that.

"I'm Calla Rose. What's your name?"

"Jane." *Plain Jane*, I say to myself, glancing down at my simple servant's uniform. I have no idea where it came from or how it got on me. Probably more of Shrink's magic. At least it's black, my favorite color, and I'm still wearing her mirrored locket and Rump's name-bracelet.

"Marcella asked me to give you this." The little girl hands me an envelope.

I tear it open. Inside is a note with instructions scribbled in red ink.

TO-DO LIST FOR THE BALL

1. *TOP PRIORITY! Arrange for the delivery of all*

2,552 invitations. Make sure you handwrite a little note from me on each one: "Can't wait to see you there~xoxo Marcella"

2. *IMPORTANT! Find out what every princess is wearing. I don't want to be caught dead wearing the same thing. BTW, I haven't gotten a new gown yet. HINT! HINT! Please handle.*

3. *SHH! Set up private dancing lessons for me. Find out where those twelve dancing princesses go. Keep your mouth shut about this. I want to surprise The Prince. SCRATCH THAT! He won't be surprised when he gets the bill.*

4. *DO ASAP! Contact the Fairytale Tattler. Make sure they cover the ball. Tell them I want a front page story about me soon, or I'll cancel my subscription.*

5. *EXTREMELY URGENT! Research the latest diet fads. I need to lose five pounds FAST! A liquid diet potion would be best.*

6. *DON'T FORGET! Set up a spa appointment on the day of the ball. Be sure to include the following: mani-pedi, facial, massage, and makeup. And don't forget excess hair removal. Convince them to throw that in free.*

7. *REMINDER: Tell The Prince to pick out my engagement ring. It had better be at least ten carats. P.S. Make sure it's flawless.*

8. *MANDATORY! Find a babysitter for Calla on the night of the ball. On second thought, don't bother. That's YOUR job.*

Whoa! I've barely set two feet into this house, and I've got all this to do? Damn Shrink for sending me here.

"If I were you, I wouldn't bother doing any of this stuff," says Calla. "You'll probably be fired by tomorrow."

Good. I'm already packed to leave.

Calla flashes me a dimpled smile. "I like your hair."

I run my fingertips through my scalp to see if it's magically grown back. It hasn't.

The little girl skips away, leaving me alone to explore the castle.

The interior is nothing like my dark, drafty castle. Bathed in sunlight, it's a vision of blissful domesticity—in fact, it feels more like a cottage than a castle despite its grandness. Brightly colored floral fabrics cover the seating and drape the windows. The furnishings, though formal, look lived-in and comfortable. Vases of white roses and lilies are everywhere and fragrantly scent the air. I stop to smell a bouquet sitting on the fireplace mantle.

"Hello. You must be my fiancée's new assistant," comes a voice from behind me.

Startled, I swivel around and see a tall, strikingly handsome man, about my age with a short flaxen ponytail, descending the sweeping staircase. He looks a lot like Calla except his skin is bronzed and his eyes are blue. He must be the child's father. The Prince. Marcella's husband-to-be.

"Yes, I'm Jane," I say, gazing into his eyes as he strides toward me. They're the bluest eyes I've ever seen. The color of aquamarines.

"Pleased to meet you." He bows. "I am Prince Gallant."

Gallant? I swear that's the prince Lady Germaine mentioned before her untimely passing. How weird!

"Nice to meet you, too, My Lord," I force myself to say. Even after Faraway, humbleness doesn't come easily to me. I half-heartedly tack on a quick curtsey.

"The formalities are not necessary. And I prefer to be called by my first name."

Gallant. That's a pretentious name. It must go with his personality.

"Is there anything I can get you?" he asks.

Funny you should ask. How about some basics for making evil potions and a magic mirror? I'm regressing so quickly. *Get a grip, Jane.*

"I'm fine," I say instead.

"Good morning, my love," I hear a shrill voice call out.

Good morning? Judging by the light, it must be close to noon.

A curvy woman in a body-hugging purple gown slinks over to The Prince and flings her arms around him. If I had to guess her age, I'd say she was trying hard for thirty. She's very made-up, very blond, and very busty. In fact, I've never seen such big boobs. They're cannonballs.

Gallant introduces me. "Marcella, this is Jane, your new personal assistant."

The PIW bats her charcoal eyes several times as if she's shocked to me.

Silence. Her eyes clash with mine. Her gaze grows so scathing I don't dare move.

Finally, with a snap of her perfectly manicured red-lacquered fingers, she says, "Get to work."

The PIW wasn't kidding when she said get to work. She hasn't given me a moment's rest since my arrival. And I haven't even started on her To Do List.

"Step on it," she hisses.

I'm standing in her huge, ostentatious chamber, knee-deep in beauty magazines and *Fairytale Tattler*s. Now that I've made her gold-leafed four-poster bed a dozen times, picked up her crusty underwear, and thrown out a week's worth of vermin-infested leftovers, she wants me to arrange her reading material alphabetically and in chronological order.

Fuming inside, I begin to organize the magazines. They must go back ten years. I recognize some of the beauty magazines from my dungeon days.

Marcella, meanwhile, sits in front of her vanity, fluffing her perfectly coiffed shoulder-length hair.

I have to admit she's extremely attractive in a brazen way. I, on the other hand, must look like a rag doll. I don't need a mirror to tell me. Even if I were brave enough to take a peek.

Marcella is so consumed with her own reflection, she doesn't notice me. Fine by me. I hastily stack the magazines in two random but neatly arranged stacks. Chances are she'll never know the difference.

Done. I'm out of here. As I skulk away, I hear something behind me crash. Then, OW! Something hits me hard in the head. I wheel around. Marcella has snagged a magazine from the middle of one of the piles, causing it to collapse like a brick tower, and thrown it at me. The nerve of her!

"Where do you think you're going?" She folds her arms under her cannonballs. "My closet needs a makeover."

With a snap of her fingers, she points to the closet. I drag myself over to it. She swings the door open and shoves me inside.

My eyes pop. Her closet is the size of a store. Gowns and shoes are everywhere, except on hangers and shelves.

"I want you to clean up the mess left by my last total-waste-of-time assistant." The PIW kicks a pair of shoes out of her way. "And I want everything color coded."

Is she kidding? This will take hours. The PIW stomps out, slamming the closet door in my face. A shoe topples onto my head. *Click. Double click.* I twist the doorknob. She's locked me inside.

"And don't forget to pick out something fabulous for me to wear tonight," she calls out. "The Prince and I have been invited to Cinderella's palace for dinner."

This is the best news I've heard since I've been here. I'll be free of her tonight! Hastily, I arrange her gowns and shoes.

Every gown is a version of the one she's wearing—shiny, slinky, low-cut. And there's a pair of shoes to match each one. I want to burn them all.

Twenty minutes or so later, I hear the door unlock. Marcella struts in and scrutinizes the closet. Silence. "What did you pick out for me to wear tonight?" she says at last.

Rage is bubbling inside me. Randomly, I grab a purple gown that resembles the one she's wearing, except for the feather detail on the bottom.

She rips it off the hanger and tosses it in the direction of her bed. She misses. One more thing for me to pick up.

I'm beyond exhausted, but there's no rest for the weary. Marcella orders me to clean her powder room.

Another major disaster area. Scattered all over the pink marble counters are open tubes of lipsticks, powders, and other beauty essentials. Dirty towels are crumpled on the tiled floor, and both the massive tub and sink are lined with green rings. It's in a word: revolting.

"When did your last assistant quit?" I venture.

Marcella fires a scathing look at me. "Your orders are to speak only when spoken to." She huffs. "Well, if you really must know, yesterday."

Only yesterday? I don't visibly react, but inside I'm registering shock. She's capable of this much damage in only twenty-four hours?

"Make it snappy." She grabs a red lipstick and storms out.

Battling fatigue, I file all her makeup in a cabinet above the sink. There's another, floor-to-ceiling cabinet against the wall behind me, but it's sealed with a padlock. I wonder what she keeps inside it. I'm probably better off not knowing. Just more work.

Getting down on my knees, I scrub the grungy tub with a filthy, smelly sponge that's lying inside it—a welcoming present from Marcella's previous assistant. Memories of my mother-the-slave-driver flood my head. I got down on my hands and knees so many times they were permanently bruised. Trying to wash away the memories, I scrub harder until my knuckles are red and raw. Finally, I conquer the green grime—and just in time. Marcella reappears and inspects the bathroom. I hold my breath. To my relief, she nods approvingly.

I'll live without a thank you. I'm done for the day. I dismiss myself, telling her that I want to get to work on her To-Do List. Honest truth, I want to find a place to collapse. Somewhere. Anywhere. Far away from her.

The PIW beats me to the doorway and blocks it with outstretched arms. A patronizing smirk crosses her lips. "Haven't you forgotten something?"

What could I have possibly forgotten? I've done everything asked of me. Okay. So, I cheated on the magazines, but I've got to restack them anyway.

She sneers. "I expect a curtsey every time you see or leave me."

What! She's not even a princess yet. She should be curtseying to me! I am still, after all, a queen!

Gritting my teeth, I force myself to curtsey. Marcella moves to the side and shoes me away with a dismissive wave of her hand.

I've had it. I hate this job. And I hate Marcella. I want to poison her. So much for fairy-tale rehab.

———⋘———

Thank goodness, I managed to get Marcella dressed for her soirée and out the door with The Prince. I'm able, at last, to retreat to my chamber. It's small but cheerful. There's a single bed with plump pillows and a thick flowery duvet, a nightstand, and a dresser. But no mirror. I'm sure Shrink's doing.

I set Elz's "Best Friends Forever" card on the nightstand, sink into the bed, then blow out the candles. After all of Marcella's abuse, I'm craving a good night's sleep. The comforter envelops me, soothing my tired, aching body. I haven't slept in such a comfy bed in years.

I close my eyes, but can't fall asleep. Indignation is raging inside me. After all I went through, the nerve of Faraway to place me with an idle, stiff-lipped prince, a pesky, know-it-all child, and that lazy, self-centered PIW. I have no idea what any of this has to do with finding the true meaning of beauty. Or what "interpersonal skills" this so-called apprenticeship is testing except my willpower not to kill someone. It's just another one of their tricks. To make me suffer. Poor Elz and Winnie. I bet they're miserable wherever they are too.

This time, I'm not going to let that waste-of-time rehab center get away with it. First thing in the morning, I'm going to write Shrink a letter demanding to stay in my castle until she finds a new position worthy of me. Like being an assistant life coach. I would be good at that! Even enjoy it!

That's fair. And truthfully, it'll do me good to be home. I'm sure my magic mirror's still there. Pining for me. We'll rebuild our relationship after I lay down the rules. Keep it short; keep it simple; and just tell me what I want to hear. But wait! What if my smart-ass looking glass talks back and tells me Snow White's still *Fairest of All?*

A loud knock-knock-knock at the door stops me in my thoughts. Dragonballs! It must be Marcella. Now, what does she want me to do?

Lighting a candle, I stumble out of bed and unbolt the door. A petite, golden-capped figure looks up at me. It's Calla.

"I'm scared of the dark." Her big brown eyes are begging me to let her in. "Can I sleep with you tonight?"

I'm taken aback. "Why don't you bother Marcella?"

"Because Marcella wears earplugs and never hears me knocking." She pauses. "And besides, I don't want to sleep with her."

"Fine." I'm too tired to argue.

The little girl follows me back to my bed and crawls under the covers with me. She clasps her hands together and mutters something quietly to herself.

"What are you doing?"

"I'm praying Marcella doesn't fire you."

Please pray she does.

"Jane, would you give me a goodnight kiss?"

Now, she's really pushing it and getting on my nerves.

"Go to sleep," I tell her impatiently as I lean over to blow out the candle.

"Okay," she says. "Sweet dreams." Just like Elz.

"Sweet dreams to you." I'm surprised how the words flow out so effortlessly.

In no time, she's sound asleep. I close my eyes and am finally lulled to sleep by the little girl's soft breathing.

Deep into my sleep, I have a dream. A tall chiseled man with a full-face black mask tiptoes into my chamber, startling me. He puts a finger where his lips should be, signaling me not to scream. I say nothing. He takes my hands in his, his grip warm and firm. I should be afraid of him, but strangely I'm not and give myself to him. In a heartbeat, we're soaring into the sky, floating like two bubbles, toward clouds. I ask the masked man, "Who are you and where are you taking me?"

A shrill voice snaps me out of my dream. "JAAAANE! I need you!"

Blinking my eyes open, I bolt to a sitting position. Calla is gone from my bed. Did I oversleep?

"JAAAANE!" the voice screeches again. "Where's my liquid diet potion?"

Damn it! It's Marcella! My second day back in Lalaland is about to go from bad to worse.

CHAPTER 21

I can forget about writing a complaint letter to Shrink. I simply don't have the time. Seriously, compared to what I have to do now, my days at Faraway seem positively enchanted.

In less than twenty-four hours, I've learned that being Marcella's personal assistant means doing all the stuff she doesn't want to do. Which is everything except sleeping, preening, and reading gossip magazines. I've already lost weight from running her errands and picking up after her. Plus, I have calluses the size of toad warts from handwriting so many invitations. And I'm only up to the B's.

To add insult to injury, on top of all my chores, I'm expected to entertain Calla. Marcella, her soon-to-be new mother, wants little do with the child. Actually, make that absolutely nothing.

At lunchtime, Calla begs to go on a picnic. Marcella backs off. She has a private dance lesson—one thing off my To-Do List. After that, she's going to spend the afternoon in bed, scanning magazines for ball gown ideas. So, I'm stuck with the picnic thing.

"It's going to be so much fun," says Calla as we head out the door.

Believe me, hanging out with an irksome imp is so not my idea of fun.

Calla leads the way. I keep my eyes on her as she skips across the front lawn of the castle toward the gated entrance. Her long golden tresses fly behind her, and her sheer dress bellows in the early autumn breeze. Birds and butterflies follow her as if they're magically drawn to her.

As I trudge along carrying a blanket and picnic basket, I feel a tinge of envy. Not so much of her youth and beauty, but rather her freedom and joy. I'm also a little jealous that her fair skin is impervious to the sun while I'm probably getting another layer of freckles. Okay. I confess. I'm a lot jealous.

Crossing a field of flowers, we come to a sparkling lake. Lake Sunshine. That figures. Calla finds the perfect spot for our picnic—under a large, leafy tree, not far from the shoreline. She helps me spread out the blanket. Famished, we both dig into the picnic basket she's filled with fresh fruit and muffins. Suddenly, it just happens...

A fart! The longest, loudest, stinkiest fart I've ever heard. Mine!

"You're the one who dealt it. But I'm the one who smelt it!" Calla bursts into laughter.

Mortified, I'm at a total loss for words. Until Calla farts right back at me. I, too, laugh uncontrollably.

The two of us cannot stop rolling with laughter. I've never laughed so hard in my life. I laugh so much it hurts.

"Are you okay?" asks Calla, fighting her giggles.

"I'm fine." I laugh harder.

Finally, after the stench of my faux pas and hers has faded into the fall air, we're able to calm down.

"What do you think of Marcella?" asks Calla, picking a dandelion.

Skank. Bitch. Wench. Witch.

"She's okay," I say instead. "How do you feel about her?"

"That woman's a FREAK!"

Good one! This kid is growing on me.

"I don't know why Papa likes her." She twirls the fuzzy flower. "It's as if she has some kind of spell on him."

My curiosity is piqued. "How did your father meet her?"

"Papa hired her to be my governess. She speaks French, at least she thinks she does. Her accent's so fake! Then I guess he figured I needed a new mother and decided to marry her."

"How do you feel about that?" I ask, deepening my inquiry and sounding a little Shrink-like.

"C'est tout à fait stupide!" she says with a perfect French accent. Though I don't speak much French, what she's said is obvious.

She raises the dandelion to her lips. "Do you know that when you blow on one of these flowers, you make a secret wish?" With a single breath, she scatters the fuzzy petals all over our blanket.

I pick a dandelion of my own and blow on it. Silently, I wish for Marcella to magically disappear. I bet Calla wished for the same.

Eager to get off the subject of Marcella, Calla suggests we play hide-and-go-seek. As she animatedly explains how the game works, I unexpectedly flashback to myself at her age… hiding under my bed or in the closet from the loud, squalid men my mother would bring home. Hoping they would *never* find me. I tremble for a moment, but Calla doesn't notice.

The game is simple and actually fun to play. Way more fun than Grimm's stupid tree-hugging game. We take turns hiding. The best part is finding the other person, which always results in an explosion of laughter.

It's Calla's turn to hide again, and my turn to find her. Slowly, I count to ten. "Ready-or-not-here-I-come," I yell.

Finding Calla hasn't been that difficult, but this time there's no trace of her. I call out her name, wanting to know if I'm getting warmer or colder. No response. I'm getting worried. It's nearing dinnertime. Marcella will go off the deep end if I'm not back in time to supervise the cooks and lay out her evening wear. Where can Calla be?

I make my way closer to the lake, looking behind every mossy tree trunk and up at every leafy limb. *Calla, where are you?* This game is so not fun anymore. As my worry turns to anger, a cry makes my heart jump—Calla!

"Help! Help!" she keeps shouting. Where on earth is she?

I frantically turn my head in every direction. Finally, I find her. Oh my God! She's in the middle of the lake, flailing her arms. She's drowning! I sprint to the water, dive in, and swim at breakneck speed.

She sees me and desperately calls out my name.

"Hang on, Calla!" I shout out to her. An image of my floating puppy flashes into my head. I swim faster, my arms and legs pumping as hard as my heart.

She is finally within arm's length. Blue in the face, she's gasping for breath.

"Hold on to me!" I tell her, reaching out my hand. Her icy, little fingers grasp mine, and I breathe a deep sigh of relief.

Towing her back to shore is much more difficult than I anticipated. Her added weight (though she's a mere waif) slows me down, and the current is strong and moving against me. My lungs are burning and so are my limbs. Each stroke I fear will be my last.

The current grows so strong we start drifting backward. Calla clings to me as I battle to stay afloat. Suddenly, something beneath the water tugs at my body. I kick my legs furiously but can't break free. Panic grips me. It must be a water serpent!

My life is passing before me. I can already see the *Fairytale Tattler* headline: *"Evil Sea Monster Devours Rehab Queen and Princess Fartsalot!"* Wait! What am I thinking? I'm *not* going to see this headline; I'm going to be dead!

With a forceful splash, the serpent's head bolts from the water. Its eyes meet mine. I gasp. It's not a monster. It's The Prince!

"Papa!" exclaims Calla.

Shit! I'm in such deep water—and I don't mean the lake. The Prince will have my head! A sea monster might as well have eaten me alive. My life is over any way you look at it.

Wrapping a strapping arm around the two of us, The Prince combats the fierce current and pulls us back to shore.

"Papa, that was such a fun ride!" beams Calla as if nearly

drowning was a carnival attraction.

The Prince hugs her. "My Little Princess, thank goodness you are alright."

The look in his eyes is intense, loving, and all-encompassing. I look on with envy and sadness, never having known that gaze myself. From a mother *or* a father.

His turns toward me, his expression drastically changed. His chiseled jaw is tight, and his piercing blue eyes are shooting daggers my way.

He is beyond furious. How could I have let Calla go into the lake? Didn't I know the child couldn't swim? How could I be so irresponsible? So stupid? Every word is a stab wound.

Calla cuts him short. She recounts her adventure. Vividly with no detail spared. In full drama queen mode.

"...And so, Papa, I tripped on a rock and fell into the water, and if Jane hadn't found me and jumped in—with her clothes on and everything!—I would have been a drowned rat. Well, not really a rat. But you know what I mean."

The Prince's face softens until any trace of anger is gone. "Jane, I am beholden to you for saving my daughter's life," he says with sincerity. "I lost her mother; I cannot lose her."

"Forget it," I say, unable to meet his gaze.

My eyes shift to Calla, who is back to being her free-spirited, inquisitive self, searching for bugs amongst the rocks that dot the shoreline. The sun plays its own game of hide-and-seek, disappearing behind a cloud. Cold and soaked, I hug myself to keep warm. Oh no! I'm missing Shrink's mirrored locket. It must have fallen off in the lake!

A wave of despair washes over me, and then Calla runs up to me. "Look what I found!" She unfolds her small hand.

My locket! A smile of relief spreads across my face.

"Thanks," I say, resisting the urge to hug her. I slip the necklace over my head.

"Jane, you are shivering," observes The Prince. He gently drapes the jacket he left on shore over my shoulders. The soft, rich royal blue velvet warms me.

My eyes survey his bare, toned, golden-haired chest and matching arms and make their way to his regal face. His nose is straight, his jaw strong and angular, and his lips, lush and full. And then...those eyes. Those gemstone eyes. He catches me staring at him and meets my gaze.

"Thank you, My Lord," I stammer, taken aback by his unexpected kindness. And manliness.

"Jane, please call me Gallant; I insist."

Fine. I've got to get used to saying his pompous name.

As the sun emerges from its hiding place, we head back to the castle on Gallant's white stallion. Calla is tucked snugly into her father, loving every minute of the ride; I'm behind him, my arms locked around his strong, rippled body. His moist hair, loose and wild, glistens in my face. A sudden gust of wind reminds me that I'm heading into a storm. The Wrath of Marcella.

CHAPTER 22

W here have you been?" shrieks Marcella. "And why are you so wet?"

The PIW's lounging on her lavish bed, surrounded by piles of *Fairytale Tattler*s.

"I took a bath," I lie. The lake incident is none of her business.

"Do you realize the ball is less than two weeks away, and I have absolutely nothing to wear?"

Hello! Has she done a reality check lately? Her closet is so stuffed with gowns and shoes she could turn it into a resale shop. Except for the fact it's always such a pigsty, no matter how often I straighten it.

"Chop! Chop! Let's get to The Trove before it closes." She throws off her fur coverlet and pushes me out the door. I'll have to pick up the dozens of tabloids strewn all over the floor later.

The drive to The Trove, whatever the hell that is, is awful. The road is full of bumps, and I have to put up with Marcella's non-stop babble about her ball gown. Her Royal Skankiness is so wrapped up with herself she doesn't notice me gazing out the coach window.

Lalaland seems different from how I remember it. Then again, I didn't get out much so maybe I missed a few things. Everything seems cleaner, newer, and bigger. More than once,

I notice the name MIDAS blazing across monumental buildings in big gold letters. MIDAS Memorial Hospital…MIDAS Publishing…MIDAS Realty… MIDAS Free Clinic…MIDAS Orphanage for Lost Boys. Whoever this Midas guy is, he must be mega-rich.

And then, about a half-hour into the ride, I leap out of my seat. To the right, perched high on a cliff, the silhouette of a massive castle with towering turrets and shooting spires comes into view. I recognize it immediately. *It's mine!*

"Stop the coach!" I scream out.

Marcella shoots me a dirty look. "Jane, I'm the one who gives orders. Driver, step on it!"

The coach speeds up. While Marcella buries her head in a *Fairytale Tattler*, I gloomily watch my castle fade into the distance. Soon, I'll be back there. Just not soon enough.

The coach turns down a wide cobblestone street. Midas Drive. A giant fortress with multi-color turrets, towers, and spires is straight ahead of us. Coaches are lined up to get inside the gilded gates.

Marcella looks up from her tabloid. "We're here. Finally."

We join the long, slow-moving line. "Can't we cut ahead?" growls the PIW, her arms folded tightly under her cannonballs.

"Remind me, Jane, to fire this driver!" she says as we finally pull up to the valet. Yet another thing to add to my To-Do List.

"And one more thing. While we're here, buy a toy for Calla and tell her it's from me."

———————

A large banner with blazing gold letters greets us as we enter the complex.

> **WELCOME TO THE TROVE**
> **ANOTHER MIDAS MALL**

Midas again! Before long, I bet Lalaland will be called Midasland.

"Move it," shouts Marcella, giving me a shove.

She takes off as if launched by slingshot. I follow her, dragging my feet. Why do I have to put up with her before I can return to my castle? It's just not fair.

Losing sight of Her Royal Skankiness, I mope through the mall, taking in my surroundings. The Trove is like nothing I've ever seen. It's a retail fantasyland catering to the whims of royals and wannabes alike. There's a store for everything, from crowns to corsets. The shops, one after another, line a pristine walkway that's packed with princesses, princes, and other assorted nobles, all chicly dressed and carrying eye-catching shopping bags. They all seem so happy. Of course. No one's banned them from their homes.

The PIW is literally prancing when I catch up to her. "I love shopping!" she croons. Finally, another activity she loves besides torturing me.

In fact, as I quickly discover, if there's such a thing as an addiction to shopping, she's got one.

For openers, she drags me into a bookstore. Barons and Nobles. Wasting no time, she immerses herself in the latest tabloids. "I don't understand why I'm not front page news!" she grumbles. "Jane, get on it!"

While she tears through the tabloids, I browse through the store. There are so many books. Near the entrance, a crowd is clamoring for copies of a thick hardcover book that are piled up high on a table. *Grimm's Fairy Tales: Based on True Stories*. What! That glum-ugly head doctor wrote a book about us!? Sasperilla was right. He was spying on us the whole time! Using us for his own publish or perish ends! I'd better not be in there or I'm going to sue! Elbowing my way through the mob, I grab a copy.

"Put that rubbish down!" barks Marcella as I flip through the pages. She thrusts a heavy bagful of magazines at me and yanks me out the door. "We've got major shopping to do."

Can this day get any worse?

A few doors down, she shoves me into another store. Forever Princess. We're the only shoppers over twenty; everyone else is no more than sixteen. The youthful fashions and gorgeous, young royals make me feel old. And jealous. I avoid looking at myself in a mirror.

Marcella, unfazed, holds one frock after another up to her curvaceous body. "Jane, how do I look in these?"

What I want to tell her is they don't make her look a day over forty. What I end up saying is they make her look like she's twenty-one.

"Perfection! I'll take them!" She jerks me out of the store, loading me down with six more overstuffed shopping bags.

Next door is a lingerie and sleepwear store. Aurora's Secret. Marcella snaps her fingers, signaling me to follow her inside. Aisles of the skimpiest undergarments I've ever seen line the store. Royals, regardless of shape or size, can't seem to get enough of them. While I stand frozen in shock, Her Royal Skankiness snatches up a dozen frilly briefs with matching corsets in assorted colors. I have no idea how they'll hold up her cannonballs. She also can't resist a leopard-print negligee that's trimmed with feathers "The Prince will love it!" she coos. It's the cheesiest thing I've ever seen.

A pretty, young maiden bags her purchases. Marcella pouts. "I need coffee! All this shopping is wearing me out."

That makes two of us. And actually, I haven't had a cup of coffee since I've been back here. Marcella briskly leads the way to a nearby café, The Coffee Queen, and orders two black coffees. The cheap bitch makes me pay for mine. To add insult to injury, when I put the hot beverage to my lips, I don't want to drink it. Everything—the smell, the taste, the color—repulses me. I'm outraged. Thanks to Faraway, I've completely lost my taste for coffee.

Marcella finishes her coffee and mine. I struggle to follow her as she charges out the door and races through the mall. She's obviously gotten a coffee buzz. A major one. Bogged down with her purchases and exhausted, I can't keep up with her. In no time, I lose her.

Mmm. Something smells delicious. Unbelievably delicious! Following my nose, I'm lured inside a charming bakery. Sparkles. Behind the counter are dozens of the most amazing cupcakes I've ever seen. Each one, a little work of art—piled high with frosting and topped off with sparkly sprinkles. I can't resist, and fortunately, I have just enough money to buy one.

When I lick the rich chocolate frosting, I practically melt. It arouses memories of my chocolate-fest with Elz and Winnie. I'm instantly in a much better mood. Recharged to resume my shopping expedition with Marcella, who's nowhere in sight.

I'm quickly detoured again. Still on my chocolate high, I stumble upon The Enchanted Spa.

"Spaaaaah!" Just saying the word makes me relaxed. I've got to check it out. Maybe this will be the real thing. A spa experience is exactly what I need after my depressing castle encounter. I deserve it! I'll squeeze in a facial. A quickie. Before the shopaholic discovers I'm missing.

Inside, The Enchanted Spa is everything I wanted Faraway to be and more. Luxurious! Pampering! And magical! "Can I have a facial?" I ask the dewy-skinned nymph at the reception desk.

"Jane, what are you doing here?" The voice is familiar.

I whirl around. Marcella!

"I'm setting up your spa appointment—#6 on your To Do List," I stammer. It's a lucky thing I remembered.

"Good. When you're done, meet me at The Ballgown Emporium." She tears out the door.

I set up her spa day, then arrange for my facial. When I find out how much it costs, I slink away.

Right next door is a toy store. Mother Goose. I'm re-minded that Marcella wants me to buy a toy that she can give to Calla. I eye a beautiful porcelain doll in the window. Calla will adore it. And Marcella will score points with The Prince. There's nothing like buying love. I think about my mother and how she used to buy all kinds of presents for Snow White—whom she secretly despised—to impress The King. Using the money *I* earned. And, of course, she never got a thing for me. Not even a tiny toy.

Inside, the store is a child's dream-come-true playroom. Amazing toys, games, and crafts are everywhere. Wow! There's even a princess dress-up kit. I would have loved that as a child.

I gasp. Smack in the middle of the store, a menacing life-size green dragon soars to the ceiling. It's just a toy, of course, but still, it reminds me of my life-and-death encounter with the real thing at Faraway. A little boy in velvet knickers (obviously some young prince) is trying to slay the beast with his pretend sword, much to the dismay of his worn out nanny.

A trim woman, holding a large staff and wearing an enor-mous bonnet that hides her face, marches up to the little boy. She slams down the staff.

"Excuse me, young man. You're going to hurt the dragon. Mother Goose says to put down your sword," she says in a threatening, put-on voice.

Startled, the youngster drops his sword and flies into the arms of his nanny. He sticks his tongue out at the big bonnet woman. What a brat! Mother Goose doesn't flinch; she simply steps down hard on the dragon's foot. The dragon roars and, out from its fanged mouth, shoots a breath of fire. I jump away. It's way too real! Yelping, the little brat and his nanny bolt out of the store.

Pleased with herself, Mother Goose walks away from the dragon. Her face is finally visible. It's freckled, and she has long red pigtails. Oh my God. Can it be?

"Winnie!" I scream.

"Jane!" she screams right back at me.

I drop all of Marcella's purchases and run over to hug her. Our arms tangled, we jump up and down like two little kids in a toy store.

"What are you doing here?" I ask.

"I'm on a late lunch break. I'm actually doing my post-rehab apprenticeship next door at Sparkles."

A bakery? And no ordinary bakery. Why would Shrink and Grimm put a woman with an overeating problem to work at a place filled with zillions of tempting sweets? There must be a reason to their madness because Winnie looks fabulous. She's half the size of when I saw her last.

"I come over here during lunch because I enjoy helping out with the children. Plus, I get a big discount whenever I buy something for Hansel or Gretel. What are you up to?"

Quickly, I tell her about my PIW position. How awful it is.

"Marcella makes Sasperilla look like a sugarplum fairy. At least, the skinny bitch didn't boss people around like she owned the world." I tell her the only good thing about my job is Calla. "I want to buy her a doll. That one in the window."

"A great choice!" Winnie heads over to the window and scoops out the doll. When she returns, she gently places it in my arms.

I examine the beautiful doll, noticing that it bears an uncanny resemblance to me, once you get past her long, silky hair and richly detailed royal attire. Sewn into the backside is a label that puts a big smile on my face. "Hand Made by Pinocchio" *Pinocchio!* He must be out of Faraway, doing his post-rehab apprenticeship nearby. With luck, I'll run into him.

Winnie carefully wraps up the doll, then hands it to me in a shopping bag bearing the store's insignia, a golden goose. She glances down at her watch. "My lunch break's almost over. I'd better get out of this costume and back to Sparkles."

And I'd better catch up with Marcella before she sends a pack of big bad wolves after me. After hugging Winnie, I hastily gather up Marcella's purchases and dash out of Mother Goose. I can hardly wait to give the doll to Calla; she'll love it. Shopping's put me in a much better mood. And, at least, I know where to find Winnie. I can't wait to see her again.

Wandering through the mall, I bump into Her Royal Skankiness as she breezes out of a palatial store called Lordstrom. Yet another shopping bag.

"Where on earth have you been?" she snaps. "And what do you have in that silly goose bag?" She cranes her neck to peer at Calla's present.

"It's a d—"

"Whatever! I've wasted valuable shopping time looking for you. Let's go!"

She points a finger at The Ballgown Emporium and shoves me along. "Move it before some princess wannabe gets the dress I want!"

❦

The Ballgown Emporium is dazzling. As big and grand as a palace ballroom, it's built on three levels, with a sweeping spiral staircase connecting each one. An enormous crystal chandelier hangs in the center.

All around it, spectacular gem-colored ball gowns dangle from the soaring ceiling, ready for their first dance. Weird! The gowns are multiplying. My eyes dart around the store from corner to corner. I see myself everywhere. What's going on? Then it hits me. The walls of The Ballgown Emporium are mirrored from floor to ceiling. Wall-to-wall mirrors! Everywhere! My heart quakes; my body shakes. All the bags I'm carrying fall to the floor.

Get a grip, Jane! I inhale deeply and attempt to meditate. But it's too late.

"Mirror, mirror on the wall,
Who's is the fairest one of all?"

The mirrors respond:

> "You, My Queen, are the fairest at the mall,
> But a golden-haired child is fairer than us all."

"Who are you talking about?" I cry out.

Silence.

"Tell me!" I yell louder. "TELL ME!"

"Dahling, are you okay?"

I snap my eyes open and find myself sprawled on a purple velvet fainting couch. A burly man, in a sequined chinoiserie robe, looms above me, fanning me with a peacock feather. I must have passed out. Collecting myself, I sit up. I tell him I'm fine. That the mirrors made me feel a little dizzy. No big deal. *No big deal?* They've turned me into a delusional basket case. Wait! Can these mirrors be magic too?

"I love your style," the flamboyant man says effusively.

I glance down at my plain black dress. He's got to be kidding.

"Black is the new pink, but no one believes me. I'm Emperor Armando. Let me know if I can show you something for the ball."

He thinks *I'm* going to the ball? *He's* the delusional one.

"You're quite the shopper; I placed your bags over there." The Emperor gestures to a corner. I'm relieved to see Calla's gift among them.

"Later, dahling." He sashays over to hug a buxom, regal woman with short white spiky hair, a small gold crown, and a crimson heart-shaped dress that pushes her barrel-sized chest up to her chin. She looks and sounds strangely familiar to me.

"Armando, dear, how's my ball gown coming along?" she asks in a deep, booming voice.

"It's to die for!" gushes The Emperor. He takes her by the arm and whisks her away.

Where's Marcella? To be dead honest, I don't really care. The wall-to-wall mirrors are still making me dizzy. Not moving from the couch, I close my eyes and banish them from my sight. Before I know it, I drift off…straight into my dream from the other night.

Wearing an ethereal ivory tulle gown, I'm floating like a feather, high in the sky. Birds flutter around me. Suddenly, the mysterious man with the black mask leaps out from behind a cloud. I float toward him, right into his arms. He swirls me around our heavenly dance floor, our bodies moving in perfect harmony. Like we've danced this way forever. "Who are you?" I ask, my heart pounding. Silence. And then an earth-shattering scream hurls me back to reality.

"AAAAARGGGH!" shrieks The Emperor. "What are you doing?"

My eyes flit to Marcella. She's recklessly yanking down the dangling gowns with both hands.

"You know, mister, I could use some customer service around here," the PIW grumbles.

Armando frantically gathers up the gowns scattered on the marble floor, crumpled up as if they've swooned.

"Do you know who I am?" Marcella huffs. "I am the future wife of Prince Gallant, and my ball's the only reason you're still in business."

The Emperor doesn't care who she is. Doesn't she know how much these gowns cost? *(Thousands!)* How much time it takes him to make them? *(Years!)* How each one is a work of art? *(They should be hanging in museums!)*

"Whatever," replies Marcella. She demands to try them on.

Practically in tears, The Emperor escorts her to the fitting room, located on the third level. Marcella looks down from the spiral staircase and snaps at me. "This is no time to be resting!"

Jumping at her beck and call, I exchange a rescue-me look with the distraught Emperor.

Dressing and undressing Marcella is a nightmare. As if the complexity of the gowns isn't enough, I've got to contend with the cannonballs on her chest. Plus, she's a total slob. Hasn't she ever heard of hanging things up neatly after trying them on? I'm on major damage control, terrified that she'll ruin one of The Emperor's magnificent creations.

The Marcella fashion show is no less challenging. The PIW parades before the mirrored walls in one gown after another. She hates everything. No matter how stunning the dress, there's something wrong with it. From being too frou-frou ("Who the hell wants to look like Bo Peep?") to being too blue ("Ugh! It's so Cinderella."). I have to swallow my tongue when she complains that the last one makes her look flat-chested. Trust me, an army of giants could trample over her without flattening out those cannonballs.

The Emperor's beside himself, and I'm exhausted. After trying on a dozen more unacceptable dresses, Marcella lights up with an idea. She wants Armando to custom design her dress.

Armando rushes off to get his sketchpad, then sketches one incredible gown after another. Not one of them works for Her Royal Skankiness.

Finally, a dozen sketchpads later, Marcella has a vision. She can see it now. A dress, the reddest of reds—the color of blood—body-clinging with a halter neckline and a detachable twenty-foot long train. Size 6. Armando madly sketches away.

When the PIW sees the finished sketch, she bubbles. "Look at what it does to my cleavage! The Prince will love it. And I'll be the envy of every princess at the ball."

The Emperor breathes a sigh of relief. And so do I.

She scowls. "One last thing."

The Emperor pales.

"It had better be ready for the ball." She eyes me with the contempt that's reserved only for a servant. "I'll send my new assistant to pick it up."

"How will you be paying for it?" asks The Emperor, clearly relieved.

God knows how much this custom creation will cost.

"Send the bill to The Prince." She smiles smugly and dashes off.

"Chop! Chop!" she shouts out to me. "We need to get new shoes."

You mean *you* need to get new shoes. *I* need to get a new job.

Emperor Armando, back to being his effervescent self, hugs me good-bye. "Jane, dahling, I'll see you soon."

How does he know my name? I don't recall telling him.

The shoe store, a few doors down, is called The Glass Slipper. Its motto: *"For the Perfect Fit Shoe."*

Whereas The Ballgown Emporium was large and grand, this store is small and intimate. A boutique. Dainty, candle-lit chandeliers bathe the upholstered pale blue walls in a warm glow and make the shoe samples scattered on glass shelves sparkle like jewels. The boutique's namesake centerpiece—a giant glass slipper sculpture—sits smack in the middle of a large, circular silk couch.

The couch is lined with dozens of royal women, trying on stacks of shoes. An army of elves runs helter skelter, assisting the demanding customers. I bet every princess in Lalaland must come here. My heart skips a beat. What if I run into Snow White?

Marcella strolls around the store in a trance, salivating over every pair of shoes. I should have brought a bucket.

"Hello, can I help you?" comes a voice from afar.

That voice! I know it! Again, it can't possibly be…

From a back room, in lopes a tower of a woman wearing white, jeweled cat-eye glasses. She looks at me. I look at her. We scream simultaneously, then run to hug each other. I can't believe it! Elzmerelda!! This is too much. First, Winnie. And now Elz!

"I love your spectacles!" I tell her. She's one of those

people who actually look better in glasses than without them. They make her nose seem smaller and draw attention away from her other homely features.

"Thanks!" says Elz in her singsong voice. "I designed them myself."

Marcella shimmies up to us. "Do you two like know each other?"

"We're old friends," I reply.

"Good! You can get me a discount."

You don't pay me enough, skank.

Elz asks Marcella her shoe size.

"Can't you tell? I'm a sample Size 6!"

A six, my foot! Her feet are the size of overgrown bananas.

Marcella demands to try on every shoe. Without flinching, Elz retreats to the stock room. She returns with two towers of glass boxes, all marked Size 6. Marcella goes at them like a vulture. With grunts and groans, she tries to squeeze her long, veiny feet into one pair after another. No matter how hard she tries, she can't; they're simply all too small.

"These shoe boxes are either mismarked, or you've carelessly placed the wrong size shoes inside them," Her Royal Skankiness grumbles. She orders Elz to bring her another pair of Size 6 shoes in every style.

On the floor is a mountain of discarded shoes. *Pig!* I help Elz match up the shoes and return them to their proper box. Carrying the twin towers of perfectly stacked glass boxes, she heads back to the stock room.

"What's taking so long?" asks Marcella. Steam is shooting out of her nostrils. She's going to blow. *Hurry, Elz! Hurry!*

Just in time, Elz reappears with two new stacks of shoes. Something's weird about the boxes. It takes me a minute to figure it out. I know. They're upside down. The top lids where Size 6 is marked are now on the bottom. Ha! The shoes are actually Size 9 (6 upside down!). Marcella doesn't notice; she tries them all on, in rapid-speed succession. They fit her perfectly.

"Told you I was a perfect sample Size 6!" she gloats. "I'll take them all."

I can't believe it. She still hasn't figured out the shoes are really Size 9. As she waltzes around the boutique in a pair of her new shoes, Elz and I shake our heads in astonishment.

Suddenly, Marcella screams out, "I've got to have them!" She's discovered yet another pair of shoes she can't live without. A pair of sparkly ruby slippers. The perfect shoes to wear with her new red ball gown.

"They're Size 6!" she squeals. "And they're ON SALE!"

"They're the last pair," says Elz.

Just as Marcella's about to swoop them up, the portly, white-haired woman I saw earlier at The Ballgown Emporium snatches them. "Ring them up," she commands Elz in her familiar booming voice.

"Those are MINE!" shrieks Marcella. "I saw them first." Do something!" she yells at me.

I'm clueless. What exactly does she want me to do? Tackle the woman? And then I gasp.

Her Royal Skankiness charges at the buxom woman and slams her to the ground. She grabs for the shoes, but her opponent refuses to let them go and kicks Marcella smack in the groin. Marcella kicks her right back, catching her heel in the folds of the woman's jutting stomach.

Holy crap! I don't believe this—a shoe fight! Marcella and the older woman are at each other like two fire-farting dragons. Clawing! Biting! Hissing! Kicking! The ruby slippers go back and forth between them, like a pair of hot potatoes. Elz bravely tries to break the twosome up, but Marcella won't stand for it. Dodging a punch in the gut, Elz finally gives up.

The other royal customers crowd around the dueling divas and cheer them on. This is insane! The battle rages on in the buxom woman's favor. But right when she thinks she's got the shoes tucked safely in the thick fold of her cleavage, Marcella lunges at her and tears her gown down the middle. The spectators let out a loud "ooh." I'm not sure if they're appalled or amused. Pouring out of her corset, Marcella's opponent is one overstuffed pastry puff. As she fumbles to cover herself up, Marcella snatches the shoes.

"Bitch!" roars the woman. "You can have them!" The crowd gasps.

"Bigger bitch!" retorts Marcella, clutching the ruby shoes.

Her opponent turns crimson. The crowd gasps louder.

"Awf…awf…awf." The woman blows out short puffs of air, as though she's trying to calm herself down.

Not bothering to try on the shoes, Marcella triumphantly tells Elz she'll take them. "You know what they say. If the shoe fits, buy it."

Holding the edges of her torn gown together, Marcella's defeated opponent marches out the door. Her body jiggles with rage.

I think Elz just lost a customer. Her hands shake as she rings up Marcella's trophy shoes.

"Wrap them up with the others and send the bill to The Prince," orders Marcella. "And don't forget the discount you promised."

That's my discount, skankface! Don't I get a thank you?

Elz shoots me a look that wavers between deep compassion and utter disgust. "I'll have them delivered to your coach," she says, sparing me the job of having to lug them myself.

It takes an army of elves to carry the glass-encased shoes out the door. Marcella fluffs her brassy hair and refreshes her makeup.

"Let's go!" She snaps her fingers at me.

Finally! We're done with shoe shopping.

The PIW yanks me out the door, leaving me no time to say good-bye to Elz. Schlepping her boatload of bags, I follow Her Royal Skankiness back to the valet. Our coach pulls up, and I let our poor soon-to-be fired driver help me load the bags into the shoe-filled carriage. Wait! One's missing. The bag with the golden goose. Calla's doll! I must have left it at

The Glass Slipper. Panic grips me.

"I'll be right back," I tell Marcella, without any explanation.

"Make it fast!" Thankfully, she's still in a pretty good mood from shopping.

I tear through the mall. My heart races. I hope no one's taken the doll.

I fly into The Glass Slipper. Oh no! The bag with the doll is gone! My heart sinks.

"Looking for this?" Out comes Elz from the stock room, with the bag in her hand.

"You're a lifesaver!" I give her a huge hug.

As I turn to leave, my eyes are drawn to a pair of shoes. They're black and shiny with six-inch high spiky heels. I cradle them in my hand. They're wickedly beautiful. I even love the little bow near the pointy toe.

"They're part of my new Fall Stiletto Collection," beams Elz.

I continue to admire the shoes, imagining what they'd look like on my feet.

"Try them on, Jane," insists Elz. "They're calling your name."

Talking mirrors. And now talking shoes. I've spent way too much time at the mall. Besides, though I happen to be a sample Size 6, I don't think any pair of shoes would fit my tired, swollen feet.

"Next time," I say.

Out of the corner of my eye, I catch glimpse of a dark-haired woman wearing a big red bow. My heart skips a beat. Snow White?

"Elz, I've got to go." I say nervously.

She frowns, but then her face brightens.

"Winnie and I are having a Girls' Night Out tomorrow. Come with us!"

Obviously, she and Winnie have connected since leaving Faraway.

"Count me in!"

"Great! My coach will pick you up at nine o'clock."

A reunion! I can't wait! The only question is how will I escape Marcella.

CHAPTER 23

Calla's bedroom is nothing like the rat-infested closet where I slept as a child or the servants' quarters where I kept Snow White. It's fit for a princess with a whimsical hand-painted mural filled with fairies and flowers, a velvety pink rug, and a shelf full of children's books and stuffed animals. Curled up on her lacy canopy bed, she cuddles her new doll.

"It's a gift from Marcella," I say.

Calla gazes at me sheepishly.

"What are you going to name her?"

"She's so pretty and nice." She pauses to hug the doll. "Lady Jane!"

I'm touched. She knows the truth. This little girl's even smarter than I thought.

"Let's get you ready for dinner," I say. Grabbing a silver comb from her night table, I sit down next to her and run it through her long golden locks. As I admire her beauty, the memory of that other beautiful little girl unexpectedly flashes through my mind. Snow White. And then I flash forward to the poisoned comb I sold her. The image of Snow White collapsing makes me shudder. Calla's comb slips out of my trembling hand and onto the bed.

"Can Lady Jane come to dinner? Please, pretty please with a cherry on top?" begs Calla, unaware of my inner state.

Marcella bursts into the room and snaps me back to reality.

"Jane," she says in a panicked voice, "the cook and his staff have just quit so I need you to get downstairs and prepare dinner. Now!"

Okay, so *now* in addition to being Marcella's personal slave, I'm also the family cook.

"And FYI, I'm on a major diet. I want to look fabulous in my new ball gown!"

"What's a diet?" asks Calla, innocently as she retrieves the comb.

"Something you'll never have to worry about." I quickly finish combing her hair.

The castle kitchen is enormous. Way more elaborate than the one at Faraway. There's a giant built-in hearth, a huge iron cauldron, hundreds of meticulously arranged pots hanging from the ceiling, and a gazillion utensils lining shelves—most of which I've never seen before. Large wooden tubs, clustered on the paved stone floor, overflow with flour, grains, assorted fruits and vegetables, and fresh eggs. Chopping blocks, workstations, and storage closets are scattered everywhere.

Meals at Faraway, along with Fanta's cooking class, were based on the principles of rustic cooking. Simple, good, old-fashioned home cooking. While I mastered basic culinary skills there, I'm not prepared to cook a meal fit for royalty. I have no clue where to begin.

Okay, think. Think! I know. I need a cookbook. I'll find an easy recipe, the kind that you can whip up in no time. You don't have to be a culinary genius to follow directions.

I search the shelves for a cookbook. Nothing. There's got to be one somewhere. I open a storage closet. Aagh! Two large gutted animals dangle before me. Maybe, they were going to be tonight's main dinner attraction. Not anymore! I slam the door shut.

After several more dead ends, I finally find a cookbook in a workstation drawer: *The Joy of Royal Cooking*. I open to the first page and begin to read.

INTRODUCTION

Blood, choler, phlegm, and melancholy, the elements found in all living things, and their corresponding natures—hot, dry, wet, cold—must be considered by the cook whenever making any royal recipe. BEWARE! Food not prepared with its humors in mind is unhealthy and can cause death to the person who consumes it.

Blood! Choler! Phlegm! Who wrote this cookbook? They sound like ingredients for an evil potion. I randomly flip to one of the recipes—Page 172, Roasted Tail of Boar with Jellied Eels. Eww! That's it. I've read enough of this royal crap and toss the book in the garbage. Where it belongs.

Outside the large kitchen window, the sun is setting. I feel the onset of panic. Help! What am I going to do?

Think, Jane, think! Suddenly, I know. I'll do what I know how to do. I'll make The Prince and his family (hmm…I'm not sure if Marcella counts) some "rustic" dishes I learned how to prepare at Faraway. A hearty soup, a fresh salad, and a crusty loaf of bread. And maybe a simple dessert.

My spirits perk up. Singing "lalalala," I prance around the kitchen in search of anything I can throw into the giant bubbling cauldron. And what riches I find! Tons of fresh vegetables, grains, and herbs. With a long wooden spoon, I stir the ingredients. In no time, the broth starts to smell delicious. You simply can't go wrong with soup.

While the soup simmers, I start on the bread. A quick rising one. I find all the ingredients I need and mix them together. The dough is perfect—soft but not too sticky. Now, on to my favorite part—kneading. For three delicious, stress-releasing minutes, I massage the dough, pressing and pulling it in different directions. How good it feels to plunge my fingers into the warm, stretchy mixture. I flashback to the first time I made bread with Winnie and remember I should be thinking about someone I hate. Marcella! *Dough, it's time for you to feel some pain.* I tug wickedly at the dough, enjoying every minute.

After letting it rest for a few minutes, I shape the dough into a round loaf, slash the top with a sharp knife—*did you feel that, Marcella?*—and place it into the hearth.

While the bread bakes, I quickly pull together a salad in a large ceramic bowl. I throw in a bunch of assorted fresh greens and then top them off with a dash of oil and vinegar. I take a taste…not bad! Marcella will appreciate it. Salad, the sustenance of Sasperilla. The perfect diet food.

Okay. Now for dessert. Hmm. What can I make? The desserts we prepared at Faraway were limited and usually made from the fresh fruit we picked. Searching through the myriad of barrels, I stumble upon a mountain of apples. Beautiful, rosy red apples.

An evil thought lurks in my head. Maybe, I should poison one of them and give it to Marcella. My mind is racing. Yes! I'll concoct an evil potion using a recipe from that bogus cookbook and dip one of the apples into it. Then, at dinner, I'll convince Her Royal Skankiness to eat the poisonous fruit by telling her that apples are good for your health. *They can even help you lose weight!*

"Stop it!" shouts a voice inside my head. "STOP IT!!" the voice says again louder. *Okay, I hear you! Enough!* Taking a deep breath, I force myself to stay focused on making dessert.

I know. I can bake an apple pie. I made one once with Winnie at Faraway. Okay. Confession. Winnie did most of the work. I merely cut up the apples and swished them around in the sugary mixture. But I think I can handle it. I mean, how hard can it be to add a little crust? If my calculations are correct, it'll take me twenty minutes to make the pie and an hour to bake it. My dessert will be ready just when The Prince, Calla, and that woman finish the soup and salad. Warm apple pie! Won't they be impressed!

I gather up the ingredients Winnie used and then quickly peel the apples. As I cut them into thin slices, Shrink's theory of good vs. evil pops into my head. On an apple scale of one to ten, Marcella's definitely a one—rotten to the core. Calla, on the other hand, is a ten—unblemished. God's perfect fruit. I'm not so sure where The Prince fits in. And come to think about it, nor where do I. Maybe, like Snow White, the human hand poisoned me. My mother's. Trembling, I almost cut myself with the knife.

Jane, get a grip! Focus! Stop thinking about all this nasty stuff! Cooking's supposed to be fun and get your mind off things. I take another deep breath and scoop the slices into a bowl. I add the other ingredients, except for the flour and the butter. *Swish. Swish.* I pop one of the sugarcoated slices into my mouth. Yum! So far, so good!

On to the piecrusts. Winnie told me a proper apple pie needs two crusts—one on the bottom to cradle the apples and one on the top to blanket them. "The apples are like the baby," she said.

Using a well-floured rolling pin, I roll out two crusts. I don't get it. Why won't the dough roll out into perfect circles like Winnie's? Mine are ugly, jagged blobs. Oh, well. They look enough like piecrusts.

I transfer one of the crusts to a deep round earthenware dish, pressing it firmly into the bottom and over edges of the rim. Easy enough. I load the apples onto the crust, piling them high in the center, precisely the way Winnie did. And now the tricky part…placing the second crust over the heap of apples. Carefully, I lift up the limp dough and edge it over the top of the pie. But then it happens. The dough breaks apart. I manage to glue the two pieces together, but I can't make the patched-up crust cover the filling no matter how much I stretch it. Losing my patience, I tug harder and harder. The dough, now as thin as parchment, breaks into a dozen jagged pieces. I have no clue how to splice them together, and there's no time to make a new crust. I want to cry.

Putting the sad-looking pie aside, I run over to the cauldron to taste my soup. I'm instantly cheered up. The ingredients have blended to perfection. I dash over to the hearth to check on my bread. The crust is golden brown, and it smells scrumptious. Time to take it out and put in the wannabe pie.

Dinner, my friends, is about to be served.

———◆———

The Prince, Calla, and Marcella are seated around a long formally set, candle-lit table in the dining hall. The Prince, dressed in a billowy white linen shirt and royal blue velvet vest, is on one end; Marcella, wearing a tacky, low-cut hot pink gown, is on the other, and Calla's in the middle. Right beside her is Lady Jane, propped up on pillows in her own chair. A carafe of red wine graces the table.

"Marcella, thank you for my dolly!" exclaims Calla with a big fake smile. *She's good!*

The PIW glowers at her. "Child, what on earth are you talking about?"

Calla rolls her eyes, then exchanges a wink with me.

Chuckling inside, I have to steady the heavy silver tray that's holding my three-course dinner. I plunk it down on the table, nearly spilling the tureen of soup on Marcella.

"Jane, I want my dinner served on the table, not my lap," she sneers.

Duh! I serve the salad first. I hold my breath as everyone takes their first bite.

Bad news. Her Royal Skankiness spits it out and screams. "There's dressing on this salad! I told you I was on a diet!" She shoves the plate away.

"Yum!" says Calla. "Can I please have more?" I serve her a second helping. She alternates between gobbling the salad and pretend-feeding some to her new doll. "Lady Jane loves it too!"

The Prince's face brightens. "It has always been a struggle to get Calla to eat her greens." I take his words as a compliment.

I clear the salad plates, then serve the hot soup and bread.

The Prince dips his spoon into his steaming bowl and lifts it to his lips. I hold my breath again.

"Mmm! What do you call this?"

Crap! I have no idea what this concoction of vegetables is called. *Think! Think of something quick!* "Um, uh Potage de Meeshmash," I stutter.

"Ah, it's French." He scoops up another spoonful. "Where did you learn how to cook like this, Jane?"

Rehab. No, wait! I can't tell him that. "I went to cooking school in France," I stammer.

"*Vraiment?*" comments Marcella, her tone snippy.

Whatever. I smile at Calla who's giving little "tastes" to Lady Jane.

Marcella hasn't touched a thing. She's practically frothing at the mouth, watching Calla and The Prince wipe their bowls clean with the crusty bread. Finally, she can no longer take it. In one swift swoop, she grabs her bowl of soup and scoffs it down. Then she snatches the bread and bites off one chunk after another. Sheesh! How much can she stuff into her mouth?

"Marcella, you hogged the rest of the bread!" sulks Calla. "Not fair!"

The PIW's eyes narrow; her lips pucker, and her fists clench. "Jane, why did *you* let me eat all that bread!" she yells as if I'm responsible for her lack of will power. "You've made me fat!"

Rescue me! She's way worse than Sasperilla! The skinny bitch, at least, had self-control and didn't blame others for her shortcomings. The smell of something burning cuts my thoughts short. The apple pie! It's still in the oven—probably burnt to a crisp!

I hurry back to the kitchen to check on the pie. The good news is…only the edges of the crust have burnt. The bad news is…the filling is now the consistency of applesauce. And it's starting to bubble like molten lava.

Panicky, I jerk it out from the hearth and yelp. I've burnt

my hand on the red-hot dish. To my horror, my flesh is glued to the rim. I peel it off. Ow! Why am I such a doof in the kitchen? I flashback to my finger-cutting incident at Faraway, then flash forward to my reunion tomorrow night. I can't wait to see Elz and Winnie. It gets my mind off the pain.

Using my good hand and a large potholder, I bring the once-upon-a-time pie to the table. "My *pièce de résistance*," I say in my best French accent.

I have to admit the aroma is tantalizing and wonder if it will taste as good as it smells. I slice a generous piece for everyone. What I really need is a ladle.

"Pass!" grunts Marcella, raising her hand like a stop sign and turning her head.

"Jane, this is simply wonderful!" says The Prince after his first bite. Taking another forkful, he savors my apple mush as if it's his last morsel of food.

Calla's equally ecstatic. "Super duper yummy!" she squeals. "Papa, may Lady Jane and I have another piece? Please? Pretty please?" she implores with the coquettish charm that only a little girl can get away with.

The Prince cannot say no to his little princess. I serve Calla and Lady Jane their second helping. There's only one piece left.

Marcella stares at it, her mouth watering. I'm enjoying every minute. *Suffer, you wannabe skinny bitch!*

"Jane, I shall have the last piece," says The Prince. "This splendid pie should not go to waste."

As I serve The Prince, he notices the burn on my hand; it's now a big red ugly welt.

"What happened to your hand?" He sounds genuinely concerned.

"Oh, it's nothing," I reply. "*Un petit* cooking *faux pas.*" Am I kidding myself? My hand is killing me!

"Let me take care of it before it gets infected." He reaches into his vest pocket and pulls out a white monogrammed silk handkerchief. He gently wraps it around the burn. My hand trembles and my heart pounds. I'm weak. It must be a more serious wound than I thought.

Out of the corner of my eye, I notice Marcella rolling her eyes in utter disgust.

"That's much better." Proud of his makeshift bandage, The Prince holds my hand in his. I keep it there longer than I need to, then hastily pull away.

"Thank you, My Lord." I quiver. "I mean, Gallant." Our eyes meet briefly. My heart races; my body tingles. I don't know why I feel so weird and wonderful.

What I do know is that I've learned a valuable lesson: *When life gives you apples, make apple pie.*

———

After dinner, The Prince sends Calla up to her room; she's had a big day and needs some sleep. The little girl protests but finally acquiesces.

"I love you, Papa." She gives her father a big hug.

"I love you, too, My Little Princess," says The Prince, holding her tightly.

Their embrace gives me the chills. Maybe, it has something to do with never having a father to kiss me good night. Knowing my mother's taste in men, it's just as well I didn't.

"Good night, Marcella," says Calla coldly before heading upstairs.

Marcella pays no attention to the child and dismisses herself from the table.

"My love, I need my beauty sleep with the ball so close." She blows The Prince a kiss, then slinks off.

Ball. Shmall. Personally, I think Her Royal Skankiness wants nothing to do with clean-up. To tell the truth, neither do I. I don't want to think about how much there is to scrub.

And then I have one of my brainstorms. When they're all upstairs asleep, I'll toss all the plates. Tomorrow, I'll tell The Prince I accidentally broke them and blame it on my burnt hand. That's sure to get his sympathy. And, come on, he can easily afford a few new dishes. In fact, I bet he and the PIW will get an entire set of new china for a wedding present.

I'm such a creative genius. Okay, so not all my plans work—the poison apple scheme bombed as did my escape from Faraway—but this one's a sure-fire no-brainer.

Singing "lalala" to myself, I start hauling plates and serving pieces into the kitchen. The Prince orders me to stop.

"Please share some wine with me," he says.

"I have to clear the dishes," I reply, slightly taken aback. Seriously, I wish he'd go upstairs. I want to get going on my kickass toss-and-clean plan.

"There is no need," says The Prince, already pouring two goblets of the red wine. "The cook and his staff shall be here in the morning. Trust me, they must have had another spat with Marcella. They always quit and come back the next day."

Holding the wine, The Prince escorts me through double doors that open to a small but beautiful garden. It's filled with hundreds of lilies and roses, in varying shades of white. Fireflies, a holdover from the summer, dance around the blooms like sprinkles of fairy dust. The Prince leads me to a stone bench, where we sit and sip the wine.

I inhale the sweet scent of the flowers and the fresh night air. The wine, the first I've had in ages, is soothing and as smooth as velvet. It goes down easily (perhaps too easily) and makes me relaxed.

"What a lovely garden," I say. On second thought, maybe I should have said, "What lovely wine." I'm not thinking one hundred percent straight.

The Prince's expression turns wistful as he refills my goblet. "My late wife designed this garden herself. Lilies and roses were her favorite flowers. She named our daughter, Calla Rose, after them. After she died, I scattered her ashes here."

Eww! I've been walking on the remains of some dead person. I want to dust off my shoes. "How long has it been?" I ask, careful not to show my disgust.

"A little over five years." There's sadness in his voice.

The power of the wine enables me to prod further. "How did she die?"

"A snake bit her. Right here in this garden."

I nervously survey the grounds to make sure no snakes are nearby. Phew! Not one in sight.

The Prince pauses; his eyes grow hooded. "I could not save her," he says at last.

Not knowing quite how to respond, I ask, "Does Calla remember her?"

He sighs. "No. She was too young."

"Perhaps, it's for the best."

The Prince creases his brows. "What makes you say that?"

Because my mother was a witch! She used and abused me. I wish I could erase every memory of her! I wish she never existed! That's what I want to say, but instead I settle for some clichéd comfort.

"It'll be easier for her to move on. To accept a new mother."

"I hope you are right." He sips his wine. "She is having difficulty warming up to Marcella."

Marcella. The mere mention of her name makes my stomach churn. Maybe, now's a good time to tell him how Calla *really* feels about her prospective new mother.

"She'll adjust," I say instead. "She's an amazing girl."

"She is indeed. I cannot thank you enough for saving her life today."

A smile flashes across The Prince's face. Dimpled like Calla's, it's dazzling. I can't get my eyes off him.

He plucks a perfectly formed lily from the earth. "This is for you."

I hold the flower to my nose and inhale its intoxicating scent. I don't know what's happening to me. I gaze up at The Prince's chiseled face, but words get stuck in my throat. I can't even squeak out a simple "Thank you." My head is swirling, and little explosions rock my body inside. It's got be the wine.

It's got to be!

"My daughter seems to have a special affection toward you," says The Prince. "Perhaps, you can help me out with something."

Anything you want. Anything, Gallant! My Lord! My Master! What is wrong with me?

"Calla's seventh birthday is in three days. I would like to throw her a surprise party. Originally, I asked Marcella to plan the event, but with all the arrangements for the ball, she has had no time to handle it. So, I am hoping you will take over."

I feel like I've been hit over the head by a brick. A birthday party!? He wants *me* to put together a birthday party? Does he have any idea of how big my workload is? And he actually thinks Marcella is handling the details of the ball? Between ball preparations and Marcella's other ridiculous requests, I barely have time to breathe. Or pee.

"No problem." I must be out of my mind.

I chug the rest of my wine. On second thought: *When life gives you apples, dip them in poison. All of them!*

CHAPTER 24

I can't sleep; my hand is throbbing, and my head is spinning from the wine. The intoxicating smell of The Prince lingers on my bandaged hand and mingles with the sweet scent of his lily, now in a vase on my nightstand. Why didn't I toss the damn flower after he asked me to plan Calla's surprise birthday party? I'll do it tomorrow. And make sure he's watching. That'll send him a message.

I finally doze off and enter dreamland. The masked man is back. Our heavenly dance continues, his brawny arms wrapped tightly around my waist. Wordlessly, he draws me closer to him. The heat of his breath seeps through his mask. "Why do you wear a mask?" I ask, growing flushed. Silence. That's it. I want to know what he's hiding. I curl my fingers, readying to yank it off…

And a pounding on my chamber door wakens me. It's got to be Marcella. Dream wrecker! What can she want at this wee hour of the night—or is it already morning? I'm sure she's not here to discuss birthday party arrangements.

I light a candle and unlatch the door. Once again, it's Calla. She's clutching Lady Jane and trembling.

"Can Lady Jane and I sleep with you? I begged Marcella to tell me a good-night story, and it gave me a really bad dream."

"Of course, you can." I put an arm around the frightened child and usher her into my room.

We climb into my bed together. I give her one of my pillows and pull the thick down cover over us. We lie side by side. The blackness of the night embraces us.

"What was Marcella's story about?" I ask, surprised that the lazy skank actually told her one.

"Oh, it was soooo scary," replies Calla in full drama queen mode. "It was about this really, really mean woman who turned little children into rats if they didn't go to sleep. And if the rats didn't go to sleep, she sent a giant snake to eat them!"

"Oooh, that's awful!"

"Snakes really scare me. You know, a big ugly snake bit my Mama and killed her."

I know.

"Do you remember anything about your mother?" The Prince said she didn't, but I'm curious to find out for myself.

"No, but everyone says she was really, really pretty," Calla replies.

My fingertips caress her exquisite face. I'm not surprised.

"So, tell me about your dream," I say, eager to move away from a sensitive subject.

"I don't remember it!" she giggles.

"I don't remember a lot of my dreams either…especially the bad ones." *Liar!* I could fill a book with all the unforgettable, horrid dreams I've had.

"Will you tell Lady Jane and me another story?" begs Calla. "Please! Pretty please!"

How can I say no and let her down? The truth is, I don't know any. My mother was not one for tucking me in at night and telling stories. Actually, most nights she never came home.

"Calla, why don't you get me started?" I say, stalling.

Calla jumps right in. "Once upon a time…"

And then I continue. Having no idea where I'm going...

"…there lived a little girl who was very lonely. None of the other girls in the kingdom would play with her because they thought she was weird. What they didn't know was that she was actually very sad because she

had to take care of her sick mother all the time. One day a fairy godmother came to visit the girl and told her she could have three wishes granted. The girl thought for a moment and then said: 'I wish for all the stray dogs and cats in the world to find happy homes. I wish for kingdoms to stop fighting. And finally, I wish for my mother to be well again.' The fairy godmother granted the little girl all three wishes. The little girl soon became the most popular girl in the kingdom. Everyone wanted to be her friend, even the girls who used to be mean to her. She was never lonely ever again."

"THE END." I'm exhausted. It's as though I've given birth to my imagination.

"Jane, what happened to the little girl when she grew up?" asks Calla, inquisitively.

Dragonballs. I didn't get that far in my head. How am I supposed to know the life story of someone I fabricated only a minute ago? *Okay. Think. Think harder!* Yes! Of course!

"She married a handsome prince and lived happily ever after."

"Wow! I loved that story. Can you tell me another one?"

Don't push your luck. "It's time for you, Lady Jane, and me to go to sleep."

Without her asking, I plant a kiss atop her head. She's sound asleep before I can wish her sweet dreams.

Lady Jane is tucked in her arms. Calla's slender body is cradled in mine. Our hearts beat together as if we are one.

Like a thief afraid to be caught, I steal a glance at her luminous face. How peaceful she looks. Like an angel. I caress her golden curls and hope the demons that brought here won't return. Sweet dreams, my sweet girl!

Sadness blankets me as I close my weary eyes. If only I could have had someone to comfort me in the darkest hours of the night. If only I could have had a fairy godmother to cure my mother of her sickness. If only I could have had the chance to live happily ever after.

CHAPTER 25

The next morning I awaken at the crack of dawn, greeted by a headache and dread. I slip out of bed, careful not to disturb Calla, and tiptoe downstairs. My spirits lift quickly. Tonight's my Girls' Night Out! I can hardly wait. Only I still have no clue how I'm going to escape Marcella.

When I wander into the kitchen, Gallant-Shmallant is already there. Damn it! I left his stupid lily upstairs. A missed opportunity to shove it down the drain.

"Can I pour you some tea?" he asks.

"Fine," I say in spite of myself. Maybe, it'll help me get over my hangover.

"How is your hand?"

"I'll live." I've taken off his handkerchief. Mental note: Burn it in the hearth tonight. And make sure he's watching.

Gallant hands me a cup of tea. A fragrant blend of orange blossoms, rose petals, and lavender trickles into my nose. I take a sip. It tastes delicious, almost magical. The Prince gazes at me with his piercing blue eyes. I get that tingly-all-over feeling. My teacup shakes in my hand.

"Jane, I shall be visiting my father tonight. So, please tell the cooks there is no need to prepare dinner for me. They should be back any minute."

"Is Marcella, by chance, going with you?" How perfect would that be.

"No, it is official kingdom business." A resentful tone accompanies his words.

So much for wishful thinking.

The Prince furrows his brows. "Please excuse me. I must prepare for the meeting. My father shall be displeased if I do not come with a formal agenda." Taking his tea, he marches toward the kitchen door. He turns to me before exiting.

"And, Jane, please keep me posted about Calla's birthday party."

I want to throw my teacup at him but spill the remains down the drain instead.

Despite my anger and queasiness, my stomach begins to growl as soon as Gallant is gone. I'm starving. I grab a handful of oats and search for the barrel of eggs.

"Jane, you poisoned me!" comes a deep, raspy voice from behind me.

Startled, I swing around. It's Marcella. She's almost unrecognizable. Her brassy blond hair is plastered to her head like a helmet, and her complexion is a ghastly shade of green.

"I didn't sleep a wink last night," she croaks.

How could she have in that clingy leopard-print duster? It's bursting at the seams. And those feathers would have driven me crazy.

"It's all your fault! It had to be something I ate!" *Ha! Serves you right for hogging the bread, you pig.* "If it weren't for the fact that I think I've lost three pounds, I'd fire you right now!"

"Can I get you something?" I don't know whether I want to laugh or punch her.

"The only thing I want is my liquid diet potion. And if you don't have it by tomorrow morning, you will be fired!"

Great! Tomorrow could be my lucky day.

"I'm going back to bed. I'll be there all day. Whatever you do, don't disturb me!"

Let's hope she'll be there all night. And I promise, I won't disturb her.

As she staggers out the door, the cook and his staff return.

With Marcella in bed all day, I'm able to get a lot done for the ball. I start working on the seating arrangements. It's weird. I can't seem to find Snow White's RSVP. In fact, I don't recall seeing her invitation. It must have been among the two thousand or so I sent out. Marcella invited every princess in the universe. I make myself another mental note: Talk to PIW about Snow White's invite status. On second thought, why bother? The less I have to do with my stepdaughter, the better.

Next, Marcella's liquid diet potion. I have no idea what to do. Or where to get it. That sorcerer who sold me that bogus evil potion? Nah. He's probably out of business. And then, *bing!* A brainstorm! Another one of my genius ideas. I'll make it myself.

Returning to the kitchen, I throw together sugar, lard, honey, and some cocoa. I pour the thick gooey mixture into a bottle and label it "*Lose Pounds Fast.*" It's going to be the best tasting liquid diet potion ever. And the most fattening. Hee-hee. Her Royal Skankiness will love it!

Dinner is just Calla and me. Gallant's gone to his meeting with his father, and Marcella still hasn't left her room. All Calla wants to talk about is her birthday. A mixture of guilt and anxiety eats away at me. I still haven't had a chance to get going on her surprise party. The truth is, I don't know where to begin. The only surprise birthday party I ever had was at Faraway. And that doesn't really count.

"I want a puppy for my birthday," says Calla. "Did you ever have one?"

I tell her about my little pup Bambi, leaving out all the painful, sordid details. Tears sting my eyes.

"Jane, why are you crying?" asks Calla.

"Because I still miss him," I sniffle, thinking about his

cruel fate.

Calla gives me a hug. It makes me feel better.

After dinner, I put her to bed. I make up a cute story about Bambi, bid her sweet dreams, and kiss her good night.

Perfect! I couldn't have planned it better. With Gallant gone, Marcella locked in her room, and the cooks back to take care of Calla in case she wakes up, I can escape for a few hours and have my GNO with Elz and Winnie.

———❦———

I sneak out of the castle a little before nine o'clock, and before I can even inhale the crisp night air, a coach pulls up, almost running me over. The vehicle oddly resembles a giant gilded pumpkin. "The Glass Slipper" is scrolled across it in big flowery letters.

I'm shocked to see Elz in the driver's seat. Winnie, seated next to her, looks relieved to see me. I climb aboard.

"Whee-Ha!" shouts Elz, slapping the horses on the rear. The coach takes off like a bolt of lightning. I'm not sure about this.

Elz is a total speed demon. Who would have thought that this shy, timid girl would ever be driving a coach? And like a maniac! Then again, she's the one who wanted to go on a high seas adventure with Hook. As we race through the dark, bumpy countryside, the wind rips through me, threatening to blow me away. I exchange a this-is-it look with Winnie and cling to her for dear life.

I have no clue where Elz is taking us. Or if we'll make it there alive. Finally, we come to a small tavern called Puss 'n Boots somewhere in the middle of nowhere. Elz brings the coach to a screeching halt, causing my stomach to lurch forward. Grateful to still be alive, I heave a sigh of relief. So does Winnie.

Inside, the tavern is dark and smoky and reeks of piss, puke, and vinegar. Loud, swarthy men line the bar along with an assortment of your usual fairy-tale freaks. Their eyes swivel our way as we head toward the counter. We're the only women here.

The nauseating stench is getting to me. It reminds me of the men my mother used to bring home. The boar head on the wall is not helping. I bet my damn Huntsman donated it.

"How did you find this place?" I ask Elz, wishing we could leave.

"Hook. We come here all the time."

My eyes widen. Is Elz seeing Hook? Before I can find out, she orders each of us a mug of beer. The beverage is cold and refreshing. I chug mine and get an instant buzz. I order another.

"I'm convinced Shrink placed us in our post-rehab positions for a reason," says Winnie, nursing her beer.

"What makes you say that?" I ask, silently cursing the thinks-she-knows-it-all therapist for placing me with Marcella.

"Since I've been working at Sparkles, I've lost my craving for sweets. I haven't had any for weeks."

"Wow!" chirps Elz. "I can't believe you can resist those yummy cupcakes, especially the ones with the creamy surprise inside."

I know exactly what she's talking about, and it's making me ravenous. Damn! There aren't even any munchies around this joint. Time to change the subject.

"How's it going with John?" I ask.

"Now that I'm working, he's pitching in a lot more." Winnie smiles. "And he's paying a lot more attention to me."

"He should be. You look amazing!" Her weight loss really is astonishing.

"Thanks."

"She's had to buy a whole new wardrobe," chimes in Elz.

I hope she's burned her fat-girl frocks, destroyed them for good. "How are your kids doing?"

"Hansel and Gretel are doing great. I really want you to meet them."

Her sage eyes glisten. Winnie and her family have obviously put the past behind them.

"I'd love to," I say and switch subjects again. "So, Elz, how's life in the shoe biz?"

"Crazy busy!" She launches into her story.

"When I got there, the store was going out of business. I couldn't believe it. I mean, women can never have enough shoes, right? Customers complained the shoes weren't fitting properly. They were either too big or too small. And they didn't care for the dated styles."

Winnie takes over. "So, Elz started to design fashion forward shoes and worked with John to perfect the fit. He developed a new concept—half sizes—for those in-between feet."

Elz continues. "I begged the owner to let me give the store a makeover and stock it with our chic, comfy shoes. I came up with a new name—The Glass Slipper—and John came up with the catchy motto '*For the Perfect Fit Shoe.*' Within twenty-four hours, we were sold out."

"John is now Elz's business partner," adds Winnie, proudly. "He also thought of the see-through glass boxes. It makes it a lot easier to find your shoes, especially when you have hundreds of them. And they help preserve them."

Little glass coffins. Like the glass coffin the dwarfs built to watch over Snow White. I shudder and take another swig of beer.

"You'll never guess who came in!" exclaims Elz.

My heart stands still. I bet she's going to say Snow White!

"Cinderella!"

"No way!" I say, relieved.

"See, Jane, it's all meant to be," says Winnie.

"I told her how sorry I was about being so mean to her. She couldn't have been nicer. She was even sorry to hear about my mother."

Her story is getting better by the minute.

"And guess what, she was so wowed by my collection of

hard-to-find Size 4 1/2 heels that she loaned me money to buy the store."

"And her old coach," adds Winnie.

Too bad she didn't throw in driving lessons.

Elz pauses to slurp her beer, then tells us she has some other news. Her face lights up.

"I'm seeing Hook; we're kind of a couple."

I have mixed feelings about the news. Hook's such a pompous asshole. Maybe he's changed. Maybe.

"What's Hook up to?" I ask.

"Oh, he's working at an orphanage," beams Elz. "He's like a mother to all these poor lost boys."

It must be that orphanage built by that Midas megalomaniac.

"What about Sasperilla?"

Elz's face loses its glow. "I'm not sure she ever got out of Faraway. It's weird, but I miss her."

"Because she's still family," says Winnie.

Ah! Winnie's words of wisdom.

Elz brightens and signals for another round of beers.

I guzzle mine. Elz and Winnie are so happy. Their post-rehab stints are perfect for them. Elz is using her artistic talent and has finally become her own boss, and Winnie has managed to control her eating and improve her marriage. Mine, however, in a word, sucks.

I fill Elz and Winnie in on everything I've had to put up with as Marcella's personal assistant. "She's a total nightmare!"

Elz, having met the skank, vouches for me. "With all you're doing, that's so mean of her not to invite you to the ball," she singsongs.

I seriously want to shake her.

"Don't worry about Calla's birthday party," says Winnie. "I'll take care of everything. It'll be a piece of cake."

That's a relief! At least, another thing on my To-Do List will get done. Thank goodness for best friends.

"Shrink promised I could go back to my castle once I complete this rotten gig," I go on, "but I'm not going to survive Marcella."

"Hang in there," says Winnie. "Trust me, everything's happening for a reason."

Trust me, I can't think of a single good reason to be slaving for Her Royal Skankiness. I'm supposed to be finding some meaning and light, but I don't even have the time to find my way to the bathroom.

"I should poison the bitch!" I say, rage rising inside me.

Winnie and Elz shoot me a don't-go-there look.

"I don't understand what The Prince sees in her."

"She's blond, busty, and brazen," says Winnie, the relationship guru.

And I, former Miss Fairest of All, am overworked, rundown, and as flat as an unbaked loaf of bread.

"What's Gallant like?" asks Elz.

The mere mention of his name makes my stomach flutter and temperature rise. What's wrong with me? It must be the beer. It has to be.

Elz's attention suddenly turns to someone else.

Hook. He pushes through the crowd toward the bar. Elz's bespectacled eyes sparkle.

"Yo, Ho, Ho," Hook says to the bartender. "Give these fine ladies another round and throw in a bottle of rum for me."

The swashbuckler chugs his rum and sets the bottle down hard. So much for Faraway's cure.

"Whatch'ya been up to, babe?" Hook leans in close to me, pressing his thigh against mine. Something hard digs into me. I glance down and gasp. A massive ivory-handled sword is lodged inside his belt.

I take a gulp of beer and edge away. With a flick of his hook, the swine yanks me back to him. Elz frowns. Shit! I wish he'd leave me alone. Or that a one-eyed ogre would come up to me and start a conversation.

My rescue-me prayers are answered.

"Give everyone another one on me!"

All eyes turn toward a dashing, long-legged man who has burst through the front door with such force the room quiets. He's dressed in formal military attire and wielding an intimidating sword. My heart drops to my stomach. It's The Prince!

My pulse goes into overdrive. I can't let him see me here of all places. I quickly hide my face behind my mug, but it's too late. Recognition flickers in his eyes. Sliding his sword into his belt, he heads in my direction. I chug my entire mug of beer in one gulp. I feel sick. Very sick.

"Jane, what brings you here?" he asks, brushing up against me.

A giant lump forms in my throat. Swallowing hard, I ask him the same question.

"Just letting off a little steam." He orders a beer and downs it. "I had another argument with my father; he does not understand me. I always stop by here after seeing him. It is quite refreshing to be with real people instead of a bunch of headstrong royals."

"Introduce us to your friend," insists Winnie.

My lips quiver. "This is Prince Gallant."

All Winnie and Elz can say is "Oh."

Oh is right. I'd better get out of here. Fast!

Gallant grabs me by the elbow, holding me back. "Please don't leave, Jane. I need someone to talk to."

He gazes at me. His blue eyes are glazed over. He's drunk. Really drunk. I struggle to break free from his tight grip.

"Leave the lady alone!" says Hook, slurring his words.

"Who is she to you?" asks Gallant.

"None of your bilge sucking business!"

And then the unthinkable happens. Hook takes a whack at The Prince, and The Prince whacks him right back. Holy crap! They've begun a bar room brawl!

"Remember what they say," says Gallant. "The wise man hits first; the better man hits last."

"Well, I'll show you who's better," responds Hook. He

packs a powerful punch that sends The Prince to his knees, gasping for air.

"You like pain? I'll you show you pain," says Gallant, getting back on his feet. At full force, he charges at Hook and knocks him down. Pinning his opponent to the sawdust-covered floor, The Prince delivers a series of hard blows, one right after the other.

Poor Elz winces with every blow and, finally unable to stomach it any more, buries her head in her arms. My heart hammers. Gallant's going to do the pirate in!

Suddenly, Hook whips out his sword with his good hand and slices Gallant across his neck. The Prince recoils, freeing Hook. Oh my God. Blood is trickling down his neck. I'm going to be sick.

Undeterred, Gallant staggers to his feet and draws his sword. "I challenge you to a duel for the fair maiden's heart!"

I can't believe this is happening! The Prince must be drunk out of his mind.

"My pleasure," says Hook. Without wasting a second, he lunges at The Prince, who ducks his assault.

Clinkity-Clink. Our Girls' Night Out has now turned into a life-or-death jousting match minus the horses. The pub-goers crowd around the dueling duo and cheer them on. They're even placing wagers.

"Round 2 goes to the challenger," someone shouts out. Gallant gives a nod of acknowledgement as he holds off Hook.

Elz peeks up at the fight and bites her lip. "It's all my fault," she says tearfully. "I should have never brought you guys here."

Winnie consoles her with a hug. "Life happens."

"But Winnie, what if death happens?" asks Elz, her voice shaking.

"Good question." Winnie ponders. "Let's think on the bright side."

Forget it, Winnie! There is *no* bright side! If Gallant kills Hook, Elz will never forgive me. And if Hook kills Gallant?

Oh, God! I can't even begin to imagine the consequences. And then, there's the third scenario: they kill each other...

A loud gasp from the crowd stops my thoughts cold. Gallant has knocked Hook's sword out of his hand, sending it flying across the room.

"You think you've got me?" says Hook, red with rage. "Well, you're wrong!"

The Prince doesn't see it coming. Neither do I. In the blink-of-an-eye move, the pirate whacks Gallant in the head with his heavy metal hook. The blow is more than The Prince can bear. He crumples to the floor as I gasp.

Hook retrieves his sword with his good hand and brandishes it victoriously above his head. "This time, drinks all around on *me*!" he shouts boastfully.

The crowd charges to the bar as I race over to the unconscious Prince.

"Hook! You've killed him!" screams Elz, in hysterics.

"He's alive!" I yell on the top of my lungs. "Help me get him out of here!"

Winnie and Elz rush to my aid. Elz calls out to Hook for help. He ignores her. He's too busy drowning himself in another bottle of rum.

Elz fights back tears. The poor girl! I despise the swine more than ever.

"Come on, Elz. Let's get The Prince into your coach and take him home," I say, surprised I can still think straight. Or think at all.

Winnie and Elz each take a leg while I take his arms. On Winnie's count of three, we lift him up.

"He must weigh a ton!" grunts Winnie.

"He doesn't look like he weighs that much," says Elz. "What do you think, Jane?"

I want to smack her. Who cares! All I care about is getting him home.

Somehow, we manage to carry him out the door. There's only one "little" problem: Elz's coach is no longer parked outside the tavern. It's gone!

"Read that!" says Winnie, pointing straight ahead at a road sign.

> **TOW AWAY ZONE**
> **PARK AT YOUR OWN RISK!**

We silently read it together. Winnie and I shoot Elz a scathing look that reads something like: We're going to kill you even if you're our best friend.

Elz shrivels with guilt. "That sign must be brand new," she squeaks meekly. "I've parked here dozens of times."

We are so screwed. Now what are we going to do? Maybe we should toss The Prince's body into the gutter and make a run for it.

And then, out of the corner of my eye, I spot a handsome white horse parked just outside the tow-away zone. I recognize the animal instantly. It's Gallant's steed. What good luck! We'll get him on the horse and send them both home.

Using all the strength we have left, we hoist up The Prince and slide him over the saddle. His arms and legs dangle lifelessly over the beast's flanks. The horse doesn't mind.

"Beat it, horsey!" I give the animal a slap on his rear. "Go home!" I don't think the horse understands me. He doesn't budge. Damn it! I wish I knew the horse's name. Maybe that would help.

There's only one solution. I'm going to have to ride the horse and take The Prince home. While I've ridden a few times, I'm not what you would call an experienced equestrian. Coupled with the fact that I've had a couple of beers or three or four or more, this is *not* going to be fun. Oh, and did I mention, I have no idea where we are? Let's hope the horse will know the way back to the castle since Gallant mentioned he's been here before.

"What about you guys?" I ask Winnie and Elz.

"Don't worry about us," says Winnie with her usual optimism. "We'll figure out a way home."

"Maybe I can get someone to take us to the local impound," chimes in Elz. "It'll be easy to spot my coach."

Winnie and I roll our eyes. Remind me never to come back here.

Except for the fact that my inner thighs are killing me, the ride back to the castle goes smoothly. Lucky for me, the steed indeed knows his way and gallops confidently across the dark countryside. I'm just nervous that The Prince, who's draped over the saddle in front of me, will fall off. Or that I will in my tipsy state.

I let out a big sigh of relief (and so do my thighs) when we at last reach the gated castle. Gallant is still out cold. The guardsmen let us in without saying a word. It's as though they've seen The Prince like this before.

I lead the horse to the front entrance. So far, so good. Suddenly, something spooks the animal. A snake! Hissing, it slithers across the cobblestone path. The steed rears up, catapulting us to the ground.

It takes me a minute to come to my senses. I'm straddled on top of The Prince, his torso rising and falling beneath me. With every breath he takes, his taut chest presses deeper into my ribs. Even in this lifeless state, he's so strong. So powerful. I gaze at his moonlit face. The blow he received from Hook is beginning to swell, but other than that, he looks so peaceful. And so handsome. I resist the urge to run my fingers over his fine features.

In the distant meadow, the horse is grazing. "Get your ass back here, horsey!" I shout, staggering to my feet.

The animal trots off. It doesn't really matter because there's no way I could have gotten The Prince back up on it by myself.

Okay. So, now what am I going to do? I can't leave him

here. I mean, a wild beast could come along and eat him alive. Or a storm could erupt, and he could drown or get struck by lightning. Or that snake could come back and bite him. Poor Calla would never get over it if he died just like her mother.

Think! Think! The problem is I'm exhausted and have had way too much to drink. I can't think. Luckily, the obvious comes to me. I take hold of The Prince's muscular arms and drag him face up to the castle entrance. Cripes! He *is* heavy!

The front door of the castle is unlocked. I kick it open and pull him inside, hoping not to wake up Calla. She'll freak out if she sees her father in this state. Marcella doesn't concern me. I remember what Calla told me. She sleeps with earplugs. Nothing could wake her. Not even a cannonball blowing through her window.

Taking a deep breath, I rest for a moment. Now, all I have to do is get The Prince up to his chamber. Forcing myself back to work, I slide him across the entry hall, then lug him up the grand staircase. Each step is torture. Pure torture.

Finally, we reach the top of the stairs. I'm a sweaty, wheezing, woozy mess. I take another breather, then haul him down a long, dark corridor. It seems much longer than I remember. And he seems to be getting a lot heavier. His chamber is unfortunately at the very end. When my head slams against a wall, we've hit a dead end and made it.

The door to his chamber is unlocked. Swinging it open, I poke my head inside. It's pitch-black; the drapes must be pulled. I can't see a damn thing. I glance down at The Prince lying by my feet; he's still out cold. It'll be easier to leave him here at the doorway and come back for him after I locate his bed.

This is my first time inside Gallant's personal quarters. The room must be very spacious because I can't find his bed. Stumbling blindly, I knock into chairs, tables, candelabras, and statues. When I dip my hand into a water tank filled with finger-nibbling fish, I almost take a fall. Let's hope he doesn't have any loose swords lying around.

A thought crosses my mind. A new problem. If I ever find the bed, how will I remember my way back to it with Gallant in tow? I remember the story Winnie told me about her two kids. How they got lost in the woods and left a trail of bread crumbs to find their way home. That's what I'll do! But wait, I don't have any crumbs or bread. Maybe I can find some parchment and make spit balls.

But why get ahead of myself? I still can't even find his bed. Weary and wasted, I'm about to give up when I stumble over what could be a boot and tumble head first into a mound of fluffy down. Heaven! Gallant's bed! It's fit for a king with its luxuriously thick duvet and array of luscious, plump pillows. And it smells so fresh and inviting. I wish I could curl up right here, right now, and call it a night.

I force myself to get up. Rolling out of the bed, I knock something over. *Crash!* It must have been a vase because water is seeping through my shoes. I scoot down, find the vase still luckily in one piece, and fumble for the flowers scattered on the plush rug. They smell like roses. And there's dozens of them. Brainstorm! Forget stinky beer-breath spitballs. I'll scatter rose petals along the floor. *Jane, you clever, clever, girl!*

Creating a fragrant path with the velvety petals, I crawl back to the entrance and retrieve Gallant. With one hand gripping his collar and my nose to the floor, I inch back across the rug, sniffing away. My little plan is working though not exactly like a charm. By the time we get to the bed, my knees are stinging from rug burns; the smell of roses is sickening me, and I'm exhausted from lugging Gallant. I actually wouldn't be surprised if my arms fell off.

Staggering to my feet, I gaze down at Gallant. How the hell I'm going to get him into the bed? Without over thinking, I grab him by his wrists and miraculously manage to heave him onto the duvet.

Okay, I can get out of here. I so need to get sleep. My head is swirling, and I don't know how much longer I can stave off waves of nausea. As I creep away, Gallant groans. He groans again, this time louder. Of course! He must be miserable in his tight britches, those boots, and that buttoned up jacket.

I start with the jacket. Yet another challenge. Fumbling for the buttons, my fingers run down his chest, feeling the ripple of every finely honed muscle along the way. My fingertips feel like they're on fire. With each button, I find myself growing hotter and fighting the urge to rip the jacket right off his body.

Grabbling for the last one, my fingers graze a hard bump between his legs. This is *not* a button. I hastily pull my hand away.

Suddenly, Gallant comes to.

"Branch, I want you. Come to me," he mutters. At least, that's what I *think* he's saying. Holy crap! He's into that tree-hugging game too?

I'm out of here. As I pivot around, he grips my arm and pulls me on top of him. To my shock, he gropes my breasts and strokes my neck with the tip of his warm tongue as if he's painting me. The sensation arouses a divine tingling deep inside me. Moving his fluttering tongue to my chest, he wraps his muscled arms firmly around me. I struggle to break away, but he's too damn strong for me in his drunken stupor. Or I'm too damn weak in mine. Rhythmically, he slides his body against mine. Up and down. Slowly. Then faster. I find myself rocking in perfect harmony. Inside, I'm throbbing. Moaning. I don't want him to stop. It feels good. So good. Oh God! Too good!

The Prince lets out a long, loud sigh and falls back to sleep. I tiptoe out of the room, careful not to knock anything else over and relieved that I didn't take his britches off first.

I hope The Prince remembers none of this tomorrow. And I hope neither do I.

CHAPTER 26

I wake up early again the next morning with a pounding headache and my tongue pasted to my palate. How many beers did I drink last night? I stopped counting after the first.

Downstairs in the kitchen, I encounter the last person I want to see. Not Marcella. Gallant!

Given all he went through last night, he looks miraculously good. There's only a faint bruise on his forehead where Hook whacked him and a small, almost indiscernible gash on his neck from Hook's sword. But that's all. Even his blue eyes have regained their clarity. Let's hope his memory hasn't.

"I must have fallen off my horse last night," he says, sipping a cup of that fragrant tea.

Oh shit! He remembers!

"I am sore all over." He rubs the back of his head. "And I have this bump. But I honestly cannot recall when or where it happened."

Phew! He doesn't. I do and turn my head away. After last night, I can't look him in the eye.

He pours me a cup of the tea.

"After learning how much Calla enjoyed her picnic with you, I have decided I need to spend more quality time with her. So I have planned a special outing."

Great. He's going to take her shopping at The Trove. I saw lots of fathers and daughters there.

"We are all going apple-picking this afternoon."

What?

"It should be great fun." He finishes his tea. "You, me,

Calla, and Marcella."

Marcella? Great fun? This is what I call misery. Pure misery.

"And perhaps tonight, you can make another delicious apple pie."

I toss my tea into the sink.

"I can't wait to go, Papa!" squeals Calla as we finish lunch. She's already holding a basket with Lady Jane tucked inside.

Marcella, on the other hand, isn't the least bit excited about apple-picking. She protests it will wear her out for the ball.

"The exercise will invigorate you," says The Prince.

"My love, picking apples is for peasants."

Great! Her Royal Skankiness hates apple-picking. Maybe she won't go.

Her face brightens as she gulps down the last bit of my liquid diet potion. "On second thought, my love, you're so right. I'll burn lots of calories and lose weight!"

Dragonballs! She's coming along. I think of Winnie's mantra: "Look on the bright side." An image of Marcella falling out of an apple tree and breaking her neck pops into my head. Maybe it will be fun.

"The coach is waiting," says Gallant, rising from the table.

Why are we taking the coach when there's surely an apple orchard on The Prince's property, only a short walk away?

Inside the coach, Calla and I sit opposite The Prince and Marcella. I gaze out the window to avoid eye contact with Gallant. The bumpy ride does little to calm my nerves.

Calla rattles off her secrets to finding the best apples. The best ones are always on the tree; the "yucky" ones on the ground.

Marcella, bored to death, sips more of her "diet" (Ha!) potion and reads the latest *Fairytale Tattler*.

"I can't concentrate," she grumbles. "Calla, can you *please* shut up."

Calla makes a face but complies. Maybe it's because Marcella said "please" for once.

The PIW tears through the tabloid pages. "Jane, why isn't there any gossip about what I'm wearing to the ball?" Venom fills her eyes.

I make a mental note. Add to To-Do List: Leak Marcella's gown.

The route we're taking is familiar. It's as though we are going to The Trove. We pass Midas this and Midas that. I swear the number of Midas properties has multiplied since I last traveled down this road. When I get back to my castle, maybe I'll invite him over and have a little chat about expanding my empire.

My cliffside castle soon soars into view and that burning desire to reclaim it surges inside me. My eyes grow wide when the coach turns into the narrow road that leads to it. *What is going on here?*

The road is long and lined with potholes, bumps, and debris. With each fault we pass over, my heart slams harder against my chest. Is this some kind of surprise? Am I finally free to live in my castle?

"Are we there yet?" asks Calla.

"Almost," smiles the Prince.

We're at the base of my property. The moat is gone, completely filled in. No big deal. It was a nuisance to cross anyway. My eyes travel up the jagged hillside to my majestic castle. It's shrouded by a thick, billowy cloud.

My eyes stay peeled to the window as the coach circles halfway around the mountain. I want to jump out, run up to my home. As the coach comes to a sudden halt, my stomach lurches.

A large sign with bold, gold writing is posted into the earth.

> **SOLD!!**
> **ANOTHER MIDAS LUXURY**
> **HOTEL COMING SOON!**

What! They've sold my castle to this Midas creep? Without asking me? My mouth opens so wide I think everything inside me will leap out.

"There is an amazing apple orchard here," says The Prince.

I should know. This is *my* castle!

"The owner shall not mind," Gallant continues.

Why don't you ask? my head screams. *You're looking right at her!*

The apple orchard is exactly as I remember it. Hundreds of trees ripe with fragrant red fruit line the base of the cliff. As I stand in its midst, memories mingle with madness.

I'm going to sue that Midas bastard. Take him to court. With luck, I'll get that whack-job judge, and she'll take off his head.

On second thought, forget about suing. It'll take too long. I'm going to hunt him down and destroy his life the way he's destroyed mine. Poison him if I have to. Whatever it takes, I'm going to get my castle back.

"How about we have a contest to see who can pick the most apples," says The Prince, oblivious to the rage blazing inside me.

"That's ridiculous," scoffs Marcella.

For once, she's right. I'm in no mood for fun and games to say the least. Unless the prize is Midas's heart.

"Papa, I'm going to win!" shouts Calla who's already

running to a tree abundant with fruit. Using a long stick she's found, she knocks off several apples.

"Look, Papa!" she says with excitement. "I already have five apples!"

"Excellent!" says The Prince.

Marcella rolls her eyes. She clearly can't wait for this day to be over. Neither can I.

The four of us scatter around the orchard. I spot The Prince and Calla in the distance, but Marcella's nowhere in sight. She's probably gone back to the coach to read her tabloid.

I wander aimlessly from tree to tree. Rage mixed with shock is ravaging me. Just wait until I get my hands on that Midas!

My heart skips a beat. Straight ahead of me is that one unforgettable tree—the tree that bore that one unforgettable perfect apple. The apple I picked and dipped into poison. The apple I gave to Snow White.

Calla, carrying her basket with Lady Jane, runs over to the tree.

"Don't pick apples from that tree!" I sprint up to her, almost knocking her down.

"What's wrong with this tree?" asks Calla, puzzled.

"Nothing."

Yes, nothing. Except the thought of eating apples from this tree is making me even sicker to my stomach. Ignoring my plea, Calla shakes the tree, and an apple falls into her basket. A big red rosy apple. Exactly like the one I gave to Snow White.

"Jane, look at this apple!" exclaims Calla. "It's perfect!" She raises it toward her rosebud lips.

As her mouth descends on its shiny exterior, I yank it out of her hand and toss it as far as I can.

Calla gives me another bewildered look. "Jane, you're acting all weird today. Are you feeling sick?"

"No, I'm perfectly fine." *Perfectly fine?* Chances are I'll never make it through this day.

What has this madman Midas done to my castle? I'm desperate to find out.

When Calla skips off to check on her father, I hurry off. Every nerve in my body is charged with anticipation as I stomp up the steep, winding road that leads to my home. Yes, *my* home! Kicking rocks and debris in my way, I'm surprised how easy it is for me to make the climb. The daily trek up to Shrink's office has gotten me into better shape than I've ever been. I can be thankful to Faraway for that. But that's all. Shrink led me to believe I could go back to live in my castle, but now that's just another wicked lie.

The cloud cloaking the castle lifts as I make the ascent, and by the time I get to the top, my home is in full view with its myriad of towers, spires, and towers.

My heart plunges. Walls are crumbling; windows are cracked; the vegetation runs wild. It's a ghost of its former glorious self.

As I circle around to the rear, I hear whistling. And then I see them. Seven little men busily working away. Hammering! Sawing! Bashing! Trashing! I can't believe my eyes. It's those abominable dwarfs! First they wrecked my life. Now they're wrecking my castle!

Desperation overtakes me. I furiously gather up an armful of rocks. I'm going to pummel those runts before nothing remains of my former life.

Then one of them spots me.

"Hey, lady, what are you doing here?" he says, not recognizing me. "This is a construction zone."

What am *I* doing here? *Hey, Grumpster, this is my property, and you're destroying it! I should get you arrested and thrown into jail! That same dark, dreary dungeon you sent me to!*

I aim a rock at his ugly oversized head but stop when, out

of the corner of my eye, I notice one of the home wreckers hauling something out of the back entrance. My heart goes haywire. It's my magic mirror!

"Where are you going with that?" I cry out.

"Taking this piece of junk where it belongs." He sneezes, blowing boogers all over my beloved looking glass.

Letting go of the rocks, I race after him, but it's too late. He hurls the mirror into a dumpster. I hear it shatter.

A loud voice inside my head urges me to leave. "Jane, don't go there!" it says. It sounds like Shrink's. I ignore it.

Frantic, I hoist myself up into the dumpster. On top of the rest of my bashed up furnishings is my treasured mirror. I heave a loud sigh of relief. It has only broken into six chunks. I'm able to piece it back together.

My magic mirror! We're together at last. Unable to resist, I look into it. And scream. I'm horrified by my reflection. The cracks, snaking across my skin, have disfigured my face. I'm dizzy, weak. Almost faint. It's as if the mirror is possessing me. *Tell me:*

> "Mirror, mirror once on the wall,
> Who's the fairest one of all?"

Silence. I bet it doesn't recognize me. How could it?

I ask again, this time louder. "Tell me!" I scream. "TELL ME!"

The mirror at last responds. Its voice sounds strangled.

> "You, My Queen, are still fair, I suppose;
> But the answer to your query is Calla Rose."

"Calla?" I gasp. "What happened to Snow White?"

No response. I grow impatient. "Tell me, you smart-ass looking glass!"

To my horror, the mirror's cracks multiply. A terrifying cobweb of cracks spreads across my face. I'm a monster! As

I shriek, the mirror shatters into a million little pieces. Tiny shards of glass are scattered everywhere. There's no way I can put it back together. It's beyond repair! Ruined! Gone forever!

Shaking all over, I climb out of the dumpster. Shock gives way to rage. Everything inside me is screaming. That two-timing, worthless piece of glass! It betrayed me again! My former best friend, still nothing but a traitor! And now, I have to compete with Calla!

Still trembling, I take one last look at my castle. Someone behind me tugs my arm. I spin around.

It's one of those damn dwarfs. The tiniest one. He's holding a shovel that's double his size.

"What do you want from me, you little twerp?"

The dopey-looking runt says nothing. He keeps pointing to the ground as if he's trying to tell me something.

I glance down and gasp. Winding its way toward me at wicked speed is a monstrous green and yellow snake. I take a giant step backward. Then another and another…until I'm standing at the cliff edge of my property. A nauseating feeling of déjà vu shoots through me. There's nowhere I can go—but down! But this time, there's no river to rescue me.

Picking up its pace, the snake slithers right up to my feet. It fixes its unblinking yellow eyes on me. One hiss and I know. I'm going to be history!

The snake flicks its forked tongue on my ankle. It tickles, but I desperately want to scream. Frozen with fear, I can't find my voice. It flicks its tongue again; I don't need to look down to know it's going to strike. And then, just as its venomous fangs prick my skin, the tiny dwarf charges toward me with his shovel. In one swift, seamless move, he scoops up the snake and tosses it over the cliff.

I'm too stunned to say anything.

The mini-mute makes a wavy motion with his free arm, snaps his teeth, and rests his head on his hands as if pretending to go to sleep.

What is he trying to tell me now?

Confused, shaken, and wanting nothing to do with any of these Snow White fanboys, I flee. And don't look back.

Back at the orchard, my jittery fingers pluck out slivers of glass embedded in the threads of my dress. I wish we had never come here. My castle belongs to another, and my magic mirror has betrayed me again. In the course of a few minutes, my emotions shift from despair to anger and then to self-pity.

A voice coming toward me distracts me, and I stab my thumb. Damn that mirror!

"Guess what! I think I won the contest! Look at how many apples I have!"

It's Calla...Calla with her cascading curls, her angelic face. She *is* fairer than me. But why am I not consumed by that insane, flesh-eating jealousy that used to besiege me? Why do I feel a lightness in my heart as I watch her skip toward me?

Full of energy and excitement, she pokes her head into my empty basket. "Jane, don't worry. I'll give you some of my apples so that you don't come in last." She fills up half my basket with her apples.

I don't get it. I'm supposed to hate this child—want her out of my life—but I don't. I can't. How could anyone loathe a child so sweet and pure?

I wish I'd never talked to my mirror. My stupid, stupid big mouth mirror.

Calla adds a few more apples to my basket. The cherubic smile on her exquisite face completely melts me. I kneel down beside her so that we're face to face. I can see my reflection in her twinkling eyes. The image of the person I have become.

And then it hits me. The truth. Hard. Direct. Pure. Shrink was right. My mirror was never magic. It was just a worthless piece of glass that messed with my head. And played with reality. Why could I not see this before?

I draw Calla closer until we're heart to heart. Every part

of me tingles. Calla is what's magic.

She adds yet another apple to my basket.

"Thank you, my sweet girl." *Thank you for everything.*

"Time is up. Let us determine a winner," calls out The Prince, striding up to us.

I spring to my feet. So much of me wants to share my amazing revelation with him. But he'd never understand. He'd probably think I'm a nutcase and have me confined to some mental institution. Ha! Faraway!

The Prince's basket is loaded with apples, but he clearly doesn't have as many as Calla. Even after sharing her apples with me. We each do a count. Calla comes in first, The Prince, a close second, and me, a not-so-distant third.

"Hooray! I won! I won!" exclaims Calla, jumping up and down.

"Not quite yet, My Little Princess," says Gallant. "You shall have to wait and see how many apples Marcella has gathered."

On cue, Her Royal Skankiness staggers toward us. A thick coat of dirt covers her from head to toe. She must have taken a fall.

Calla cups a hand over her mouth to suppress her giggles. I risk a smile. Gallant, too, is amused.

The little girl runs up to Marcella and then races back to us.

"Six! I counted them! Marcella only has six apples, and they're all rotten! That means I'm the winner!"

"Get me out of here!" screeches Marcella. She flings her basket, sending the apples flying in all directions.

Fighting her clingy gown and high heels, she inches toward the coach.

Calla calls out, "Watch out for that—"

Rotten apple. But it's too late. Marcella trips over it. She lands face down, smack on her cannonballs.

This time Calla cannot contain herself. She explodes with laughter. I adore this child; I really do. Screw my stupid, piece-of-junk mirror! I'm glad it's history.

"What are you laughing about?" Marcella struggles to stand up. "Can't you see I'm hurt?"

She brushes herself off, adjusts her gown, and begins to hobble. She's faking. I know because it's exactly how my mother taught me to feign a limp. To over-exaggerate it and make believe you're in a lot of pain. "Pity breeds generosity," she preached. Her scheme worked like a charm. Whenever I begged for money, passersby would always give me an extra coin, thinking I was a cripple. She even forced me to carry a crutch, which came in handy the day she kicked me hard in the shin.

"My love, I don't think I can make it to the coach," moans the PIW.

Gallant wraps his strong arm around her, letting her lean on him for support. I want to ram her back onto the ground.

"Papa! Look over there!" exclaims Calla, pointing straight ahead of us.

Out of the clearing comes a young spotted deer—Bambi! I'd recognize him anywhere. Recognizing me, he prances over to us. The sweet animal eats one of my apples. With gleeful laughter, Calla offers him one of hers.

He nibbles her apple, then butts his budding antlers against Marcella. She freaks. "My love, save me from this flea-ridden beast!" She takes several giant steps backward. So much for her twisted ankle.

Still falling for her act, The Prince gallantly sweeps the bogus bitch into his arms. I want to puke.

"Papa, can we take him home?" begs Calla. "Please! Pretty Please! He could be my prize for winning the contest. Or my birthday present!"

"My Little Princess, I'm afraid he already belongs to someone else."

At the edge of the clearing, another elegant young deer appears. Bambi leaps over to her and nuzzles her head. She must be his new mate. Side by side, they prance into the orchard.

The Prince carries Marcella back to the coach. "My hero," she says, with a smug smile directed at me.

Calla and I exchange a despondent look. She takes my hand in hers, squeezing it gently.

I glare at Gallant. He, too, belongs to someone else. I have another startling revelation. No, it's not Calla I envy. It's Marcella.

CHAPTER 27

Thank goodness for Winnie. She's planned Calla's entire surprise birthday party right down to the party favors. After yesterday's apple-picking excursion with all its extreme ups and downs, there's no way I could have handled it, even if I'd had the time. My battered heart has shut me down.

As I sit on the edge of Calla's bed, braiding her hair, I wonder for the umpteenth time: *what am I doing here?* Shrink promised that I could go back to my castle if I completed my apprenticeship. But now, what's the point? My castle belongs to that Midas creep, and my mirror is no longer of any use to me. When Marcella (walking perfectly fine) flung a shoe at me this morning for not delivering her daily *Fairytale Tattler* to her in bed, why didn't I throw it back and just call it quits?

"Do you think Papa's going to get me a puppy?" asks Calla, snapping me out of my funk.

Gallant. I can't get him out of my head. Though I've tried to avoid him, he did mention at breakfast that he and Marcella had something very important to do today, and now they've been gone for hours.

"I hope so," I sigh. "I'm sorry I haven't had the time to get you something," I add with remorse.

Instead of a frown, Calla's lips curl into a dimpled smile. "You are a gift."

Her unexpected, beyond-her-years words light up my heart, and I smile despite myself.

Calla has no clue about her surprise birthday party. My job has been to keep her occupied until Winnie gives me the

signal to bring her into the courtyard. We've played check-
ers, read a book together, and given Lady Jane a bath. In my
gloomy state, it's not been easy, and I'm running out of ideas.

Just as I finish with her hair, a rock hits Calla's bedroom
window. Finally, the signal.

"Come on, birthday girl. Let's get some fresh air and play
hide-and-seek." Calla reaches for Lady Jane, then takes my
hand.

The warmth of her little hand in mine radiates throughout
me. She's the reason I'm still here.

"Surprise!" shouts Winnie and a group of one hundred or so
children, mostly boys, I've never seen before.

"Happy Birthday, Calla!" I say, joined by the others.

Calla is overwhelmed. "Wow!" is all she can say.

Wow is right. Winnie, dressed up as a fairy godmother,
has created the ultimate Princess Birthday Party. There's a
magic castle playhouse, pretend tiaras and crowns for all the
children, and a pony ride. She's even brought along that giant
dragon from the toy store. How did she manage to get it here?
I'm probably better off not knowing.

"Who are all these children?" I ask.

"They're from the local orphanage," replies Winnie. "I
thought it would be more fun for Calla if she had other children to play with."

Despite Winnie's good intentions, my blood runs cold. I
bet they're from that Midas Orphanage for Lost Boys. I hate
that Midas!

I recognize one of the children—that unruly boy I saw
the other day at Mother Goose. Much better behaved today,
he's showing Calla how to make the dragon roar by stepping
on its foot.

"Who's that?" I ask, pointing at him.

"That's Curly," says Winnie.

"He's an orphan?" I'm surprised. "Didn't I see him with his nanny the other day?"

"Oh, that was his latest foster parent. He's been in and out of the system for years. No one wants to keep him." Winnie pinches her lips together and shakes her head. "It's sad because he's really not a bad kid."

The boy makes Calla roar with laughter. After her initial shock, she can't get enough of the fire-breathing dragon. What a wonderful birthday she's having. Sadly, I can't remember turning seven. In fact, I can't remember any of my childhood birthdays. It was just another day to scrub floors and beg for money. My mother didn't give a damn. She didn't buy me a thing; she was too busy shopping for new clothes for herself and seducing men. In a way, I was an orphan too. Maybe, worse off.

Winnie forces me back to the present by bringing two youngsters over to meet me, a boy and a girl. "These are my children, Hansel and Gretel." Of course! They look just like her with freckled faces and flaming red hair. The little girl's the spitting image of her brother, except she has long thick braids. I bet they're twins.

"Pleased to meet you, Your Majesty," they say in unison as they bow before me.

Huh?

"I told them you're a queen," Winnie whispers in my ear.

I smile at the two children. "Just call me Aunt Jane." Why not? Winnie's like a sister to me. "And the next time you see me, I'd prefer a hug to a bow."

The two of them giggle.

Winnie waves her pretend magic wand over them. "Now, children, magically disappear."

Hansel and Gretel giggle again. After hugging Winnie, they scamper off to play with Calla and Curly. Winnie squeezes my hand and smiles. How lucky Hansel and Gretel are to have her as their mom. And how lucky she is to have them.

To the children's absolute delight, Winnie is a one-woman show. She sings; she dances, and she even juggles cupcakes. For her finale, she tosses the cupcakes into the audience. Just like at the Faraway talent show that now seems like ages ago. The rapturous children clamber to catch and eat them.

Taking a much-deserved break from entertaining Calla and her newfound friends, Winnie sits down with me on a stone bench, ironically the one where Gallant first asked me to arrange this party. Finally, a chance to tell her about my castle and mirror.

With out a single interruption, she listens intently as the words fly out. By the end of my story, my mouth is dry, and my throat is burning with anger.

"It's all meant to be," she says.

Is that *all* she can say?

"Elz and Hook broke up," she says before I can tell her about my plan to hunt down Midas.

Poor Elz! I knew that sleazeball would break her heart.

"Don't feel bad for her." She's such a mind reader. "Elz dumped Hook."

Good for her! After how he treated her the other night, he deserved it. I'm proud of my roomie. She's really taking control of her life.

"How's Elz doing?" I ask.

"She's doing great. It's Hook who's a shipwreck."

"How are my young mateys doing?" comes a familiar voice from behind us. Talking about the devil…

It's Hook! Who invited him? Then I remember. He's in charge of the children at the orphanage. The Midas Orphanage…maybe he can lead me to the bastard.

Hook surveys his wards at play. "It looks like they're having a whale of a time," he smiles. "But their ship is about to sail."

"Please let them stay a little longer," begs Winnie. "At

least to have some birthday cake. Which reminds me, I need to get the cake ready."

Winnie dashes off, leaving me alone with Hook. I have to admit he looks like a wreck. With his bloodshot eyes and thick layer of stubble, he probably hasn't slept for days.

"Do you know Midas?" I ask him right away despite his sorry state.

"Never met the bloke."

Dragonballs! My mouth twists with disappointment.

"I'm sorry about the other night," he says in a surprisingly humble tone.

The other night…I flush at the memory.

"I've gone cold turkey. I'm off booze for good."

"That's great." I wonder how long that'll that last.

He moves much too close to me. "Now, that it's over between me and Elzmerelda, maybe we could give it another shot."

God, he just won't give up. "Hook, let's just be friends, okay?"

"What do you mean by that?" he asks, sounding confused.

Luckily, I don't have to answer his question. Calla comes to my rescue.

"Jane, it's almost time for my cake. Where's Papa?"

Good question. Where is The Prince? I can't believe he's missing his daughter's birthday party.

The sound of singing fills my ears. "Happy Birthday to You." It's Winnie with the cake—a glittery castle made of hundreds of chocolate cupcakes with colorful candles stacked to look like spires. How creative of Winnie! She must have had it custom made at Sparkles. Unfortunately, it makes me think again about my castle and that Midas monster. I can't wait to get my hands on him.

All the children gather around the cake and sing along with Winnie. Hook joins them and finally so do I. Hook's beautiful baritone voice harmonizes with the choir of children. Calla, holding Lady Jane, beams with joy.

"Calla, make a wish and blow out the candles," says Winnie.

"I'm only seven. So how come there are eight candles?" asks Calla.

"One's for good luck," says Winnie.

With any luck, The Prince will show up before this party's over.

On Winnie's count of three, Calla takes a deep breath, winks at me, then blows out all eight candles. Everyone shouts "Happy Birthday."

"What did you wish for?" I ask her.

"I wished that Papa would—"

Winnie cups a hand over Calla's rosebud lips and then reprimands me.

"Shame on you, Jane. Don't you know that if you say what you've wished for, it won't come true?"

Right! I should have known that from my "birthday party" at Faraway. Silly me!

A bellowing voice in the distance diverts my attention.

"What is going on here?"

The Prince. Finally! With Marcella hanging on his arm, he lopes over to us.

"Where have you been?" I ask, not hiding my anger.

"We went shopping!" croons Marcella. "Want to see what I—"

Gallant cuts her off. "Who are all these children, and what are they doing here?"

"They're children from the local orphanage. They're here to celebrate Calla's birthday," I reply.

"Eww, orphans!" says Marcella as if they're rabid rodents.

"Get them out of here. Now!" orders The Prince. "I cannot have my daughter exposed to all these germs. Who knows where these gamins have been!"

"But Papa, they're my new friends!" protests Calla.

"My Little Princess, this is none of your concern." Gently pushing her aside, he accidentally knocks Lady Jane out of her hand. The doll tumbles onto the cobblestones.

Calla crouches down to pick up her precious doll. "Papa! Look what you've done!" she cries. The doll's beautiful porcelain face is cracked all over.

In a fit of tears, Calla runs off, Lady Jane dangling from her hand. Her sobs are like pins in my heart.

The Prince stands there motionless.

"My love, it's only a stupid doll," says Marcella. "She'll get over it."

She moseys over to the cake and dips a finger into the frosting. As she licks it off, I want to strangle her.

"Well, I guess the party's over," says Hook. He gathers the orphans. "Ahoy, my mateys. It's time to sail."

"Aye, aye, Captain," respond the orphans with a salute.

They form two straight lines. To Hook's credit, they're all exceptionally well behaved and respectful. Curly included. Perhaps, Hook, too, has found his meant-to-be calling.

"Children, don't forget your party favors," says Winnie.

She hands them each a woven gold name bracelet. They're almost identical to the one Rump made for me. The children's faces brighten. And for a fleeting moment so does mine. Rump must be back in Lalaland.

"Hook, I'll go back with you," says Winnie. She takes Hansel and Gretel by their hands.

I'm sad to see them go.

Before departing, Hook strides up to Gallant. "By the way, matey, sorry about the other night."

The duel! My heart leaps to my throat.

Gallant glares at Hook. "Sir, I have no idea what you are talking about."

Phew! He still doesn't remember anything about the other night.

"She's a great woman," continues Hook. "Definitely, worth fighting over."

"Why, thank you!" says Marcella. The stupid cow has no clue Hook's referring to me.

Hook struts off and catches up to Winnie. They lead the children off the grounds of the castle. Calla's birthday party has ended disastrously. My blood is churning. It's time for me to give Gallant a piece of my mind. Prince or no prince.

"You can't keep Calla in a bubble forever," I bark. "She needs to be with children her own age. She needs friends."

The Prince furrows his brows. "And Jane, how do you know all this?"

"Because I *didn't* when I was her age," I say hotly.

Gallant is taken aback. I'm not done with him.

"And on your little shopping trip with Marcella, I can only hope you remembered to buy your 'Little Princess' a present. In case you don't know, she wanted a puppy."

The glimmer in his blue eyes vanishes. He lowers his head. He can't hide his guilt and shame. At least not from me. Let him sulk. He deserves to feel bad.

"I am going inside to pour myself a drink," he says finally and marches off. So he thinks he can drown his sorrows. Ha!

Pleased with myself, I clean up the mess the children have left behind. Marcella saunters up to me, stuffing her face with a gigantic piece of cake. So much for her diet. In fact, she may be over it. She's silently crooning laddi da da.

"Jane, look what I got!" The PIW thrusts her left fist under my nose. On her fourth finger is a sparkling diamond, the size of rock.

My heart sinks to my stomach. I'm numb all over. But not for long. The numbness gives way to madness. I want to tear the ring off her finger and shove it down her throat. And watch her choke on it.

"Congratulations" is all I say.

Back inside the castle, The Prince is slumped at his desk, nursing a drink. Sensing my presence, he gazes up at me with forlorn eyes.

"Calla is inconsolable. She refuses to see me."

"What do you expect? You blew it."

"I was somehow unable to break away from Marcella."

There's regret in his voice, but the mention of her name makes bile bubble in my throat.

Gallant's eyes do not leave mine. "Please, Jane, I beg of you to talk to her."

"What do you want me to tell her?" I ask, my tone softening.

"Tell her that I am sorry for everything and that I shall buy her a new doll. A hundred of them, if she wants."

"I'll do what I can." No matter how much I want to stay mad at him, I can't.

Calla's chamber door is locked. Muffled sobs seep through the thick slab of wood. I knock gently.

"Calla, can I please come in?"

"No!"

"Pretty please with a cherry on top?"

"Maybe."

I take that as a "yes" because I hear the door unlock.

Back on her bed, Calla is curled up with Lady Jane, her face soaked with tears. She caresses the doll's cracked face.

"Your father feels really bad about today," I say, sitting down beside her.

"All he cares about is Marcella," she wails.

"That's so not true. He loves you more than anyone in the whole world."

"How do you know that?"

"Because I just do."

We share a stretch of silence. Calla's sobbing reduces to whimpers.

"Your father told me he'll buy you a new Lady Jane," I continue.

Calla bursts into tears again.

"I don't want a new Lady Jane. I only want this one!"

I examine Lady Jane. The doll's once perfect porcelain face is now lined with a maze of cracks. Its close resemblance to my reflection in my cracked "magic" mirror sends a shockwave through me.

"I wish she was still beautiful," sobs Calla.

"She is," I say, calming down.

"I don't believe you."

"I'm going to prove it to you." I pull out Shrink's mirrored locket from under my dress and snap it open.

Intrigued, Calla stops crying. "Who gave that to you?"

"Someone special. It's magic."

That really gets her attention.

"Now, I want you to let Lady Jane take a look at herself in my magic mirror."

Calla props her dolly up in front of the mirror, then peers at Lady Jane's reflection. "What's so magic about that?" She frowns. "Her face still looks all cracked."

"Keep moving back, but make sure Lady Jane can see still see herself in the mirror." Calla, holding Lady Jane, slides back on the bed as far back as she can go. "Okay, stop!"

A shocked Calla blinks her eyes several times. "I can't see Lady Jane's cracks anymore. They've disappeared!"

"See, I told you my mirror was magic. Lady Jane *is* still beautiful."

A bright smile replaces Calla's frown. She kisses the doll on her cracked cheek.

I smile too, proud of my "magic." Scooting next to her, I fold an arm around her thin shoulders. "Now that you're seven, I want to tell you a grown-up secret. Do you think you're ready?"

Calla's eyes light up as she nods.

"Someone once told me that beauty's not in the face; it's in the heart," I whisper in her ear. Okay. Those weren't exactly Shrink's words, but close enough.

Calla cocks her head like a puzzled puppy. "What does that mean?"

Dragonballs. Now, I've got to makeup something. I still haven't figured out what Shrink meant.

"It means that you must love Lady Jane even more. Especially now that she's a little hurt. Do you think you can do that?"

Remarkably, what I've said makes sense to Calla. She nods again and hugs the precious doll.

"Time for you to go to sleep." Smiling, I tuck her under the covers and plant a kiss on her forehead.

"Sweet dreams," I say softly.

Clutching Lady Jane in her arms, Calla closes her eyes.

Quietly, I slip out of the room. As I close the door behind me, Calla's sweet voice calls out to me.

"By the way, Jane, thank you for my birthday party. It was the best one I ever had."

The memory of another little girl who turned seven flashes into my head. Snow White. How could I forget? It was on that fateful day my "magic" mirror first played with my head, warning me that she would one day would be fairer than me. As I descend the staircase, I tremble, wishing that mirror had never existed.

———

Gallant is still at his desk. The blaze in the fireplace basks his face in a warm amber glow. Hearing my footsteps, he rises.

"How is she?" he asks, moving toward me.

"She'll be fine." I gaze at his face and my body quivers.

The Prince places his strong hands on my shoulders and meets my eyes. "Jane, I am forever beholden to you."

"It's no big deal," I reply, tingling from his touch.

"Jane, you know so much about children. Have you taken care of them before?"

"No," I stammer and look away, shamed by my past.

How horribly I treated poor Snow White. She was a sweet little girl—an orphan—who cared nothing about beauty and asked for nothing. She was always so kind to me. But I wanted nothing to do with her. I dressed her in rags and made her sleep with the servants. And as she grew older and more beautiful with every passing day, I wanted her out of my life. I even I tried to kill her. How's that for my child-care experience?

And then there was another child. My beautiful stillborn son. The child I never got a chance to care for and know. Perhaps if he had lived, my life would have turned out so differently. The King would have loved me, and we would been one big happy family.

Tears prick my eyes as guilt and grief rip me apart.

With his thumb, The Prince brushes a tear off my cheek with a tenderness I don't deserve. "What is wrong, Jane?"

"Nothing." *Everything.* "You're so blessed to have Calla."

"I know and that is why I overprotect her." The Prince pauses reflectively. "But you are right, Jane. I have to let go. She needs to have friends. Perhaps, you can help me find a good school for her."

"My love, I know the perfect school for Calla. Lots of royal tykes go there."

Marcella! My body stiffens as she glides toward us.

"Tell me more," says Gallant.

"It's a boarding school in France." Her tone is as obnoxious as the big fat diamond on her finger. She throws her arms around The Prince and shoots me a patronizing smile that clearly says, "He's mine!"

I eye her frostily and step away. "Good night. It's been a long day."

The PIW twists her ring. "Jane, didn't you forget something?"

Screw her curtsey. I stalk out of the room.

"Jane, wait!" shouts Gallant.

I do not turn back to see his expression.

CHAPTER 28

I wake up early the next morning with the bad taste of Marcella still lingering in my mouth. Tucked under my chamber door is one of her scribbled notes. I bet she's firing me. I crawl out of bed and retrieve it.

> *J—Missing my emerald earring. Need it for tonight's dinner party at The King's palace. Check the shed; it could have fallen off there. Don't bother coming back until you find it. And BTW, don't tell The Prince about this.—M*

I crumple the note in my fist. Yet another thing to do. Maybe Calla *will* be better off going to a boarding school faraway from her selfish, self-centered mother-to-be.

As I make my way out of the castle, the sun is rising. Its rays mingle with the early morning mist, creating the illusion of fairy dust.

Having no idea what shed Marcella's referring to, I stumble upon a pebbled path and follow it. This is the first time I'm actually exploring the vast property on my own. I feel like an adventurer staking out a newly discovered land. It's rather empowering and gets my mind off Marcella.

Following the meandering path, I'm awestruck by the beautiful gardens. The flowers and shrubs are artfully arranged—indeed, someone's well-thought-out vision. Most likely, I bet, the handiwork of The Prince's late wife. There are potted plants, flowers of all colors, grapevines, and orchards.

The scents blend to form a fragrant chorus.

Further on, I pass by horse stables, a wishing well, and a carriage house. Shortly after crossing an olive grove, I come upon a small, shingled structure with several boarded up windows and a thatched roof. Maybe this is the place Marcella means.

The door is unlocked. I venture inside cautiously. My mouth drops. It's not a shed. It's a museum!

There are paintings everywhere. Landscapes, still-lifes, portraits, and more. Hanging on the walls. Stacked in corners. Standing on easels. If I had to guess, two hundred paintings, at least.

The paintings are astounding. You don't have to be an art scholar to appreciate them. Each one is a masterpiece.

The artist has managed to breathe life into all his subjects with his masterful strokes and a subtle but beautiful use of light. I pause to admire a garden scene—a luminous patch of white lilies. The droplets of dew on the outstretched petals are so well done they seem touchable, practically real. Wait! They are real! What I mean is that I remember seeing this very patch of flowers in Gallant's late wife's garden.

Obviously, the artist must be someone in the service of The Prince. I recognize a portrait of his white stallion that's so full of action the horse is practically leaping off the canvas. There's another equally splendid portrait of The Prince himself. His blue eyes stand out, glistening with a vibrancy that's missing now.

Rummaging through the stacked canvasses on the floor, I discover a charming portrait of a beautiful, brown-eyed infant with gilded curls. It's unmistakably Calla. The artist has admirably succeeded in capturing her magic, even at this tender age.

In the far corner of the room, I come across what must be a large canvas propped on an easel. It's hidden from view by a sheet of thick damask. Curious to see what lies beneath, I carefully edge down the fabric.

"STOP!"

I freeze, then wheel around. Gallant! His eyes are narrow; his lips tight.

"What are you doing here?" he asks.

"I'm searching for one of Marcella's earrings." I act calm but inside my heart is racing. "I thought it might be here." My question is: What is *he* doing here?

"This is my studio," Gallant says solemnly.

The Prince painted all these works of art? I'm in awe. I had no idea he was so talented.

"I'm sorry to be intruding on your space and time," I say humbly.

The Prince apologizes for his outburst. "Please continue your search. I only came by because one of the guards reported hearing a strange noise in here last night."

"I'll leave. I don't want to distract you from painting." He must be working on the covered canvas.

"I no longer paint," he says wistfully.

He goes on to tell me that after the death of his wife, he could not bring himself to pick up a paintbrush. The world lost all its color. Everything seemed so futile.

The sadness in his voice moves me deeply. He lost both his true love and passion.

The Prince's eyes grow distant. "After she died, I could no longer find the true meaning of beauty in the world."

The true meaning of beauty. Shrink's haunting words echo in my head. So, Gallant knows the answer. Or at least, once he did. Now, is he searching for it like me?

I yearn to ask him, but the words stay trapped in my throat. I pivot toward the door.

The Prince places his strong hands on my shoulders, stopping me in my tracks. "Jane, please stay."

To my delight, his mood brightens, and he gives me a whirlwind tour of his studio. He springs to life as he talks about the inspiration behind each painting. Never having seen him so animated and passionate, I find myself engrossed in his every word. Stimulated. Sharing my reactions and interpretations. Asking him questions. Challenging him. Challenging myself.

"You're a master," I say, meaning it. "Your paintings belong in a museum for the world to behold, not hidden from the human eye."

Finally, we come to the covered painting. "What's under there?" I ask with curiosity.

The Prince takes a deep breath, then sweeps off the damask cloth. Before me stands a large canvas. It's obviously a work in progress. A portrait of woman picking flowers, still at the outline stage.

Gallant's eyes, glimmering just moments ago, are laced with melancholy. He turns away from the canvas and remains silent.

"My last painting," he says at last. "A portrait of my wife. I was going to surprise her with it on her twenty-first birthday. But she died before I could complete it. I have not been able to paint since then."

So, grief shut him down. Is that what love does?

"My Lord, you should finish the painting. You owe it to yourself. You owe it to Calla." I stare at the unfinished portrait. "And you owe it to her."

With a sigh, Gallant carefully re-covers the painting and changes the subject.

"Forgive me. What did you say you were doing here?" he asks as if we've just met up.

I tell him again about Marcella's missing earring. Uh oh. I was supposed to keep this under wraps. Oh well. Whatever the consequences, I can't undo what's been done.

"I am sure it is not here," says Gallant. "My studio is off limits to everyone, including Calla.

"Then I'd better get going." Truthfully, I don't want to leave him.

A mutual loss for words forces us to lower our eyes.

"Look!" We say it simultaneously. As if we had timed it.

There it is on the ground…Marcella's emerald earring. Right under the easel holding the unfinished portrait of Gallant's wife.

We squat down together. Meeting face to face, we're very close—our eyes just a palm's width apart. His warm, sweet breath blows on my face. My cheeks grow flush, and I'm getting tingly hot all over. My heart thuds so loudly I can hear it.

The Prince studies my face. I gaze at my reflection in his piercing blue eyes. What does he see in me?

With his long, skilled fingers, he delicately traces my features. It's as if he's drawing me. My skin prickles from his touch, but I don't dare blink an eye.

His mouth curls into a smile that renders me breathless. "You are meant to be painted."

I don't know what to say. No one's ever said that to me before. Not even my "magic" mirror.

We each reach for the sparkling earring. Our fingers touch; a spark flies between us, and then we quickly pull apart. I let Gallant pick it up. As he hands me the jewel, our fingers interlock. This time he doesn't pull away.

"I've got to go," I stammer, struggling to my feet before my knees give in.

"Jane, please do not leave yet," he says, tightening his grip.

"Marcella will have my head if I don't get back," I force myself to say.

As I finally manage to pull away, a rustling sound distracts me. It's coming from outside. Has someone been watching us?

I hurry to the door. Clutching Marcella's earring, I sprint back to the castle and wonder—how did it end up where it did?

CHAPTER 29

Me

T hose are the two colossal gilded letters carved into the daunting gate outside The King's palace. Can you imagine—ME!—how more egocentric can you get? Well, I suppose if it were my palace, I wouldn't exactly inscribe "YOU" on the front gates. *My house is your house.* Now, there's a concept.

"Papa! We're here!" squeals Calla with excitement.

"Jane, calm her down," snaps Marcella as she fiddles with her emerald earrings.

She never even thanked me for finding the missing one. The ungrateful skank! I hope Calla chews her ear off. It would serve her right. She went off the deep end when Gallant asked me to come along—especially since it was going to be her first time meeting his parents, recently back from their six month diplomatic trip abroad. Finally, she backed off when he told her it was more of a babysitting gig. I could occupy Calla while they enjoyed an "adult evening" with The King and The Queen.

The paved road leading into the King's palace goes on for miles. Seated opposite Gallant, I stare at his handsome face. He looks tense. Almost withdrawn. He catches my eyes on him, and suddenly I feel embarrassed, like I've been trespassing on his private space. I quickly turn my head and peer out the window.

The palace comes into view and gets my mind off Gallant.

It is a castle of monumental proportions—much grander than mine—with countless towers, turrets, and spires. Lit by the full golden moon, it resembles a gigantic, gilded jewel box.

A drawbridge leads to a stone gatehouse, where two armed guards greet us. They're delighted to see The Prince and Calla. I get the feeling they are like family though they're only hired help. Our carriage lets us off in front of the palace, where we're met by a fleet of welcoming valets.

Inside, the palace is equally grand. It's filled with fresco-painted walls, richly embroidered draperies, and sumptuously upholstered furnishings. Gilded touches are everywhere, including a massive candle-lit chandelier that hangs from the high vaulted ceiling. I bet it's made of real gold.

An elderly, barrel-sized man, holding a golden staff, descends an elaborately carved gilded staircase. He is, undoubtedly, The King. He has the same sharp blue eyes as Gallant and, beneath his neatly trimmed beard, the same square jaw. And once upon a time, I bet he sported the same lean, athletic body.

"Grandpa! Grandpa!" shouts Calla. Her face lights up as she runs over to him.

"*Bambina*!" beams The King, lifting her high in the air.

Bambina? How odd to hear that word again after so many years. Could he possibly be the man who gave me a gold coin on that fateful day? Even if he were, he'd never remember. I'll never forget.

"Hello, father," says The Prince, his voice cold and distant. He's clearly on edge tonight. What's eating him?

"Son, introduce your guests to me says," says The King.

Marcella tugs at her clingy green gown, then puffs her chest. "My love, what are you waiting for?" She elbows Gallant, jolting him out of his other worldliness.

The PIW cringes when he turns to me. "Jane, this is my father, King Midas."

King Midas!? The Prince's father is King Midas!? The ruler of the Midas Empire. The me behind the ME. The man with the golden touch, who owns just about everything in La-laland, including my castle! *My house is your house*, I scream silently.

Every muscle in my body clenches as my mind transforms into a raging inferno with Midas trapped inside. I force myself to curtsey as I mentally char the bastard to a crisp. *Nice to meet you, Mide-ass! Now, give me back my castle!*

"I've heard so much about you," says The King.

You won't live long enough to find out more. I exert so much control to keep my mouth clamped—and my hands to myself—my neck may snap.

Marcella shoots The Prince a dirty look. "What about me?"

Hastily, Gallant introduces Marcella to his father, not mentioning she's his fiancée.

"*Enchantée,* Your Majesty." The PIW's cannonballs shoot out of her deeply décolleté gown as she curtsies.

"The Prince didn't tell me that you're so svelte," she says in the most sickening kiss-up voice I've ever heard.

"Oh, Marcella," chuckles the hefty King, his eyes glued to her chest. "You know exactly what to say to make my day."

And what to do. She loads her ammunition back into her gown.

A horrifying thought flies into my head. Holy crap! This slut will one day own my castle if I don't get it back. Burning bile rushes to the back of my throat.

While Gallant remains silent and detached from the conversation, Calla jumps right into it, unaware of the turbulent emotions raging inside me. "Grandpa, Jane's made a yummy pie with apples we picked at that spooky castle."

"Ah, my new property," says The Kings.

My old property, I seethe.

The bastard claps his thieving hands. "Splendid. I can't wait to eat it!"

Dragonballs! Another missed opportunity. Had I known I was going to meet the property thief, I would have figured out a way to poison his slice of pie. One bite and he would have been history.

Marcella plumps up her breasts, then clears her throat with an attention-getting cough. "Your Majesty, I've also brought you a yummy dessert. Homemade vanilla cupcakes."

Homemade cupcakes? You had me order them from Sparkles, you lying witch!

Marcella shoots me a nasty keep-your-mouth-shut look.

"I can't wait to bite into one," says The King, his eyes exactly where the skank wants them to be.

"Trust me, Your Majesty, after you eat one of *my* cupcakes, you'll *never* want to eat that apple pie."

Flaunting her boulder-size engagement ring, The PIW slaps me with a smirk. As much as I want to kill Midas, I want to kill her more. Much, much more.

———

"Grandpa, where's Grammy?" asks Calla as we gather in the great room for pre-dinner cocktails.

"You know, Grammy," chortles The King. "She can never make up her mind what shoes to wear."

At that very moment, a buxom woman, with skunk-white hair and a scarlet satin gown, makes a grand entrance. "Hello, everyone," she says in a thundering voice.

"Grammy!" Calla races over to hug her.

Wait! I know this woman. She's the one Marcella battled at The Glass Slipper! For those glittery ruby slippers! She's The Prince's mother!? The wife of King Midas. Marcella's future mother-in-law?

Marcella also recognizes her. Her body lurches forward, and her eyes almost pop out of their sockets. She seriously may have a seizure.

"This is my beautiful wife, The Queen of Hearts," says King Midas affectionately.

Marcella practically tumbles out of her chair to curtsey.

To my astonishment, The Queen doesn't recognize Marcella, who has her hair, blonder than ever, pulled back in a regal chignon. Maybe she's blind as a bat or suffering from some extreme form of dementia. Whatever it is, she's as gracious as can be. Relieved, Marcella plasters a sickening smile on her face and puts on her *enchantée*-I-speak-French act.

"Your Majesty, your shoes are so *très* faboo! You must tell me where you bought them."

I want to vomit. Oh God. Can this night get any worse?

The banquet table in the grand dining hall is ornately set for eight. A huge vase of exquisite heart-shaped red roses graces the table. On the wall facing me is a striking, life-size portrait of The Queen. I recognize the artist's hand instantly. Gallant. He has transformed his matronly mother into an immortal beauty—albeit, with a few nips and tucks.

We take our seats, but two chairs remain empty.

"Where is Cinderella and that other son of ours?" roars The Queen.

Prince Charming is Gallant's brother? What other family surprises do I have in store?

"Dear, you know that Cinderella. She is always late," replies The King.

The Queen pounds a fist on the table like a gavel. Everything shakes, including me.

"I'm going to sign that girl up for a time management class once and for all," she says though clenched teeth. "In any event, we're not waiting for them. I'm famished. Let's eat!"

She still looks and sounds so familiar to me. But my mind is too jammed with Midas madness to figure out how I know her. I stop dwelling on it when an army of servants brings an elaborate meal to the table.

Wine begins to flows as The King and Queen pass an assortment of delectable tarts, purées, and breads. Being in the same room as Midas has killed my appetite. I feel sick. All I manage is some wine. I'm not alone. Gallant, seated across from me, isn't eating either.

"We are vegetarians," says The King, helping himself to a generous portion of everything. "Although sometimes I could die for a good leg of lamb."

I make a mental note: Be sure to bring an *entire* lamb the next time you see the property thief. That is, *if* there's a next time.

The Queen, draining her second goblet of wine, loosens up. "Dear, what have you done to your hair?" she asks Gallant, noticing for the first time that he's wearing it loose, instead of in its usual ponytail. "I rather like it."

Actually, I do too, my mood lifting just a little from the wine.

Gallant speaks for the first time since we've sat down. "Thank you, Mother. It is quite liberating."

"Well, I think it makes you look like a girl!" grumbles The King.

Let me at him.

The Queen turns her attention to the skank. "Marcella, do you like croquet?"

"*Mais oui.* It's one of my favorite dishes," she mutters, stuffing her face.

Calla's about to burst out in laughter but claps a hand over her mouth just in time. Despite myself, I want to laugh too.

"And how are the arrangements for the ball coming along?" continues The Queen after another gulp of wine.

Her Royal Skankiness barely looks up from her plate as she wolfs down her meal like a starved stray. I guess she forgot her "diet" potion.

"Oh, Jane's handling all the details. She can tell you better than I," she says, helping herself to another whopping serving of everything.

The Queen looks my way.

"Great," I say. *Great?* The ball is only a week away, and

there's so much to do...flower arrangements, finalizing the menu, selecting the music...and let's not forget squeezing Marcella into her ball gown. And squeezing the life out of Midas.

"Excellent!" says The King. "I'm expecting this to be our biggest-ever Faraway fundraiser."

Faraway? What does this ball have to do with Faraway? I thought it was to celebrate Gallant's engagement to Marcella.

Then it hits me. Of course, Gallant's going to announce their engagement to his parents tonight. I gulp. That's what's been on his mind.

"Father, Mother, I have an important announcement to make."

And here it comes.

Marcella's eyes light up like lanterns. She lurches so far forward her that her cannonballs graze the gravy on her plate. It's her big moment. By tomorrow, her official engagement to The Prince will be headline news in the *Fairytale Tattler*. Everyone will know.

My heart sinks as the Prince rises.

"Father, I don't want to rule the world; I want to paint it."

My heart bounces back up. A tremor of excitement ripples through me.

"Son, what are you talking about?" shouts the shocked King.

Only Marcella is more horrified. Her jaw hangs wide open, her mouth spilling over with mashed up bits of turnip pie.

"I want to abdicate my right to the throne." Gallant's voice rings with confidence. "I want to be an artist, not a king."

I smile; Marcella gags.

"I told you, dear, he took after my side of the family," beams The Queen, eyeing her portrait and obviously pleased with her son's decision. "He wants to use his God-given gift to make the world more beautiful. How marvelous!"

The King rants on. "Son, you have spent your entire life preparing to take my place!"

"No, Father," responds The Prince, holding his own. "You have spent *your* entire life preparing me for a life *I* have never wanted."

Oh God. He's more handsome and powerful than ever. I desperately want to fling my arms around him and tell him how proud I am of him. Calla, too, is glowing with pride; almost nothing he does can disappoint her.

"Charming can rule the Kingdom. He's perfectly capable," continues The Prince.

Midas fumes. "Charming is such a cow—"

Marcella jumps up and cuts Midas off. She's frothing at the mouth like she's gone mad.

"My love, you're out of your mind!" she shrieks. "You think I'm going to let that ditz Cinderella become Queen? *You* are going to become King, and *I* am going to be crowned Queen and that's that!"

Suddenly, a guard charges into the room. My jaw drops. The Huntsman! The one person whose life I want to destroy more than Midas's and Marcella's combined. What is he doing here?

I break into a cold sweat. What if he recognizes me? He'll tell them everything! I quickly hide my face in my napkin. To my relief, he pays no attention to me. Something far more urgent is on his mind.

"Your Majesty, the palace of Prince Charming and Cinderella has caught fire!"

"Have the stable boys prep the carriage. We must go at once!" commands The King, showing himself to be a fast-thinking, in-control leader.

"Have Calla stay behind with the help!" orders The Prince.

"No, Papa," cries Calla. "I want to go with you."

There's no time for Gallant to argue with his little girl. I grasp her hand and follow the royal family out to their carriage.

"Jane, how dare you leave me alone with all this food!" shrieks Marcella. With her mouth stuffed, she joins us.

CHAPTER 30

As the King's carriage races through the countryside, we huddle next to each other in silence. Even Marcella doesn't say a word. I manage to smother my loathing for Midas by keeping my gaze focused on Gallant. His anxious eyes never leave mine.

Within minutes, the blaze is visible. Colossal puffs of orange smoke light up the night sky. As we get nearer, I see flames shooting out of the palace. Everywhere!

Upon entering the palace gates, the flames and turmoil freak out the horses, and we are forced to come to a halt. The Prince, the first to jump out, whips each of us out of the carriage. The smoke is intense; embers are flying everywhere. My eyes sting, and I cannot stop coughing. Calla, too, is choking. I drape her head with my shawl to protect her.

Chaos surrounds us. Servants and villagers run back and forth, armed with hoses and buckets of water to quell the flames. Some lead spooked animals away from the palace while others carry the royal couple's salvaged treasures to safety.

"Brother!" chokes a voice in the near distance. It must be Prince Charming.

Gallant runs over to him. For a second, I think I'm seeing double. Except for his cropped hair, Charming is the spitting image of Gallant. They must be identical twins.

"Where is Cinderella?" asks Gallant.

"She's still in the palace." Charming winces as a villager wraps gauze around his raw, blistered hands. "I'm going back in to find her." Coughing, he breaks away from his attendant.

Gallant holds him back. "Brother, you can't in your condition. Let me go."

"No!" roars The Queen. She blocks Gallant with her boulder-like body, but The King pulls her away.

"Gallant must do what he needs to do," says Midas solemnly. He places his large hands on The Prince's shoulders. "May God be with you, my son."

Gallant embraces his father and takes off. As he sprints toward the blazing palace, he becomes a silhouette in the clouds of smoke.

"Papa, come back!" cries Calla, bursting into tears.

I lift her in my arms and hold her close to me.

"He'll be okay, my sweet girl," I say, smoothing her hair. The tongues of flames licking the sky tell me something else. The truth. The Prince may die! My heart almost stops as I squeeze back tears of my own.

Marcella marches up to me, shielding her face with her forearm. To be honest, I forgot about her.

"Where the hell is Gallant?" she hisses.

"Inside the palace, searching for Cinderella."

"Stupid idiot!"

Is she outraged because Gallant may die or because he may rescue the future Queen? It doesn't matter. She makes me sick. I need to get away from her. Still carrying Calla, I make my way through the bedlam over to The King and Queen. Standing close to Charming, they hold hands in silence, awaiting Gallant's return. Worry is etched deep into their faces.

Suddenly, Midas bolts into action to help a villager fill up a bucket with water from the nearby well. Rolling up his sleeves, he immediately gets to work.

The King looks our way as he fills up yet another bucket. With a sincerity that moves me, he says, "We must help these kind, brave people put out the fire."

"I want to help Grandpa," says Calla, wriggling out of my arms. The Queen joins the courageous little girl, and putting my hatred of Midas on hold, so do I. Charming, too, pitches in despite his burnt hands. We've formed an assembly line. The King catches Marcella slinking by us and tosses her a bucket. "I can't believe I'm doing a peasant's job!" I hear her mutter.

The laborious work gets my mind off the fate of Gallant and Cinderella. I don't stop, not even to wipe the sweat and soot off my face. And then, an enormous explosion almost knocks me off my feet. A fireworks-like display of embers shoots into the sky. Oh no! The main tower of the castle has collapsed!

"Cinderella's private quarters!" cries Charming.

"Papa's dead!" sobs Calla. I cradle her in my arms, but nothing I do or say can comfort her. An unbearable sadness swells inside me.

"We must call for a clergyman," says The Queen, her eyes brimming with tears. The King, near tears himself, draws her in close. Grief, as mighty as love, has united them.

Something moving slowly toward us catches my eye. A disoriented beast? Blinded by the dense smoke, I can't make it out. It gets closer, and finally, I can tell it's a person...a man... and he's carrying something...or someone...in his arms. Oh God! Please! Can it be...?

"Look!" I shout out, pointing in their direction.

"Papa!" It's Papa!" cries Calla. She scrambles out of my arms and races toward him. The King, hopeful yet skeptical, commands the rest of us to stay put.

We wait anxiously in silence. The minutes pass like hours. At last, The Prince returns to us, carrying Cinderella in his arms and Calla piggyback style on his back. He's weary and battered. Like a worn-out soldier returning from battle.

Our smoke-filled eyes connect. I so badly want to run up to him, caress his ash-covered hair, and bathe his seared face.

"Welcome back, son," says The King, clearly proud of his heroic would-be heir. The relieved Queen gives Gallant a king-size hug.

"I thought I'd never see you again, my darling!" chokes

Prince Charming, taking Cinderella into his arms. Even covered in head-to-toe soot, she's stunning. A pang of jealousy stabs me. Yet another beautiful princess rescued by a handsome prince.

Marcella darts up to Gallant and dramatically throws her arms around him. "My love, you had me so worried. I simply couldn't imagine my life without you!"

Of course, you were worried, you two-faced cow! You *could* imagine your life without him. NO humongous castle! NO closet full of extravagant gowns and matching shoes! NO kingdom to bow down to you. And NO Jane to do all your crap!

I'm burning up inside. The palace blaze meanwhile begins to subside. Miraculously, most of the castle has survived.

"Cinderella and Charming can stay with us while they rebuild their palace," Midas tells the Queen.

I think about my palace. I want to hate this man for destroying it. Instead, I'm moved by his kindness and strength.

Thanking villagers and servants for their help, Midas leads the way back to our coach. We haven't gotten far when a guard runs up to him. I don't believe my eyes. The Huntsman. Again! I quickly lower my head, not trusting the thick smoke to mask my identity.

"Your Majesty, we have apprehended a suspect."

"Bring him to me at once," The King commands. "I want to know who he is."

The Huntsman rushes off and then returns with the suspect in chains. Except the suspect is not a he; *it's a she*. Holy crap! It's Sasperilla!

"It's you again!" says Prince Charming, his voice shaking. "I should have known. Why can't you leave us alone?"

"I'll never leave you two alone until you're MINE!" shrieks the stalker, scary-skinnier than ever.

Foaming at the mouth, she lunges at Cinderella. The Huntsman, acting quickly, pulls her back. She lunges again. This time at me. Her wretched eyes clash with mine. She recognizes me! I stand frozen in time as she shoots me that same scathing smirk she's sent my way so many times before.

I'm doomed! She's going to reveal my identity. In a matter of moments, everyone will know I'm The Evil Queen! Just as the sicko's parched lips part, The Queen of Hearts roars.

"Off with her head!"

Off with her head! Oh my God! I know how I know this woman. Of course! She's the hotheaded judge who sentenced me to one hundred years in that dark, dreary dungeon! One hundred years! How could I forget? Her hair's white now and she's two chins thinner, but still. Maybe, I didn't want to remember. But it's no wonder she hasn't recognized me. I *am* so different now.

A sudden chill in the air sends a shiver through me. Is this all meant to be? That The Prince's father is the man who took away my castle….and his mother, the woman who took away my life. Seven years of it! I should destroy them for what they did to me. But strangely, I feel no hate. I feel no anger. All I feel is emptiness.

Midas wraps his ample arm around his wife. "Dear, let's not go that far! You don't want to go back to anger management classes." The Queen inhales deeply and calms herself down as The King orders The Huntsman to take Sasperilla away. "Lock her up once and for all. No more second chances!"

Poor Elz! How will she feel when she finds out about her sister? At least, Midas spared the skinny bitch her life—and The Queen mine, once again, in a way. I breathe a deep sigh of relief. Safe for now. But how long will it be before my past is revealed? I can't hide it forever.

The near-tragic night comes to an end. The King and The Queen walk toward the carriage, arm in arm. Prince Charming helps Cinderella mount his stallion and follows them. Gallant swoops up Calla in his arms and falls hopelessly under Marcella's spell yet again.

I'm left standing all by myself. Once more, I'm that little girl. Alone in the dark. Afraid of evil.

CHAPTER 31

The day of the ball comes fast and furious. Though exhausted from all of Marcella's demands, I wake up earlier than usual. Gallant's already downstairs in the kitchen when I get there. He's forgone his usual cup of tea yet he's especially upbeat and energized. Of course. Tonight, he and Marcella will at last officially announce their engagement to the kingdom. A heart wrenching pain hits me deep in my gut.

"Jane, there is something I need to show you," Gallant says eagerly.

I try to beg off. The ball's only hours away, and the last minute details are overwhelming. First on my list: Picking up Marcella's gown from Emperor Armando. Okay. The truth. I can't bear to be with him.

Gallant won't take no for an answer. I bet it's yet another last-minute thing Marcella wants done for the ball. I'm surprised when he instead leads me outside. His white stallion awaits us, ready to ride. He lifts me up onto the saddle, then mounts the majestic horse. This time I'm sitting in front of him, his brawny arms wrapped tightly around me. My heart is galloping. Where's he taking me?

As the sun rises, we trot down a familiar path. I know—the path that leads to his studio. Great! I'd love to see his paintings again. Maybe he's painted something new.

Gallant's been a different person since breaking the news to his father about his true ambition. He smiles often and laughs. I've even heard him sing. What a voice! Best of all, to Marcella's chagrin, he's been spending a lot more time with

Calla—playing with her, telling her stories, and helping her with her French. He even took her shopping at The Trove. Ha! You should have seen the expression on the PIW's face when her future stepdaughter came back with a coach full of new clothes—including a gown for the ball. So much for Calla not going and me having to babysit her.

I was right. Gallant has taken me to his studio. He unlocks the door and lets the early morning sunshine slip in. The streak of light makes the paintings more radiant than I remember. My eyes bounce from one canvas to the next. Each, be it a portrait, landscape, or still life, moves me more deeply than before.

The studio smells different this time. I can't identify the scent. Then I see an easel. Tubes of paint and various size brushes are scattered on it. Ah-ha. Gallant *has* begun to paint again.

In the back corner, the unfinished portrait of his late wife is still mounted on an easel and covered. Has he worked on it? Before I can ask, The Prince takes my hand and pulls me over to it. In a single swoop, he sweeps off the damask and reveals the canvas. Oh my God! I'm going to pass out!

Gallant has completed the portrait of his late wife. It's a masterpiece. A woman, whose beauty is beyond all others, smiles at me as she picks a bouquet of lilies and roses. Her wavy dark hair is held back by a big red bow while her matching red cloak floats in the summer breeze. What's most outstanding is her milky-white skin. It's fairer than the blooms she's holding.

The Prince beholds the painting with pride. "Jane, you inspired me to follow my dream, my passion. And to complete the painting that means the most to me."

I'm paralyzed. I can't get my mouth to move or my brain to think.

Gallant turns to me. "Jane, you look as if you have just seen a ghost. Are you okay?"

Am I okay? Is he kidding? I *have* seen a ghost. And not

just any ghost.

"I'm a little overwhelmed by the painting," I stammer. *A little overwhelmed?* That's got to be the understatement of all times. I'm in a state of shock!

"Be honest, what do you think?"

I think I'm going to die! I can't move. I can't breathe. I can't even feel my heart beating.

"Jane," he continues, "I want to hear your thoughts. You have such a keen mind when it comes to art."

"She's the most beautiful woman I've ever seen," I manage to say.

"Yes, she was," says Gallant with growing excitement. "Tell me more. What about the colors?"

"Th-they're perfect," I splutter. "Her skin's as white as snow; her hair as black as ebony, and her lips as red as blood."

"Amazing!" Gallant's blue eyes sparkle. "That is exactly what I wanted to convey."

The Prince pauses to smile at the portrait. "Jane, I am beholden to you. Completing this painting has made me feel whole again."

I, on the other hand, feel like a million little pieces. Like a jigsaw puzzle that can't be put together. Or a shattered mirror.

"I have even started to work on another painting," he adds, his face beaming.

Out of the corner of my eye, I glimpse another large canvas across the room—the beginnings of another portrait. I'm too shaken to focus on it.

"I've got to go." I hurry toward the door.

"Jane, wait!"

Gallant dashes after me. Hooking his arm around my waist, he stops me in my tracks. He spins me around and draws me to him. Our bodies meet. We're so close I can't tell whose heartbeat is whose. Cradling my face in one hand and holding me tightly against him with the other, he lowers his head and presses his lips on mine. Our tongues dance. A fire rips through my body, awakening every part of my being. It's like nothing I've ever felt before. No matter how much I will it, our lips will not separate. To be truthful, I don't want it to end.

Suddenly, The Prince pulls away. I feel like I've been catapulted out of a dream. My head is spinning, my body throbbing.

Gallant lowers his eyes and steps back. "I could not help myself. Please forgive me, Jane, if I have offended your honor or dignity."

Offended me? I've just kissed the husband of the woman I tried to murder! My stepdaughter. Gallant's wife. SNOW WHITE!

———⊸⊷———

I spend the rest of the morning pacing the castle in a state of total panic. My lungs are burning; my stomach's churning, and my head is whirling. I should be working on last minute ball preparations, but I'm too distraught from my shocking discovery. It's all I can think about.

Why didn't I figure it out? I should have known that The Prince's late wife was Snow White. I mean, the clues were in my face. Right there in front of me!

> **Clue #1**: Calla's snow white skin; A dead giveaway; no pun intended.

> **Clue #2**: Calla's red velvet bow. They're probably a dime a dozen, but still.

> **Clue #3**: That despicable Huntsman showing up all the time. A coincidence? Not!

> **Clue #4**: Those damn dwarfs. No wonder, they worked for The King.

Clue #5: That unforgettable night when The Prince, drunk out of his mind, called me Branch. Now, I know what he was trying to say— *Blanche,* French for white. Damn it! I wish my French didn't suck.

Clue #6: The cottage-y feel of the Prince's castle. Okay, it wasn't a giveaway, but still a clue.

Clue #7: The unfinished portrait. I should have recognized the outline of Snow White's signature cloak and bow.

Clue #8: Marcella's obsessive collection of old fairy-tale tabloids; they must be filled with Snow White gossip. Of course, she'd want to know everything about The Prince's #1 wife. With the exception of me, what #2 wife wouldn't?

Clue #9: One of the most obvious clues of all. No RSVP to the ball from Snow White. Dead people don't do balls.

Clue #10: My stupid-ass looking glass. No wonder, my "magic" mirror didn't mention Snow White's name in the dumpster. Duh! She was history!

And, of course, only her gorgeous little daughter Calla Rose could take her place. How could I be so stupid? So clueless! So totally clueless! If only in the dumpster, for that one time only, my mirror had been magic. It could have said something, and I wouldn't be in this horrible, horrible mess.

Questions pummel me like rocks, each one coming harder at me than the one before. What am I going to do? How can I stay possibly stay here? What am I going to tell The Prince? And Calla? *Oh, by the way, sweet girl, I forgot to tell you that I despised your mother and tried to kill her. Not once. But three times. Actually, four times if you count The Huntsman. Oh and do you want to hear something else? I kissed your Papa today! And guess what! I liked it!*

Who am I kidding? I *more* than liked it! It wasn't me who pulled away! Oh God, why did I have to run into The Prince this morning? Why did Shrink make me work at this castle? Why did I have to do rehab at Faraway? The Huntsman should have let me rot in that dungeon or done me in when he had the chance. None of this would have ever happened. None of it! This *wasn't* meant to be!

I'm an emotional wreck. I desperately need to talk to someone. Someone who can help me navigate my way through this miserable maze of confusion, guilt, and shame. *"Oh, Gallant, I've got a little confession to make…"* No, NOT The Prince! I need someone like Shrink who could listen with her "third ear" and offer me advice.

What's the point of dreaming? It's futile. There's no one I can talk to. *No one.* I've got to get my mind off what's happened. "Hard work makes strong minds," the Badass Fairies preached at Faraway. I compulsively start straightening and polishing everything in sight. When I glance down at the polished surfaces, I see my reflection. My evil self! Aagh! I try a couple of bars of "lalalala." That'll cheer me up. Forget it. I know. I'll try meditating. Perhaps, if I can silence my mind, I can…

"JAAAANE!" My meditation is shattered by Marcella's shrill scream. Still sitting cross-legged on the floor, I pop open my eyes and find her looming above me.

"Where's my ball gown?" she snaps. "And what are you doing in that ridiculous position?"

Oh no! I've totally forgotten about Marcella's gown. I've got to get to The Trove before it closes and pick it up from Emperor Armando.

The Trove! A glimmer of hope flashes before me. Yes! I'll talk to Winnie and Elz. They'll know what to do.

CHAPTER 32

T his is awful!" says Elz.
"It could be worse," says Winnie.

"How could it be worse?" I gasp. I've just relayed my recent, life-shattering events at an emergency meeting with my two best friends at Sparkles. A plate full of chocolate cupcakes lingers on the table. No one has taken a bite.

Thumbing her lips, Winnie ponders my question. Finally, she says, "You're right. This is bad. *Very* bad!"

Let's face it. My life is a disaster. A living nightmare beyond all nightmares. "What should I do?" I plead to my friends.

Elz thinks I should tell Gallant the truth. The truth is always better than not telling the truth. I remind her of the time she confronted her mother with her true feelings and sent her to her grave. Tears well up behind Elz's spectacles.

"How could you say that!" yells Winnie. "Especially after what happened last week with Sasperilla."

Yes, the fire was headline news. Elz bawled her eyes out over her sister's heinous crime. I hate myself for making the cruel comment about her mother. I apologize. I'm not in my right mind.

Truthfully, I'd be better off dead. I should stick my head in the hearth or jump into the lake with a boulder strapped onto my body. Wait! It's simple. I can whip up an evil potion—I'm sure I can rustle up the right ingredients—and chug it. I'll fall to the ground and die instantly. People will say I died by my own hand. She got what she deserved. That's it…

"I'm going to kill myself!"

"SHUT UP!" shout Winnie and Elz in unison. I've never seen them so angry with me.

"You're being irrational," says Winnie. "There has to be a reason why this is all happening."

I adore Winnie, but I've had it with her "everything's meant to be" attitude. Shrink had no clue what she was doing when she placed me in the Prince's household. There's only one reason this is happening: I'm evil! I'm being punished for all the terrible things I've done.

"Come on, Jane. Look on the bright side," she continues.

And enough with this bright side crap. For once, can she not say that? There is no bright side. I want to explode! Self-destruct!

"Winnie has a point," chimes in Elz. "He kissed you."

Oh God, the kiss! That unforgettable kiss. A fire resurges inside my body.

"What was it like?" asks Elz, with wide-eyed curiosity.

My heart pounds madly. The truth is, I've relived it all day. His mouth parting my mouth, my breath warmed by his, our bodies one.

"I can't explain it." The magical kiss that saved Snow White has awoken every fiber of my being. Yet, I'm at a loss for words.

"Why do you think he kissed you?" asks Winnie.

I don't know. I just don't know.

"I'll tell you why," says Winnie. "Because he's in love with you."

Her words reverberate in my head. *The Prince…in love with me?*

"And you, girlfriend, are in love with him."

Me…with him? Why does Winnie always have to be right? Oh my God! *I am! I'm in love!*

I burst into tears. Unstoppable, scalding tears.

"What should I do?" I splutter. "He's marrying Marcella!"

"Don't let him go," says Elz. "Your prince comes along

only once in a lifetime."

How does she know? Hook doesn't count.

"Elz is right," says Winnie, the relationship guru. "Don't let him go."

Don't let him go. The words whirl around in my head and cloud my thoughts. Only one thing is clear. If Gallant were mine, I could never live with myself knowing what I did to Snow White. *Never.* A greater force has conquered my desire. My conscience.

Remembering Marcella's gown, I leap up from the table without saying good-bye to my friends. Or thanking them for their advice. This time, girlfriends and chocolate did not have magical powers.

With tears storming down my face, I stagger about the mall, unsure if I'll make it to The Ballgown Emporium. I hate Marcella but hate myself more. So much more.

Armando's Ballgown Emporium is pure mayhem. It's packed with last minute shoppers, buying gowns for the ball. As I stumble into the store, I bump smack into The Queen of Hearts. Folded over her blubbery arm is an extravagant heart-print gown.

Trying to stay calm, I hastily curtsey before her. I keep my head bowed, hoping she won't notice my tear-soaked face. She doesn't.

"My dear, are you here to pick up your gown for the ball too?"

She actually thinks *I'm* going to the ball? *Me?* The woman whose head she wanted for the attempted murder of her late daughter-in-law?

My lips quiver. "Um, I'm actually here to pick up Marcella's gown."

"I understand she and Gallant are making a very important announcement tonight."

I fight back tears. Of course. Their engagement before the entire kingdom.

"Ta-ta," says The Queen with a dainty little wave. "See you at the ball."

Aided by a swarm of sprightly pixies, Armando is crazy busy with last minute alterations. He has a tape measure around his neck; a pair of shiny scissors in one hand and, in the other, a felt cushion filled with pins and colorfully threaded needles. Oh God! Why does the pincushion have to be a big red apple with bright green leaves? And remind me of Snow White?

As I'm verging on another onslaught of tears, The Emperor spots me. He sashays up to me, planting his signature kiss on both cheeks.

"Dahling, what's wrong?" he asks. "You look like you've lost the love of your life."

I *have* lost the love of my life. How did he know that? I catch a glimpse of myself in one of the mirrored walls. With my swollen red eyes and tear-streaked cheeks, I look beyond terrible. This is all too much for me.

"I'm here to pick up Marcella's gown," I say feebly, averting his question

"I just finished it!" He orders his pixie assistants to retrieve it.

With a thumbs up, the tiny fairies zip off. In seconds, they're back with the red satin gown. It takes more than a dozen of them to hold up the twenty-foot train, their wings drooping from the sheer weight of it. The Emperor relieves them of their burden.

"Isn't it to die for!" he gushes.

Totally. It's a work of art! Marcella will indeed be the belle of the ball. And how fabulous she'll look on Gallant's arm. Tears flood my eyes yet again.

The Emperor carefully places the gown inside a long,

protective muslin bag and folds it over my arm. It's almost as heavy as my heart.

"Dahling, I must go." He gives me a big hug. "I'll see you later."

Later? He must mean when Marcella shows up tomorrow to order her custom wedding gown. My blood churns.

"And dahling, please don't cry. It's so bad for your complexion," he shouts out as he rushes off to help a princess in distress.

Dragging the gown, I slump out of the store. A flurry of pixies surrounds me.

"Lalalala!" they sing in perfect harmony. "You've just won our 'Be Our Guest' sweepstakes." One of them hands me a flyer.

HOORAY FOR YOU!
Be our complimentary guest at
The Enchanted Spa.
Offer expires Sept. 30th

September 30th? That's today! My chest tightens. What am I going to do? The ball is just hours away. I've got to get back to the castle with Marcella's gown. And get her ready.

I read on about the spa's services...a relaxing aromatherapy massage with magic hot crystals...a soothing mineral bath in their mermaid lagoon...a deep cleansing facial. And that's just for starters.

God, this sounds divine. And it's all mine—FREE! Temptation gnaws away at me. Maybe, I can squeeze in a visit—it's exactly what I need to clear my head and figure out my complicated mess of a life. A little voice in my head says, "Go for it!" "GO FOR IT!" it says again, this time louder. Yes! Hooray for me! My decision is made.

The Enchanted Spa is all that I remember it to be and more. A luxurious, tranquil wonderland with creamy marble walls and floors, gurgling fountains, and lush lounging areas. Scented candles are everywhere.

Several gorgeous princesses, holding muslin bags like mine, are reading beauty magazines on a plush velvet divan. One of them looks up at me and makes a horrified face. Do I look *that* bad?

I recognize the front desk receptionist—that peachy-skinned nymph from my previous brief visit. Her head is buried in her reservation book. "What time is your appointment?" she asks me, without lifting her head.

"I don't have one."

"Sorry. We're all booked up today because of the ball."

I slap the flyer down in front of her. She takes one look at me and shakes her head. "I'll squeeze you in."

I *must* look that bad. My fairest days are definitely over.

"Beauty is our duty," says Miss Peaches and Cream. She tosses me a white fluffy robe and whisks me off to my first treatment…a deep cleansing facial.

Inside a small, sterile room, an attractive woman, who calls herself Fiora, plunks me down on a pink leather reclining chair. She applies a hot towel to my face. It feels good.

"Beauty is pain," she says. Removing the towel, she squeezes my pores.

OWW! She wasn't kidding.

"Your complexion is beautiful," she says, still poking my face. "I know so many princesses who would kill to have skin like yours."

The irony of her words tenses up every muscle in my body. I think of Snow White again. Of how I so envied her fair skin. Her incomparable beauty. I wanted her dead, out of my way. My body quakes. How can I ever face Gallant again?

I can't get Snow White out of my head. That is, until Fiora transforms into an ogress right before my eyes. I almost fall off the chair from shock.

"Don't freak. It happens every day at this time," she says. "My husband loves me this way. He's an ogre too."

I don't want to know more. Then I make a connection. That dumb-ass dungeon guard—more bad memories!—was an ogre. He told me his wife worked at a spa and got all the latest beauty magazines free. It had to be Fiora! This is too freaky. Why is this all happening?

Fiora slaps my face. "Very good for circulation." Then she tells me my facial is over.

I can barely stand up. My face stings. And my body is a contorted bundle of nerves. Maybe coming here was a bad idea.

"You desperately need a massage," says Fiora.

No kidding.

She escorts me to another similar room where Urma, a brawny woman with inky-blue spiked hair and a strand of coral beads around her neck, awaits me. She has eight strapping arms like an octopus. I guess the more the better for a killer massage.

She orders me to remove my robe and lie face down on a body-length, padded table. I take off everything except Shrink's mirrored locket and Rump's name bracelet. These gifts never leave me. *Ever.*

"Are you going to *zee* ball tonight?" Her heavily accented voice is deep and raspy.

"Yes," I lie. I'm in no mood for conversation.

"It *eez* fundraiser for Faraway," she says. "Very worthwhile cause. I was sea witch before rehab there."

Octo-mama's a Faraway grad? This is beyond weird.

"You, very stressed out." She rubs some warm, soothing oil on my back. "I give you Urma's enchanted deep tissue massage."

With her eight powerful hands, she begins to knead my body like dough. Angst oozes out of me. I'm beginning to feel relaxed and wonderful. I only hope she doesn't imagine her worst enemy and press too hard. Too late! I yelp as she pounds the base of my spine. Surprisingly, she releases a lot of tension.

Half way into the massage, she scatters hot crystals on my back. "Sea salt," she says.

The crystals must be magic because all my problems miraculously melt away. I feel like a new person.

"I throw *een* aromatherapy for you." She dabs some warm oil under my nose. "Take deep breath and relax."

I inhale. The aroma of the oil rushes into my nostrils and jolts me upright. It's a blend of lilies and roses. The essence of Snow White! My anxieties charge back into my body like an onslaught of flaming arrows.

Urma tells me I look faint; she says many of her clients get lightheaded after her deep tissue massages. "You need restorative mineral bath—hydrotherapy."

Wrapping her eight strapping arms around me, she practically carries me to my next stop—a tropical lagoon. A dozen gorgeous twenty-something women are soaking in the hot, bubbly water—probably all rich, spoiled princesses wanting to be the fairest at the ball. One of them is a pretty redheaded mermaid who waves at Urma, then at me. I ignore her.

Holding onto Urma to steady myself, I glide into the bubbling bath. AAAHH! The warm, soothing water unlocks every muscle in my body. I feel wonderful again.

Closing my eyes, I let the therapeutic water wash away all my worries. At last, there's no more Gallant, no more Marcella, and no more Snow White living in my head. I'm in a state of total nirvana.

A cheery voice snaps me out of my mindlessness.

"Hello," says a spa fairy, carrying a gilt tray. "Can I offer you a refreshing apple?"

A refreshing apple!? I almost vomit. The last thing I want to eat is an apple! Forget massage therapy, aromatherapy, or hydrotherapy. I need real therapy. I need Shrink! Help! Get me out of this place!

But I can't leave. I'm a prisoner! Two portly one-eyed

ogres yank me out of the water and drag me to the sauna. One of them pours water over the hot rocks. The other adds a drop of eucalyptus, a scent I recognize from Faraway's Enchanted Forest. An invigorating steam fills the chamber.

Sitting on a cedar bench, I inhale deeply. On the exhale, I once again feel tension release from every part of my body. A woman, wearing a white towel, matching turban, and blue facial mask, sidles over to me. The steam clouds my vision, but I can tell she could stand to drop a few pounds. Or more.

Plopping down next to me, she says, "I bet you're going to the ball tonight."

That voice! I recognize it instantly. Oh no, no, no, no, no! It's Marcella! What is she doing here? Then I remember. When we went shopping, I arranged a spa day for her—on the afternoon of the ball—just like she requested on her To-Do List.

In a panic, I bury my head between my sweaty knees so she doesn't recognize me.

"It's going to be divine. I planned the whole thing myself," she continues.

You planned it? You didn't do a damn thing, you lazy cow.

"What are you wearing?" she asks.

"Something plain and simple," I mumble, masking my voice. "I'm actually a reporter covering the event for the *Fairytale Tattler*. What made me say that?

"Perfection! Emperor Armando custom-designed my gown. You're going to die when you see it."

I have seen it. And you're not going to be able to get your fat ass into it!

"Well, since you're a reporter for the *Tattler*, I might as well give you the scoop since my waste-of-time assistant didn't."

Her waste-of-time assistant!? I want to drown her in her sweat.

"Tonight, Prince Gallant's going to make a very important announcement."

A very important announcement. The exact words spoken earlier by The Queen of Hearts.

"He's going to say 'I do' in front of the entire kingdom. Well, at least, everyone who's anything. We're getting married!"

They're getting married? Her words hit me like a firing squad. I'm going to black out.

"You're hyperventilating," says Marcella. "You've probably been in here too long."

Way too long. I can't cope with this. Any of it! I've got to get out of here. Now!

Dripping with sweat, I spring to my feet and sprint out of the sauna. Marcella's shrill voice trails behind me. "See you at the wedding."

The spa *was* a bad idea. A really, really bad idea.

CHAPTER 33

W here have you been?" shrieks Marcella. "And why does your skin look better than mine?"

I shuffle into her chamber, her red gown in its bag draped over my arm. I don't know or care how she got back to the castle before me. My shock, rage, and despair have succumbed to numbness.

Clad in her feathered leopard negligee, she's seated at her vanity, doing her makeup. I catch a glimpse of her face in the mirror. With her plaster-white skin, blood-red lips, and serpentine brows, she looks more like a monster in the making than a bride-to-be.

"I spent a fortune at that ridiculous spa," she hisses. "Why didn't you make them throw in free makeup and hair?"

Choosing to ignore her, I silently hang the bag with her gown over her closet door. Her chamber is a pigsty. It's as if never existed. Her bed's a mess; clothes are strewn every-where, and fairy-tale tabloids are scattered all over the floor. Straightening things up, I come across an old front-page story that makes my heart jump:

SNOW WHITE TESTIFIES: EVIL QUEEN DOOMED!

A Fairytale Tattler Exclusive by H.C. Anderson

The Evil Queen, charged as a possible suspect in the near-fatal poisoning of Snow White, was convicted today. Minutes before sentencing, Prince Gallant, who saved the beautiful princess—often thought to be the fairest in the land—told reporters, "I hope The Evil Queen gets what she deserves."

Oh, God. I have gotten what I deserve. Death would have been a kind punishment compared to what I'm suffering now. I force myself to read on.

Medical tests have revealed that The Evil Queen poisoned Snow White with a rare snake venom, that caused her to go into a deadly, deep sleep.

Snake venom? Wait a minute. This shoddy reporter got his facts all mixed up. My evil potion, the one I used for the apple, was made with powdered stinkweed, bulbadox juice, and dragonstone extract. I didn't use any snake venom. Not a single drop!

Before I can read more, Marcella eyes me in the corner of her vanity mirror. "This is no time to be reading gossip magazines!" she snaps. "You're supposed to be dressing me!"

I let go of the magazine and slump over to her gown. Carefully, I remove it from the garment bag. The long train puddles on the floor.

Marcella gives it the once-over. "Perfection! Now, get me into it."

Ripping off her negligee, she exposes her corseted body. My eyes pop. Who knew what really lurked beneath that towel in the sauna. Her tummy bulges as if it's hiding a loaf of bread; saddlebags line the sides of her cottage cheese thighs, and her cannonballs are the size of small planets. She's easily gained fifteen pounds, thanks to my high caloric diet potion. Yet, another one of my brilliant plans gone bad. Getting the skank into her slinky gown is going to be a lot harder than I imagined. A contest of mind over matter. War.

Then, *ding*, a little bell goes off in my head as I'm undoing the fastenings. So what if it doesn't fit her? She won't have a wedding gown. No gown. No wedding. I'll be the victor. And to the victor belongs the spoils. Could I...?

"What are you waiting for?" growls Marcella, cutting my tempting thoughts short. Impulsively, she grabs the gown out of my hands and steps into it, feet first. She slides it up her legs. Damn it. So far, so good. But once it gets to her hips, it won't budge. Not even an inch.

"Do something!" she screams.

"Squeeze your butt. And suck in your gut," I tell her. *Good luck.*

Ha! No matter how hard she squeezes or sucks, the dress won't give. Losing her patience, she begins to yank at it, stretching it in every direction. The taut sound of seams bursting sends a shiver down my spine.

No matter how much I hate her, no matter how much I cannot bear the thought of her marrying Gallant, I can't let her destroy Armando's masterpiece. *I can't.* With both hands, I pull the dress down. It bunches on the floor like a red ball of fire.

"What have you done?" she screeches. "I'm going to be late for the ball!"

She splays her knuckly fingers across the bulges of her corseted hips. Eyeing her monstrous, flashy diamond, I get an idea. A brilliant one.

"This is going to work." I smile wickedly. With a single yank, I pull in the strings of her corset, so tightly that her eyes bulge out of their sockets.

"What are you doing?" she gasps.

Isn't it obvious? I'm suffocating you, wench!

Marcella moans. A memory of Snow White flickers in my head. This is exactly how I once tried to kill her. I tremble and quickly loosen Marcella's corset.

She lets out a deep breath.

What's wrong with me? I just had the opportunity to kill the woman who's made my life so miserable and is marrying the man I love. But I didn't.

Marcella's expression turns to rage. "Get the dress on me. Now!"

My eyes travel up and down her distorted body. It's time for a new plan of attack. I tell her to step out of the gown that lies crumpled at her feet.

"Now what?" she snaps.

I detach the long red satin train and lay it lengthwise on her bed. Then carefully, I slip the gown over Marcella's head and gently pull it down.

"You're going to ruin my hair and makeup!" she shrieks.

Truthfully, I'm much more concerned that her over-the-top makeup will ruin Armando's work of art. I pass the first hurdle—getting the gown past her cannonballs. Very carefully, I edge it over her balloon of a belly. Success again. And then, the final challenge—getting it past her fat ass. Slowly, with little tugs, I manage to lower the gown to her feet. The feeling of victory eludes me as I reattach the twenty-foot train.

Shoving me aside, she struts up to her vanity and admires herself in the mirror, oblivious to her rolls and bulges.

"Perfection!" She blows a kiss at her reflection. "Gallant will love it."

The mention of Gallant's name makes my heart ache. I fight back tears. *Why didn't I pull those strings until she dropped? Why?*

"Jane, I need my shoes!"

I should have killed her.

Reluctantly, I search her room-size closet. There must be over three hundred boxes of shoes, stacked helter-skelter plus another two hundred pairs scattered all over the floor. Thank goodness for Elz's innovative glass coffin shoeboxes. I spot the ruby slippers right way.

Marcella snatches the shoes from me as I step out of the closet. She cuddles them, then tosses them onto the floor. I enjoy every grunt and groan as she tries to squeeze her big feet into the dainty shoes. No luck. She tries stretching them to make the fit. No luck.

"Jane!" she yells. "My feet are swollen. Why didn't you get me a foot massage?"

Ha! She'll never get her Size 9 feet into the Size 6 shoes.

"Don't just stand there! Get me a bucket with hot water so I can soak my feet!"

Biting my lip to keep from laughing, I scurry to her powder room.

When I return with a bucket of water, Her Royal Skankiness is glued to her bed, massaging her red, swollen feet. I set the bucket on the rug. She plunks her feet inside.

"AAAAGH! This water's scalding hot." She yanks her feet out of the bucket.

I deserve a big laugh after all I've been through today, but I refrain.

"Quick! Get me my *Miracle Foot Potion,*" she shouts. "It's in the medicine cabinet."

I hurry back to the powder room. I search the cabinet above her sink but only find makeup. About to leave empty-handed, I notice that the large cabinet against the wall, which is usually locked, is ajar. Could her *Miracle Foot Potion* be inside?

Whoa! This is no ordinary medicine cabinet. It's practically a factory of potions, lotions, and herbs. Crammed with my bogus *Lose Pounds Fast* diet potion is a slew of other magical potions. To name just a few:

> ***Forever Young Youth Potion****: Knock years off your age. Use daily for best results.*

I shake the bottle. There's nothing left.

> ***B-Cup No More Potion****: Rub gently on breasts and watch them grow before your eyes. CAUTION: DO NOT OVERUSE.*

Obviously, the skank didn't read the warning.

> **Smooth and Silky Skin Potion**: *Apply liberally all over. Gets rid of dry scaly skin. Important! Use frequently to prevent scaly build up and recurrence.*

> **Go-Blond and Beautiful Hair Potion**: *Covers unsightly gray and leaves hair manageable. Blondes have more fun!*

I knew it! She's one big fake! Her hair, her skin, her boobs. And I'm sure that's not all. I shudder. I bet her love for The Prince is fake too! But what does it matter? She's marrying him in a matter of hours. Sadness and despair tear through me again. I clench my stomach.

"Jane, what's taking you so long?" I hear Marcella screech. "I need my *Miracle Foot Potion*!"

I try to focus. Randomly, I pick up another bottle

> **Love Potion #13**: *Put magic into your relationship. Brew daily for long-lusting results. Expires 9/30*

I wrench it open. The scent of the herbs rushes to my nose. I recognize it instantly—a blend of orange blossoms, rose petals, and lavender. The tea Gallant drinks for breakfast! Oh my God! Marcella *has* had him under a spell! What am I going to do? The effects wear off today, but it may be too late!

Marcella screams at me again. Panic-stricken, I grab another bottle.

> **Magic Lip Plumper Potion**: *Apply liberally for fuller, more kissable lips. He won't be able to resist!*

Choke! The thought of Gallant kissing Marcella sends me over the edge. I want to rip the slut's phony fat lips right off her face, pull out her bottle-blond hair, and punch her inflated boobs. I feel evil! So over-the-top evil! And there are no little voices in my head telling me what *not* to do. Damn it! Why didn't I create a potion to end her life a long time ago?

Brainstorm! One of these potions *has* to be poisonous, and I'm going to find it. I'll take the slut by surprise and force it down her throat. *Drink it and die, bitch!* I can't wait to see her take her final breath. I'll blow her a kiss good-bye. Then I'll cover my tracks with a fake suicide note. Something simple like...*Dear People: Changed my mind about marrying The Prince. He didn't really love me. So I took my life. Love—M.*

Yes! I'm back to being an evil genius! So much for rehab. It was a total waste of time.

Madly, I tear through the racks of potions, examining one bottle after another. Damn it! Nothing! Then, unexpectedly, I come upon her foot potion.

> ***Miracle Foot Potion***: *Heals, soothes, and smoothes swollen feet. Satisfaction Guaranteed.*

I look closely at the fine print. *"Caution! Poison! Keep out of the reach of children!"*

The sweet irony of it all! It's funny how things sometimes work out for the best.

I wrench the bottle open and take a whiff. Whoof! Nasty stuff. I can't wait to pour it down the skank's throat. Ha! I'm finally going to give her a dose of her own medicine. A fatal one!

Suddenly, my hands shake. Violently. The bottle slips out of my fingers and crashes to the floor, cracking in half. A rancid odor fills the room as I numbly watch the potion snake across the tiles.

"Look what you've done!" screeches a voice behind me.

I wheel around. Marcella. Barefoot in her red gown. The train trailing out the door.

"Rub some on my feet. Now!" Her voice is as toxic as the potion.

Still quivering, I squat down and smear the potion all over her skanky feet. I ask myself for the second time: *Why? Why didn't I kill her when I had the chance?*

A nauseating mixture of confusion, anger, and despair seeps into my veins as Marcella hobbles back to her chamber. She plops down on her bed. The dainty ruby shoes sit on the floor, waiting for a pair of feet to claim them.

I confess. I haven't prayed since I was a child. Why bother when my prayers for a loving mother were never answered. Now, it's all I can do. To pray. To pray that her *Miracle Foot Potion* doesn't work. That she'll never be able to get her bone-ugly feet into the dainty ruby slippers. It's the only hope I have left to stop her from going to the ball. And from marrying Gallant before the effects of her love potion wear off.

I hold my breath as she steps into the shoes. She wiggles her feet; she pushes. She wiggles again, pushes harder. She grunts. She groans. I smile slyly, but not for long. To my utter astonishment, the skank manages to stuff her big, red, puffy feet into the little slippers.

"Ha!" She smiles triumphantly. "They fit like a glove."

A miracle. My heart sinks like a boulder.

Marcella parades again before the mirror. I hate that mirror! I want to bash it. Instead, I dash out of her chamber before I dare do it.

Marcella screams at me. "Get back here!" I shut my ears to her shrill cry.

After tonight, Marcella will no longer be a PIW. She'll be a real princess. Gallant's princess. Tears spill from my eyes.

Marcella yells out to me again. "Jane, one last thing. Remind me to fire you after the ball."

———⋙———

Gallant is downstairs at his desk, sketching. My heart flutters. How handsome he looks in his navy velvet suit and white blousy shirt, opened far enough to expose his tawny, chiseled chest. He gazes up at me with a fleeting smile. I blink back tears and meet his eyes. I so desperately want to run over to him and sink my body in his. The only thing that's stopping me is shame. That and the fact that he's marrying another in a matter of hours.

Calla skips down the staircase and breaks our tense silence. Clutching Lady Jane in one hand, she runs over to her father to give him a hug. Her beauty has no equal. In fact, she's more beautiful than ever, in the gown Gallant bought her—a white lacy confection that's accented with a yellow satin sash. The sash matches her golden curls, that are held back by her ever-present red velvet bow…the bow that once must have belonged to Snow White. How much she resembles her mother, with her flawless alabaster skin, rosebud lips, and twinkling chocolate eyes. An insufferable pang of guilt stabs me. How could I have…?

"Jane, why aren't you dressed for the ball?" asks Calla.

Caught off guard, I falter for an excuse.

"Big parties are not my thing." *That sounded stupid.*

"But you came to my birthday party!" *She's got me.*

"I don't really know how to dance." *That sounds better though not true.*

"I can teach you!" *She's got me again.*

"I have nothing to wear." *Well, that's the honest truth.*

"You can borrow something from Marcella." *She's got a point.*

"I don't think she'd like that," I stammer. Truthfully, I can't imagine myself in any of Marcella's sleazy gowns. Except for The Emperor's magnificent creation with a few major alterations.

Aware she's getting nowhere with me, Calla turns to her father and implores him to make me go the ball. I wonder if she knows that it's more than a ball. That tonight she's getting a new mother. Marcella!

Gallant's face lights up. "Jane, it would be an honor to

have you as my guest."

My gaze meets his. I'm burning up with desire. Even my conscience can't quell the flames.

"Thank you, My Lord," I say, holding back tears *and* my body. "But honestly, I don't want to go." *Liar!* "Plus, I can use the night off to catch up on some of Marcella's chores."

"Did I just hear my name?" comes a coy voice from the staircase.

Marcella! She slithers down the steps, the long train of her gown trailing behind her.

"My love, do you like it?" she asks, stopping to pose in front of her husband-to-be.

Color drains from Gallant's face, and his eyes morph into sharp blue daggers. I've never seen him like this before. Can her spell possibly be over?

"Where did you get that?" he demands, his voice powered by anger.

"At The Ballgown Emporium. It's an Emperor Armando original."

"No, that!" He points to the long red velvet cloak that she's added to her ensemble. I recognize it immediately and shudder.

"Oh, I borrowed it from your closet. It goes so well with my outfit. Don't you agree, my love?"

"Take that off. NOW!" Each word is a sharp staccato. "That cloak belonged to Snow White!"

"Whatever," says Marcella, not the least bit miffed. She unhooks the fastening and lets the cloak slide off her.

The Prince catches it before it falls to the floor. Cradling it in his arms, he lowers his lips to it. My body goes numb. This time his kiss will not magically bring back Snow White from the dead.

Gallant turns to me. Guilt and shame consume me. I can't look at him.

"Jane, please put this cloak back where it belongs after we leave," he says stiffly.

"Yes, My Lord." I cannot tell him how much I dread touching it.

As he hands me the cloak, our fingers interlock over the blood-red velvet. His heat courses through my veins, searing every part of me. I try to pull my hand away, but he won't let it go.

"Jane, please come to the ball," begs Calla again, this time clasping her little hands in prayer. "Pretty please with a cherry on top?"

"Get over it child," snaps Marcella before shooting a wicked smile my way. "Servants do not attend wed—I mean, balls."

Her words slice me like razors. I turn my head so neither Gallant nor Calla can see the tears forming in my eyes.

"We're late!" shrieks Marcella. She yanks The Prince away from me and shoves Calla to the front door where their coach awaits them. Calla glances back at me, unable to mask her disappointment.

I long for Gallant to turn his head.

He doesn't. He doesn't. He does!

I hold his gaze in mine as if I'll never see him again. Then he's gone.

"These shoes are killing me," I hear Marcella moan outside. So much for "Satisfaction Guaranteed." *I hope you suffer all night!*

Clickety clack. Clickety clack. The sound of the coach fades into the distance. I bury my head in Snow White's lifeless cloak and cry.

CHAPTER 34

The cooks have the night off. Technically, I have the night off, too, since Marcella's not here. I should enjoy my freedom, but instead, the great swimmer is drowning in a sea of sorrow. The thought of Gallant marrying that woman is suffocating me, pulling me under. But what does it really matter? Even if he doesn't really love her. A colossal wave of hopelessness washes over me. The truth is, I can't hide from my past forever. Eventually, Gallant will find out. The minute he learns that I'm The Evil Queen, the witch who tried to kill his beloved late wife, I will no longer be Jane. My life, as I know it now, will be over. I'll be as dead to him as Snow White.

Tears pour down my face. I don't know if it's heartache or shame. There's only one thing I can do. I cannot wait until Marcella fires me. Or until my past is revealed. I must leave this house at once. Before Gallant returns from the ball. Before I ever have to face him again.

With my eyes watering, I pack my bag. It doesn't take long as I have few belongings. Where will I go from here? With my castle a forgotten dream, I'm not sure. All I know is that by morning, I will be far away, moving on to another chapter of my life. Putting this all behind me.

Just one last thing I have to do—write The Prince a note. He deserves to understand my actions. And maybe, just maybe, it will give me a sense of closure.

Slowly, I make my way to his desk, every step an effort. The sketch he was working on faces me. It's a portrait of

Calla. My beautiful, sweet girl. Carefully, I tear it out from his pad and place it in my bag next to my treasured "Best Friends Forever" card from Elz. I'll cherish my memories of Calla forever.

Lowering myself to his desk chair, I gently tear out a clean sheet of parchment from the sketchpad and put a quill to it.

"Dear Gallant," I begin. This is not easy. Tears flood my eyes and fall onto the words I've written. I watch as they dissolve into an illegible black blur, a fitting reminder of my miserable life.

I rip out another sheet and start over. Brushing my tears away, I write my farewell letter.

> *Dearest Gallant~*
>
> *By the time you read this letter, I will be gone. I can no longer bring myself to stay in this house and be of service to you and your family.*
>
> *I have a confession to make. Several years ago, I caused your late wife Snow White great harm. It's too painful for me to go into the details, but rest assured, I am profoundly sorry for the grave damage I caused. I can only pray that you'll find the strength in your heart to forgive me.*
>
> *I will never forget my stay here and the kindness you have shown me. Most of all, I will miss Calla. She's a very special little girl. Please give her my love and take good care of her. I hope you and Marcella live happily ever after.*
>
> *Forever~Jane*

I put down the quill and read over my letter. Tears blur my vision, but I'm careful not to let them spill onto my words.

They're perfect, but what made me write "Forever~Jane"? I could have signed it, "Sincerely," or "Best Wishes," or even "Good-bye." Instead, I chose "Forever." Whatever. It's written. I fold the letter, seal it in an envelope with my tears, and place it in the top desk drawer. Some day, My Prince will find it.

My tears subside. I take a deep breath and close my eyes. The ball. I can picture it in my head. All eyes are on Marcella in her gorgeous scarlet gown. On the outside, she's all smiles, but inside she's dying in her three sizes too small shoes. Suddenly, her feet give out. She's going down! Yes! And then, no! Just in time, Gallant comes to her rescue, scooping her up in his arms. He carries her up to the altar where The King pronounces them husband and….

I snap open my eyes, and the dam holding back my tears crumbles. An endless river rages down my face. I wish I were at the ball! I wish I could stop Gallant from marrying Marcella! I wish! I wish! *Damn it, Jane. Just admit it. I wish it were me!*

I can't stop the tears. Searching for something to wipe them away, I find one of Gallant's handkerchiefs tucked inside a drawer. I dab my face. Its heavenly scent reminds me of the time he tenderly bandaged my burnt hand and brings on more tears. Other memories swirl around in my head. Our first encounter…My "sea monster" adventure with Calla… That outrageous night of drunken folly…And then, that one unforgettable kiss.

Oh, God. How I ache to peer into his jewel-blue eyes, to feel the ripple of his muscles beneath his shirt, to caress his saffron hair. Most of all, I want to kiss him. One more time before I leave. One last time. I no longer need to fool myself. I know why I signed the letter "Forever~Jane." Because simply, I will always love him. *Forever*, as in as long as I live.

My tears puddle on the floor. Heaving, I tell myself I must leave. *I must.* I take a deep breath, and finally, I head toward the front door for the very last time. *Good-bye, My Prince.*

Good-bye!

"Dahling, do you need another hankie?"

Startled to hear a familiar voice behind me, I spin around before I have a foot out the door. Standing before me is Emperor Armando, in a long white sparkly robe and a matching cone-shaped hat. A hankie is one hand and a shopping bag in the other.

My teary eyes are as round as marbles. "What are you doing here?" I sniffle.

He gives me his signature double cheek kiss. "Fashion guru by day; Fairy godmother by night!"

He's a fairy godmother? Okay. Whatever. So happy to see him, I throw my arms around his bear of a body and bury my face in his cushy chest.

"Careful, dahling, don't ruin my new outfit with your tears. It took weeks to make!"

I take his hankie and blow my nose. After one giant honk, my tears subside.

The Emperor looks me over. "My little muse, we're going to have to work quickly to get you to the ball on time!"

The ball? I'm going to the ball? Huh!?

"Dahling, I hope you like it." Like *what?* What is he talking about?

I'm even more mystified when The Emperor pulls out a shiny sewing needle from a pocket. "Say hello to my magic wand."

He must be kidding.

He waves the needle over me. Just as I expected, nothing happens.

"I don't get it." He frowns. "I can work magic with a sewing needle at my emporium."

"Maybe you have to say an incantation. Or it's not big enough," I murmur, skeptical of his powers.

"Good thinking, dahling." He squeezes his eyes closed. "Ippity-bippity-boppity-boo. Make this needle as big as can be."

"I thought incantations had to rhyme."

The Emperor opens his eyes. "Cut me some slack, dahling. This is the first time I've come out as a fairy godmother. I haven't gotten the rhyming part down."

It doesn't matter. The two-inch needle morphs into a two-foot glow stick! I gasp.

"Dahling, let's try this again." The Emperor waves the sparkling wand over me.

Nothing happens. I shrug my shoulders. Suddenly, a shower of fairy dust pours over me.

It *is* a magic wand! Before my eyes, my plain black dress transforms into a ball gown. An incredible ball gown!

"Whoever said 'it's not the size of the wand but the power of the magician that counts' should have his head examined," says The Emperor.

I gaze down at the gown. Two little spaghetti straps hold up a form-fitting bodice that gives way to cascading layers of silky black satin and tulle. Sparkles coat the top layer of tulle as if it's been dipped in fairy dust. It's the most magnificent dress I've ever seen.

"I call it my LBD—my Luscious Black Dress," the Emperor gushes. "I designed it especially for you."

"Can I really wear black to the ball?"

"Trust me, dahling," says the Emperor. "Black is the new pink. When all those frou-frou princesses see you in it, it'll be all the rage. I can't bear to think of how busy I'll be tomorrow!"

Tears of joy trickle down my cheeks. I expect the Emperor to brush them away, but instead he waves his magic wand over me one more time. I gasp again. My tears have turned into a magnificent pair of diamond teardrop earrings! They're floating before my eyes.

"FAAAbulous!" Armando clips them onto my earlobes. "They go perfectly with your bling."

I almost forgot about Shrink's locket. Still around my neck, it grazes my beautiful gown.

The Emperor glances down at my feet. "Sugarplum fairies! I almost forgot…these are from Elzmerelda. She says you've *got* to have them!" He reaches into the shopping bag.

Oh my God! It's the killer stilettos with the pointy toes and little bows. The wickedly beautiful, shiny black shoes I coveted! The Emperor places them by my feet. Holding onto his shoulder, I step into them. Instantly, I'm six inches taller.

"How do I look?" I ask.

"Let's face it, dahling. Everyone looks better with six more inches. Everywhere."

I would kill to see myself in a full-length mirror.

"Dahling, you don't need a mirror-shmirror on the wall to tell you that you'll be the chicest at the ball!"

How did he read my mind? And know what I used to imagine my "magic" mirror to say? Well, not exactly, but more or less. I suppose it's just another one of his magical powers. What's next?

"Now, let me see you walk," says The Emperor.

I've never walked in such high heels—or in such an extravagant dress. I teeter; I totter. My ankles wobble.

"There's no way I can do this!" Seriously, how does he expect me to walk in these shoes when I can barely balance in them?

"Dahling, come on now. Get in the moment. You can do it."

I try again and almost topple over. Forget it! I can't walk in them.

"Dahling, don't give up."

I force myself to take another step and then another. Yes! I'm doing it! I'm strutting in my killer heels and my LBD! In no time, I'm prancing like a cat.

The Emperor claps his hands with childlike glee. "I think I'm having a Cinderella moment."

I'm not quite sure what he means, but who cares. I'm ready to go the ball!

But wait! There's one little problem: how am I going to

get there? The coach that took The Prince, Marcella, and Calla is long gone. I wish I had a pumpkin and a couple of mice handy so The Emperor could do some more Cinderella magic. My heart sinks. I guess I won't be going to the ball after all.

"Dahling, stop worrying. They don't call me a clothes horse for nothing."

With one little jab of his magic wand, he magically transforms into a white stallion. My mouth drops. This is no ordinary horse. It's a sparkling unicorn with wings. And it can talk!

Straight from the horse's mouth come the words, "Dahling, time to PAR-tay!"

The equine emperor lies down, allowing me to mount him easily. Spreading his wings, Armando leaps to all fours and charges through an open window. I cling to his silky mane.

Holy crap! We're flying!

So much for my not-so-fairy-tale life. I'm going to The Prince's ball! As we eclipse the grinning moon, King Midas's palace, the crown jewel of Lalaland, comes into view. That's when reality throws a spear my way. I'm not going to your everyday fairy-tale ball. It's going to be the wedding of all times. Generations will read about it. Forever and forever.

My sky-high joy takes a nosedive. The Prince is marrying Marcella!

So much for *my* fairy-tale life

CHAPTER 35

I can't do this!" I tell Armando. The Emperor has transformed back to himself, and we're about to make our grand entrance into Midas's palace.

"I'm not even invited," I add, my blood pounding in my veins.

"Dahling, stop worrying. I'm on the A-list. And you're my guest."

The ball is in full swing. It's a glittering spectacle with everyone who's anyone in Lalaland. I marvel at how it's all come together, thanks in large part to me. Searching the crowd, I spot the Queen of Hearts mingling with King Midas; Cinderella sharing champagne with Prince Charming; and Calla frolicking with Lady Jane. Missing in action are Marcella and The Prince.

"Seriously, I can't do this," I whisper to Armando as we step onto the red carpet.

"Dahling, relax. Just stay in the zone. Head high and tummy in."

The Emperor interlocks his arm with mine. In my six-inch heels, I tower over him. I nervously play with my mirrored locket with my other hand.

A chorus of trumpets blows announcing our arrival. My stomach muscles clench.

"Royal Ladies and Gentlemen, the distinguished fashion

designer Emperor Armando and his guest…"

"The faaabulous Jane Yvel," bellows The Emperor.

The crowd gasps. I smile halfway. My confidence soars when I see Calla jumping up and down and waving at me. She blows me a magical kiss. A big smile spreads across my face. I *can* do this!

All eyes are on me as we do the walk. The Emperor, loving every minute of this spectacle, blows kisses to his adoring fans. He was right. They're all buzzing about my dress.

Without warning, my heart skips a beat, and I almost trip. Straight ahead of me is a vision in red. Marcella! And beside her, The Prince.

Gallant's eyes connect instantly with mine. He jerks his arm free from Marcella's grip and steps away. "Where do you think you're going?" shrieks the PIW.

Ignoring her, Gallant strides up to me. My heart flutters; my body trembles; my legs wobble. Thank goodness, The Emperor is holding me up.

The Prince clasps my hands and gently draws me close to him. In my six-inch heels, we're face to face. He gazes at me with his blue eyes, more vibrant than ever, and breaks into that dazzling smile.

"Jane, you look beautiful."

I'm tingling all over. For the first time in my life, I *feel* beautiful.

"Thank you, My Lord." I curtsey before him, one hand still in his.

He lifts my hand to his lips and tenderly kisses the back of it. My heart leaps to my throat.

And then it sinks to my stomach as Marcella lurches toward us in her three sizes too small shoes. Her twenty-foot train trails behind her, collecting dust along the way.

"What the hell is *she* doing here?" she asks Gallant.

"Language, language," scolds The Emperor. He inspects Marcella's ill-fitting gown and shakes his head side to side. "Dahling, you should have gotten the Size 12."

Marcella's jaw drops to her cleavage and doesn't move as The King makes an announcement.

"I want to thank all you all for being here tonight for this very special evening. Instead of gifts, my son, Prince Gallant, has requested you make a donation to a special cause that is close to my wife's heart and mine…"

Aghast, Marcella elbows The Prince. "But I registered for a palace full of stuff! You know how much I wanted that monogrammed silver chalice for my Liquid Diet…."

"Faraway!" The King says proudly.

Faraway?

Midas continues. "By supporting this venerable institution, you will make a difference in someone's life."

Actually, I do remember Midas mentioning something about Faraway and a fundraiser at that disastrous dinner last week. And so did Urma, my masseuse. I don't get it, but this is hardly the time for a little Q&A session.

The crowd applauds wildly and breaks into "Go, Faraway" cheers.

The King takes a humble bow. "Thank you all, my friends. Now let's get this party started!"

The orchestra begins to play. Marcella yanks Gallant onto the dance floor. My heart tanks.

"Dahling, shall we dance?" asks The Emperor. Not waiting for my response, he whisks me onto the dance floor and swirls me around to the flow of the music. I follow him with ease though I've never danced like this before. My eyes all the while stay glued on Gallant.

And across the expansive ballroom, his eyes stay locked on me. Noticing what's going on, Marcella's eyes shoot poison darts my way. Except they keep missing.

The music stops. Armando and I find ourselves brushed up against the soon-to-be newlyweds. Venom pours out of Marcella's eyes as Gallant's stay fixated only on me. My heart is slamming against my chest. Any second, it may actually spill out.

The music starts up again.

"Your Royal Highness, may I have the pleasure of dancing with your lovely Princess-in-Waiting?" asks Armando.

"The pleasure is mine," says Gallant brightly.

Marcella gapes. Before she can get out a single word, The Emperor waltzes her away. Crippled by her shoes, she can barely keep up with him. Her face contorts with agony. And if that's not enough, everyone keeps stepping on her long train.

Alone, Gallant and I gaze at one another, each afraid to make a move. My heart is throbbing. My knees are buckling. I don't know how much longer I can take it. Minutes feel like eternity. Finally, My Prince sweeps me away…

And I'm his Princess. Melting in his arms, I lose sight of everyone around me. My body follows his as if we're sewn together. As if we've danced this way forever somewhere in another world. A world where he's now taking me. I'm no longer in this ballroom, and my feet no longer touch the ground. I'm in heaven, floating with him across the clouds. Just like in my dream. Only this isn't a dream; it's really happening. And in place of a mask, I see the face of The Prince. My beautiful Prince.

The music stops and sends me crashing back to reality. The King has another announcement. Gallant grips my hands in his. His pulse is racing.

"My beloved royal friends, it is my pleasure to announce that tonight you will witness the marriage of my son, Prince Gallant, to his lovely princess to be, Miss Marcella Méchante."

My heart has just been tossed off a cliff. It plunges into darkness as Marcella hobbles up to Gallant. She shoves me aside. Everything inside me is dying.

Marcella grabs Gallant's hand. "Come, my love. It's time."

The Prince stands there motionless. And then he turns to look at me one last time. With such longing, I'm brought back to life.

"Do you, Marcella, take this man to be your lawful

wedded husband?" asks The King.

"You bet your royal… I mean, I do," says Marcella.

I'm dying again. How am I still standing?

"And do you, my son, take this woman to be your wife? To have and to hold from this day forward, for better or for worse, for richer or—"

"Hold it right there," butts in Marcella. "Your Majesty, can't we just cut to the chase!"

The Prince turns to face Marcella.

My heart is about to implode. It takes all I have to stay on my feet.

"Father, I d…"

Suddenly, a voice screams out from the crowd.

"Papa, you can't!" It's Calla! In tears, she runs up to her father and flings her arms around him.

"Beat it, you little imp," screams Marcella, grabbing Calla by the hair. Gallant forcefully shoves her away.

He lifts Calla into his arms. "What is it, My Little Princess?" he asks, his voice tender, loving, and full of concern.

"At my birthday party, I wished that you would marry Jane! Please, Papa. Pretty please! Make my wish come true!"

Gallant's eyes find mine in the crowd. The King turns my way. So does The Queen. Soon, all eyes are on me. My body doesn't know whether to freeze with shock or melt with joy.

Marcella is so red she clashes with her dress. "Ha! You little brat. You told your wish, and now it won't come true!"

Calla pokes her tongue out at the skank. Mentally, I do the same.

"You'll pay for that!" Marcella seizes Calla. The little girl screams.

"Marcella, let go of her!" pleads The Prince.

"You're too late, lover boy!" Marcella's raspy voice is almost unrecognizable.

To my horror, her skin starts to peel off like a snake's. Her face dissolves into a ball of wrinkles; her bottle-blond hair goes gray and wiry, and her plump lips grow thin and cracked. Her body shrivels, and her skin turns scaly. Even her cannonballs shrink, until they're no more than droopy, dried out sausages. Her minutes-ago clingy gown hangs loosely on her hunched, skeletal frame.

All her magic potions must be wearing off at once! She's turning into an old hag! But not just any old hag! Oh my God! This can't be happening! It can't! But it is! *She is turning into my mother!* My evil mother...Nelle Yvel!

The Prince stands frozen with shock as the woman, he almost married, grips Calla by the neck. Calla's porcelain face turns blue, her breathing shallow. She's suffocating! I can't let my mother hurt this precious child! *I can't! I can't!*

"You may have destroyed my life!" I shout. "But you won't destroy hers!"

Taking her by surprise, I plow into her and knock her to the marble floor. She lets go of Calla.

"Run, Calla!" I yell. Out of the corner of my eye, I see her run safely into Gallant's arms.

My mother staggers to her feet. "You bitch! You were always a problem child!"

"No, you witch!" I scream back. "I was always there for you!"

"No, you just got in the way! You were too beautiful for your own good."

Me? Plain Jane?

"I could have married a king if it wasn't for you!"

"I didn't—"

"Shut up! When that prick banned me from his kingdom, I vowed I would get revenge by destroying you. And that beautiful child of his."

What is she saying? That *she* always intended to kill Snow White?

Catching me off guard, she rakes her brittle fingernails down my face. I wince as warm blood trickles down my cheek. Another scar, but what's one more when I have so many.

Recharged, she goes at me with ruthless force. Kicking.

Clawing. Punching. Pinching. Defending myself against her vicious assault, I accidentally tear off the detachable train of her gown. It meanders across the room like a river of blood.

"You've ruined my dress!" she shrieks. "Now, you're really going to pay!" Slamming me to the floor, she claws at my beautiful black gown, shredding it to pieces.

"Stop it!" I scream. But she keeps at it.

I have no choice. Without thinking twice, I clamp my fingers around her withered neck and, with all my might, start squeezing the life out of her. I squeeze tighter and tighter. As she writhes and wheezes, a terrifying reality sets in. I'm strangling my own mother!

"You can't destroy me," she hisses.

"Yes, I can," I hear myself say. I've wrestled with evil long enough. Now, this battle must end.

Her face turns gray. Her body convulses. The heels of her ruby slippers bang to the beat of her life as it ebbs away. Transfixed, as if under a spell, I watch her take her final breath. Her body quiets, and her lips spread as if she's about to shoot me one last smirk.

Suddenly, a monstrous green and yellow snake bursts out of her mouth. I bolt back in horror as Gallant cries out my name. As it endlessly slides out, the lifeless shell of my mother disintegrates like a crumbling rock. All that's left of her are her ruby slippers and a heart-shaped mound of black dust. And the smell of rotted flesh.

As I struggle to my feet, the ghastly serpent—it must be fifty feet long!—slithers across the shimmering red train, heading straight toward The Prince. Its deafening hiss sends everyone running except the royal family. Gallant protectively shields Calla.

Lifting her head, the serpent lets out a loud, hoarse laugh. "I'm coming for you."

"Leave Calla alone. It's me you want," Gallant says stoically.

The hideous monster flicks her long, black forked tongue.

"Yes, my love, it is *you* I want."

My heart freezes in shock as she springs forward and snatches him. Coiling her body around him like a whip, she hoists him high into the air. Almost to the gilded ceiling of the multi-storied ballroom.

"Papa!" cries Calla. The King holds her back.

I watch with horror as my monster mother brandishes Gallant like a trophy. He tries desperately to twist himself free from her powerful grip. But it's futile.

"My love, it's finally time to say 'I do'." Her evil tongue grazes The Prince's strong chin. Repulsed, he jerks his head away. Our eyes meet, his burning into mine.

I read his lips. "Jane, I love you."

No one has ever said that to me before. *No one.*

My heart clenches as I cry out the words, "I love you too!"

"Gallant, my love, you belong to me!" hisses my mother.

"No, Mother, his heart belongs to me!" I shout back.

"Not this time, you wicked child." Her jaw opens wide, exposing her venomous fangs. They're as long and sharp as daggers.

My heart is thudding in my ears. I can't let her take My Prince away from me. I can't! With all the strength I can muster, I throw myself at her, attempting to tear her away from Gallant. The attack takes her by surprise. She lets go of Gallant, sending him flying. He lands head first in an unconscious heap. Crumpled and lifeless.

Calla screams. My heart stops. Oh my God! He's dead!

"Jane, Jane, Jane," my mother hisses. "Always messing up my life. It's time for you to pay for being born!"

Uncoiling, she goes after me with hell-bent speed. I run. Faster than I ever have in my six-inch heels. I'm almost safely out the door when the unimaginable happens. One of my heels catches in the shreds of my once voluminous dress. I go flying across the marble floor, landing next to Gallant.

My Prince! My poor darling Gallant! He's as pale as a corpse, yet he is as beautiful as ever to me. I gently run my fingers over the contours of his soft, peaceful face, making the outline of a heart. Red-hot tears tumble onto his ice-cold flesh. Heartache tears through me. I can't resist. Cradling his head, I lean in close to him. And kiss him. *One last time.*

His lips, still warm and delicious, melt every fiber of my being. *I love you, Gallant. I always will. If only my kiss could bring you back to me.* Magic exists. Maybe not in a mirror, but in my heart, I know it does.

Running my fingers through his tousled hair, I press my lips deeper into his. *Oh, please wake up! Please!* He doesn't move. Somewhere in my head, Calla's voice calls out to me, but I can't let go. I can't! And then, without warning, a waft of cold air blows on the nape of my neck, sending a chill down my spine. I twist my head around and gasp. My mother. The monster!

"Now, Jane, kiss your mother good-bye," she hisses in the same wicked tone I remember from my childhood.

Her breath of death is upon my cheeks. I'm terrified. *Oh, God. Think, Jane, think!* Without thinking, I rip off a shoe and scrape the sharp stiletto heel across her thick, scaly skin. The sharp sound of her leathery skin ripping apart is music to my ears.

She winces with pain, her head swinging wildly. "You evil girl! How could you do that to your mother?"

Ha! It was easy. I do it again. This time harder and deeper. A putrid green goo oozes out of her wounds. She sinks back to the floor, still twisting and turning. I slide back as she tilts up her head and glares at me with her wretched eyes.

"Jane," she hisses, her voice almost a whisper, "it's time to say good-bye to your mother." Her movement has reduced to a sporadic jerk. She's dying. But why does it sound like she's mocking me?

Suddenly, she springs back to life and whips her body around mine, so tightly I can't move. She's tricked me! And now, I'm her prisoner. Just like I was as a child.

"Why didn't you kill me before?" I ask, choking out the

words.

Her wicked eyes flicker like two bolts of lightning. "I would have but I needed you. To take care of that meddlesome imp."

And to do all her other shit just like I did as a child. If only my rage could empower me to break free of her bone-crushing grip.

She hisses. "Actually, I missed my big opportunity a long time ago. I should have finished you before I attempted to off that other imp."

Other imp? Then it hits me. That snake I encountered in the forest on my way to giving Snow White the poison apple.

"It was you in the tree?" I gasp.

She laughs wickedly. "Such fond memories." Her tongue flickers. "Too bad you don't have a big red juicy apple now. It would make such a nice dessert."

Her grip tightens. I can't move a muscle. Her cackling laughter echoes across the room as she crushes me with her powerful body. Oh the pain! As I fight for my life, other memories reel around in my head, before connecting like pieces of a puzzle:

The snake that spooked The Prince's horse the night of the duel…

The scary good-night story Marcella told Calla about the snake that ate children…

The snake that mute dwarf tossed off the cliff…Marcella caked with mud…

The rustling sound outside Gallant's studio and the intruder the previous night…

The *Fairytale Tattler* story about the rare venom that put Snow White into her deep sleep…

The deadly snake that ultimately killed the fair Princess in her garden…

How could I have not seen it until now? My mother is a cold-blooded murderer. She killed Snow White. And now, she's going to kill me!

That's it! Whatever it takes, whatever the consequences, it's time for her to come face to face with her evil self. Rolling side to side, I manage to wiggle one of my hands free from her grip of death. I tear Shrink's locket off my neck and snap it open.

"Look at yourself!" I shout.

I shove the tiny mirror into her monstrous face. Shocked by her reflection, she jerks away.

"Look what you've done to me!" she shrieks. Flailing madly, she loosens her grip around me.

"And look what you've done to me!" With both hands now free, I rip open what remains of my gown and expose a lifetime of scars, each a souvenir of her loathing. If she's going to kill me, she's going to face the truth. All of it!

"No, Mother, it's time for *you* to say good-bye to me."

At last able to free myself completely, I leap to my feet. With all the muscle-power I have left, I stab one of my killer heels deep into her head, smack between her wicked eyes. A volcanic burst of venom spurts out and spatters me. She lets out a deafening scream. Nothing stops me. I dig my heel into her again and again and again until I've made hole as big as the one she's left in my heart.

"Jane, you naughty girl," she hisses hoarsely. "It's time for another whipping."

Without warning, her thick tail whips around and whacks me with a force so great it sends me crashing to the floor. My head cracks against the cold marble as Shrink's locket goes flying out of my hand.

I can't move. I'm paralyzed. Unable to blink an eye, I

look up at my mother's viperous, split-open head hovering two inches above me. A repulsive mixture of venom and slime spews out of her puncture onto my face. She glowers at me with her wretched, jaundiced eyes, then flicks her evil tongue across the tip of my nose. Terror fills every crevice of my being.

"Say good-bye, Jane. It's such a shame we didn't get to know each other better."

As my mother's deadly fangs sink into my skin, an explosion rocks me. There's a flash of white light...Then blackness.

CHAPTER 36

Wearing layers of black tulle, I'm dancing miles high in the sky. I pirouette from one cloud to another. A shadow appears behind one of them. He's back! The man with the black mask. He leaps through the cloud, grabs me around the waist, and our waltz begins. Our bodies float in perfect harmony like always except this time we're flying too close to the sun. The heat makes me dizzy. He draws me nearer to him, leaning his head forward close to mine. The heat of his breath makes my temperature rise even more. I can't take it anymore. I'm going to unmask him. Find out who he is. With a sharp tug, I yank off his mask. I scream. He has no face! It's a hideous, flesh-colored, gooey mass with deep sockets and crevices where his eyes, nose, and mouth should be. A revolting reddish substance oozes out of the openings and drips onto my hands, burning them like molten lava. I jerk away from the monster, and my heart drops. Oh my God. I'm falling from the sky!

Still plummeting, I hear a chorus of muddled voices around me.

"She's okay," says one.

"Our spell worked!" says another.

"It's a miracle," says a third.

I flutter my eyes open. It takes me a moment to adjust to the bright light that envelops me. Where am I? Everything is so familiar. The dingy yellow walls, the simple wood furniture, the barred up window. Can it be? I'm back at Faraway?

Three plump, winged women surround my bed. The

Badass Fairies: Fanta, Flossie and Fairweather. They break into a chorus of "lalalala." A bird flies in through the open window and chirps along. I'm *definitely* back at Faraway!

"You survived a harrowing experience," says Fanta.

"I read all about it in the *Fairytale Tattler*," says Flossie.

"Fanta, let me borrow it!" says Fairweather.

Since when were gossip magazines allowed at Faraway?

I'm not sure what's going on. What I do know is that my head is throbbing. I rub my forehead and discover what must be a two-inch scab above my left eye. This is not going to be pretty. I fumble for Shrink's locket to take a peek, then gasp. My treasured keepsake is gone!

Fractured memories of the events that brought me back here drift in my head, creating a hazy montage. The ball. My beautiful black gown. My dance with The Prince. The serpent that ended my life...

Wait! I'm supposed to be dead!

"We used our magic to put you into a deep sleep," says Fanta

"We didn't think we could still do it," chimes in Flossie.

"Dear, it saved your life," adds Fairweather.

"How long have I been asleep?"

In unison: "Three weeks."

I gasp again. So, I've been in a deep sleep. Like Snow White. Except I woke up by myself. What happened to the handsome prince who was supposed to wake me with a kiss? Then it hits me like a stoning. My Prince is dead! Killed by Marcella! My mother! The monster! Sorrow, deep, raw, and ruthless, rocks my body. Gallant is gone forever!

"Dear, don't cry," says Fanta, dabbing my tears with her apron.

"We understand it's been a very emotional experience," says Flossie.

"You'll feel better after you meet with Shrinkerbell," says Fairweather.

Shrink. I so desperately need to talk to her. The Evil

Queen who had no heart now has a heart that's broken.

———————

I'm lying on the tattered velvet chaise lounge, the same place where I've spent countless hours revealing my fears, my secrets, and my sorrows. How many tears have I shed on it? Only a few compared to what I've just shed waiting for Shrink. Gallant's beautiful face fills my head. But his piercing blue eyes stab my heart. I keep bleeding tears.

Shrink, at last, comes buzzing in, sprinkling her fairy dust all over me. It was magical enough to transport me to another world, but it doesn't numb my pain. I'm afraid there's no magic in the universe that can do that. Like my mirror that shattered into a million little pieces, my splintered heart can never be mended.

Through my tears, I notice that Shrink's blond hair hangs loose, and she's not wearing those ridiculous bug-eyed glasses. Her tiny arms are stretched around a thick, hardcover book.

"What's that?" I sniffle, doubtful that it's some kind of cure.

"It's my new book—*The Peter Pan Complex: Why Some Men Never Grow Up*. Tink gave me the idea."

I half-heartedly listen. My mind is already back on Gallant.

"I begin my book signing tour tomorrow," she continues. "But enough about me; we're here to talk about you." She pauses. "Jane, why are you crying?"

Drowning in my tears, I manage three words. "I lost someone."

"Ah, yes, I heard," she says in surprisingly matter-of-fact voice. "We'll get to that later. Right now, let's talk about something else."

I'm taken aback. I so need to talk about Gallant. Isn't she here to help me? Truthfully, I don't know how much longer I can bear the pain. The heartbreaking, gut-wrenching pain.

Shrink grows impatient. "Jane, surely, there must be something else. So much has happened to you since we last met."

Yes, so much. Yet, all I can think about is Gallant. My beautiful Prince.

"Well, Jane, we don't have all day."

My tears have wiped out everything else, except my dream. Somehow, I find the strength to relay it. I ask her what it means.

"The dance could symbolize your relationship with evil," Shrink says in an analytical tone. "The man you unmasked was likely your mother."

"My mother?" I shudder. "Where is she?"

"Your mother is dead."

I'm confused. "Did I kill my own mother?" I cry out.

Shrink's silence answers my question. A deep, unexpected sadness, one that has nothing to do with Gallant, sweeps over me. I bury my head in my hands.

"Jane, look at me."

Slowly, I lift my head. Shrink is in my face, a blur from all my tears.

"Jane, you did *not* kill your mother."

"But I must have!"

"No, Jane. The Huntsman shot her."

The Huntsman? His gunfire must have created that explosion I heard.

"And I suppose he brought me her heart as a souvenir?" I ask with sudden bitterness.

"Your mother had no heart. She was a monster."

I force myself to ask, "Was she born that way?"

"We'll never know. Perhaps, she was the victim of some evil sorcerer's spell."

I'm overwhelmed with emotion. Sorrow. Remorse. Confusion. Relief. Maybe once my mother was a decent person. Shrink lets me collect myself and remains silent.

"Jane, you're finally free of evil," she says at last.

I'm free of evil? I'm speechless. I don't know what to say.

"Come, Jane. I want you to take a look at yourself." She whizzes over to a standing object at the far end of the room. It's covered with a sheet.

Of course, it must be a full-length mirror. I dread seeing myself. After my ordeal and all this crying, I must look beyond terrible. The large scab on my face won't help.

Hesitantly, I get up from the chaise and make my way over to it.

Shrink carefully pulls off the cloth, letting it slide to the floor. I gasp. It's not a mirror. Before me is a large painting on an easel. A portrait of me holding Calla in my arms. Gallant's last painting—the one he was working on in his studio. He must have completed it before the ball.

A rush of fresh tears cascades down my face as Gallant's words from that extraordinary day float in my head. *"You are meant to be painted."* All too sadly, My Prince will never paint me again.

"What do you think?" asks Shrink.

"It's magnificent," I choke.

"I've heard you've become quite an art critic."

I wonder how she knows that.

"Tell me," she continues, "what is the artist trying to communicate about the woman in the painting?"

My weeping eyes study the painting. I look closely at the woman's radiant face and tender hands. A mirror might bare your face, but a work of art will bare your soul. My throat thickens.

"That she is warm and caring and loving," I say slowly.

"I agree," says Shrink. "Can you elaborate more on the relationship between the woman and the child?"

"The little girl is a bright light in the woman's heart." My words surprise me.

"Again, I agree with you." Shrink smiles. "Now, can you infer from the painting how the artist feels about his subjects?"

My moist eyes stay glued on the painting. In the lower

right corner, there's an inscription, painted in red. Bleary-eyed, I move in closer to make out the words. I hear myself say them aloud. *"Forever in my heart."*

The words echo in my head. *Oh, my beautiful Prince, you will never leave me. I will love you forever. Yes, forever.*

"Well, Jane," says Shrink, with a hint of impatience, "I'm waiting for your answer."

"I…believe…he…loves…them." I squeeze out the word between sobs.

"Yes, he does," says Shrink, using the present tense. *Doesn't she know Gallant is dead?*

A too familiar chime sounds. Time's up. Our session is over.

"I'll see you tomorrow at the same time," says Shrink.

Tomorrow? They must be readmitting me. No more second chances! I'll be here for the rest of my life. And never see Calla again!

"Where?" I sniffle. My brain is mush. I'm not thinking straight.

"At my first book signing. At some bookstore called Barons & Nobles. I'll be disappointed if you're not there."

What? I'm going back to the land of fairy tales? Before I can say anything, Shrink disappears behind the painting. She reappears, hiding something behind her back.

"I believe this is yours." She hands me the object.

My mirrored locket! I slip it over my head.

There's no time to thank her. At lightning speed, Shrink spins around me, creating a whirling dervish of fairy dust. Magically, I'm gone. Far, far away.

CHAPTER 37

O ne minute, I'm in Shrink's office; the next, I'm in a cavernous room somewhere in Lalaland, sitting next to Elz and Winnie. Hugs all around. It's so good to see them again. The compassionate look on their faces tells me they know about the recent tragic events in my life. What they can't possibly know is the depth of my pain—a fiery, bottomless pit.

I learn from Winnie that I'm attending my first EPA meeting—Evil People Anonymous. It's a mandatory weekly support group for Faraway alumni who've recovered from their addiction to evil.

I'm shocked by how many people are here. And by who's here. Not surprisingly, I see Hook, Rump, The Wizard, and my sweet Pinocchio. But sitting in the front row are King Midas and his wife, The Queen of Hearts. To the right of them is The Emperor, who blows me a kiss. I also see my old buddy, that green ogre from the dungeon, and my roommate Gothel, who, seated next to Hook, eyes me with distrust. And lastly, Urma the masseuse, who waves to me with all eight arms.

I'm anxious, not knowing what to expect. And then, I get another shock when familiar, heavy footsteps drum in my ears. The Huntsman! What is *he* doing here? My eyes follow him as he heads toward the podium.

"Welcome," he says. "Who would like to begin today and share their story?"

The King rises and marches up to the podium.

"My name is Midas, and I'm addicted to evil. My first wife was a social climber. To make her happy, I let a fairy grant me a wish: everything I touched would turn into gold. My wife was thrilled; she couldn't spend the gold fast enough. Meanwhile, I began to throw my power around, hurting people around me. And then something terrible happened."

He takes in a deep breath, wiping off a patch of sweat above his brow. I've never seen him like this. I'm not sure if he'll continue. He inhales one more time and, on the exhale, picks up where he left off in a voice that's now soft and wistful.

"I had a daughter. A beautiful *bambina* named Marigold whom I loved more than anything or anyone. Every morning, I would start my day by giving her kiss. And then one morning when I kissed her, my *bambina* turned into gold."

Bambina. The word echoes in my head as the group gasps. Midas must have been the man who gave me that gold coin. I'm certain now. I'm all ears as he continues.

"I was devastated. I hated myself. I begged the fairy to break the spell. She granted me my wish and Marigold became a little girl again…"

The group cheers.

"But my angry wife ran away with her."

The group quiets. What a tragic story!

"Did you ever see them again?" asks Winnie.

"No," says Midas, his voice cracking. "I wanted to end my life when I heard about Faraway. I checked myself in and had the good fortune to learn how destructive my greed was. And to meet my lovely second wife who bore me two wonderful sons."

Only one son now. Fighting back tears, I wonder how The King and Queen have dealt with their loss and pain. I'm sure they're taking care of Calla. Thank goodness. When I'm ready, I will ask them if I can visit my sweet little girl.

Midas, composing himself, continues. "While I have been blessed with success, I learned at Faraway that the power of giving is mightier than the power of gold."

The Queen beams at her husband. Now, I understand why the ball was a fundraiser for Faraway.

"Dear, tell everyone about your latest project," urges The Queen.

"Yes, I almost forgot. In lieu of building a luxury hotel on a site occupied by a former castle, I have chosen to build a school for boys and girls."

I can't believe my ears. He's turning my former residence into a public school. Calla will have a place to learn and be with other children. Maybe they'll dedicate it to Gallant. *The Gallant School for Boys and Girls*. His spirit will live in both my heart and my home.

Fraught with emotion, I stand up and applaud Midas. So do the others.

The Emperor volunteers next. Flamboyantly dressed as usual, he sashays up to the podium.

"Hello, dahlings. My name is Armando, and I'm addicted to evil."

How could my darling fairy godmother be addicted to evil? I find out as he tells his story of how his addiction to clothes caused him to ignore his kingdom.

"I'm the original shopaholic. I changed my clothes every hour of the day. And I wouldn't be caught dead in the same outfit twice. My palace was my closet."

He confesses that an embarrassing incident led him to Faraway.

"What happened?" asks Elz.

Armando blushes. "Dahling, let's not go there."

He continues. At Faraway, he took a class that changed his life—Flossie's sewing workshop. He discovered he enjoyed making clothes more than buying them. When he was sent back to Lalaland, he apprenticed as a tailor and worked his way up to being every princess's favorite designer. The former shopaholic is now a workaholic.

"Remember, dahlings," he concludes, "clothes don't make the person; it's the person that makes the clothes."

A vision of myself in Armando's magnificent black gown, floating in Gallant's arms, fills my head as the room echoes with more cheers and claps. The Huntsman takes the podium again. He casts his eyes in my direction, bringing my fantasy to an abrupt end. I look away.

"I'd like to welcome two new Faraway graduates, Rumpelstiltskin and…"

Here it comes. He's going to say it. *The Evil Queen.*

"Jane." I take a deep breath. My real name.

"Who would like to go first?" asks The Huntsman, still staring at me.

I don't think I can do this. To my relief, Rump stands up and teeter-totters to the podium.

"R-Rumpelstiltskin is my n-name," he stutters. And I-I'm addicted to evil." The stuttering stops. "I threatened to take away a queen's firstborn child."

My heart jumps with shock as the group gasps. Rump used an innocent baby as a means of extortion? What dark demons inside him would drive him to do such a terrible thing? Pity, not anger, fills me. My poor little man! How much pain and guilt he's had to endure!

Red in the face, he limps off the stage.

Silence. Until Hook gives him an ear-piercing whistle.

"Way to go, matey!" He leaps to his feet and mimics an applause with his good hand and hook. I follow him, clapping my hands zealously. One by one, the others join in.

Rump, overwhelmed, breaks into a toothy grin. Lifting his stumpy arms above his head, he does a happy little jig.

"Isn't he adorable?" Elz whispers in my ear. Her face flushes. She's clearly got a crush on him.

My throat tightens. It's my turn to talk. Winnie gives my hand a gentle squeeze as I rise. The walk up to the podium feels like an eternity.

Facing my Faraway friends, I'm helplessly, hopelessly sad. Memories of Gallant dance in my head. I still don't know if I can go through with this. Battling tears, *please no more tears*, I begin.

"My name is Jane, and *I'm* addicted to evil."

And then the words ebb and flow out of my mouth. I talk about my love-hate affair with my mirror and how it drove me to evil. How it made me hate Snow White and want to destroy her. I also share what I learned about friendship at Faraway and how another beautiful little girl named Calla changed my life. But I deliberately stay away from talking about Gallant. I'm not ready to go there.

The group is mesmerized by my story. Throughout, The Huntsman's eyes stay glued on me.

"What did you learn from the little girl?" asks Urma.

There's one answer. One word. "Love."

The true meaning of beauty. I step down from the podium, feeling strangely exhilarated.

Everyone cheers. Elz and Winnie jump to their feet. The others follow.

"Way to go, babe!" whistles Hook. Gothel elbows him. We could become fast friends.

"Time's almost up for today's meeting," announces The Huntsman, returning to the podium.

I guess the others will tell their stories in the weeks to come. The Huntsman remains at the podium. His eyes, still locked on me, grow misty.

"My name is Beau, and I'm addicted to evil. Many years ago, I fell prey to a beautiful, bewitching woman. I conceived a child with her—a beautiful daughter. I made a terrible mistake and was forced to abandon this little girl. I know this caused her great suffering. But she's always been there in my heart. I'm sorry for what I did and pray she can forgive me."

His words move me like a tremor in the earth. Our eyes connect. His, green and wide-set like mine. Oh my God! Can it be? In a heartbeat, he vanishes.

Holding a torch, I follow the group through a dark, damp underground passageway. Pinocchio clasps my hand as we march in silence. I shiver. I can't stop thinking about what The Huntsman said. Too much has happened in one day.

We tread up a steep flight of steps, and one by one exit

through a trapped door. I'm surprised to find myself at the entrance to The Trove.

A harvest moon lights up the night sky. It does little to brighten my spirits. Realizing I have no place to go, I ask Winnie if I can stay with her.

"I don't think you'll need to," she smiles.

My eyes look up, and my heart almost stops. Heading toward me on a majestic white stallion is the most beautiful man I've ever seen. He's alive! Gallant's alive!

He swoops me up and we gallop away.

It's not a dream.

My Prince has come.

CHAPTER 38

D ahling, it's so beyond," gushes my fairy godmother Armando, wearing a gold brocade caftan and matching beret.

He fluffs the fountain of sequin encrusted ivory tulle that pours down from my waist to my ankles. I look down. He's right. My wedding gown is a work of art. And so are my matching shoes, custom made by Elz. Believe me, it wasn't easy convincing her to keep the heel size down to three inches.

Armando stands back and admires his creation. "When the *Fairytale Tattler* gets wind of this gown, knockoffs will be showing up everywhere."

Holding a large straw basket full of fragrant petals that surround Lady Jane, Calla, my flower girl, gazes up at me. "You look like a Princess Bride," she beams, referring to "Uncle Occhio's" new blockbuster doll line.

Bending down, I kiss her in the center of the floral garland that circles her golden curls. A few tendrils of my hair, now several inches longer, escape my matching garland and fall into my face. My stomach bunches up with nerves. It all seems so unreal. I'm about to marry My Prince.

The Queen wanted to do a lavish event in the ballroom of their castle. Personally, I had experienced one too many weddings there. And so had Gallant. We insisted on to doing it right in our own backyard—in Snow White's rose and lily garden. And to keep it small. More like a Faraway reunion plus some close family members and friends of the royal family. Winnie, God bless her, handled every detail, right down to the icing on the cake.

For a moment, I think about my first wedding—if you want to call it that—a loveless, perfunctory arrangement—witnessed only by a little girl hiding in the back of a somber, damp chapel. Snow White. The bittersweet irony of it all sends a shiver up my spine. And then I relax. How different today is. Where there was dark, there is light. Where there was cold, there is warmth. And where there was emptiness, there is joy.

The sound of harp music outside signals my cue. A tingling mixture of nerves and joy races through me. Calla hands me my bouquet—a single white lily that Gallant handpicked. The symbol of everything I love. The French doors swing open and in walks the man who will give me away to my Prince. Standing proud and tall. The Huntsman. Beau. My father.

My eyes meet his in a warm embrace as we lock arms and take our first steps across the threshold. His strong hold and steady gait make me feel at ease. Calla follows us, tossing petals from her basket.

The high noon sun is shining brilliantly; the white blooms glisten, and chirping birds circle in the sky. My feathered friends who woke me up every morning at Faraway are singing me a love song. I smile, and then my heart skips a beat.

Straight ahead of me is the man I love. Gallant, in his billowy white blouse and creamy leather britches, more beautiful to me than ever. Standing to his left are his best men, Hook and Charming and to his right, my maids of honor, Elz and Winnie, both beaming. Behind him is King Midas, his gold crown gleaming,

Holding onto my father, I walk toward them slowly, taking in everything and relishing each magical step. I catch glimpses of the small crowd out of the corner of my eye. Shrink is hovering in the fragrant air between Grimm and the Badass Fairies. Gothel, Hook's date, is seated in the back. Rump, who's promised to take Elz on her long awaited high seas adventure—a honeymoon cruise—is seated in the second row next to Winnie's husband John and their children, Hansel,

Gretel and Curly, whom they adopted. Pinocchio, who graciously declined being a best man, is seated next to Peter Pan, whom he met at Shrink's book signing party. They've become inseparable and do volunteer work at the Midas Orphanage for Lost Boys. Occupying every seat in the front row are the Seven Dwarfs; wearing matching hooded robes. Wow! They actually dressed up. The tiny mute one gives me a thumbs up as Cinderella breezes in, late as usual, and takes an empty seat next to the disgruntled Queen. That seat was originally meant for Oscar, the Queen's new croquet partner, who unfortunately had planned a retirement party from wizardry.

The walk up to Gallant feels something between eternity and the blink of an eye. His whole face lights up as he takes me from my father. He clasps his hands firmly around mine, and my smile meets his. The butterflies inside my stomach flutter away. I'm floating like a feather as Midas begins.

"Royally beloved, we are here to unite two people who have magically found each other. I will let them speak for themselves."

Gallant's piercing blue eyes burn into mine as he delivers his vow.

"My beloved Jane, where there has been cold, you have brought warmth; where my life was dark, you have brought light. From this day on, I promise to laugh with you in good times; to struggle with you in bad; to wipe your tears with my hands; to comfort you with my body; mirror you with my soul and love you until our lives shall come to an end."

It's my turn. I swallow hard, forcing the rising lump in my throat to go away.

"My beloved Gallant, I enter into this marriage with you, knowing that the true magic of love is not to avoid changes, but to embrace them. Let us commit to making each day of our lives more different and beautiful than the one before. Let me be the light inside your heart that brings out the best in you always until death do us part."

Gallant squeezes my hands. Elz is positively bawling, and

there's a chorus of sniffles in the crowd as Midas envelops us with his burly arms.

"Do you, my son, take this woman…?"

"I do," says Gallant with a bright smile.

"And do you, Jane…?"

"I do," I say without the slightest tremor.

Midas removes two identical gold bands that are stacked on Hook's hook and slips them on our ring fingers. Inscribed inside each of them is one word: *Forever.*

"I hereby pronounce you husband and…"

Before Midas can say "wife," Gallant's lips consume mine. I surrender myself shamelessly. Neither of us pulls away.

Amid applause and cheers, Calla runs up to me and gives me a huge hug.

She reaches into her basket, still half-full with petals, and pulls out something from under Lady Jane.

"This is for you." Her chocolate eyes twinkle.

My heart swells with joy. It's another one of Rump's woven name bracelets. But this one says "MOMMY."

As my sweet little girl slips it over my hand, I'm the happiest I've ever been in my entire life. I no longer need a mirror to tell me who I am.

EPILOGUE

Everyone's life is a fairy tale written by God's fingers.

—Hans Christian Anderson

S oon after our wedding, Gallant and I donated all of my mother's possessions to a resale shop, including her ruby slippers. I told Gallant that I sure wouldn't want to be in her shoes. Yesterday, the *Fairytale Tattler* reported that a house fell on the woman who bought them and killed her. I knew those shoes were cursed.

After all she did to me, I sometimes miss my mother in a strange, inexplicable way. I'm glad Shrink left me with the hope that she might have been born a good person. Yet, I'm still not sure if people are born evil or if it's the events in their lives that make them that way.

What I do know for sure is that fate is meant to be. But it's not a *fait accompli.* Fate, in fact, has a way of writing its own twisted version of happily ever after. In my fairy tale, had I not gone to rehab, I would have never found the light inside me.

Shrink was right about so many things. About letting go of the past and looking deep inside myself for the future. Even about starting a career as a writer.

Having unleashed my imagination, I'm writing a children's book. Gallant's doing the illustrations. It's a fairy tale called *Dewitched.* You can guess what the story's about. As usual, I'm having writer's block. But, at least, I've written the last line…

…And they lived happily ever after.

~THE END~

ACKNOWLEDGEMENTS

As I hit home plate, exhausted and elated, I realized there are so many people who helped me get there. Yes, it takes a team to write a novel, and mine, in this digital age, came from around the world. BIG, heartfelt thanks...

To my mom, the best mother ever.

To Dana, my best friend and fellow writer for her never-ending belief in me and terrific edit.

To novelist and new friend Artemis Hunt, who gave me insightful advice and the courage to self-publish after much deliberation.

To my dear friend Shelley Miles, who had no idea that she inspired me to write this book one day at lunch after sharing a first-time novelist's success story.

To Cheryl Ferguson, who helped me grow as a writer and graciously accepted my decision to self-publish.

To Wendy Engelberg, who gave me the perfect words when I could no longer find them.

To Angela Weltman, my sister Laura, and the fabulous women of the LACMA Costume Council Board, who supported me with unwavering enthusiasm.

To my ever-patient formatter John Ling, a perfectionist and bestselling novelist himself.

To my passionate cover and website designer, Glendon Haddix of Streetlight Graphics, who gave me sanity when I thought I'd lost it.

To Siri, who showered me with unexpected love and kindness when I most needed it.

To Khalil Gibran for his beautiful, inspirational quote: "Beauty is not in the face; beauty is a light in the heart." (Okay, he's not really part of the team, but he deserves a mention.)

To the always supportive and helpful community of writers on Kindle Boards Writers' Café, especially Dalya Moon and Liz Grace Davis.

To my stepkids, Cristina and Nicholas for helping me debunk the evil stepmother myth.

To, most of all, my family—my husband, Danny, my constant sounding board, who helped make the action scenes jump off the page, and my twin daughters, Lilly and Isabella, who put up with an obsessed mommy and way too many frozen dinners.

It's been a long, jittery journey with lots of ups and downs, but I believe I made the right decision to take the road less traveled. I hope I will make you all proud.

Last but not least, a HUGE shout out to my readers. I hope you enjoyed *Dewitched* and will give it a positive review.

Thank you, all. I couldn't have done it without you.

Love~ els

ABOUT THE AUTHOR

Ellen Levy-Sarnoff, writing under the name E.L. Sarnoff, has enjoyed a prolific career in the entertainment industry, creating, writing, and producing television series, including the original *Power Rangers*. She lives in Los Angeles with her Prince Charming-ish husband, twin teenage princesses, and a bevy of pets. She's also the stepmother to two grown-up children, who don't think she's that evil. When she's not writing in her PJ's, she likes to dress up and pretend she's Hollywood royalty.

Ellen would love to hear from you. Connect to her at:

http://www.elsarnoff.com
http://www.facebook.com/ELSarnoff
en.twitter.com/#!/elsarnoff
elsarnoff@gmail.com

COMING IN OCTOBER 2012

*Un*hitched

Jane's journey continues as she deals with a two-career marriage, the baby issue, and a woman from Gallant's past—Sleeping Beauty.

Made in the USA
Lexington, KY
17 February 2014